Wanton Regard

Geoffrey Neil

I0680849

Copyright Information

Priorities Intact Publishing

8306 Wilshire Blvd., #7076
Beverly Hills, CA 90211

3680 Grant Drive, Suite N
Reno, NV 89509

Text copyright © 2014, by Geoffrey Neil
Cover art by Geoffrey Neil
Edited by Christina Dominguez
Printed in the United States of America

9 8 7 6 5 4 3 2 1

ISBN-13: 978-0985022341

Table of Contents

For Busk. You win.

"All extremes of feeling are allied with madness."

—Virginia Woolf

One

IF THE CUTE barista turned out to be stronger than she looked, it wouldn't matter. That's the wonderful thing about fate. What was supposed to happen was about to happen. Gage could feel it. His sweaty fingers twiddled the keys in his pocket as he leaned against the window inside Hot Perks. Sunlight poured into the crowded coffee shop, and patron conversations competed with the sounds of hissing steamers and gurgling coffee machines.

He watched her make thirteen drinks in a row before she looked up once—a record for her. He loved the ponytail. It flitted and flopped so playfully when she tilted her head to pour milk or leaned to scoop ice. She did most of her work framed under the *Pick-Up* sign. The irony made Gage smile. What a treat she'd be.

He wore a new brown parka, blue jeans, and year-old work boots that looked as though he had purchased them yesterday. Well-groomed hair and refined facial features complemented his outfit to make him look like an executive on his first day of a blue-collar job.

"Have you ordered, friend?" An elderly man nudged him from behind. Gage shook his head and pointed to the rear of the line, keeping his eyes locked on the barista. Today, she must have forgotten her nametag, but Gage knew her name. He had gathered more trivia about her than he needed. In less than a week, Gage learned that she was 20 years old, left-handed, worked 10:00AM to 5:00PM weekdays, respected authority, lived alone, quit college, went to more concerts than she could afford, had a growing affinity for alcohol and had rejected three customer date requests in two days. And he also knew her missing nametag had *Marissa* engraved on it. All these facts were useless. Only three things mattered today—Marissa had short-trimmed fingernails, she would ride her bicycle home after dark, and her route included a road with sparse traffic.

His best estimate from a distance was that she stood about shoulder height to him. Her breasts were difficult to assess under the stained bib apron, but it was a safe bet they'd be acceptable. The skin on her face was a little pasty, but nothing that putting her face-up in the sun for a couple of hours couldn't fix. Although she wasn't a perfect specimen right off the shelf, she'd more than suit his needs after a few adjustments.

He got in line and inched his way to the *Order Here* sign, where he paid for a medium, half-caf, no-foam, non-fat, vanilla soy latte. He dropped his change from high above the tip jar. The piercing coin crash failed to make her look his way. He moved along the display of cupcakes, croissants, and gift cards to a chocolate-bar rack beside the worn countertop where Marissa placed her finished drinks. He pulled an oversized chocolate bar from the rack and pretended to read its label. Then Gage put the candy bar back, slipped his hand behind the rack, and removed a magnetic bug the size of a bottle cap from the backside. He had only needed four days of its seven-day battery.

"I have a large chai latte for Jim," Marissa called out, sliding the drink to the counter's edge. Her voice, in person, was always richer than it sounded in the tinny recordings.

As she scooped vanilla powder into a large cup, Gage stepped closer and said, "Pardon…"

Marissa looked at him and raised her eyebrows, inviting his question. Her inquisitive expression made him smile.

"Has anyone ever told you that you favor Hailey Vaughan?" he asked.

Color flowed into Marissa's cheeks. "I'm sorry. I don't know who that is."

Gage winked at her. "That's okay, darling. She comes in here every day without fail. Dresses impeccably. She has auburn hair like yours and lights up a room like you wouldn't believe."

"I still don't know her, but she seems like a great person to look like!"

"Trust me, you do. And the two of you have something else in common…" Gage threw his hands up in surrender. "Let's just say that when God created your smiles, he was just showing off!"

Marissa's blush deepened. "Thank you." She stepped away, wiped a steamer nozzle with a damp cloth, and then pulled an empty cup for a new order. While serving the next drink, she noticed Gage still waiting and watching her.

"Does she wear business suits and carry a shoulder satchel?" Marissa asked.

"That's her."

"I think I know who you're talking about. She orders a medium half-caf, no-foam, non-fat, vanilla soy latte. I know my customers by their drinks!"

Gage pointed to a monitor above Marissa's head that displayed the drink queue. The next order was for a medium, half-caf, no-foam, non-fat, vanilla soy latte. She laughed and said, "I always joke with her it must taste good because it's as hard to say as it is to make. Looks like she's gotten you hooked on it, too."

Gage rubbed his chin. "Oh, yes. I'm hooked."

• • •

The reflection of a brilliant sunset slid down Wenshire Harbor's tallest buildings. Below, Gage sat parked at the curb in his yellow Chevy Blazer. He had emptied the rear compartment of its stacked tool boxes, wire spools, and electronics. Only a tattered comforter remained spread edge to edge, foam stuffing protruding from several tears in its lining.

Days earlier, he discovered this parking spot with a perfect view of the rear alley exit for Hot Perks Coffee Shop. He checked his watch at 5:02 p.m. The headlights of passing cars blinked on as the sky darkened. Like clockwork, Marissa emerged from the alley on her bike and stopped at the curb to put on her helmet. Gage whispered, "Good girl."

Marissa plugged an earbud into each ear, checked for oncoming traffic, and pedaled onto the street for her ride home, which should take anywhere from eighteen to twenty minutes.

Gage started his Blazer and waited. He didn't need to keep her in sight—yet. He knew her route. He knew her speed. He knew the night would be darker when she reached the two-mile stretch on Route 6 between Mantle Tavern and the driveway to her apartment building.

After waiting ten minutes, he began his drive, joining the same traffic Marissa had. He stayed in the slow lane, carefully monitoring his speed. Turning onto Route 6 gave him a bigger rush than he had imagined. "Finally!" he said, wiping his hand on his lap.

The outskirts of town had only sporadic traffic, which Gage chalked up to another wink from fate. In his rearview mirror, he saw two sets of headlights. He soon recognized his prize in the distance. A red safety light under Marissa's bike seat fluttered, dimming and brightening with each rotation of her pedals. Before getting too close, he pulled to the side of the road, briefly flashing his hazard lights. The two cars behind him passed. He rechecked his mirror and saw the darkness that promised time—a limited amount, but plenty for what he needed to do.

As he drove his Blazer back onto the road, he pulled two pairs of flex cuffs from the glove box and put them beside a first-aid kit on the passenger seat. He drummed his fingers on the kit as he closed in on Marissa. She pedaled in strong, even strokes. Her head moved side to side as she bounced to her music. He pulled up beside her and slowed to match her speed. His Blazer came within an arm's reach of her left handlebar. She looked toward him as his passenger window slid down. He turned on his interior light to disarm her with his smile.

"Excuse me," he shouted.

Marissa released one hand from the handlebars and held up her finger for him to wait so she could remove an earbud. Gage jerked the wheel hard to the right and then straightened. He heard the metallic thump against the passenger door and the briefest scream. He saw her go down in the right rearview mirror, arms, and fingers spread to break her fall. He slammed on his brakes and then shoved the gearshift to reverse. He backed past her, then pulled forward and parked, his bright headlights illuminating Marissa amidst a swirling cloud of dust.

She sat upright on the road's shoulder, rubbing her knee. She cupped her hand toward the car to shield her eyes from the headlights. Her bicycle lay on its side a short distance away, the rear tire slowing to a stop.

She yelled something that Gage didn't hear.

After watching her momentarily, he tossed the first-aid kit onto the rear seat and got out, tucking the flex cuffs into his back pocket. He walked toward her, gravel crunching under his boots.

Marissa fingered hair from her face and said, "What's your problem? You almost killed me!"

Gage said nothing, closing in on her.

Marissa waved him away. "I'm okay. You can keep going. I'm good to go. No harm done." She tried to stand and grimaced when she put weight on her left leg, so she sat down and resumed rubbing her knee.

Gage continued past her.

A chill shot through Marissa. He hadn't even asked if she was okay. She leaned back to see if any cars approached from behind the man's vehicle. There was only blackness. She fumbled in her sweatshirt pockets. Both were empty. To stave off panic, she took a couple of quiet, deep breaths.

Gage slipped his hands into his pockets and examined the toppled bicycle, its front wheel turned backward.

"You can just leave it there," Marissa said. "Seriously, I'll be fine. I don't want to hold you up."

Gage picked up her phone from the asphalt near the bicycle. He pried open the back cover and popped out the battery. Then something else caught his eye. A pen-sized pepper spray dispenser with its cap missing. He picked it up and turned toward the headlights for a better view, illuminating his face.

Marissa said, "Hey, aren't you the guy in Hot Perks today?"

Gage stood motionless, staring at her.

"You said I look like that other woman, right?" Marissa wished he would say something—anything.

Gage pulled the flex cuffs from his back pocket. He strolled toward her, and his boots resumed their crunch, crunch, crunch.

Marissa said, "You know, if you didn't like the drink, we replace it for free. You didn't have to run me down!" She squeezed out a nervous laugh. "Listen, I don't need any help. I just need my phone."

Gage separated the flex cuffs and pinched one pair between his teeth while he loosened the other, grinning at her.

Marissa's eyes widened, and she screamed, "No! Please!" as she tried to scoot away.

As it turned out, the cute barista wasn't stronger than Gage expected, but she was much louder.

Two

Three months later.

THIRTY-THREE-YEAR-OLD Hailey Vaughan sat at her desk in her spacious office, where she ran her successful business consulting practice. Her stellar reputation with clients made her a sought-after speaker at many executive retreats and conferences.

She swiveled to her coveted view of Wenshire Harbor. Six stories below, bustling shops and eateries arced around a harbor dotted with sailboats and fishing boats on sparkling blue water.

She pawed in her purse and pulled out her phone. It was still warm from having held it a few moments ago. She swiped her finger across the screen and saw the voicemail message was still open. Her finger hovered over the *Play* arrow.

She felt a pang of shame for having enjoyed the message. Hailey would have deleted it without a second thought on any other day. But another argument with her husband, Mason, that morning made the message's timing both awful and perfect.

She heard the elevator open in the reception area outside her office. Her assistant, Robert, was returning from a late lunch. She went to her doorway and saw him sitting at a small desk facing the elevator. He popped his gum while studying his mobile phone.

"I'm going to make a few private calls," Hailey announced.

"Got it," Robert said, not looking up.

Hailey closed the door and returned to her desk. Then she stood again, returned to the door, and locked it before returning to her chair. She attached the voicemail message to an email, addressing it to her best friend, Felicia Blakner, double-checked the *To:* and *cc:* fields, making sure she hadn't accidentally included any other recipients before she sent it. Then she turned off the speakerphone, tapped *Play,* and pressed the phone to her ear.

Hello, Ms. Vaughan. I'm calling to tell you that you forgot your notepad at the Marriott yesterday. I tried to catch you after your presentation, but you ran off! I will leave it at the hotel's front desk. I am positively miserable that I can't return it to you in person! You really connected with me. Forgive my forwardness. Life is short. I could not take my eyes off you. Your presentation was absolutely beautiful, and so are you. In fact, when God created your smile, he was just showing off! Bye-bye now.

Hailey caught herself smiling. She wondered why the caller hadn't given his name in the message. The omission ruined any chance of Googling any scoop on him. "…absolutely beautiful, and so are you," Hailey said out loud. She leaned back in her chair and sighed, resting her chin in her hand. She closed her eyes, trying to remember the attendees of the Small Business Growth Expo at which she had given her presentation yesterday. She could probably recite a hundred names of people she recognized there, but when linking the caller to someone in the audience, her memory retrieved only a mass of attentive faces, none distinct.

She did remember having left her notepad and lecture notes, but at the time, she didn't feel they were important enough to return for. The caller's kindness in notifying her and his flattery created a perfect reason to call and thank him.

Her phone rang. Felicia's name flashed on the screen.

Hailey answered. "Hi, Felly. That was fast. Did you listen to it?"

"Yes, do you know his name?"

"No, but his phone number showed."

"He's flirty. You *sooo* don't need to call him back. Mason would blow a gasket if he found out."

"Look, I don't even know who this guy is. I only know his message was considerate and flattering—"

"And flirty. Stay away, Hale."

"Oh, relax! I'm not planning to meet him, but wouldn't you want to know what he looks like if I did? I could screen him for *you*."

"I don't have your looks. I don't need the rejection."

"You never know. You could be this guy's type."

"Hale, I'm erasing the message from my phone, and you need to do the same. If Mason ever hears it, you're dead."

"Mason doesn't touch my phone. And you're acting like I'm planning to sleep with the guy! It's harmless to call and thank him for returning my notes. Where's your faith in me?"

"I know you're strong. It's just that his voicemail paves an easy road to a bad decision. The guy is hot for you. And if he is truly hot, you'll get hot, and that's way too much heat."

Hailey laughed. "Oh, give me some credit, girlie. I gotta go."

"Okay. Call me later. And by the way, if you ignore my warning, yes, I do want to know what he looks like."

Hailey laughed again. "Bye."

She needed to resume work, but the voice message became too distracting to focus on anything else. She couldn't remember the last time Mason complimented her, much less referred to her as beautiful. She imagined him hearing the message and shuddered.

He often wrongfully accused her of cheating with Robert and was so adamant about her unfaithfulness that Hailey finally gave up trying to convince him otherwise. Their spat this morning ended when Hailey invited Mason to mount cameras in her office to watch her whenever he wished it would make him feel better. That's when he stormed out of the room, shouting, "You could be banging him anywhere!"

Hailey held out her hand and spread her fingers. She saw the slight skin indentation where her 2-carat platinum diamond wedding ring was supposed to be. Maybe this was the reason the caller felt so comfortable flirting with her. Last week, Hailey lost the ring, and Mason noticed it missing the following day while they ate breakfast. It was only the second time in their marriage that he saw Hailey's finger without the ring, and he threw a tantrum with a fresh reason to accuse Hailey of infidelity. She tried to calm him. "I am *not* cheating on you. The missing ring doesn't mean I'm married to you any less."

"I worked harder than you know for that rock," Mason said.

"And your sacrifice means a lot to me, Mason—really. If the ring doesn't turn up soon, we can have a new one made."

"We? It was fifty-grand. 'We' don't have that kind of money lying around—unless you want to run to your dad."

"I don't need my father to replace the ring, Mason."

"Why not? He could swipe a pen and fix the problem for you." Mason rolled his eyes and snapped open a newspaper.

"I make plenty of money on my own," Hailey said. "Why pull my father into this?"

"I'm just saying … your dad gave you a generous supply of clients and gifted this house as a wedding present, so why wouldn't he have one of his people buy you a ring to replace the one I worked a year for?"

"Can you please drop the sarcasm? My family has money—I can't help it. The ring is lost. What do you expect from me?"

Mason folded the paper and slapped it down. "Maybe you could start off by being a hundred percent wife instead of a hundred percent 'Vaughan.'"

Hailey shrugged, keeping her shoulders up. "Where does this come from?"

"The ring was a symbol of our marriage," Mason said. "Now that's gone, and we don't even share a name."

Hailey sat back and crossed her arms. "So that's what this is about—the name."

"It's part of it … If we are married, your last name should be Barger."

Hailey sighed. "We've talked this to death, Mason. My last name *is* Barger. Using Vaughan was a big advantage for starting my business."

"I'll say." Mason got up and walked to the den to cool off.

"Mason, you're impossible," Hailey said. "I'll find the damned ring."

"Oh, now it's a damned ring?"

"You know that's not what I meant."

Mason grabbed a sofa pillow and threw it, knocking a picture from the wall near Hailey. He left the room with a maniacal look on his face. For the first time, Mason's eyes had scared her.

Hailey rocked in her chair, contemplating whether to go home early for the day. She hadn't been productive, and her thoughts kept returning to her mystery caller. Despite Felicia's concern, the idea of a brief conversation with him grew on Hailey. She was well aware of her own boundaries and never crossed them. She'd rather rot in a lousy marriage than admit she couldn't succeed. She was committed to Mason until death parted them, no matter how excruciating the journey. Remembering this commitment brought her some clarity. She decided not to call, but she didn't delete the message.

. . .

The faded green *$7 All Day Parking* sign was rimmed in the white splatter of gull droppings. Below it, a uniformed parking attendant counted a folded wad of cash while he paced at the entrance. The public lot was six stories below and across the street from Hailey's office window. The lot would be full before 5:00PM as evening diners flowed into Wenshire Harbor.

A yellow Chevy Blazer with tinted windows sat parked in its special space near the back. As usual, Gage had paid the parking attendant ten bucks extra to reserve this particular spot for him. Gage put his double-meat, double-cheese burger on the center console, removed his Giants baseball cap, and aimed a pair of binoculars upward. His smile grew, a smear of ketchup on one side.

"That's more like it," he said. His anger subsided because the damned glare of the afternoon sun on the building's reflective windows finally sunk low enough for him to see into Hailey's office window again. He adjusted himself into his seat, excited, as if watching the opening credits for his favorite movie.

As fate would have it, Hailey pivoted into view, centered perfectly in her window. She rocked in her chair while holding her phone to her ear. Gage's binoculars were powerful enough for him to detect a smile on her face. He watched her rest her chin on her hand. When she closed her eyes, Gage said, "Yes, baby, yes! Are you listening to my message? You deserve it. You *are* beautiful. Drink it in."

When she swiveled from the window, Gage put the binoculars on the passenger seat and picked up his burger. He wiggled his mouth around an oversized bite. His position allowed him to see into her office window and provided a perfect view of her building's garage exit across the street. He watched every car that entered and exited, noting the familiar ones. He knew Hailey's red Lexus IS250 wouldn't exit for a while. He knew she had never left work before 5:00 p.m. Usually, the exit arm lifted for her car between 5:15 and 5:25 p.m. Gage wouldn't miss her car for anything. He was used to waiting for her. She was worth every minute, and he had all the time in the world. If she worked late, he knew he could watch footage of her for hours, and at least they could be together that way.

He took another bite of his burger and then propped his phone at an angle on the dashboard. He tapped its screen several times to launch a slideshow. His Blazer was aimed perfectly to enjoy his dashboard slideshow without missing any vehicle that exited the garage across the street.

Images of Hailey from Gage's massive collection faded in and out every five seconds on the small phone screen. One telephoto shot showed her walking out of her lobby to get her daily medium, half-caf, no-foam, non-fat, vanilla soy latte at Hot Perks Coffee Shop next door. The next photo captured her return, her lips puckered as she blew into the cup's tiny sip hole. Gage pressed pause. This was one of his favorites. "Yes, blow! It's hot, don't burn those lips, lover!" he said, grinning.

He put the last hunk of burger into his mouth and crumpled the wrapper. He exited the Blazer and tossed the sack and an empty soda cup into a nearby dumpster. Returning to his driver's seat, he pulled two sani-wipes from under his armrest and wiped his face and hands. He wiped down the steering wheel, door handle, and center console where the burger sack had been. Finally, he rolled down the windows and turned on the vent to clear the Blazer's air of the fast-food smell.

He picked up a framed 8 x 10 photo of Hailey from the passenger seat. The frame had no glass. He drew his finger across her cheek and then gently kissed her. When he pulled back, he saw a dab of ketchup on her cheek. "Dammit!" He slammed his hand on the armrest and craned his neck to check his face in the rearview mirror. He pulled out a third sani-wipe and cleaned his face again.

After taking a deep breath, he exhaled slowly and used his pinky to swipe the ketchup from her cheek. He then carefully painted it onto her lips. After he sucked his fingertip clean, his forehead wrinkled with concern. "I'm sorry I got you a little messy, baby. Can you forgive me? You see how I turned a mess into something beautiful for you? Do you know how beautiful you are? Yes, that smile tells me you do." He kissed her nose and placed the photo back on the passenger seat. He reclined and resumed the phone's slideshow, ready for whatever wait was required.

Three

HAILEY SHUFFLED THE paperwork on her desk, did some billing, and then spent some time fine-tuning her presentation points for a workshop she would facilitate next month. She searched her desk drawers and picked up her satchel from the floor. She rifled through it and pressed the intercom on her desk phone. "Robert?"

"Yes?"

"Did you file a theft report with management about my iPad?"

"Sure did."

"Great, thanks."

During the last month, two valuable items went missing from Hailey's office. When the iPad disappeared, Robert fingered the janitorial staff even though they had cleaned Hailey's suite for years without incident.

A few days later, her phone disappeared from her desk during a brief trip she took to Hot Perks. Later, Robert confessed to stepping out and leaving the door unlocked for a few minutes. Again, he blamed the janitorial crew, but such a carefully timed midday theft was virtually impossible. After Hailey reprimanded Robert for leaving the unlocked office unattended, he promised to keep the door locked at all times and had Hailey's phone replaced that same day.

Hailey jumped when her phone rang. She turned from the window. The caller ID displayed *Home*.

"Hi."

"I have your ring," Mason said.

"You do?" Hailey jumped up from her chair.

"Yes."

"Oh, thank God!" Hailey's voice wobbled as she teared up. "Where was it?"

"Dora found it on our bedspread after she folded clothes."

"See? I told you I took it off to mix meatloaf by hand. I must have put it on a dishtowel that went through the wash."

"Yes, I get it. That's probably what happened."

"Probably?" Hailey bristled and stopped herself, taking a big breath. "I'm so relieved. She deserves a finder's fee, a raise, or something."

"No kidding," Mason said. "Listen, sorry about this morning."

"Let's forget it," Hailey said, even though she didn't want to forget it.

She'd love for Mason's discovery of the truth about the missing ring to resolve it. Ignoring their arguments was always easier than hashing them out and facing their issues.

Mason cleared his throat. "Our discussion shouldn't have, you know, ended that way, with the door slamming and all that."

"The door didn't slam. You slammed it. Own your behavior, Mason."

"I know. Please don't make this harder than it needs to be. You're right, and I'm sorry."

"Thanks," Hailey said. She appreciated his rare apology. "I know there isn't much in the fridge. I haven't had time to go to the market. Want to meet for dinner? Maritime Bistro? Or Mexican?"

"I'm going shooting before work tonight."

"Right," Hailey sighed. "The guns."

"Hale, you know I've been going to the range on Monday nights for weeks."

"Mason, I didn't argue with you. I just thought it would have been nice to have dinner. I've told you before that I sometimes feel that your weapons pull rank on me," Hailey said.

"Really?" Mason answered. "You're going to make my hobby the issue even though it takes up a fraction of the time you spend at work?"

Hailey pulled the phone from her ear and strangled it. When she put it back, she heard Mason say, "...is exactly what our problem is, and you call *me* the jealous one."

"Just forget it, Mason."

"Why is it that when you get pissed off, you want me to forget it right away, but when I get upset, like this morning, you remember it and rub it in my face forever? I was the bigger person this time. I called to apologize. You didn't."

"You're right, I'm wrong," Hailey said. "Have fun with your guns." Mason didn't hear her. He had hung up.

Hailey dropped the phone onto her desk, grabbed her hair, and said, "Ughhhhh! You're *impossible!*"

After calming down, she took her phone and scrolled to the mystery man's voicemail. There was no better time to call and thank a considerate man for saving her notepad. It would make her feel better. A green *Call* button illuminated beside the phone number. She nibbled her cheek while her resistance drained.

• • •

Gage tapped his phone screen to zoom in on a photo of Hailey in the lobby of her building last week. He had taken it with a tiny camera on a timer tucked under his arm. The image showed Hailey standing beside the elevator, looking up at the illuminated floor indicator. It was a perfect profile photo of her chin raised to feature the tremendous beauty of her throat and smooth necklines—two of Gage's many favorite features. He was about to scroll to the next photo when his phone rang. The caller ID read *Private.*

"Hello?" he answered.

"Hello. I'm sorry, I don't know your name. My name is Hailey Vaughan. Are you the person who left me a voicemail message earlier today?"

Gage sat up straight. "Oh, yes—yes, I did. A pleasure to talk with you, Hailey!" He grinned. "My name is Gage." He tapped *Speaker* on the phone screen and gently set it on his lap.

"Well, Gage, thank you for returning my notepad from the conference," Hailey said.

"You're very welcome." Gage raised his binoculars and quickly honed in on her window. He saw the back of Hailey's chair as she sat at her desk, phone pressed to her ear. "Have you already picked it up from the hotel front desk?" he asked, shaking his head to answer for her.

"No, as a matter of fact, I was going to stop by the Marriott after work. I just wanted to call and thank you for your kind voicemail. I'm so glad you enjoyed my talk, and your compliments made my day."

"All that I said was true. And I meant what I said about your smile. It's special." He watched Hailey swivel her chair toward the window and cross her legs.

"Thank you, I appreciate that. It was a fun group, and I truly felt the enthusiasm."

"Say, is there any chance your presentation was videotaped?" Gage asked.

"Not to my knowledge. The Small Business Growth Expo coordinators seemed to be handling all the logistics for the event. You might check with them."

Gage reached under his seat and pulled out a high-definition mini-cam chock full of video footage of Hailey. "Yes, I might."

"Well, I'll keep this call short and sweet. Thank you again, Gage. It is nice to meet you," Hailey said.

"Likewise," Gage said. "Uh, one more thing, Hailey…"

"Yes?"

"Is there any chance we could meet when you stop by the hotel? I could buy you a drink."

Hailey cringed. It was time to clarify her status in case her missing wedding ring caused any confusion. Gage's flattery felt terrific, but she knew there was a limit to how much she should enjoy. "I'm sure a drink would be enjoyable, but ... I'm meeting my husband tonight," she said.

"Bring him."

"I beg your pardon?"

"Bring Mason. We'll have a great time."

Hailey paused. "How did you know my husband's name?"

"You mentioned him in your presentation yesterday, remember? You used your marriage to illustrate healthy boundaries between interdependent roles. Mason loves guns like you love your gym membership. He doesn't make you shoot, and you don't make him run. It was the perfect illustration."

"Right. I forgot about that. Still, I'll have to take a rain check on the drink since this evening isn't going to work."

"Rain check it is! You should know that I'll only be here until the weekend. If you change your mind, you'll let me know, won't you?"

"Absolutely. Thank you, Gage."

"Bye-bye, for now!"

Hailey tucked her phone into her purse. She knew Gage was enamored, but hadn't been prepared for him to actually ask her to join him for a drink during their first conversation. Even so, he had proven to be as charming as he sounded in his voicemail.

Since she would be home alone this evening, she took some work so she could at least be productive. Hailey left her office after stocking her satchel with some files and her laptop.

Four

WHEN HAILEY STEPPED from the elevator into the lobby, she saw two well-dressed gentlemen standing by the planters near the street exit. They carried clipboards, and when they saw Hailey, one elbowed the other, sending him hurrying toward her. Hailey noticed his approach and prepared to deny any solicitation request.

"Excuse me, ma'am. Can I talk to you about a life-changing peace and joy that you can have through truth and justice?" the young man asked. He was thin, with dark, short-cropped hair and black-rimmed glasses. His face was enthusiastic, as if the correct answer from Hailey might win him a prize.

She stopped. "I have no idea what you are talking about," Hailey replied.

"Thank you for your curiosity. We believe that truth and justice can raise every aspect of your life to a new level. It has changed our lives and can change yours, too. We've reached a higher echelon. We're Echelonians."

Hailey recognized the name. The Echelonian movement recently swept through the city of Henderton and its surrounding communities. For reasons that were a mystery to Hailey, their bizarre message struck a powerful chord with locals, and Wenshire Harbor seemed to be a new outpost for them. Their odd way of speaking and the pushiness with which they approached anyone who would listen was off-putting.

"Well, I already believe in truth and justice. How's that?" she said, walking to the garage elevator.

"Fantastic," the young man said, beaming. "My name is Isaac. Can we book a time to talk with you more?"

Hailey pressed the garage elevator button three times and said, "No. And you shouldn't be soliciting in the building. You should leave."

"The building management agreed that we could spread our message to those who need it, provided we remain in the lobby."

"Forgive me, Isaac. I have no interest in your religion or whatever you people are doing."

Isaac kept his smile while some hope vanished from his face. "Some souls aren't ready yet. Have a fantastic evening, ma'am." He backed away and then returned to his partner by the planters.

The garage elevator opened. Hailey didn't get on. She walked around the corner to the building's management office.

Jonah Chaney, the management supervisor, sat inside a small makeshift office space that was a converted closet the size of a jail cell. A horizontal line of brown scuff marks and paint scratches lined the wall at chest height where mops and broom handles once leaned. Two facing desks and one tattered chair for a guest left only a narrow aisle of visible floor.

Hailey entered the doorway. "Do you have a minute?" she asked.

"Certainly, Ms. Vaughan. What can we do for you?" Jonah replied.

"These truth and justice folk out in the lobby—are you letting them solicit in the building?"

Jonah stood. "They are here only for a short while. Have they caused you a problem?" He looked concerned.

"Not yet. If they are permanent, I certainly don't want to be interrogated whenever I go through the lobby. Am I being unreasonable?"

"No, of course not. I'll speak to them, Ms. Vaughan."

"How can you let them do this? Isn't the building private property?"

Jonah shrugged. "They asked permission from the owner, Mr. Handel, and he gave the okay. I'm so sorry if it has been an inconvenience."

Dissatisfied with Jonah's answer, Hailey left the management office and took the elevator to the garage. She drove out the exit, turning right on North Harborcrest Avenue. At 5:30PM, traffic was heavy, so she turned on her favorite jazz station and settled in for the drive to the Marriott hotel on the opposite side of town.

She called Felicia and opened the conversation with, "Felly, I'm on my way to the Marriott."

"Oh my God, Hailey. You're going to meet him, aren't you?"

"No, I'm only getting my notepad. Besides, I've already talked to him on the phone."

"You did? Who is he?"

"His name is Gage."

"Gage, who?"

"I didn't ask. Look, it was just a brief thank-you call. He did ask me to join him for a drink."

"See? I *told* you he's hot for you."

"Oh, calm down! He invited Mason, too."

"Now that's just weird."

"Anyway, none of that matters because it's all over. I'm just picking up my notepad from the front desk. I'll call you later. By the way, thank you for the Godiva milk chocolate caramels. You know my weakness. I *love* them and ate them until I was almost sick last night."

"You're welcome. Be careful. I'll talk to you soon."

Hailey hung up and shook her head. She loved Felicia, even though she was too high-strung.

A few minutes later, Hailey heard her phone chime with a text notification. She guessed it would be Felicia with more questions about Gage. Mason's name showed on the screen. She slowed her car to read it.

Sorry about dinner. Back from shooting by 10. You got a package…

Hailey wasn't expecting any deliveries at home. She hit reply and typed:

What type of pac—

Before she could finish, she collided with a pickup truck that had stopped in front of her. Her torso flew forward, restrained by her seat belt. Her head slammed back into her headrest. "Oh God, oh God, oh God," Hailey said. From her driver's seat, the hood didn't look bent. She saw the pickup driver looking at her in his rearview mirror, and then he began pounding his dashboard with his fist. He pulled his truck to the side of the road and motioned for Hailey to follow. She did and parked behind him.

Her satchel had flown from the passenger seat, spilling papers and her laptop onto the floor. She tasted blood on her lip. She didn't know if she had bitten it or if her face impacted the steering wheel. Her first thought was to call the police. She searched the seat and the floor for her phone, but couldn't find it.

The pickup driver threw his door open and got out, screaming, "What the hell were you doing? Are you blind, or are my damned brake lights broken?" He stomped back to check the rear end of his truck. After checking it, he turned to Hailey and said, "What's your problem?"

Hailey froze with fear, watching him. She stayed in the car to assess whether this man would become dangerous. She rolled down the window only enough to shout, "I'm so sorry!"

The man approached her window and said, "Get your ass out of the car. *Get out!*" He pointed to the ground outside her door as if she should obey like a dog. "Get the hell out, and I want all your information. You better be insured, dammit."

"I am. Please relax, sir." She rested her hand on the door handle, waiting for him to calm down before she got out. She'd feel more comfortable exchanging information after the police arrived.

"Relax? You're lucky my daughter wasn't with me in my truck, bitch. Now, get out!"

Hailey let go of the door handle, turned on her interior light, and searched for her phone in earnest this time. The floor was dark, and she couldn't see or feel where it landed.

The pickup driver circled Hailey's car, taking photos with his phone, and continued to shout at her. He squatted in front of her car to take a close-up of her license plate and then moved back to the driver's side of the windshield, snapping two photos of her VIN. "Still waiting for you to get out, bitch," he said.

With no way to summon help from inside her car, Hailey took her purse and opened the door enough to put one foot out. The man grabbed the handle and flung it wide, screaming, "I told you to get out!"

"Please calm down. This is all going to be resolved," Hailey said as she stood.

"Move!" the man said. He pushed her to the side, knelt in her driver's seat, and began searching.

"Excuse me!" Hailey yelled. "What are you doing? Get out of my car!"

"I better not find a cell phone that ain't hung up," he said.

Hailey took a deep breath and closed her eyes for a moment. She heard the cars passing and considered flagging down another driver for help.

"You need to get out of my car. You're trespassing," she said.

The man backed out of her car and stood up. He towered over her and then leaned close to her face. He pointed his finger close to her nose. "You're a crap driver, and I *still* don't see your license or insurance information."

Hailey stepped back. The man stepped closer, staying in her face.

"Hey, leave her alone," a woman said from a passing car. The man flipped her off.

"The paint job is new, and you ruined it," the man said, pointing to his truck.

"I have excellent insurance. I'm telling you, it won't be a problem."

"It's already a problem," he said. As he raised his finger to Hailey's face, they heard footsteps running toward them. A man wearing a Giants baseball cap ran past Hailey and shoved the pickup driver away.

"What the hell is your problem, buddy?" the pickup driver said. "We're working something out here."

The baseball cap man grabbed the pickup driver's collar and slammed him against Hailey's car, saying, "You need to keep your hands off my wife."

Hailey watched, stunned.

The pickup driver fought to get free while pinned face down on

Hailey's car hood. The baseball cap man turned to her and asked, "Are you okay, sweetheart?"

Hailey was as confused as the pickup driver. She nodded, "Yes—yes, I am. If we could call the police, that would be a better way to handle all this."

"Look, no offense to your wife, but I just need her information, and she's not giving it," the pickup driver said, his cheek pressed against the car.

"Go get your information, and then we'll give you what you need." He lifted the man and shoved him toward his truck. When the pickup driver was out of earshot, Hailey said, "Thank you so much, sir. I don't want you guys to fight. I only want to clear this up."

"We won't fight. I'll help you get out of this mess." He lowered his voice and added, "Make sure he believes I'm your husband, okay?"

Hailey nodded. The brute strength of this man combined with the husband and wife charade seemed to diffuse some of the pickup driver's temper, so she didn't mind going along.

The pickup driver returned and held out an insurance card for baseball cap man who said, "Did you ask my wife if she was hurt?" Before the pickup driver could answer, he held up his hand to stop him.

"Darling, are you hurt?"

"No, Dear," Hailey said.

"Thank God. You wait in the car, darling. We'll be right back." He helped Hailey back into her car and turned to the pickup driver. "Show me the damage."

They went to the front of Hailey's car, and the pickup driver pointed to several parts of his bumper. Hailey couldn't hear the conversation. She saw baseball cap man hand something to the pickup driver, who got into his truck and sped off.

"What happened? Why did he leave?" Hailey asked as she got back out of the car.

Baseball cap man didn't answer. Instead, he took her arm and gently turned her to face the headlights of oncoming traffic. "My God, do you know who you are?" he asked.

"Pardon?"

"You're Hailey Vaughan!" he said. "I can't believe it!"

"Have we met?" Hailey asked. She couldn't get a good look at him with only the brief flashes of passing headlights on his face.

"We just spoke on the phone. I'm Gage!"

"What? That's impossible!"

"I swear it! It must be fate!" He reached out and shook her hand. "I just happened to be headed back to the hotel after a late lunch."

"I, I—okay!" Hailey stammered, shocked by the coincidence. "Wow, out of nowhere, here you are! Thank you for the fast thinking, by the way."

"My pleasure. While approaching your car, I saw that man berating you. It seemed I could be of service."

"Your timing was perfect. He was about to lose control over a minor bumper tap. I can't thank you enough."

Gage smiled and tipped his hat. "Sure, you can. You could reconsider having a drink with me if it wouldn't cause you a problem with Mason."

Hailey winced and checked her watch. She wanted to get home sooner rather than later, but Mason would likely be gone even if she rushed home now. And after Gage had diffused such a potentially dangerous situation, rejecting his second request to share a few minutes to talk could seem less than gracious. She smiled and said, "I'm not sure how I can say no after such a timely rescue."

Gage gave a two-fisted cheer. "Then don't say no. Where are you headed?"

"To add to the coincidence, I was going to the hotel to pick up the notepad you left for me."

"That's perfect. I'll meet you there." He helped Hailey into her car.

Before she rolled up the window, Hailey said, "Excuse me, Gage. You didn't say why that guy left. I'm going to need his information."

"I've got all the information you need on him. I'll explain at the hotel. Let's go where it will be safer to talk. I'll be right behind you." He patted her car's roof with his hand and then jogged back to an SUV parked a short distance behind her. The headlights brightened when he started the engine. Hailey saw a Chevy emblem on the grill. She couldn't make out the exact model.

The drive to the hotel gave Hailey some time to gather her thoughts. The bizarre coincidence of Gage showing up out of nowhere was eclipsed by the relief she felt for his intervention in her dilemma. Still, meeting him for a drink at the hotel was not something she usually would have agreed to, despite feeling indebted for his kindness. She'd keep their meeting short and then brace herself for the ribbing Felicia was bound to give her.

Five

BY THE TIME Hailey turned into the Marriott parking lot. No cars followed her. She wondered if Gage may have gotten stuck at a traffic light or arrived ahead of her. She parked and scanned the parking lot, looking for him. She saw no other people walking to or from it.

She knew Mason would be angry if the car was damaged, especially if she was at fault, so she checked the front of her car. There was no visible scratch on her car, at least none more distinct than the dried splatters of insects on her bumper.

She entered the lobby and felt the same shame she experienced at enjoying Gage's voicemail message. Mason would be angry if he found out she didn't tell him about an automobile accident. His anger would double if he found out she was having a drink with Gage afterward.

She stopped beside a beautiful floral centerpiece and looked around. After she realized Gage was not in the lobby, she sat by the concierge desk, picked up a sightseeing brochure on the wall beside her, and fanned her face.

She regularly met with powerful CEOs, yet, at this moment, her hands felt clammy, and Felicia's stern warning replayed in her head. She tried to dismiss it.

A family toting luggage entered the lobby from the parking lot. As the doors closed behind them, she considered maybe it wasn't too late to scrap the idea of a drink. She could leave Gage a message, telling him something had come up. No, that would be impolite. She had given her word. Besides, Gage may well have saved her from a physical assault. Sharing a few minutes of her time to show proper gratitude wasn't a big deal. It was good manners.

She went to the front desk, and the clerk greeted her.

"I'm looking for a notepad that was left for me. My name is Hailey Vaughan."

"I'm sorry, ma'am, your husband picked it up a few minutes ago."

"My husband?"

"Hailey?" a voice came from behind. Gage hurried toward her from the direction of the elevators, her precious notepad in hand.

"Here's your notepad," he said, holding it out to her.

Hailey took it. "Thank you. Did she say 'husband'?"

Gage waved it off, saying, "She must have assumed it." He wore a sports jacket with a pressed shirt under it, having somehow dispensed with the baseball cap and parka. Hailey glanced at her watch and said, "You must tell me your shortcut to get here… I can't believe you had time to change your clothes."

"No shortcut. I'm just quick," Gage said, smiling.

Hailey noticed a faint scar the size of a dime beside Gage's left nostril. While there was something familiar about his face, she had no memory of him from the conference. He had dark hair and distinct smile wrinkles beside his eyes and lips.

Hailey loved the look of his outfit. She constantly told Mason how good he looked in a jacket each evening before leaving for work. Gage, too, was attractive, but not stunning.

"Shall we?" Gage asked, motioning for Hailey to lead the way to Concetta of Italy, the hotel's restaurant with an attached lounge. A young hostess greeted them at the door, inviting them to sit anywhere. Soft jazz played in the background. Gage selected a corner table, and when they neared it, he stepped ahead of Hailey and pulled out her chair.

Hailey said, "Why, thank you!"

"The pleasure is mine," he said. After Hailey was comfortable in her chair, he sat while keeping his eyes on her face. "My God, you are even more beautiful when you aren't standing in traffic!"

Hailey laughed and patted the back of her hair, a rare nervous gesture because she was rarely nervous. Gage's flattery felt good, though it fanned her uneasiness.

"Thanks for that compliment, too. Between saving me from an assault and rescuing my notepad, you've been incredibly helpful tonight. I can't get over the coincidence of you following me."

"Oh, I wasn't following you. I happened to be passing by. In any case, my daddy always told me, 'Fate don't negotiate. It knows what it wants and always gets it.' Fate happened tonight!"

"Interesting," Hailey said. "I'm so thankful my fate didn't include a longer amount of time with that angry pickup driver."

"I wouldn't have let him hurt you," Gage replied, placing his phone beside his plate.

Gage's charm was refreshing, and his protectiveness felt good, reminiscent of the early years of her marriage. It was a time when Mason was still the heartthrob she had fallen for, who charmed her with gifts and attention. Then, his high-powered attention evolved into hair-trigger jealousy.

Gage folded his hands on the table and stared at Hailey with a slight smile, making her pat her hair and shift in her seat. "So, you are the mystery man who left me the thoughtful voicemail message," she said.

Gage raised his right hand and said, "Guilty as charged!" He removed a soft plastic pouch from his pocket and pulled out an antibacterial wipe. He cleaned the thin drink menu left by the waiter. Hailey watched intently until he stopped wiping and said, "Oh, it's a ritual for me. You never know who's been holding your menu. Do you know how rarely restaurant menus are washed? I hope this doesn't make you uncomfortable."

"Oh, not at all," Hailey said. "I find it fascinating that you arrive with a supply of cleaning tools."

Gage drew the wipe along the edge of the table nearest him, then pointed to Hailey's menu and said, "Would you like me to…"

"Sure," she said, handing it over. Gage sanitized it for her and gave it back.

A young woman wearing a uniform arrived with a pen and pad to take their order. Hailey ordered an ice water with lemon, and Gage a glass of Cabernet.

"So, where did you have lunch that led to our meeting?" Hailey asked.

"I was on my way back from Wenshire Harbor."

"No wonder," Hailey said. "My office is in Wenshire Harbor."

"Really?" Gage asked. "Anyway, this afternoon, I got a craving for some shrimp scampi. The concierge here recommended Shiney's Shrimp Shack. I have to say it was the best—"

"Unbelievable! I love Shiney's. It's literally across the street from my office!"

"You must be kidding me!"

"I'm serious. Did you love it?"

"Love it? I want to marry it!"

Hailey threw her head back, laughing.

"I can't wait to go back," Gage added.

Hailey recognized this as an invitation, but agreeing to join him for a drink tonight more than met any obligation she felt. She changed the subject, saying, "Gage, there's something I need to know from you, if you don't mind."

"Anything," Gage replied.

"What did you say to the angry truck driver? He left so abruptly."

"Oh, that," Gage said. The waiter brought his glass of wine and Hailey's water. Gage swirled the wine and then raised the glass to see it in the light. "You won't have to worry about that guy," he said. "I handled the situation for you."

Hailey cringed, and then folded her hands on the table. "While I appreciate that, Gage, the guy took a lot of photos, and I have to tell you

I'm concerned about my liability if he makes an issue of the accident. I have no police report, which could be a problem. He went from demanding my information to suddenly driving away. What were your magic words?"

"I didn't use words. I used currency."

"What do you mean?"

"As you know, I'm in town for the Small Business Growth Expo, so, as luck would have it, I'm carrying traveler's checks. I explained he was upsetting my wife and that there was no way in hell that a scratch too faint for me to see on his bumper was more than a $100 touch-up. He said the repair would cost $200. Handing him $300 infected him with a case of accident amnesia."

"You paid him money for me?"

Gage nodded and sipped the wine while watching Hailey process the good news.

She cleared her throat and said, "Thank you, but you shouldn't have. And I insist on paying you back."

She reached for her purse. Gage held up his hand. "Not a penny."

Hailey shook her head and said, "I have to be honest, Gage, I'm uncomfortable with that." She opened her purse on her lap and pulled out her wallet. "I truly appreciate what you did, but I prefer to pay my own debts, and I feel terrible having put you out."

Gage opened his arms to reason with her. "Listen, there was no way I would let that guy bully you. Rather than get into a fistfight with him, I decided to see if appeasing him would work, and it did. Listen," Gage looked up in thought for a moment. "I have a proposition that should address any concern you have."

Hailey had her checkbook open and pen ready. Gage reached across the table and tried to close the checkbook. Hailey pulled it away. "Before you write that check, hear me out," he said. "I'm going to be expanding my business soon, and, to be frank, I'm nervous about it. There will be so many decisions. I could use your help to prioritize the important issues and refining my business plan. I'm hoping you'd be willing to coach me. You can consider our first session something of a trade agreement that fully pays me back."

"Coaching?"

"Yes. Personal coaching is featured on your website, which you mentioned in your presentation. I've never had a professional coach. After your presentation and our fateful experience tonight, I have even more trust in you, and I'm ready to try it."

Though Gage's words flattered her, something about his delivery felt odd. "I suppose we could discuss that, Gage, but that man took many photos before you showed up. He could still come after me for damages if he changes his mind."

"He won't."

"How can you know that? I should have at least gotten a police report."

"Did you get his license plate number?" Gage asked.

"No."

"Neither did I, so if we call the police, what info can we give them?"

Some of the tension left Hailey's face. She closed her checkbook and folded her hands on it.

Gage said, "Please trust me. The guy isn't going to say a word. And if you need me to be a witness, I'll honestly say I saw him drive away from the accident scene before we did."

Hailey sighed and said, "Okay. As rude as that truck driver was, I still want to keep everything above board, you know?"

"I'd expect nothing less from you," Gage said. "I apologize if my intervention made you feel uncomfortable. You seem disappointed."

"Thank you for the apology. I'll only be disappointed if this situation somehow escalates."

Gage's apology and assurances eased Hailey's concern, and during the next half hour, Hailey answered questions Gage had about the key points she had given in her presentation the previous day. She learned he was an even bigger fan of hers than he had indicated in his voicemail message.

Gage's overall appeal and sincerity had begun to grow on her. He was terribly generous with a touch of protectiveness that was easy to become comfortable with. Even his scar added a certain charm. And when he smiled, he had the deepest dimple on his left cheek.

"It's been a pleasure getting to know you, Gage. I'm afraid it's time for me to get going," Hailey said.

"Aww, it's ended too soon," Gage said, smiling. "I think I warned you I'm rather forward, so I'm going to go out on a limb and take a big educated risk, just like you suggested in your presentation yesterday." He rubbed his neck a few times while searching for the best words and then said, "Is there any possibility you could stay here a little longer if I treat you to dinner? The Italian food here is consistently on Zagat's 'Best of' list."

Hailey grimaced and looked at her watch.

Before she could answer, Gage added, "If you need time to think about it, you can do that while we're ordering."

Hailey laughed. She smelled the savory aroma of garlic, sauces, steak, and many grilled delicacies. She sighed. "It is tempting, Gage, but my husband is probably already wondering where I am." She braced for Gage's disappointment.

"Call him. He'll join us." Gage grinned.

It was the second time Gage's invitation to include Mason caught Hailey off guard. At least Gage respected she was married. She loved Italian food and, frankly, didn't feel like preparing a meal at home. Mason would go straight to work after his date with his guns, so he wouldn't miss her.

"You won't be sorry," Gage prodded. He flagged down their waiter and requested dinner menus.

• • •

Hailey studied the menu, comprehending none of the words. A moment of rationalization reminded her this was the beginning of a professional business relationship and put her in a more comfortable place. Besides, if dipping a toe into a pool isn't swimming, dinner together was certainly not an affair despite what Mason would say about it—if he were to find out.

She lowered the menu to see Gage. His menu was closed and set aside. He was watching her.

"Have you decided what you're having already?" she asked.

"I know what I want," he said with a wink.

"I'd better hurry up," Hailey raised the menu again, hiding the blood rush to her face. She felt like she was thirteen years old. She looked around the restaurant. Although the Marriott primarily hosted out-of-town visitors, there was some risk someone she knew might see her with Gage.

The waiter came to their table to take their order. "And what may I bring the lady?" he asked Hailey.

"So many dishes look tasty. I might need another minute to decide." She flipped the menu over to read the back.

Gage ordered an appetizer of creamed spinach dip and chips. "I'll take your salmon and please bring her a Venetian Caesar salad to start." Hailey opened her mouth, and Gage held up his hand before she could speak. "If you want something different, take the salad with you."

Hailey smiled. "I was just going to say a Caesar will be lovely, and that will be all for me."

The waiter took the menus and departed.

Hailey leaned forward and said, "I adore Caesar Salad. Thank you."

"Yes!" Gage said. "I guessed right."

"I can see as part of your coaching, we will not have to work on your assertiveness," Hailey said, laughing.

"Excuse me?" Gage looked at her, puzzled.

"Taking on my auto accident problem as your own, insistence on dinner, ordering for me..."

"I'm sorry," Gage said. "I've made you uncomfortable..."

"No, not at all," Hailey said. "I appreciate the attention, and I really find it all very enjoyable. You are incredibly charming. It's just I'm not used to hearing such flattery. Maybe it's because I'm usually wearing my wedding band." She spread her fingers on the tablecloth. A tan line was clearly visible on her ring finger.

"I bet it's beautiful," Gage said. "Lost?"

"Yes. I have been going nuts looking for it, and Mason called to tell me our housekeeper found it this afternoon—thank God. We were all so stressed out by it."

As Hailey sipped her water, Gage said, "Isn't it great how wedding rings fix everything?"

Hailey coughed and put her napkin to her mouth.

"I wish that were true," she replied. Not wanting to expound on the topic with Gage, she changed the subject. "So, tell me a little about you."

"Funny you should ask," he said. He took a sip of Cabernet. "I fix marriages."

"I beg your pardon?"

"Marriages deemed irreparable, I repair. I'm a certified marriage and family therapist. In my practice, I employ a rather unorthodox method."

Hailey wondered if Gage had sensed her marital tension. From his insight, if he was a therapist, he might have concluded more from her reactions than she intended.

"Interesting," Hailey said.

"Most of the time, it *is* interesting. I came to your presentation for executive input on growing my practice. I liked your Warren Buffett quote about calculated risk: 'Risk comes from not knowing what you're doing.' I'm telling you, your presentation was worth the entire conference fee."

"Thank you. Where's your practice?"

"A couple of hours away in Denburg."

The waiter brought the spinach dip and made room on their table for it.

"Denburg isn't far away, yet you're staying here at the hotel?" Hailey said.

Gage smiled at her curiosity. "The Small Business Growth Expo had enough interesting presentations for me to book a room for the week rather than drive back and forth."

"I see," Hailey replied. "So tell me about this unorthodox method?"

"It's what I've termed Isolated Intimacy Reclamation. I train couples to recover lost intimacy by role-playing with each one individually. I act as a surrogate partner."

"I agree with you," Hailey said. She took a bite of the spinach dip.

"About what?" Gage looked surprised.

"Sounds unorthodox," she answered, covering her mouth. "You'll remember from my talk I'm all about improving business relationships through communication. I don't understand how a surrogate partner could possibly improve a marriage."

"You make a good point, but if one partner in a personal relationship cannot open up to the other, no communication will happen. I enable that communication because, with me, there's no risk."

"It still sounds impossible—no offense. You don't act as a physical surrogate, right?" A nervous laugh escaped her.

"Most couples cannot reach the level of intimacy they crave. Opening themselves up feels too vulnerable. You'd be shocked at what couples say and do to a surrogate spouse. I've saved over 200 marriages through my unique form of role-playing. All I can tell you is it works beautifully. And you've already sampled a taste of it."

"Really?"

"Yes. At the scene of the accident. We role-played a married couple. I assume your husband would have stepped between you and harm like I did."

Hailey almost laughed. She imagined Mason in the same situation. He would have been volatile. He would have fought the truck driver.

"I'm sure Mason would have protected me," she said.

"Of course," Gage said. He watched her, tallying the extra details in her expression. "There's nothing more beautiful than a spouse that will stand up for you in a healthy marriage."

Hailey picked up her water and raised it. Gage toasted the sentiment with his wineglass.

They spent dinner talking and laughing. Gage shared many common interests with Hailey, including travel to tropical locations, the board game Monopoly, and reading. He even subscribed to *Total Health Magazine* like Hailey did, confessing that the publication contained information about his goals, not his lifestyle. Hailey laughed. Gage had become more interesting to her. The similarity between their outlooks on life fascinated her.

A few minutes before ten o'clock, Hailey said, "I'm afraid I really need to get going now."

"So soon?" Gage said. They laughed. He added, "Oh, before I forget. I have something for you I hope you'll like." He reached into his inside coat pocket and pulled out a plain box the size of a Rubik's cube.

"What is it?" Hailey said, taking the box and turning it to find a label.

"I sometimes use this in my therapy. I had an extra one. Open it," Gage urged.

Hailey pulled back the flap and slid out a black box with a large green button labeled *Compliment Generator.* She set it on the table beside her plate.

"I love it," Hailey said. "Does it work?"

"Try it."

Hailey pressed the button and heard a nasally electronic voice.

You are fantastic.

Hailey clasped her hands together and laughed. "I need this!"

"I love it when that happens! Try again. It has more to say!" Gage said. Hailey pressed the button again.

You look beautiful today.

She pressed it four more times.

You're a rock star ... How did you get to be so wonderful ... You might be perfect ... Everyone should be like you.

Hailey picked up the box and said, "This is a great cure for any tough day I might have. Thank you."

"My pleasure," Gage replied. "It's a wonderful conversation starter for an office desk."

"And my desk is exactly where I'll put it. Thank you. This is great." Hailey tucked the box into her purse.

Gage walked her out to the hotel parking lot. They stopped beside her driver's side door. "Thank you for sharing your fine company with me tonight," he said.

"I had a great time," Hailey replied. "Thank you for running interference at the traffic incident tonight, for returning my notepad, and for dinner. I have to say, I'm so pleased to have met you."

"Really?"

Hailey got into her seat. "Yes, I am."

"I appreciate that more than you know," Gage said. He extended his hand, and Hailey shook it. "When can I book my first coaching session?"

"I'll check my calendar at the office in the morning and call you with a time tomorrow."

"Very good," Gage said.

"I have your number," Hailey said. "By the way, I will need your last name."

"Dolon," he replied. "Gage Dolon. And I'm ecstatic." He patted the roof of her car before Hailey drove away.

On her way home, Hailey began having second thoughts about accepting Gage's coaching request. Typically, she would have conducted a more formal interview with Gage before taking him as a coaching client. It wasn't like her to make a decision under pressure. The circumstances of her meeting with Gage were extraordinary and must have distracted her.

She wanted to call Felicia to tell her about the night, but decided to wait until tomorrow for the inevitable lecture about having dinner with Gage. She could better handle it after a good night's rest. Besides, whatever Felicia had been so uptight about obviously hadn't happened.

When Hailey got home, Mason had already left for work, as she had expected. She climbed the stairs to their master bedroom, smiling. Something about Gage's rawness and charm appealed to Hailey. That could be a real distraction. Meeting him in a more professional context would keep things in check. She would keep the coaching commitment, sleep on it, and cancel tomorrow if it didn't feel right.

Six

THE NEXT MORNING, Hailey woke up when she heard Mason downstairs entering the kitchen from the garage. As usual, he was arriving home from his all-night shift as the general manager at *Club Parlay*. He plodded up the stairs and entered the bedroom. "Did you find it?" he said, loosening his tie.

"Find what?"

Mason pointed to her bedside stand. She hadn't noticed the handkerchief folded into a square. She opened it and saw her ring.

"Thank you sooo much, Mason." She kissed him, took the ring, and slid it onto her finger.

"Sure thing," he said. Hailey watched him disappear into his closet. She had so enjoyed her conversation with Gage the night before she wished she could have the same experience with Mason. They used to talk like that every night. If only she could transfer some of Gage's fresh interest in her to Mason, it would do wonders for their marriage.

She dressed and went downstairs, leaving Mason to prepare for a day of sleep. In the kitchen, she prepared a breakfast of oatmeal, sliced banana, strawberries, and a thick slice of sourdough toast. On her drive to the office, she smiled while remembering her evening with Gage. The smile lingered as she entered her office. Robert noticed it and said, "You're cheery today."

"Because it's going to be a great day," Hailey replied. She picked up her morning mail from a tray on his desk and went to her office, closing the door behind her.

She tried to focus on work while the memory of her time with Gage intruded on her focus. Today, her memory painted him as even more heroic in handling the angry pickup driver. She wondered if sleep had enhanced his image in her mind. She had to admit he was charming. Circumstances had brought them together in such a serendipitous way— it was almost as though their introduction was meant to be. She'd keep her coaching agreement. He had become a client. Everything was fine.

She suddenly remembered the *Compliment Generator* Gage had given her and pulled it from her purse. She placed it on the far corner of her large desk and pressed the button.

How did you get to be so wonderful?

Hailey laughed, slid out her keyboard from under the desk, and began returning emails.

By mid-afternoon, Hailey felt her work momentum finally picking up, and her intercom beeped. "Jonah from building management on line one," Robert said.

"I'll take it," Hailey said, picking it up. "Hello."

"Ms. Vaughan, could you come down to our office immediately? I have an urgent matter to discuss," Jonah said.

"I'm up to my neck in work. What's it about?"

"I prefer to discuss it in person—if you don't mind. I encourage you to see me immediately," Jonah's voice was tense.

"Fine. I'm on my way." As Hailey passed Robert's desk, she said, "Jonah needs to see me. Do you know what it's about?"

"I sure don't," Robert said.

Hailey checked a wall clock behind Robert's desk. It was 4:45 p.m. "I'm not sure how long he needs to talk to me, so if you are finished for the day, go ahead and take off."

"Okay." Robert closed a notepad on the desk, scooted to the edge of this chair, and clicked his computer mouse to close his open programs.

Hailey rode the elevator to the lobby and went to the cramped building management office.

"Thanks for coming, Ms. Vaughan. I have something important to bring to your attention, and you'll understand why I preferred to discuss it in person." He held his hand toward the chair for her to sit.

Hailey looked out of place, sitting on the tattered chair in a business suit. "What's going on?" she asked, taking a seat.

Jonah closed the door of the cramped office and knelt on one knee beside her. "I have some disturbing video you need to see," Jonah said. He flipped open the cover of an iPad. A video was already queued up. He tapped *Play*. Hailey saw her assistant, Robert, standing inside the parking garage, stopping drivers who had pulled forward after taking a parking ticket. Three cars and three times, driver windows rolled down. After Robert spoke a few words, the drivers handed cash out the window, and Robert handed something back to them.

"Robert's dealing drugs?" Hailey asked. She squinted at the screen and then looked up at Jonah.

"No, he's selling your validations, ma'am," Jonah said.

Last week, Hailey had laughed when she opened her bill for parking validations. The $1,225 charge was ridiculous, and she had called Jonah's office to clear up the charges, stating that she refused to pay it. She kept parking validation stickers for the rare occasions when she met clients at her office. She could count on her fingers every client who had visited in the last six months. The total amount should not have exceeded $50.

Hailey watched the video again, unable to believe what she saw.

"Is your employee aware you buy these and they are completely traceable?"

"This is crazy," she said.

"I'm afraid it is true. We've verified the auto license plates of his customers, and they match with your validation stickers."

"I can't be liable for all this?" Hailey said.

"Unfortunately, the parking spaces were used, and Unico Parking wants their money. Building management can't waive this. He is your employee and, therefore, your responsibility."

"There must be another solution because this is absurd."

"I called Unico Parking," Jonah said. "They'll make you a deal, settling this for seventy-five cents on the dollar."

New footage of Robert wearing a different outfit on another day played on the screen. "It's coming out of his last check," Hailey said.

"You do what you have to do, ma'am. I'll let Unico Parking know you accept their settlement."

Then Hailey remembered the thefts from her office. "Did Robert file a report with you about items stolen from my office?"

Jonah shook his head. "No reports have been made."

"Dammit," Hailey said. She thanked Jonah for the bad news and left his office. As she rode the elevator back up to her suite, disbelief changed to anger. She and Robert had never really clicked. There was something about him that never felt right. She had never been entirely comfortable with him, and now she knew why.

The more she considered the situation, the more Hailey could link Robert to the other instances of theft—her phone, iPad, and right after Robert had been hired, her laptop had disappeared, too. Anyone who would fleece her by selling parking validations would have no qualms about stealing her personal belongings from her office.

She wanted to fire him on the spot, but when the elevator opened to her suite, she found the light off. Robert had wasted no time in leaving for the day. With irrefutable proof Robert was a thief, she wondered if he was also dangerous.

Back at her desk, she was tempted to call Mason. She wasn't looking forward to his inevitable gloating. Her relationship with Robert had caused repeated arguments with Mason, almost verbatim, beginning whenever Mason asked, "Why can't you just hire a woman?" His hair-trigger jealousy surfaced whenever Hailey mentioned Robert, so she stopped mentioning him. This worked until her silence about Robert fanned Mason's paranoia.

She picked up her phone and rehearsed her opening to him. It was as good as it was going to get. When he answered, Hailey cut to the chase. "Hi. I'm going to have to let Robert go." She paused, imagining the wave of pleasure Mason certainly felt at that moment.

"Why? What happened?"

"Remember the outrageous parking bill I told you about?"

"Yes. Wasn't it twelve hundred bucks or something?"

"Right. He was selling my parking validations in the parking lot."

"No way."

"Yes. Building management showed me security camera footage."

"Bastard. I told you he was no good!" Mason yelled. Hailey held the phone away from her ear for a moment.

"I bet he's the one that stole your phone and iPad, too," Mason added.

"In any case, I want him gone. I'll let him go in the morning. I'll ask building management to have the police on hand, and everything should go smoothly."

"I want to be there, too."

"Mason, I don't want this to become a scene."

"I told you I never liked the guy, and now it takes this to make you see he should never have been hired."

"Mason, I took a risk by sharing this with you because you've always had a problem with my decision to hire him. Please don't gloat."

"Fine. I still want to be there."

After the conversation, Hailey prepared a termination letter for Robert and resumed some tasks Jonah's call had interrupted.

She remembered her promise to call Gage. She wondered how he would handle her situation with Robert. As a therapist, he would undoubtedly have some insight.

She dialed.

Gage answered on the first ring, saying, "Perfect timing! I was just thinking about you."

Gage's greeting brought a grin to Hailey's face. How wonderful it would be for Mason to answer one call from her this way. "And our serendipity continues," she said. "I had promised to call you to schedule our first coaching session. I apologize for being late. Something rather uncomfortable has come up I have to deal with."

"I'm sorry to hear that. Is everything okay?"

"It'll be fine. I just learned I must let my assistant go."

"Ouch."

"Ouch, is right. He was stealing. Firing someone is never easy, but in this case, it is vital."

"Tough decisions you aren't willing to make only get tougher," Gage said, citing a line from Hailey's presentation.

Hailey laughed. "Someone's been paying attention."

"You made it easy. Did your assistant confess?"

"No. I haven't confronted him about it yet."

"How do you think he'll respond?" Gage asked. "I'm sorry for the questions. The therapist in me is coming out."

"That's okay. Robert has had a couple of temper tantrums, but I'm not very worried. Our building security is good, and I plan to have security on hand."

"Excellent. If he's vengeful, security will thwart most of his options," Gage said.

"Oh, I certainly don't think he would retaliate against me. After all, *he's* in the wrong!"

"In a perfect world, that's true. Sadly, you cannot predict vengeful behavior. Especially when a person feels spurned."

"Great. Something else for me to worry about."

"Sorry," Gage said.

"That's okay. Sometimes I'm not cautious enough. You sound experienced on this topic. Maybe I should hire you for some security consulting."

"I'd love it if that happened. I'm sensitive to security issues and learned you can never be too careful. Did this Robert have your home address?"

Hailey hadn't considered that, either. Gage's question was as reasonable as it was disturbing. "Yes, but my husband and I live in a gated community with full-time guards."

"I'm glad to hear that. The only other area in which I would be concerned is identity theft. Did he ever purchase items on your behalf?"

Hailey had to think about that. She had given Robert her credit card to purchase a few office supplies and a plane ticket for a business trip she took last month. "Yes, only recently, on only one credit card."

"You'll want to cancel the card. And as extreme as it sounds, you should also have your office door re-keyed."

"I should be okay there, too, because the only access to my suite is by elevator key card."

"Is management aware of the theft?"

"Yes, they brought it to my attention."

"Then they should replace your elevator key card as part of standard protocol."

"Gage, I want to thank you for raising my level of anxiety!" Hailey laughed.

"I apologize, Hailey. I've learned in my business that losing a job or an important person can cause some of our deepest emotional reactions. Fired employees who are angry can exhibit extreme behavior shortly after their termination. It makes sense to take precautions during the first month or so."

"I have no problem with that. I'll talk to building management right away." Hailey jotted a note on a pad. "Meanwhile, shall we book your first coaching session? I have my calendar in front of me."

"Fantastic. How about tomorrow night, 7:00PM here at the Marriott's Concetta of Italy?"

Hailey laughed at Gage's enthusiasm. "You sure don't waste time, do you?"

"Not when I've made a decision."

"Okay, same place. I'll see you then," Hailey said.

"And do let me know how it goes with your assistant," Gage said.

"I will. Thank you for your advice."

• • •

Hailey exited the elevator in the lobby. Isaac, the Echelonian, saw her and ran to meet her as she walked to the garage elevators. Hailey raised her hand and said, "No! I told you I'm not interested. *Please* don't start…"

"Ms. Vaughan, I have a message for you," Isaac said. He held out a card to her. She kept walking, rounding the corner to the garage elevators.

"I'm thrilled with my life," she said, pressing the down button. "I don't need to reach some new echelon. I'm not interested. I've heard your message."

"You haven't heard this message. I come to you with a special request from our leader." Isaac held out the laminated card to her again, and Hailey took it. It had a blue tint with the words *Hailey Vaughan* embossed at the top. In the middle, the Echelonian logo of a staircase was centered above a color photo of Hailey and the words *Personal Guest of Eusebio Xismanchitl.* The photo was one of Hailey's publicity shots of her smiling at a podium.

"What are you talking about?" Hailey said. The elevator opened. After Hailey stepped in, Isaac opened the door to finish his pitch. "Do not make me late," Hailey said, pointing to her watch.

"Our honorable leader of conscience, Master Eusebio Xismanchitl, saw a video of one of your presentations. He would like to make you an offer."

"What's the offer?" she asked, examining the card.

"Master Eusebio has indicated your public oratory was magnificent. If you would meet him, he'll discuss a business proposition. We'll provide transportation at your convenience."

Hailey's first thought was a consulting job for the Echelonians would be the perfect opportunity to be compensated for the inconvenience they constantly caused her. Her next thought questioned how effectively she could assist an organization she didn't like.

"I'll think about it," Hailey said.

"That's all we ask," Isaac said. He released the elevator, and as it closed, he added, "The offer will be generous. Please consider hearing it."

When Hailey got into her car, she immediately took a photo of the card and emailed it to Felicia. The Echelonian offer and the fancy unsolicited ID card would make great conversation.

• • •

When Hailey got home, Mason called out to her as soon as she entered the door, "Hale, I need you in here. You have some explaining to do."

She rolled her eyes as she dropped her keys on a table by the door and then went to him. She found Mason standing in their gourmet chef's kitchen, papers scattered on the granite island countertop.

He tapped his fingers on a box of chocolates decorated with an orange ribbon. Beside it was an open miniature card. Mason flicked it toward her with his finger. Hailey read it.

Sweets for a boss who gives a great "job."—Robert

Hailey gaped at the card.

"It came in today's mail," Mason said.

"I have no idea what this is about," Hailey said.

"You sure you want to fire him? Sounds like he provides employer benefits."

"Oh, give me a break, Mason! Don't be ridiculous! I'll call him right now." Hailey took out her phone.

"Forget it," Mason said. "Put your phone away. I have something more important to show you."

"Fine, but you have to believe me. We know he is a lying thief, but he's never been stupid, and sending me a gift with such an inappropriate message is stupid. I don't know what he'd gain from it. I have *not* had an affair with him."

"Look what else I found," Mason said.

Hailey's pulse raced as Mason slid some papers toward her. She picked them up. They were printouts of a paid instant background check. He pointed to the documents and said, "He's a criminal! I told you to do a background check before you hired him."

Hailey picked up one document. Robert's criminal past included shoplifting, check-forging, and a shortlist of other charges.

Mason tapped his finger on another page, saying, "He's got two assault and battery charges. The guy is violent. I wish you'd let me arm you."

"Mason, we've been over this a million times. I have absolutely no interest in carrying a firearm or even having one in my office. Besides, it's a moot point. I'm firing him first thing in the morning."

Mason gathered the papers and shuffled them. "He's dangerous. I'm going into the office with you tomorrow."

"That's really unnecessary. Building security will be there, and Jonah will arrange for the police, too."

"I'd still like to be there."

"Suit yourself."

Hailey wondered if Mason wanted to be present for her safety or simply to enjoy vengeance on a man he never liked. Either way, his presence wouldn't hurt. She remembered a few instances when Robert had blown up over seemingly insignificant problems like a broken copier. Then, there was the time when the electrician caused Robert to have to stay a couple of hours past closing time. The electrician had called Hailey the next day to share how Robert had exploded at him, throwing a pen holder to the floor because the electrical repair had taken too long.

"He interviewed so well," she said to Mason.

"Of course he did," Mason said. "The best cons do."

• • •

Hailey went to work an hour early the next day to ensure Robert wasn't in her office unsupervised. Before taking the elevator to her suite, she walked next door to Hot Perks Coffee Shop for her latte. She pulled open the glass door and entered, no longer paying notice to the photo flyer of the missing woman taped on the inside. The headline read, "MISSING," above a photo of Marissa Swenker and contact information for leads. The coffee shop featured several more posters of Marissa inside, including one on a stand by the cash register. Employees wore bright yellow ribbons by their name tags. Working at Hot Perks was the last place Marissa had been seen.

Hailey had first seen the flyer several months ago. She instantly recognized Marissa as the cheerful girl who always made Hailey's complicated drink correctly. Each time Hailey ordered, she asked if they had received more information about Marissa. Each time, she got the same answer: "No news yet."

When she returned to her office, the phone rang before she could sit at her desk. "I'm in the lobby. Robert's on the way up," Mason said.

"Thanks," Hailey replied, rolling her eyes at Mason's excitement.

She heard Robert enter the outer office. She got up and greeted him before closing her door to call Jonah. In a hushed voice, she said, "I'm ready, are you?"

"Give us five minutes."

"Got it." Hailey hung up.

Four minutes later, she went to Robert's desk.

"Would you please come with me?" she asked.

"Sure," Robert said. "Do I need to take a notepad?"

"No."

As they rode the elevator, Robert said, "We're going on our first field trip?"

Hailey gave the comment a courtesy laugh that didn't relieve the tension. Moments later, the elevator doors mercifully opened.

Mason, Jonah, and two uniformed security guards stood outside.

"Robert, I need you to come with us," Jonah said.

Robert looked at Hailey. "What is this?" he asked. Hailey eased past him. One of the security guards stepped in and took Robert's arm. "Does somebody want to tell me what this is about?" Robert asked as he stepped out.

"We'll explain everything in a moment," Jonah said.

The small group followed the security guard, who guided Robert by the arm around the corner to the management office. Robert's gait was stiff, and he hesitated at the door before entering the office at the guard's prompting.

Jonah pointed to a chair and went to his desk as Robert sat. Hailey and Mason stepped inside. The security guards stood outside the doorway.

"What the hell is going on?" Robert said, his face turning red.

"Unfortunately, Robert, I'm going to have to terminate your employment effective immediately," Hailey said.

"What? Why?" Robert's shocked reaction was convincing.

"I think you know why," Mason said.

"Mason, please..." Hailey raised her hand to him. "Robert, I've prepared your last paycheck. It's more than fair." She handed him an envelope. He wouldn't take it. She tossed it onto his lap.

"Why are you firing me?"

Jonah interjected, "Robert, we've seen you selling parking validations in the lot."

Robert crossed his arms. "That's bullshit."

Jonah turned his laptop on his desk so Robert could see. Footage rolled, showing Robert soliciting the drivers of no less than six cars, passing something into the window for something else he quickly shoved into his pocket.

Robert observed the footage. "Those aren't validations," he said to Hailey, who now leaned against the doorframe. "And *I'm* not your problem."

"Robert, we've matched the vehicle license plates with the validation stickers you sold. The evidence is clear, and you are liable for repayment of twelve hundred twenty-five dollars," Jonah said.

"It's over, Robert. You no longer work for me," Hailey said. "I'm sorry. I cannot compromise my requirement of complete honesty from my assistant."

"C'mon, please give me a break. I need the work. I can't afford to lose this job."

"You should have considered that before you put your job at risk."

"Put me on probation! I'll take a pay cut—please don't do this!"

Mason put his hand on Hailey's shoulder and said, "You've heard enough, Hale. Let's wrap this up."

"Is this because of the affair?" Robert asked Hailey.

Mason took his hand from her shoulder. All eyes went to Hailey.

"Nice try," she replied. Hailey remembered having mentioned Mason's suspicion in passing to Robert months ago. Robert had laughed at the notion. Then he said, "I should be so lucky." Hailey decided it would be best not to mention it again.

A slight smile crossed Robert's face.

Mason clenched his jaw as he looked back and forth between Hailey and Robert.

"Getting rid of me doesn't make our feelings disappear," Robert said.

"You slime bag!" Hailey shouted. "We didn't have an affair, and you know it." She turned to Mason and said, "You see what he's trying to do, right?" Mason's eyes drilled into Robert.

"I didn't say 'our' affair," Robert continued. "I meant the affair you have me cover for when you are out of town."

"Liar! Get him out of here!" Hailey said. Mason approached Robert. Hailey stopped him, saying, "Mason, I didn't have an affair, and if I did, why would I have told him about it?"

"If I did?" Mason said as he stepped out of the office.

"You've got to be kidding me!" Hailey shouted, pointing at Robert. "You believe a desperate thief? I've never cheated on you."

Robert's smile grew.

Jonah said, "I'll call the police. If you want to press charges, they'll assist you."

"Absolutely," Hailey said, glaring at Robert. His smile vanished.

"We'll hold him outside," a guard said. As they took Robert by the arms and helped him to his feet, he looked at Hailey and said, "You better watch your back, bitch."

Mason came through the open door and grabbed Robert by the collar. "Are you threatening my wife?" he shouted. The guards intervened, removing his grip on Robert.

"All I said was she needs to watch her back."

"What the hell is that supposed to mean?" Mason asked.

Robert looked at Hailey, who had moved to the doorway. "I'm not who you need to worry about. And you deserve whatever happens to you."

Robert's audience looked at one another, confused.

"You'll have plenty of time to reconsider coming clean with us in jail," Mason said.

Robert yanked his arms free of the guards and lunged toward Hailey. Mason tried to grab him but caught only his shirt as Robert slammed into Hailey, knocking her into the door frame. She dropped to her knees, clutching the side of her head with her hands.

Both guards chased Robert, who collided with a bystander in the lobby before escaping to the street. The guards ran after him until they were out of sight.

Mason knelt over Hailey and examined her forehead. She had a small cut beside her right eye, and the swelling had begun. He helped her to the guest chair in the office and said, "I'll get you some ice from Hot Perks." He jogged out of the lobby.

While Jonah waited with Hailey for Mason to return, police officers showed up, and Hailey gave them a report of the parking validation theft. Then Jonah described the incident that led to Hailey's injury.

Mason returned with ice wrapped in a towel and escorted her back to her office, nagging her to keep it pressed to her forehead.

"Why don't you take the rest of the day off?" he asked as they exited the elevator into her suite.

"It's only a small cut, and the swelling will subside. I'll leave early," Hailey promised.

They entered her office, and Hailey sat at her desk and sighed, keeping the ice pressed to her forehead.

"I talked to the guards outside of Hot Perks," Mason said. "They told me Robert got away. Make sure he isn't allowed back into the building."

"Jonah won't let him back in. I'm not worried," Hailey said. She got up, went to a wall mirror, and pulled the ice pack from her head. Her eyes welled up. "Mason, I didn't cheat. I never have."

Mason stood silently momentarily and then said, "I know."

"Thank you." Hailey took a tissue from her desk and wiped her face.

"I'm going to try to grab a nap at home before I leave for work. I have to go in early. If I miss you, I'll see you in the morning," Mason said as he went to the door. "Call me if you need me."

"Thanks. See you soon," Hailey replied.

After he had left, Mason came back to her doorway. "I still wish you'd carry," he said.

"Mason, I don't want a gun, and you agreed not to push it," Hailey said. Mason shrugged, went to the elevator, and pressed the button. "I'm sorry," Hailey hollered after him. "I know you mean well. I appreciate it."

Mason leaving early for work kept Hailey from having to explain her coaching meeting with Gage. She only wished Mason could handle that information. Since nothing questionable was going to happen, what Mason didn't know wasn't going to hurt him.

Hailey spent a couple of hours scouring websites for temporary employees until she felt completely overwhelmed by the options. Her phone rang.

"Hey, Felly," Hailey answered.

"I was waiting to hear from you. Have you called that mystery guy back?"

"Yes, and I actually met him," Hailey said. "And you probably won't believe me when I tell you how." Hailey gave Felicia a recap of her first meeting with Gage.

"I don't like it, Hale," Felicia said. "It sounds like he's roping you into a relationship."

"Stop worrying. Yes, it's a totally professional relationship, and he knows it. But *you* could have a personal relationship with him ... I think I might be able to set you up."

"What does he look like?"

"Nice. I'd say, overall, he's handsome. He's got a little scar beside his nose that could be described as adorable. At the accident, he wore a baseball cap, jeans, and a parka. He might have changed before I got to the hotel because he wore a sports jacket, and the baseball cap was gone."

"You love a man in a suit. Damn, he's good," Felicia said.

"Well, he might be good for *you*. I'll see what I can do. Right now, I have a bigger problem."

"I fired Robert."

"What? Why?"

"Theft. The police are involved. We confronted Robert, and he denied it. Then he freaked out, threatened me, and ran. Security didn't catch him. I'll tell you more later."

"What a scumbag."

"Now I desperately need a new assistant, and I have no time to find, interview, and hire one."

"Want me to help? I can post an ad for you."

"I couldn't ask you to do that."

"You didn't. I offered. I have the time. It'll take me ten minutes. Send me the job description, and I'll get you some interviewees."

"Thank you so much, Felly. I owe you."

"Let's get together. It's been too long."

"Deal. Maybe this weekend."

After the call, Hailey went to Robert's desk and stood momentarily in thought. Despite the building's full-time security and Mason's promise of availability, she felt more uneasy than she had expected after firing Robert. What had he meant by telling her she needed to watch her back? The manic rage over Robert had unnerved her and matched the sketchy background Mason had uncovered about him. If Robert were to somehow make it back up to her suite, she'd be essentially defenseless.

She called the building management office. When Jonah answered, she said, "I want to make sure Robert's elevator key card has been deactivated and all the guards on staff have been briefed about what happened."

"Don't worry, Ms. Vaughan. Everything is locked down. He won't get past the building entrance."

Hailey went back into her private office and locked the door. She was trying to get her mind back on her work when she noticed the Echelonian ID card on her desk and picked it up. For such a bizarre group, they were certainly doing something right. What a few months ago was a handful of members handing out flyers downtown was now a popular movement. During the last week, Hailey had seen new Echelonian booths popping up throughout the city at shopping centers, the local hospital, and parks. She had to admit she was curious about how their numbers had multiplied so quickly. As annoying as they could be, the opportunity to talk to their leader could be interesting, and to be paid for it would be a bonus. She examined the card. It had no phone number. She decided to take an early lunch and check with Isaac on her way out.

As Hailey exited the elevator, Isaac stood the moment he saw her and came around outside the booth to greet her.

"Hello, Ms. Vaughan," he said, smiling as he approached.

"Hi. I've thought it over, and I'd be willing to discuss the business arrangement with your boss." Hailey handed him the ID card he had given her the day before.

Isaac waved the card away and said, "Please keep your ID card. Master will be so excited about this. When can you meet him?" He beamed.

"I could meet him later this afternoon if he's available."

"Please hold on a moment while I check." Isaac stepped away to the booth, pressing his phone to his ear. After nodding and saying "yes" several times, he returned to Hailey.

"Master would consider it a privilege to meet with you today. How about one hour from now?"

"Fine. I need to get some lunch," Hailey said, checking her watch.

"We would be honored to provide transportation when you return."

Hailey smiled and said, "You're going to drive me? Sounds urgent."

"Our mission to fix and enlighten all the damaged lives surrounding us is urgent," Isaac said. "We provide a car service for our VIP guests. We'll have transportation to Master Eusebio's location when you return from your lunch. You won't be sorry."

"Thank you," Hailey said. She exited the lobby and went to a sandwich shop next door to Hot Perks Coffee Shop.

Seven

AFTER HAILEY HAD escorted Robert to the lobby, Gage heard only the faint hiss of an empty office. He removed his headphones and exited his Blazer to get some lunch. When he returned, Hailey's office was still quiet. The silence reminded him of a few weeks ago when she was out of town for three days. Gage turned his laptop's volume up as high as it would go. He longed to hear her voice again. He could usually count on some occasional banter between her and Robert as they hollered to one another about phone calls and tasks she needed to complete. Now Gage's laptop showed flat lines on each recording device. What was going on?

As noon approached, he placed his camera on his lap and fixed his eyes on the lobby exit to the Handel Towers Building. The lunch crowd descended on Wenshire Harbor, and the lot was so full the attendant had double-parked some cars, one blocking Gage's Blazer. He didn't mind because it further obscured any view of him while not hampering his view of Hailey's office window.

Gage got out his binoculars and focused on the lobby's glass doors. Inside, he saw Hailey talking to a man. Their conversation was brief yet long enough for Gage to get his camera ready. Hailey came out of the door, and Gage clicked away, getting a new series of photos, including an excellent profile shot of her looking back over her shoulder when she noticed the honking of a nearby traffic altercation. She disappeared into the sandwich shop next door.

Forty minutes later, Hailey returned to the Handel Towers' front door and entered the lobby. He opened his laptop to launch his recording software when he noticed Hailey come back outside. She crossed the sidewalk and got into the back of a black Cadillac Escalade SUV with limo-tinted windows, its door held open by a uniformed driver.

What the… Gage moved the laptop to the passenger seat and got out. The driver closed Hailey in the back seat and walked around to the driver's door. Gage whistled for the missing parking attendant. "What are you doing, baby?" he muttered to himself. He got into the Blazer and leaned on the horn for five seconds, getting the attention of the parking attendant who came running and the man who was climbing into the driver's seat of the Escalade.

Gage opened his door and yelled, "I have to get out. Move this fucking car!" He pointed at a Toyota Prius, double-parked to block him in.

"I'll get the key," the attendant said, turning and jogging back to the valet key box at the entrance.

"Hurry up, dammit," Gage yelled. He honked the horn again twice as the Escalade pulled away with Hailey inside.

The harried parking attendant moved the Prius, and Gage sped out of the lot in pursuit. He slowed to look both ways at the first three intersections. When he could find no sign of the Escalade, he pulled over and screamed at the top of his lungs, beating the steering wheel. He opened the laptop, grabbed his hair, and concentrated on breathing to avoid smashing it. He turned up the laptop's volume and clicked on an icon labeled *Hailey's phone*. If only she would make a call to someone—anyone—he could learn something about where she was going and with whom.

• • •

Hailey made herself comfortable in the back of the Escalade. She paid no attention to the horn sounding across the street. She checked her phone messages and saw a text message from Felicia:

What's with the fancy Echelonian ID? Don't tell me you joined them! Hailey replied:

I didn't. They're trying to impress me. Going to meet with their leader. Potential client. More later.

The SUV drove Hailey to the northwestern side of town, just beyond the Wenshire Harbor city limits. They pulled into a set of long buildings that surrounded a larger one.

"What is this place?" Hailey asked the driver.

"It used to be a religious private school," the driver replied. "It was shut down after successful lawsuits by parents about illegal conduct by the folk running it. The Echelonians are leasing it from the city until they find a permanent place."

They entered a circular driveway with a slightly tilted flagpole in the center, rising from a dried-up fountain. The SUV stopped at a worn curb with faded paint on it. A sidewalk with weeds pushing through its cracks led to dilapidated front doors. Three men in suits stood outside, watching them.

The driver got out, came around, and opened the door for Hailey as one of the men approached.

"May I see your ID, please?" the man in the suit said.

Hailey pulled her wallet out and flipped it open to her driver's license.

"No, I need to see a membership ID."

"Did Isaac give you another ID card?" the driver asked.

"Oh, that," Hailey said. She pulled the other ID from her purse and handed it over.

"Ms. Vaughan, thank you so much. We must be careful. I'm sure you understand."

"Certainly," Hailey replied.

"I'll be here waiting for you, Ms. Vaughan," the driver said.

The suited man led Hailey to the front doors. Shattered windows that ran along the length of the buildings were boarded up. Unbroken windows had the shades pulled closed.

The two other suited men pulled both front doors open while the first led Hailey between them into the building. Inside, the floors were polished to a shine, and the walls lined with quotes and bible verses. A massive banner over the entrance to the main corridor read, "Truth and Justice at All Costs."

They walked through a maze of hallways deep into the back of the building. They entered a large, dimly lit room that had been converted into a warehouse. Shelves were stacked high with pamphlets that had the Echelonian logos on them. Near the back of the storeroom, two more men in suits guarded a door. The man who led Hailey said, "Hailey Vaughan."

One of the guards motioned for Hailey to approach. When she came close to him, he pulled out a wand and said, "Please hold your arms out. I will not touch you." Hailey complied. The man scanned her with the metal detector and, after a few moments, allowed her to go through the door.

Inside, Hailey saw a small man with a dark complexion, wearing what looked like a white bathrobe, sitting at a grand desk. Behind him sat two more suited men in each corner of the room, watching her.

"Welcome, Ms. Vaughan. I am Eusebio Xismanchitl." When Hailey approached the desk, he didn't stand, instead offering his hand palm-down as though she should kiss it.

Hailey shook it and said, "Pleased to meet you, Mr—"

"Let's dispense with formality and save time. You can refer to me as Master Eusebio."

Hailey stopped herself from laughing when she saw Eusebio's sincere expression.

"Please have a seat," he said.

"Thank you." The men behind Eusebio kept their eyes locked on her. On her left, a wall held a painting featuring Eusebio with his hand on the forehead of a woman who knelt before him. The opposite wall had numerous framed quotations, the author noted as *EX*. "What sort of consultation are you looking for?" Hailey asked.

"I'm looking for more than a consultation. I've seen footage of several of your recent presentations, including the Small Business Growth

Expo last week. I must tell you I'm most impressed by your connection with your listeners."

"Thank you again. That's flattering."

"You're welcome. In fact, I was struck by your charisma and your honesty, too. Some of your anecdotes were so pure and your intentions so truthful it soon became obvious—it is God's will that you join us."

"God's will?"

"Without a doubt. Rarely is it so clear, and because of that, I'm prepared to offer you a coveted position within our organization."

"I see," Hailey said. She looked at the men behind Eusebio. Their eyes remained locked on her. "What sort of offer are you making? My day rate is $2,400."

Eusebio smiled as if to forgive Hailey's naivety. "Our pay will be worth much more than that."

"I see. You certainly have my interest," Hailey said with a nervous laugh.

"Ms. Vaughan, our movement is afoot. Our numbers have burgeoned, and growth is accelerating. Nothing can stop the real truth and justice we stand for. There are countless religions. We are so blessed God has given us the truth. You will be elated and elevated to a higher echelon when we show you how to live in pure truth and justice. Your salvation will be assured. Based on the philosophies you espoused in your presentation, your perspective needs only minor adjustments to align with ours."

"Sir, I don't mind providing a professional service for your group, but if doing so requires membership in your organization, I'm afraid that offer doesn't work for me."

Eusebio ignored Hailey, saying, "You are welcome to ask any of our members. They'll tell you joining the Echelonians was the best thing that happened to them."

"I'm sure they will, but—"

One of the men behind Eusebio held up his hand to stop Hailey.

Eusebio continued, "I dreamt of our movement before it began, realizing every success before it happened. I foresaw the growth we've experienced. I had visions of every good thing that has happened to us. And I now have a new vision of our future that includes you."

Hailey shifted in her seat and patted the back of her hair. "Oh?"

"Yes. I have seen you do what is right. You embraced our message. My dreams always come true, Ms. Vaughan."

Hailey stared at him. "I'm not sure what to say."

"Say you will begin learning our truth and are prepared to dedicate your God-given talent to our cause."

Hailey cleared her throat and said, "Mr.—"

"Master."

"Right. I'm flattered by your interest in me, but with all due respect, the way you've described your proposal takes away my choice and makes my decision a matter of right and wrong."

Eusebio chuckled and then said, "Please take no offense... Sometimes, the truth shoots through me before I can dress it up in a palatable way to my listeners. It's what happens when you operate on a higher level—a higher echelon."

"I see. Well, I will have to pass on your offer, thank you. I'm not a fit for your organization."

"Ah, you need more growth," Eusebio said.

"Pardon me?"

"You will join us, and at that time, we'll welcome you with open arms. Time is on the side of truth."

Hailey stood. "I need to leave," she said.

Eusebio looked slightly over one shoulder, and one of the men behind him jumped up to escort Hailey to the door.

"We'll see you when the truth makes you ready," Eusebio said.

Hailey exited without answering. Her suited escort took her back through the hallways and out to the front doors. Her driver waited by the Escalade, holding the door open for her as if he had expected her arrival right at that moment.

Eight

HAILEY DECIDED TO go straight home after she visited with the Echelonian leader. When she arrived, she went upstairs to change and, as expected, found Mason sleeping. She quietly pulled her running shoes and shorts from her closet and took them downstairs to change into. She looked forward to a good workout to settle her busy mind from the day's stress.

She jogged a quarter-mile from her house, passing the many new Turlock Heights Estates homes scooped up by Silicon Valley entrepreneurs. Each house in the development was as unique as the brick two-story she and Mason owned. At the guard gate, she turned onto Center Street, Henderton's main thoroughfare. It wound through several communities and was lined with popular shops and eateries. Fit Performance Gym was five miles away, where she typically stopped for some lightweight training before jogging back home.

A bicycle and jogging path split off and paralleled Center Street for a mile before turning in its own direction at what some locals called Scary Church. The huge, dilapidated old building had become an eerie eyesore for the locals. Its hollow windows with stained glass teeth around the edges were always dark, even at midday. A rusty cross sat on the steeple, clinging sideways, having refused to be evicted by winds. The wild weeds surrounding it gave it a foreboding appearance.

A short distance beyond Scary Church, the path went through a quarter mile of thick woods before crossing a narrow wooden bridge that spanned the Townsend River. Hailey ran along the path, rising, dipping, and zigzagging through sunlight that slivered through the tree branches. The path took her far enough from the street to silence the sounds of Henderton's traffic. She slowed to check her pulse a few times, hearing only the birds in the branches above.

After a final turn, the path opened to a vast expanse of manicured lawn. In its center sat Fit Performance Gym, a building that, from the outside, seemed nothing more than a large warehouse. As she jogged closer, the exercise equipment and mirrored interior became visible through the lower floor's full-length windows. Inside, a fitness class worked out in unison.

Originally leased to a logistics company that went bankrupt, a couple of local entrepreneurs obtained financing to convert it into a fitness center. Never intended for retail use, the only vehicle access was via a private service road that connected the loading docks to nearby Highway 73. The unusual location gave Henderton exercise buffs a gorgeous scenic jog along the path.

Hailey ran to the front door and flashed her membership card that dangled from a neck strap. Megan, the woman working the front desk, recognized her. "Hi, Hailey. Early workout?"

"Burning off some angst," Hailey said as she speed-walked by.

"Well, burn some off for me, too!" Megan laughed.

Hailey gave a thumbs-up sign over her shoulder without breaking stride. The gym was her escape. Exercise exhilarated her, giving her a sense of accomplishment and control.

After a few upper body exercises and a water refueling, Hailey exited the gym for her run home. She turned up her music and followed the path around the perimeter of the building and back into the woods. When the path rejoined Center Street, she pressed her fingers to her neck, checking her pulse, and then picked up her pace, not satisfied with the intensity of her run.

• • •

Gage sat in his Blazer on the shoulder of Center Street. He had watched Hailey disappear into the woods on the way to the gym. It was the second time she had vanished on him today. This time, he knew where she was going. He was familiar with her Fit Performance Gym exercise routine and knew she would emerge from the woods within an hour. If she took longer, that was okay. He could still be with her while he waited. He pulled his laptop from the passenger seat onto his lap and reclined his seat back a few notches to get more comfortable. He played a couple of Hailey's recent phone calls through his laptop. His eyes closed so he could fully enjoy the creamy smoothness of her voice while she talked to Felicia. He had never met a woman with a sexier cadence than Hailey Vaughan. He grinned at the part when Hailey described his sports jacket and referred to him as attractive. The compliment left him breathless for a few moments. He played it ten more times, closing his eyes for each. "You have great taste, lover," he said. "You flatter me, and you make me blush."

Forty minutes later, he saw Hailey emerge from the woods on the path. He started his Blazer and waited for her to gain some distance before pulling onto the road to follow her. A red light stopped him. He wasn't worried. She could run as fast as she wanted to. She wouldn't get too far away again.

• • •

Hailey had almost finished her run and was on final approach to the guard gate of Turlock Heights Estates. Her phone vibrated in her armband. She checked the caller ID. It showed an unfamiliar local number. She answered in case the police needed to discuss her situation with Robert.

"Yes," she said, pressing her phone to one ear as she ran.

"Hailey, it's Gage."

"Oh, hi!" she said. She smiled and turned up her phone's volume. She plugged one ear to hear him over the passing traffic.

"Sounds like I may have caught you in the middle of something."

"No, no, no!" she said, trying not to sound as winded as she was. "I'm finishing up a run. It's not a problem."

"I might have guessed you are an athlete. I'm sure if I tried to run whatever distance you did, I'd be curled up beside the road, wheezing!"

Hailey smiled at Gage's flattery and stopped to sit on a low red-brick wall that featured the Turlock Heights Estates sign.

"I wanted to call and ask if we could move our coaching meeting from seven o'clock to seven-thirty tonight," Gage said.

"Sure, that's fine."

"What a relief. I know we are meeting after hours, and I hate to make a long work day longer for you."

"It won't be a problem. After the day I've had so far, an extra half hour will help."

"Perhaps it's a bad time to ask how the firing went."

"Not well. Robert was belligerent and became furious. He shoved me while running from the building's management office. The side of my head managed to find the door frame, and now I'm sporting a souvenir of the incident."

"Oh my God, you were injured?"

"Only some swelling and a tiny cut. Fair warning: you'll see it tonight. Don't be alarmed!"

There was silence on the line. "Gage, are you there?" Hailey asked.

"I'm so incredibly sorry this has happened to you," Gage said, his voice drifting off.

"It's okay, Gage. I'm okay. My head will heal faster than my feelings. Robert said some awful things about me, which really shook me up."

Gage cleared his throat and said, "I doubt he'll be a problem for you anymore."

"Why not?"

"You are wonderful. What Robert has done to you will only hurt him."

"Thank you. By the way, if being a therapist doesn't work out, you should look into security consultancy. I'm so grateful for your advice on Robert. Thanks to you, I feel more prepared for whatever he might try."

"I'm glad to have been helpful to you. I find my patients with anger issues often get involved in situations they cannot control. And the lack of control creates more anger in a vicious cycle. They can be destroyed by their own anger. It's almost karmic if you believe in that."

"Oh, I absolutely do," Hailey said.

"Now, Hailey, could you excuse me?" Gage asked. "Something urgent has come up I need to take care of before we meet."

"Certainly. I'll see you at 7:30."

"Yes, you will."

• • •

Gage hung up, threw open the door of his Blazer, and jumped out. Spit flew from his mouth as he screamed, "Son-of-a-bitch!" He stomped around to the passenger side. He kicked gravel that peppered the side of the Blazer and grabbed his hair with both hands. He leaned against the Blazer and bashed the butt of his hand into it, denting the door. He flailed his arms for a moment, as if fighting an unseen assailant. A passing car slowed. Gage swatted at the driver to continue, and the car sped away. Returning to the driver's seat, he looked in the rear-view mirror and wiped his mouth with a tissue. His nostrils flared with each breath. He finger-combed his hair and then picked up his 8 x 10 photo of Hailey. He caressed it with the back of his shaking finger and panted, "It's going to be alright. I promise." He picked up his phone and pressed a speed dial number.

"Hello?"

"Robert, this is Gage," he said, his voice calm and steady.

"I've got nothing for you," Robert replied, "and I won't have anything more. She fired me."

"I'm so sorry to hear that." Gage switched his phone to the other ear and wiped the sweat from his hand.

"Yeah, well, shit happens. You want her home Wi-Fi password? It's the last thing I could get from her new laptop."

"Perhaps, but don't I still owe you money for getting me the first phone?"

Robert hesitated. "Yes, I think you're right. And I sure need that since I won't be getting paid by that bitch anymore."

Gage cringed and squeezed a fistful of fabric on his pants. "Take it easy. There's no need for name-calling."

"Sorry. No offense to your crush. It's just as well it's over. Her nut-job husband looked like he wanted to kill me, and I had to ditch their lame security."

"I'm sorry I put you in that position. I can't apologize enough. It won't happen again."

"Obviously."

Gage took a deep breath and said, "It sounds like you could use the money as soon as possible. I'll tell you what. Get me her home Wi-Fi password, and I'll pay $400. Will that help you out?"

"Wow. No shit? That's great. The problem is, I'm not at the building anymore and can't go back. So how are we going to do this?"

"I have an idea. Why don't I drop it off to you?"

"Fantastic. Sure!"

"I have a pen ... I just need your home address. Go ahead."

• • •

Hailey waved to the guard as she jogged past the Turlock Heights Estates guardhouse, headed for home. Gage's concern about her safety in light of Robert's firing intrigued her.

When she entered the house, she was surprised to find Mason awake, sitting on the sofa in the den, cleaning his guns. Cleaning rods, cloths, brushes, and other tools were spread out on the coffee table. A football game played on television.

"I thought you might be gone already," she said.

"Change of plans. You sound disappointed," Mason said, his voice tense.

Hailey stared at the guns. "No, not at all. I didn't expect you to still be here, that's all."

"I'm almost finished doing this," Mason said, pointing at the guns. "I didn't know you'd be home early."

"Sorry. If I had known you were awake, I would have called to warn you." She leaned against the doorframe. The resentment she felt for sharing her house with the guns spiked. She had tried to be indifferent, but seeing them on display made it impossible. Years ago, Mason had agreed to never bring them out in any of the main living quarters of the house. After this morning's stressful situation with Robert, Hailey chalked up Mason's need to clean them as therapeutic.

After setting her coaching appointment with Gage, Hailey had counted on leaving the house without explaining where she was going. Now, her departure would be trickier since Mason's work shift didn't begin until 9:00 p.m.

"Are you upset about what happened with Robert this morning?" she asked.

Mason closed one of his revolvers into a case. "Robert's criminal record, then threatening you and making a run from the guards, got me all wound up, and I haven't been able to relax since. The guy is dangerous, Hale, and I can't believe you didn't know earlier."

"I'm not a mind reader, Mason. The puzzle pieces didn't fit until Jonah showed me the videotape of the parking garage."

Mason stood and crossed his arms. "I want you to let me arm you."

"No way. I'm not even going to consider—"

"C'mon, Hale! You aren't safe."

"Mason, you know how I feel about the guns. Carrying one of those," Hailey pointed to the table in front of him, "doesn't make me feel comfortable and won't make me safer. I'd be swapping fears for no benefit."

"Guns don't kill people. Vengeful ex-employees kill people."

"Why do I need a gun in a building with full-time security guards? I'm safe."

Mason smiled and shook his head. He got up and walked past her to the kitchen.

"Where are you going?" Hailey asked.

Mason disappeared around the corner, returning a moment later, holding a small fire extinguisher he had retrieved from the kitchen. He threw it into a waste bin by the door.

"Why are you doing that?" Hailey asked.

"Why do we need a fire extinguisher in a town with a fire department?"

"That's absurd, Mason."

"Is it? Robert knows your schedule. It won't be at your building if he wants to hurt you."

"Robert won't try anything that will require a gun. I know him."

"I bet you do."

"What's that supposed to mean?"

"Never mind." Mason sat down and sighed.

"I'm sorry, Mason."

"I'm sorry, too." He placed a pistol on a towel and wrapped it. "Don't ever accuse me of not trying to keep you safe," he added.

"I won't, and I appreciate that. But I also thought we agreed about having the guns out," Hailey said, pointing at the table.

"As I said, you surprised me by coming home early. I'm sorry you had to see the guns, okay? Tell me how often you have seen them in the past decade?" Hailey didn't answer, so Mason did. "Twice? Maybe?"

"That's not the point," Hailey said. "This is an example of you not respecting our agreed rules."

Mason raised his hands and let them flop onto his lap. He picked up the rag and cleaned a revolver, tilting it in the light to examine the chambers.

As Hailey climbed the stairs, Mason said, "I'm trying to protect you, but I can't force you to accept my help. It's your move."

After her shower, Hailey descended the stairs, rehearsed and ready to handle Mason's complaint about her departure for the evening. He had left. Problem solved—for now.

• • •

Hailey made it a practice to prepare for each client meeting during her drive to the meeting. She typically recited aloud the focal points of her presentation and sometimes verbalized some imaginary dialogue to align her thoughts with the task at hand. On the drive to the hotel today, she didn't prepare to coach Gage. She still felt preoccupied with Mason's pressure to carry a gun. She remembered the attention he gave her long ago—flowers, surprise dinners out, impromptu getaways. Where had they gone? The protective attention and advice Gage gave her reminded her of what she once had with Mason.

Perhaps Gage's bizarre therapy might make sense for her and Mason. "Ha!" she laughed. Maybe Gage would consider a professional services trade with *her*. He could help her with her marriage in exchange for her coaching help with his counseling practice.

She fished out her phone from her satchel on the passenger seat and called Felicia.

"Hello?" Felicia answered.

"What are you up to?" Hailey asked.

"I've got a pint of butter pecan, a sofa, and I'm happy. You?"

"Tension on the home front again."

"Oh, no. I'm sorry, Hale."

"He tried to get me to carry a gun again. I refused. Both of us are pissed off right now."

"I thought he knew better. You sound like you're in your car."

"I'm on my way to meet a client."

"Since when do you make evening work appointments?"

"Since Gage hired me to coach him."

"Ooh, la, la! A business date?"

"Stop it. It's not a date! It's a meeting. It's strictly business."

"Does Mason know?"

"No. I was prepared to tell him, but after the gun argument, he took off."

"That's a smart move. You better hope he doesn't find out."

"He won't, and quit making it sound like I'm cheating."

"Sorry."

"Would something thoughtful like flowers or chocolate be too much to ask? Instead, I get, 'Hey, Hailey, you need to carry a gun.' I'd be over the moon if he gave me so much as a wilted bouquet."

"Be glad you have a man, Hale. I have nobody."

"You will soon. I can feel it."

"Whatever. So, where are you meeting Gage?"

"The Marriott."

"Just be careful, Hale. Seeing this guy while you're in a tough spot with Mason may not be a good idea."

"Stop worrying. Gage is totally safe, and he really respects my marriage. He's a therapist, for God's sake. I'll be fine."

"Call me."

"Okay, Felly. Thanks."

Nine

HAILEY PULLED INTO the Marriott lot and parked. Sade's *Hang On To Your Love* played through her car's stereo from her phone's oldies album. She had already replayed the song twice, singing along.

Before she got out, she examined the side of her head in the mirror. The swelling had gone down, and the barely visible cut was easily concealed by her hair.

She gathered her purse and satchel and walked to the lobby, where she saw Gage standing near the entrance to Concetta of Italy. He wore khaki pants and a navy sweater with the top opened to a crisp white collar. In his hand was a beautiful bouquet of purple and yellow flowers. As Hailey approached him, she grinned. "Hey, no bribing the coach!"

Gage laughed. "I bear gifts, not bribes."

Hailey reached for the bouquet. Gage pulled them away, shielding them with his hand.

"What are you doing?" Hailey asked.

"I'm protecting them so your beauty doesn't make them wither with jealousy."

"What a charmer!" Hailey took the flowers. She inhaled their sweet fragrance and said, "Thank you, Gage. This was so thoughtful."

Gage hugged her gently with one arm. Hailey used the flowers as a convenient prop to limit her participation in the hug, wary anyone who knew her and Mason might see her.

"Shall we?" Gage said, motioning toward the entrance of the restaurant.

"Absolutely." As they walked in, Hailey noticed Gage had a rather severe limp. "What happened?" she asked.

"I must have pulled something during the little encounter with your angry truck driver the other night. My leg ached soon after, and the pain hasn't let up."

"I'm so sorry," Hailey said. "It's my fault!"

"No, no, no. Of course not. I'm sure it will clear up in a few days. Please ignore my hobbling."

A well-dressed man by a podium greeted them, saying, "Welcome to Concetta of Italy. Table for two?"

"Yes, and could we get something for these?" Gage asked, pointing to the flowers Hailey held.

"Most certainly, sir." The man took the flowers from Hailey and called a nearby worker with instructions to get a vase. The worker disappeared with the bouquet. The man pulled two menus from a shelf and led Gage and Hailey to a table. Gage pulled out Hailey's chair for her. She said, "You've lost none of your chivalry since our first meeting."

"Pardon?"

"The chair. You pulled it out for me last time, too. You are such a gentleman—even when you are wounded."

Gage sighed as he sat hard in his chair. He pulled out his antibacterial wipes and cleaned Hailey's menu.

"I wonder if that's a habit I should adopt," Hailey said.

"It certainly wouldn't hurt." He smiled as he handed the sanitized menu to her and began wiping down his own.

A waiter came for their drink and appetizer order. Gage ordered fried zucchini and mozzarella sticks and a bottle of Cabernet. Hailey ordered water with lemon.

"Your head," Gage said, leaning forward. "I don't see a boo-boo."

"It's healing. It's there and a bit sore." Hailey lifted the hair from her forehead, showing Gage the damage.

His mouth tightened, and he shook his head. "Some men don't have the proper respect for women. Those men never end up happy."

"I don't think physically injuring me was Robert's goal. Luckily, I'm hard-headed," Hailey said. She then changed the subject and pulled her notes from her satchel. "Ready for some coaching?" She placed the notes beside her plate.

"I've never needed it more," Gage said. "But first, I have to ask you, what's it like?"

"What is what like?"

"Having such a wonderful, understanding husband?"

Hailey blurted a nervous laugh and patted the back of her hair. "Wow. I didn't expect that," she said, buying time to compose an answer.

"I ask because I see your gorgeous ring is back on your finger." He stared at her hand.

"Oh, that. Thank you." She spread her fingers on the white tablecloth, and the ring sparkled.

"I have seen the loss of a ring become a big enough issue to test a marriage."

"Yes, I'm sure," Hailey said. She picked up her fork and ran her thumbnail along the groove in the handle.

"I've upset you. I'm sorry," Gage said.

"No, it's—it's okay!" She put the fork down. "Mason is wonderful. As with any marriage, we do have our challenges."

Gage watched her while nodding slowly.

"Our issues are nothing different than any couple would have to deal with," she added. "You must know that. It's your field, right?"

"Yes, and I have my own firsthand experience."

"You're married?"

"Was."

"I'm sorry."

"Don't be. Fate drew us apart. It was the healthiest thing for us."

"Interesting," Hailey said. She didn't want to digress from her coaching agenda, even though Gage's self-disclosure intrigued her. "If you don't mind my asking, how is it the healthiest thing?"

"The infamous 'irreconcilable differences' crept into our relationship. For us, it was religion. My wife was a devout churchgoer. She wanted me to join her and eventually insisted, even though we had an understanding I was not and would not ever attend church. She couldn't respect our differences, and when she insisted, it damaged our marriage, eventually beyond repair."

"I'm so sorry. Divorce is never comfortable."

"We never divorced. She died before it was official."

Hailey covered her mouth and said, "I am so sorry."

"It's okay," Gage replied.

The waiter came to their table with the appetizers and drinks. He took their dinner orders. Hailey ordered the chicken marsala, and Gage ordered prime rib, rare.

The waiter poured a glass of wine for Gage while Hailey considered how freely Gage had described his marital problem and its tragic ending. She wanted to know how his wife had died, but couldn't think of a tactful way to ask. His wife's insistence he takes part in something he didn't like bore a striking parallel to her situation with Mason. Hailey was so distracted by her thoughts she failed to see the waiter pour wine into her glass, too.

"Oh, I won't need—"

"It's okay," Gage said to the waiter, who apologized and left. "The Cabernet is excellent, Hailey. You really should try it."

Hailey raised her hand above her head. "Designated driver, here."

"Fine. You realize a sip or two will be out of your system long before we finish tonight, but your comfort is most important to me."

Hailey said, "You know, Gage, I'm impressed you would share such a personal anecdote with me about your marriage."

"I feel safe with you." He took a sip of wine.

After thinking momentarily, Hailey said, "I'll share something personal with you."

"I'd be honored, and don't worry, we have doctor-patient privilege," Gage said.

"Of course. I forgot!" Hailey smiled. "The healthy boundary example you remembered from my presentation has become a marital challenge for Mason and me." Hailey sipped her water. "After the unsettling incident with Robert, Mason wants me to carry a gun, and I can't tell you how uncomfortable that makes me."

Gage shuddered and said, "Wow." He took another drink of wine. "I absolutely hate guns."

"Really?"

"Oh…" Gage contorted his face. "I'm terrified of them."

Hailey grinned. "No way!"

"Yes, way." Gage's expression turned serious. "I, uh," he put his head back and blinked several times. When he brought his head down, his chin quivered. "I lost a dear niece to gun violence."

"Oh, I'm so sorry, Gage." She reached across and touched his hand on the table. Great. She had focused Gage on two of his life's tragedies and brought the poor man to tears.

Gage cleared his throat and tried to smile. "In fact, my experience has driven me to become something of a gun-control freak." He began counting off facts on his fingers. "Availability of guns increases impulse-suicides. Crime victims with guns are more likely to be shot when criminals perceive them to be more dangerous. Most lunatics who go on killing sprees got their guns legally or stole them from legal gun owners, and the 2nd Amendment to the Constitution was targeted toward the militia rather than civilian individuals. I could go on and on."

Hailey said, "I'm so impressed by your informed position."

Gage raised his wineglass and said, "To the end of gun violence."

Hailey hesitated and then raised her glass for a toast. "Hear, hear!" She took a sip of wine and coughed. She fanned her face and said, "You're right. It is good."

Gage smiled. "Hailey, I'll tell you what I tell many of my clients. You deserve to be thrilled by your husband. Don't let him or anyone change you or control you."

"I promise," Hailey said.

"Enough of my prying. I'm ready for you to coach me. Where do we begin?"

Hailey sat up straighter in her chair. Sharing with Gage had been so easy and so comfortable. He seemed to understand her. No wonder he was a successful therapist.

"To determine which area of coaching we'll focus on," Hailey said, "I'll need to learn a little more about your expectations of our work together."

"I'm game," Gage said. He slid his plate aside and folded his hands on the table.

"There are several areas we can focus on, including creating compelling goals, unleashing your creative potential, reducing personal barriers and conflict—"

"That one," Gage said. "I want to eliminate barriers." He winked at her.

Hailey blushed. Gage's flirtation had lost its subtlety. "Tell me more about your interest in eliminating barriers," she said.

"Well, some opportunities come along only once in a lifetime, and I don't want to miss a single one of them."

Hailey jotted notes on her pad while paraphrasing him. "We'll work to identify your goals and anything that might keep you from attaining them." She took another drink of the wine. "I must admit, that's delicious," she pointed her pen at the glass.

Gage poured her a little more and said, "It's called *Undurraga T.H. Cabernet Sauvignon* out of Chile. Cherry and strawberry notes on the finish. It feels serious and restrained, yet young, with a long life ahead."

"Don't tell me you're a sommelier, too."

"No. You happen to be tasting my favorite. When I like a wine, I study it, learn it, and remain faithful. I consider sommeliers promiscuous."

Hailey laughed. The host returned to their table with the vase containing the flowers. Hailey admired the vase while the host poured another glass of wine for Gage. "Wow, a painted Amphora," she said. "It's gorgeous. Can we keep this?" she asked the host.

When the host hedged, Gage said, "Please put it on my room tab."

"Of course, sir." The host bowed slightly and then departed.

Hailey cringed. "Oh, Gage, this must be costly. I couldn't—"

"Not a word! It's my pleasure … Are you some vase expert?" he asked.

"I happen to collect them—promiscuously." Gage laughed as Hailey rotated the vase on the table, examining its pattern. "Specifically, I collect head vases, which are rarer. In my home study, I have shelves filled with collectible head vases from all over the world."

"Amazing." Gage grinned. "I'd love to see them sometime."

Hailey didn't accept the apparent invitation to invite Gage to her house. She knew bringing Gage to her home to see her collection was out of the question as long as Mason was in the same hemisphere. "I haven't added a new vase in a long time. This one is stunning." She drew her finger across the colorful vase's indentations. "Anyway, back to our coaching interview," she said.

"I'm not surprised you appreciate a quality floral vase—something created to contain pure beauty," Gage said.

Hailey smiled and focused on her notes. Mason had absolutely no interest in her vase collection, while Gage made her interest sound almost poetic.

"Hailey?" Gage said.

"Yes... I'm sorry," she said. "I got lost in my notes for a moment."

"You seem uncomfortable," Gage said.

"Oh, no, I'm fine." She took another drink of wine. She felt warm inside.

"Can I make a personal observation?" Gage asked.

Hailey nodded.

"I sense you and Mason have pulled off the road."

"What do you mean by that?"

"Based on what you've already told me tonight, you and Mason have entered a place I call 'inner space.' It's a place couples go when their marital enthusiasm dwindles. A person or their partner focuses on their own internal needs, creating space between them, and their relationship suffers."

Hailey looked away, picking up her fork again and sipping her wine.

"I've made you uncomfortable. I truly am sorry. I sometimes can't turn off my work. It's just that identifying and fixing that problem is my profession."

Hailey said, "It's okay. If relationships were perfect, you'd be out of work, right?"

"True. The perfect relationship doesn't exist. The perfect person for each of us *does*," Gage said. "And we always find that perfect person, eventually. My daddy always said, 'Fate don't negotiate.'" Gage tipped his glass to finish his last swig of wine.

"My relationship isn't perfect, but I cherish it. As the cliché goes, 'it's a road, not a destination,'" Hailey said.

"But when that road takes a marriage into inner space, nine times out of ten, it is because one partner suspects the other of cheating."

Hailey's fork slipped from her fingers and dinged on the edge of her plate. Gage was either lucky or had accurately profiled her relationship with Mason with almost no information. "Is that so?" she said, picking up her wine glass.

"Yes, I always see it in my practice," Gage continued. "Though common, your situation is difficult for many therapists to recognize. I've become adept at seeing it. If it doesn't offend you, I'll make a very personal observation about you."

"Go for it," Hailey said, taking a drink.

"Couples also enter inner space when a marriage is in trouble because partners let go of the seemingly trivial overtures that once made the relationship fresh and exciting. It usually begins after what's known as the seven-year itch, and if it is going to become a problem, it does so at about year eight or nine. How long have you and Mason been married?"

"Ten years," Hailey answered in barely a whisper.

"I'm sorry, I didn't hear you…"

"Ten years." She felt the wine dulling the discomfort of Gage's analysis.

He drummed his fingers on the table and said, "I'm sorry, but I'm seldom wrong about this. The good news is this is fixable and quickly, too."

"Your perception is uncanny," she said. "We should get back to your coaching, or this will become a coaching session for me."

"Trust me, you're a bigger benefit to me than I am to you," Gage said.

Hailey tried to refocus on Gage's coaching by asking him about the formation of his business and creating lists of his strengths, weaknesses, opportunities, and threats. She worked to get concrete answers about Gage's business goals. He redirected their discussion to Hailey's relationship with Mason each time. "I will say your love of discussing relationships may be a sign you've chosen the ideal profession," she said. Gage grinned.

When dinner arrived, Hailey made another attempt to establish some results for Gage's first coaching session. She helped him create a goal list for expanding his practice and offered suggestions for him to tackle them.

When Gage finished eating, he said, "Would you pardon me for a minute?"

"Sure," Hailey said. She picked up her wineglass again.

"Finish that, and I'll order more," Gage said.

"This is my last," Hailey said, feeling more buzzed than she had been for years.

Gage left, limping away to the restaurant entrance. When he rounded the corner into the lobby, his limp vanished. He went to the concierge and asked for the restaurant manager. After a brief wait, he heard someone say, "Sir?" Gage turned to find a thin, nervous man wearing a silver name badge that read *Marvin*. "Is everything okay?" he asked.

"Better than okay," Gage replied. "Can I make a musical request for the dining room? I have a special song I want to play for a special lady." He pressed some folded cash into Marvin's palm.

"Uhhh, yes. Excellent, sir," Marvin said. "Give me the title, and let me see what we can do."

When Gage limped back to his table, he saw Hailey smelling the flowers he had given her. Her wine glass was empty.

"Sorry I took so long," he said as he sat.

"No problem. Gage, I was wondering what your hobbies are? What do you do to relax?"

"I bake."

"Interesting. A chef, too?"

"I try. Greek desserts, mostly."

"Get out of here!" Hailey said, realizing she had spoken too loudly.

Gage stood up as though he was leaving. Hailey laughed and pointed to his chair, saying, "You need to stay off your injured leg as much as possible. I reacted that way because I could eat baklava until I'm sick."

"Happens to be my specialty. I've got some up in the room." Gage gestured upward.

"Hold on—you carry it with you?"

"Not always. I made a big batch last Friday and brought some on this trip. My home-baked desserts save me a bundle on room service and taste better, too. I'll send you home with a couple of pieces."

"Unbelievable," Hailey said.

A waiter brought another bottle of Cabernet and placed it on the table.

As Gage poured himself another glass, he said, "I never followed through on my dream of completing culinary school, so I began cooking as a self-taught hobby that took root."

"I think that's fantastic," Hailey said.

The music in the restaurant began playing Sade's *Hang On To Your Love.*

"Love this song," Gage said.

When Hailey recognized it, she hummed along. "I've got this album in my car."

Gage smiled.

While Hailey closed her eyes, quietly singing and swaying to the music, Gage refilled her glass. Before he finished pouring, she opened her eyes and said, "Whoa! I can't have more. I will have to wait off this woozy before I can drive."

"Don't worry. If you are uncomfortable driving, I'll call you a taxi and follow in your car so you get home safely."

Hailey wagged her finger high and said, "Are you *that* much of a gentleman?" She covered her mouth and laughed, again realizing how loudly she had spoken.

Their waiter cleared their table. Gage pulled a checkbook from his pocket and tore out a filled-out check. He handed it to Hailey.

"What's this?" she said, taking it. It was made out to Vaughan Consulting for $2,500. The check had no address, only the name Gage Dolon and a Wells Fargo Bank logo and account number.

"This should cover me for a few more coaching sessions."

"Thank you," she said, examining the check. "But I don't require a retainer."

"I'm rarely willing to pay one," Gage said. "But you are worth it. Please accept it and notify me when your billing exceeds that amount. I'll be happy to renew it."

Hailey hesitated and then said, "Okay. Thank you."

A half-hour later, Hailey finished another glass of wine at Gage's gentle prodding. Their conversation had wound through stories about the evolutions of their respective businesses to places they had lived. Gage seemed to get her. When he tried to refill her wineglass again, Hailey stopped laughing long enough to offer a serious protest, covering the glass with her hand.

"I really do need to stop, or I'll need a room here tonight," she said.

Gage pretended a waiter stood by them and said, "Can we order five more bottles, please?" Hailey leaned to her side and laughed with her hands over her mouth. She couldn't remember when she had laughed so much over dinner. Completely content in the safety of Gage's company, she knew she had indulged in more alcohol than she should have.

Gage said, "You really should try my therapy."

"Oh, that... the thing... where we pretend we're married?" Hailey said, stumbling over her words.

Gage shrugged. "I suppose you could call it that. I promise you'll be pleasantly surprised by a tiny sample we can do right here at the table."

"Okay, why not?" Hailey replied. It might be entertaining. She made a show of rubbing her hands together.

"Hailey, remember, I don't have to know anything specific about your relationship with Mason for my therapy to work. Think about it. The worst thing that can happen is it doesn't work. It certainly will do no harm."

"I'm ready," Hailey said. "But I must tell you your description of this seemed odd to me—no offense."

"No offense taken," Gage said. "I'm used to that. Let me give you an analogy that might better explain my method. Are you familiar with how vaccines work?"

"In general, yes," Hailey said. She felt her head swaying even though she was sure she was holding it still.

"Vaccines contain weakened forms of real viruses. They mimic infection, triggering the body's immune defenses so they can learn how to fight the virus. Like vaccines, my therapy provides a weakened dose of intimacy that allows a couple to learn how to fight issues that have come between them. My method works even though it may seem bizarre."

"Fine. I'll take a small sample," Hailey said, raising her finger.

Gage smiled. "I'm going to say some things to you as though I were Mason. Close your eyes so you won't confuse my face with his."

After a giggle, Hailey closed her eyes. Her whole body felt warm.

Gage said, "Since the day I met you, I've been in love with you."

Hailey tried to resist laughing. She didn't want to insult Gage.

"Losing you would destroy me," Gage continued. "You're the reason for every breath I take."

"This feels incredibly odd," Hailey said.

"Please don't speak yet!" Gage answered. "It always feels odd at first." He leaned closer to Hailey and said, "As your husband, I want to be what you want me to be. I want to excite you. I just haven't yet learned how."

Hailey's face relaxed, and she tilted her head. Gage's voice was calm and soothing. It was apparent he had practice with his therapy. He used his words like a maestro.

"Now, while keeping your eyes closed, I want you to say a simple, three-part phrase. Ready?"

Hailey nodded.

"I'm happy to be yours. Our bond is unbreakable. I love you."

Hailey inhaled through her nose and exhaled through her mouth. She laughed nervously and said, "I *am* speaking to Mason, right?"

"You're speaking to your husband," Gage answered. "Take your time and repeat it with as much feeling as possible."

Hailey took a moment to collect herself and said, "I'm happy to be yours. Our bond is unbreakable and..." Hailey stalled.

"I love you," Gage prompted.

"I love you."

Hailey opened her eyes. Gage grinned at her. "Wasn't that easy?" he asked.

Hailey felt no different about Mason. How she would feel when she saw him remained to be seen. "I'll let you know if it works," she said.

"Oh, it's already working. It never fails."

• • •

Gage's limp was more noticeable when they left the restaurant and entered the hotel lobby. Hailey took his arm to assist him despite feeling a little unsteady as she carried her purse, satchel, and vase of flowers. She questioned her ability to drive and had got a cup of coffee to-go from the restaurant before leaving. She didn't want to make Gage wait for her to sober up and felt they had spent enough time together for the evening.

Near the elevators, Gage hugged her and said, "I almost forgot … I owe you some baklava."

"You wouldn't dare forget!" Hailey said, her voice echoed, and some people checking in at the nearby front desk turned to look at her. "You know I need proof you can really make it—I mean, bake it!" She laughed.

Gage guided her toward a chair. "Forgive me. It might take a little longer for me to make it back down from my room with my limp, but I'll try to hurry," Gage said.

"Nonsense," Hailey said. "I'd feel horrible making you do all that walking. I can come to your door."

"I couldn't ask you to do that."

"You didn't. I offered," Hailey said, going to the elevator panel. She pressed the UP button.

"You're so kind," Gage said.

As the doors closed, Gage leaned against the side of the elevator and smiled. "Thank you for joining me tonight," he said.

"No, thank you," Hailey replied, gently pressing her index finger into his shoulder. "I've had such a fantastic time with you. We should do it again really, really soon."

"The pleasure is all mine," he said, smiling at the floor indicator.

"Are you sure you're not just trying to get me to your room?" Hailey asked. She squeezed her eyes shut and laughed.

Gage took her arm, and they walked the hallway to his room. When he swiped his key and opened the door, the aroma of chocolate wafted out.

"Wow! What do you have going on in there?" Hailey asked. She raised her chin and sniffed without entering the room. "It smells like a candy factory!"

Gage stepped inside and held the door for her. "Please come in for a moment. I won't bite."

As Hailey stepped inside, she looked around for the source of the delicious smell. Behind her, Gage slipped the Do Not Disturb sign on the outside doorknob. The door clicked shut.

She saw a fondue pot on a warming pad on a round table by the window.

"Chocolate is my second passion," Gage said. He quietly turned the door's deadbolt. He went to the table, opened the lid, and raised a wooden spoon from the pot. Chocolate dribbled from it, ribboning on the surface.

"That smells divine," Hailey said, inhaling deeply.

"It's Godiva Milk Melting Chocolate tweaked with a smidge of bourbon and cinnamon. I'm doing some flavor experimentation with crispy puff pastry dipping sticks. Come and have a tiny taste. You'll love it." Gage motioned for her to join him at the table.

Hailey hesitated and finally put her purse, satchel, and flowers on the floor by a luggage rack. She went to the table.

Gage handed her a small taste of chocolate on a mini-spoon. She put it into her mouth. "Mmm! You are an absolute wonder."

"I'll get your baklava," Gage said. He went to a mini-fridge on the opposite side of the room and squatted, keeping his back to her. He pulled out a white paper sack with an Ellada Bakery logo. After removing the wrapped baklava, he wadded up the sack. He went to Hailey and unwrapped two squares of the honey-drizzled dessert.

"Ummm," Hailey said when she saw it.

"I'd love to see you enjoy it. Try a bite now?"

"Well, twist my arm," Hailey said, laughing. She pinched a piece, and when she bit the corner, a string of honey sagged between the sticky pastry and her lips.

Gage gently wiped a sticky crumb from the corner of her mouth and said, "If you think that's good, hold on." He went to the table and pulled a dipper from the fondue pot. He drizzled a scribble of chocolate on a dipping stick, put it on a napkin, and brought it to her with a cup of water.

"You are really going to make it difficult for me to leave, aren't you?" Hailey said.

"Why, I'd never!" Gage replied. They laughed.

"But, please, I promise it will be memorable," Gage said.

"Okay, what delicacy have you created for me to taste next?" Hailey asked.

"Just try it. You might recognize it."

Hailey bit the cookie in half. A sweet flavor filled her mouth, followed by a bitter aftertaste. She made a face. Gage handed her the water, and she drank some.

"The pastry is a little bitter, but see how the chocolate flavor rushes back to the rescue?" Gage asked.

Hailey nodded. "Are you going to tell me what it was?"

"Sure. In fact, let me show you. I may have some you can take with you." Gage disappeared into the bathroom. "Almost… almost… almost," he said.

As Hailey waited, she felt dizziness coming on. "I really do need to get going. Maybe next time," she said. Gage peered out from the bathroom. Hailey dropped the pastry onto the floor and leaned on the table with both hands. The room spun.

She felt herself falling, and Gage's arms hooked under hers from behind, holding her up. He dragged her to the bed, her body limp. As he laid her down, he said, "Don't worry. I've got you."

Hailey couldn't hear him.

Ten

HAILEY SENSED LIGHT. She tried to open her eyes. They felt heavy, as though they were glued shut. When she succeeded, she squinted at the sunlight that poured through the curtains. She raised her head from the pillow and felt a splitting headache. After a few moments, her mental fog cleared, and she recognized she was in a hotel room—in a bed. She looked to her side and saw Gage sleeping peacefully, face up next to her. Seeing him triggered the memory of having had dinner with him the night before. *What happened?*

She sat up and slid her legs out from under the covers, expecting that her movement would wake Gage. He remained still. Her head throbbed, and a wave of dizziness hit her. She closed her eyes, waiting for it to pass. Still, Gage didn't stir.

She was fully dressed, her clothing wrinkled but intact, skirt zipped, blouse buttoned, bra on. Her dizziness subsided. She looked at her watch and clapped her hand over her mouth. 9:54 a.m. *Oh, my God! It's the next morning?* Her pulse raced. She never overslept. Mason would be home from work by now, and he'd have questions. Legitimate questions. Questions she didn't want to answer… and couldn't.

God, what happened? She looked at Gage lying there beside her and became disgusted. She remembered dinner the night before, Gage's leg injury, and riding the elevator to keep him from having to walk so much on it. She hadn't consumed enough alcohol to have blacked out—not even close. The implications of having awakened in bed with him were sickening. She had to get out of the room as quickly as possible, preferably without waking him.

She crept toward the door, watching Gage, expecting him to wake. He didn't make the slightest twitch, his eyes closed and his chest rising and falling in slow, steady breaths.

Hailey found her purse and satchel perfectly aligned on the luggage rack. On the floor beside it, her shoes were placed side-by-side beside the vase of flowers. She had a faint memory of putting her purse and satchel down but not taking off her shoes.

She no longer wanted the flowers. She stepped into her shoes, tucked her purse and satchel under her arm, and slowly turned the doorknob. A wave of dizziness swept her again, and she leaned on the door to steady herself. Her purse fell from under her arm with a thud. She grimaced and squeezed her eyes shut, waiting for Gage to wake and say something. He didn't.

She picked up her purse and slowly opened the door, willing it not to squeak. She glanced over her shoulder to ensure she hadn't left anything else and exited. She saw the *Do Not Disturb* card hanging from the outside doorknob, and her stomach knotted.

The lock's bolting mechanism snapped into place with a loud click when the door closed. Sure that the noise had been loud enough to wake Gage, she rushed along the hall to the elevator, steadying herself by sliding her hand along the wall. She was relieved the elevator opened promptly. Inside, she repeatedly tapped the Close Door button, half expecting to see Gage's hand reach in to grab the door, preventing it from closing.

While the elevator descended, she checked her purse and satchel. All her belongings appeared inside—her wallet with cash, makeup, keys, and a bottle of pain reliever. Thank God.

She exited the elevator feeling the relief of someone who had just stepped out of a nightmare. The bright morning sun that filled the foyer and the echoing voices exacerbated by the marble floor didn't help her headache.

Back at her car, she felt her senses sharpening despite an odd fuzziness that resembled a bad hangover. Maybe nothing had happened between them. Maybe everything happened. Either Gage had been a perfect gentleman, or he had completely undressed and dressed her, including panties, bra, and stockings. Either way, continuing her coaching with him was out of the question. Hailey's discomfort about last night enveloped her like a stench. Her desire for answers about what she couldn't remember was offset by a desire to not see Gage again.

Hailey got in her car and locked the doors. Before driving away, she pulled out her phone and swiped the screen. Her phone's address book appeared. She stared at it. Her phone had been set up to automatically lock the screen with a photo of her mother after two minutes of non-use. It now opened without needing a code.

As she drove out of the parking lot, she called her voicemail and put her phone on the passenger seat as her messages played through her car's speakers. There were four voicemail messages, one from the assistant of Trace Ramsey, a big client prospect. The meeting was scheduled for 10:00AM this morning. Her watch read 9:57 a.m.

"Dammit," Hailey yelled. The Ramsey meeting was a mini-boon for her. Ramsey led a group of entrepreneurs who hoped to build a co-op of referrals, and they were considering Hailey to facilitate the startup meeting to guide their brainstorming. The week-long retreat was to be held in Hawaii, and they had proposed a $3,000 day rate, expressing some urgency to discuss the details with Hailey. She immediately called Trace Ramsey's assistant and rescheduled for 11:00 a.m., profusely apologizing for missing the meeting.

The adrenaline rush of the appointment crisis cleared up more of her grogginess. She was fully awake and felt as though she had slept deeper than she had for years, yet was completely unrested. Her legs tingled, and soreness crept into her back. She couldn't remember a workout that had caused as much soreness as she felt now. She swallowed some pain relievers dry, almost gagging because her mouth felt full of cotton.

Hailey's anxiety subsided about the Ramsey meeting and her thoughts turned to Mason. If things went perfectly, he'd be home asleep, assuming she had simply left for work early. She could go into the house, clean up, and change without waking him. That she hadn't received an angry voicemail from him made this scenario very possible.

But if Mason woke up after she got home, how could she explain her all-night absence? She could tell him she fell asleep at the office. She sure looked the part—complete with yesterday's wrinkled attire, and she regularly spent long hours preparing each of her presentations.

She didn't want to compromise her honesty with Mason about Gage again. In this case, the truth was her meeting with Gage had been innocent. It was waking up in bed beside him the next morning that had created a potential crisis. Sharing that with Mason would be cruel, not to mention masochistic. If nothing happened, blabbing about it would only cause problems. It certainly wouldn't happen again. What Mason didn't know about the night before wouldn't hurt him. She hoped it wouldn't hurt her either.

The shame she felt made her want to improve her relationship with Mason. Last week, they had briefly discussed taking a few days for a vacation together. At the time, the idea had appealed to Mason more than Hailey. Although she had been managing a heavy workload and didn't want to lose momentum, a few days away with Mason could be therapeutic for them and help her forget her poor judgment with Gage last night. She decided to suggest it. Mason would be excited for some exclusive time with her.

· · ·

Hailey parked in the driveway so the garage door motor wouldn't wake Mason. *Please let him be asleep.*

She got out and peeked through the garage door crack. It was too dark to see if Mason's car was inside. She opened the front door quietly and stepped inside. The alarm didn't chirp, and the house was quiet. She smelled toast. Mason was home. She shut the door, holding the knob to keep it from clicking. She removed her shoes at the bottom of the steps to climb the hardwood staircase.

At the edge of their bedroom door, she leaned to see inside. Mason lay on his stomach diagonally across their king-size bed, still wearing his suit from the club. He must have had a rough shift to have not undressed.

She crept into her walk-in closet, placed her shoes on the rack, and quietly selected fresh clothes. Instead of using their master bath, she went downstairs to the guest bathroom. She was always considerate of Mason's sleep. More so today.

She closed herself into the guest bathroom and locked the door. If Mason caught her using this bathroom, it would look suspicious because they never used it to shower or locked the door unless they had guests. The risk would be worth it if it kept Mason asleep.

She turned on the shower and finished undressing. Seeing herself naked in the mirror returned her thoughts to Gage and the hotel room. He certainly had the *opportunity* to do whatever he wanted with her. She tried to be thankful he left her fully clothed. Or had he? Uncomfortable possibilities rushed to mind. *He respects me so much there's no way he would have...* The scene would have been entirely different if anything had happened in the hotel room. The sheets and bedspread would have been in disarray. They would have been naked with clothes strewn on the floor. The notion that anything happened was absurd.

She looked over her shoulder to examine her backside in the mirror. Her back had become sorer, yet she saw no bruising or other marks. Still, she couldn't shake her pangs of worry.

Hailey gathered her clothes. Her heart pounded. She didn't want to check her panties. She wished she didn't need to. She raised them to the light and inverted them to examine the crotch area. What she saw sent a chill of terror through her, and she gasped, "Oh, my God!" Her ring finger was bare. She looked in the mirror, the top of which had become foggy from the steam. The color had drained from her face. She dropped the panties and covered her mouth, saying, "No, no, no!"

The doorknob jiggled, and there was a hard knock on the door. Hailey jumped and let out a small scream.

"Hale? Are you okay?" Mason's voice echoed in the hallway.

Oh, shit! "Yes, uh, Honey."

The knob jiggled again. Her pulse raced as she scooped up her dirty clothes from the floor and draped them over her left hand. She opened the door a few inches. Mason had removed his suit jacket and slacks and stood in his wrinkled dress shirt and boxers.

"What are you doing down here?" he asked.

"I didn't want to disturb you."

"Since when?"

"You looked so beat. I came down here to shower so you could get some more rest." She puckered and put her face to the door's crack for an obligatory peck. When Mason pulled back, his face remained full of suspicion.

"I'll be out in a few minutes. Go back to bed. Get some sleep," Hailey said.

Mason planted his foot to block the door as she closed it. "Hold on," he said. "I came home early this morning. Your car was gone."

Hailey felt the knot in her stomach tighten. She wished she could jump into the sink and slide down the drain to escape the inevitable interrogation.

"Mason, I'm sorry, I—"

"Don't worry about it," he interrupted. "But next time you go to the gym early, tell me. I think I'm ready."

"The gym? With you?"

"Yes, I told you I'd try working out with you. Just don't expect me to be able to keep up with you. And it's only on the condition that we *drive*, not run to the gym," Mason laughed.

"I'm so sorry," Hailey said. "I promise to bring you along next time, okay?"

As Mason walked away, he said, "Remember, you promised."

Hailey laughed out the door to make sure Mason could hear it. "Get some sleep!" she said. She closed the door and sank to her knees, stunned by her good fortune. Her relief was fleeting, overtaken by the implications of her missing wedding ring. She *had* to find it and do so before Mason noticed it was gone from her hand.

In the shower, she tried in earnest to remember the details of the previous evening. How could the ring have left her finger? She had either lost it, or Gage had stolen it. There were no other possibilities. If she had taken it off and placed it on the bedside stand in the hotel room, it might still be there. The discomfort of calling Gage and explaining her stealthy departure from his room was worth the chance of getting the ring back.

Hailey wrapped herself in a towel and ran to her study, where she closed the door. She called the Marriott and asked for Gage Dolon while cupping her mouth to the receiver.

"We have no guests by that name," a female desk clerk said.

"You *must*. I was at your hotel with him this morning," Hailey said.

"May I have the room number, please?"

Hailey realized she didn't even know the room number she had rushed from. "Do you have a guest named Gage—any Gage at all? Please recheck your list."

"I'm sorry, Ma'am. We cannot disclose the last names of our guests."

"You've got to help me. Please!"

"I'm sorry, ma'am, I cannot share our guest roster. Is there anything else I can help you with?"

After the call, Hailey rushed to get dressed. If she hurried, she could reach her office in time for her 11:00AM meeting with Trace Ramsey's people.

• • •

Before she had backed out of the driveway, Hailey had Gage's number pulled up on her phone. After his phone rang five times, a computerized female voice prompted her to leave a message.

"Hi, Gage, this is Hailey. Thank you for a great time last night. You slept so peacefully this morning, so I slipped out without waking you. Listen, I have a bit of a dilemma. I misplaced my wedding ring last night, and I wonder if you've found it in the hotel room. If so, can you call or message me on my cell phone? Thanks so much. Bye."

Hailey hung up and nibbled her lip. *Please call me back, Gage.* Traffic was backed up because of road construction. She squeezed the steering wheel, willing the cars that blocked her to hurry. She checked the clock every minute. At 11:15AM, she pulled off the road and called Trace Ramsey's assistant to explain that traffic had made her late and requested a few more minutes. The assistant put her on hold, and when she came back on the line, she said, "Mr. Ramsey has postponed our work with you and will contact you if we need any further consultation." Hailey apologized profusely. She hung up, rested her head back, and sighed. A lost client to match her lost ring.

She rechecked her phone for a call from Gage. Why hadn't he called back? He should have sensed the urgency in her voice. Perhaps he was a slick jewel thief, after all. Or maybe he was pouting, pissed off that she had left him without waking him to say goodbye? She pulled out the check he had given her. It said Gage Dolon with no address on it. She pulled back onto the road and headed to the Marriott.

She entered the lobby and approached the check-in counter on the chance there had been a mistake, or another clerk could find him. "I'm looking for a guest named Gage Dolon. Can you tell me what room he is in?"

"I'm sorry, ma'am. We cannot disclose the room information of our guests."

"He's my client. I need to contact him. He wants me to contact him," Hailey said, the desperation in her voice seeped through.

"Let me ring him for you. What was the name again?"

"Dolon. D-O-L-O-N."

The clerk scrolled a touchscreen monitor through several pages of names. "I'm sorry, we have no guest by that name."

"He may have checked out this morning. Can you look at yesterday's guests?"

"Our guest list includes historical data, ma'am. If he's stayed here before, his name will show up."

Hailey nibbled her cheek. She didn't want to believe the clerk. Gage couldn't have vanished so quickly. She went through the arched entrance to Concetta of Italy restaurant and was greeted by the aroma of bacon and coffee. She saw the table where she and Gage had sat for hours.

"May I help you?" a voice said behind her. "Table for one?"

Hailey turned to see a woman with a manager nametag.

"No, I just, uh… I had dinner here last night, and wouldn't you know it, I forgot to keep my receipt. I was wondering if you could pull a duplicate for me."

"Most certainly, ma'am. The name?"

"Dolon, D-O-L-O-N."

"Please give me a few moments," the woman said before disappearing through swinging doors.

Hailey stepped out into the foyer and paced. Knowing he was in one of the rooms above her but not knowing which one frustrated her. It would be great to catch Gage sneaking out after he said he was staying until the weekend. After waiting only two minutes for the restaurant manager, Hailey got on the elevator and then paused before pressing a button. Was it the sixth floor? Or the fifth? She couldn't remember the damned floor. Her memory of using the elevator the night before was so faint. She tried the fifth floor.

Strolling down the hall, she looked at each door, hoping one of the room numbers would feel familiar. The room she suspected had its door propped open and a housekeeping cart outside. When Hailey stepped inside, a uniformed housekeeper stopped making the bed and looked at her.

"Excuse me," Hailey said. "I'm sorry to interrupt you… I may have left something valuable in this room. May I look around?"

The housekeeper said something in Spanish and then continued making the bed while Hailey began searching. She needed to find something that assured her this was the right room. She went to the circular table in the corner by the patio window. It hadn't been cleaned yet and had chocolate splatter on it.

Confident this was the correct room, Hailey scoured the top of the credenza bedside stand and then got on her hands and knees, searching under the bed and every inch of the carpet. The housekeeper stepped around her several times. Hailey looked under two soiled towels on the bathroom floor and shook them while holding her breath. The nightstand was bare. She assumed any housekeeper who had found the enormous diamond and had the vaguest idea of its value would have promptly gone downstairs and quit her job.

The housekeeper mounted her cleaning bottles to the edge of her cart and pushed it to the door. Hailey said, "Un momento por favor."

The housekeeper looked back. Hailey made a prayer sign to her and pulled the cart back to a place beside the bed. She pulled out towel after towel from the cart's laundry bin, shaking each before piling them on the bed. The housekeeper was not amused. When Hailey had emptied half the bin, the housekeeper sucked her teeth and tapped her wrist with her index finger. "I'm sorry. I'm so sorry," Hailey said, not slowing down. She pulled the last towel out of the bin and shook it. Empty. The housekeeper continued muttering Spanish while Hailey helped her heap the towels back into the cart.

Gage was gone, and so was her ring. So much for Gage spending the week at the hotel. Hailey felt sick. As she walked to the elevator, her frustration grew to anger. She called Gage's number again. After the annoying female voice prompt, she left another message, struggling to keep her voice steady and calm.

Gage, it is imperative I talk to you. Please, please call me back immediately. I need your help. It is absolutely critical. Thanks.

She stepped off the elevator and walked through the lobby toward the sliding glass doors to exit.

"Mrs. Dolon?" the restaurant manager called out to her.

Hailey stopped. Perhaps the manager had good news or, better yet, could give her a receipt with Gage's information on it. "Yes?" Hailey said.

The manager approached her and said, "We have no record of a 'Dolon' dining with us last night. I'm sorry. Are you sure you didn't use another method of payment, Mrs. Dolon?"

"No, that's okay. Thank you for trying," Hailey said. She drove away from the hotel in tears.

• • •

On the way to the office, Felicia called. "Hey, girlie!" Hailey said, trying to sound normal.

"Hi. You won't believe it."

"Believe what?"

"Resumes. Lots of them. I posted the ad for your assistant position at ten o'clock this morning, and I've already received over thirty resumes. I'll email them to you."

"That's great," Hailey replied.

After a brief silence, Felicia said, "Are you okay? You don't sound well."

"No."

"No, what?"

"I'm not okay," Hailey said. Her eyes welled up.

"What's wrong?"

Hailey couldn't answer right away. Her throat tightened up as she blinked back a second round of tears. She pulled her car to the side of the road.

"Tell me what's going on, Hale," Felicia said. "Fight with Mason?"

"No, I lost my ring. Again."

"Yikes."

"Right. And it was while I was with Gage," Hailey added.

"How in the world could that happen?"

"Felly, I've made a mistake, and now I have an enormous problem."

"How big?"

"I woke up in Gage's hotel room and don't remember anything past walking down the hallway to his door."

"My God."

"I know. I was stupid. I had a little to drink. I thought that with food, it wouldn't hit me like it did. I was so comfortable with him, and he was hurt, and I helped him to his room, and I just..."

"Hold on, Hale. Start at the beginning and tell me what happened."

Hailey told Felicia the story of the coaching meeting with Gage, the wine, and the little she remembered about walking to the room and waking up after a night she had no memory of.

"So, do you think he—you know?" Felicia asked.

"I don't know. My back and legs are sore, and I woke up fully dressed and... I'm so confused."

"Hale, you could have been seriously hurt or worse. This guy is a scumbag. I totally get a bad feeling about him."

"Oh God. I hope you are wrong. I mean, he was such a gentleman. He paid for dinner and gave me a check for $2,500 for future coaching."

"What's your ring worth?"

"Fifty grand and Mason won't let me forget that fact."

"This Gage guy is a con!" Felicia shouted. "Hale, even if the check doesn't bounce, he turned a fat profit. I'm afraid he's gone with your ring. You need to call the police."

"The police will need my address. Mason could get word of it, and you know how bad that would be for me. I called Gage less than an hour ago. I want to give him a chance to call back because that would be easiest. If he found it, I can put this behind me with a critical lesson learned."

"So you hope he didn't have sex with you while you were unconscious? And you hope he found your ring? And you hope he returns it?"

"Thank you. Now I feel horrible and unreasonable."

"Hale, I'm sorry for being such a downer. It's just that I care about you, and I don't feel good about this guy. If I were you, I'd find the best jeweler possible and get a perfect replica underway."

Hailey sniffled and said, "You're right."

"I'm going to bring these resumes to your office," Felicia said. "I want to see you. In the meantime, call me back if you hear from him, okay?"

"Okay."

• • •

When Hailey got to her office, her desk phone blinked with a new voicemail message. Excitement surged through her. She picked up the receiver to listen.

Hailey, this is Gage. I got your message. I'm so sorry I missed your call. I'll try to call you again later.

Caller ID was blocked with no phone number shown this time. He had left no callback number. Hailey slowly put the receiver down, amazed at how unhelpful and vague Gage's message was. He could have at least said whether he had the ring or not.

She dialed the only number she had for him on her phone. After it rang five times, she slammed the receiver down during the voicemail greeting.

The phone almost immediately rang. It was building security. Felicia was at the desk requesting permission to come up.

"Send her up," Hailey said. She went out to her reception area.

When the elevator doors opened, Felicia emerged. Her dark brown hair was pulled back into a messy ponytail, and a pair of sunglasses dangled from her mouth as she stepped out, counting a stack of papers.

Hailey said, "You are a sight for sore eyes."

"Sometimes things suck for a bit, and then they get better. Trust me," Felicia said and pulled Hailey into a hug. Hailey blinked away tears before taking her chin off Felicia's shoulder.

"No callback yet?" Felicia asked.

"I just got a message from him, saying he'll try again later. He said nothing about the ring."

"Bastard. I'm telling you, girlfriend, this guy is trouble."

"I know."

They went into Hailey's office. "This should cheer you up," Felicia said, handing over a stack of resumes.

"Thank you so much. I want to start interviewing tomorrow," Hailey said.

"You'd better. We have over sixty applicants."

Hailey picked up the resumes and fanned them. "Good. In fact, I will ask Mason to sort through these for me tonight. If he chooses the final candidates, he won't be able to complain about them."

"Sounds smart, but do you really want to let Mason choose your assistant?"

"Oh, believe me, if he feels like he chose the candidates, my life will be much better, and I'll still make the final selection."

"Actually, when you get your ring back, your life will be better," Felicia said.

"That too. I'll be right back." Hailey left her office and went to the restroom around the corner from the elevator foyer. Felicia sat down and draped her leg on the arm of the chair to get more comfortable. She picked up a few of the resumes and began skimming some of the applicants.

She heard a phone vibrating. She put the resumes down and stood to hone in on the sound, searching all over Hailey's desk. When Felicia realized it was coming from Hailey's purse on the floor, the vibrating had stopped. The screen reported a missed call.

When Hailey came back, Felicia handed her the phone. "You missed a call."

Hailey checked the screen. The caller ID reported *number unknown*. There was a new voicemail message. She played it on speakerphone.

Hi Hailey, Gage here. Tag, you're it! I called your office and cell with no luck. I'm interested in booking our next little get-together for my coaching. I can't tell you how much last night energized me, and I'd love to get more of the same next time. Maybe tonight? Call me!

Felicia said, "I thought you asked him about the ring."

"I *did*. He didn't say anything about it."

"That's weird, Hale. Really weird. I have two words: 'Po-lice.'"

"If he was a con man, it wouldn't make sense for him to call me anymore if he only wanted the ring."

"Good point. Are you *really* sure nothing happened between you last night? I hate to make you think about it, but maybe he wants a replay."

Hailey's face flashed disgust.

"I still think you should call the police," Felicia said.

"I don't want to freak him out—yet. If I could actually get him on the phone, I could sense whether that is necessary. If I don't hear from him in the next few minutes, I'll call the police," Hailey agreed.

"Fine. Want to go grab a late lunch?"

Hailey shrugged.

"I didn't think you'd be up for it."

The office phone rang. The caller ID read *private*.

"Hello?"

"Hi Hailey, this is Gage. How are you?"

Hailey pointed to her phone and mouthed, "It's him."

"I've been better. Listen, did you find my wedding ring in the room?"

"Yes. Yes, I did."

"Oh, God, thank you, thank you, thank you!" Relief flooded Hailey, and she grinned at Felicia. She shouldered the phone and whispered, "He has it."

Felicia silently cheered.

Hailey put the call on speaker and pressed her finger to her lips, reminding Felicia to keep quiet.

"Where was it?" Hailey asked.

"Last night, do you remember the melted chocolate?"

"I'm sorry, for some reason, I don't remember much at all," Hailey said. She looked at Felicia, who wore a shame-on-you look.

Gage said, "You didn't want to get your ring dirty, so you took it off. I put it on top of my wallet for safekeeping. I didn't want to wake you. I had hoped you would see it on the credenza."

Hailey didn't remember removing her ring but decided that fact wasn't as important as getting it back. "I'm so relieved. Thank you again!"

"I love to make you happy."

Hailey gave a courtesy laugh while Felicia rolled her eyes.

"Can I stop by and get it from you? I can be there in fifteen minutes."

"Well, that's the thing, Hailey. I've already checked out, and I'm back in Denburg."

Felicia frowned.

Hailey asked, "Well, did you leave the ring at the desk? How can I get it?"

"Oh, absolutely not. Your ring appears to be incredibly valuable. If I left it with a stranger who lost or stole it, you'd never forgive me."

Felicia squinted at Hailey suspiciously.

"So how will we do this?" Hailey said. "I hate to sound so desperate, but I really need to get the ring back immediately. Like I mentioned in my message, this is critical."

"I understand, and I don't blame you one tiny little bit. So here's what I'm thinking... Since we've had only our first of many coaching sessions, I thought we could set up the next one, and I'll bring the ring to you in person then. I think that would be safest. Does that work for you?"

Hailey looked at Felicia, who only shrugged.

"Fine. I just need to get the ring immediately."

"Not a problem," Gage said. "How soon can I see you?"

Hailey and Felicia froze, eyes locked on each other, processing the stickiness of Gage's excitement.

"I suppose I could drive there now," Hailey said. Felicia sent her a warning look.

"I'd hate to make you drive that distance," Gage said. "I'll tell you what, because this is so important to you, I'm willing to make the drive back. How about I meet you at your office and deliver your ring there?"

Felicia waved her hands and shook her head emphatically.

"Gage, my office is a mess. I'd feel more comfortable meeting somewhere else. How about Shiney's Shrimp Shack, the place across the street you loved."

"Booked. I can be there in two hours. It's 12:45 now. How about we meet at three o'clock?"

"Really?" Hailey said, surprised. If Gage had already made the two-hour drive to Denburg, he would have arrived there only minutes ago. For him to immediately turn around and come back made no sense. Not calling her about the ring before he left town made no sense. So little about this situation made sense.

"Gage, there's something else I have to ask you."

"Anything."

"I must admit I'm a bit embarrassed by it, but after having the wine last night, my memory must have taken the night off. All I remember is waking up in your room this morning..."

"Yes, right before you snuck away from me," Gage laughed.

"Right. I was fully clothed, and... I'll be frank. Did anything happen between us last night?"

"Don't be Frank, just be Hailey," Gage laughed. Hailey didn't. Felicia shook her fist at the phone.

"I'm sorry, but this isn't funny to me," Hailey said. "It is incredibly important."

"If it is important to you, then it's important to me. You have nothing to worry about, Hailey. Nothing happened that shouldn't have."

"Thank you. I'm sure you understand my concern."

"Absolutely. You are fortunate to have been with me. I'm someone who believes everything happens for a reason. There are no accidents. There is no luck. My car's position right behind you when you had an accident didn't happen by chance. Your presentation, my baklava hobby, your offer to coach me, and my unique therapy you tried were all meant to be."

Felicia used her finger to make a crazy sign beside her head.

Hailey's eyes remained riveted on the phone.

Gage continued, "Everything is a mathematical formula of the universe that doesn't involve chance. This truth makes me happy. It takes away the scary randomness involved with important things that happen to us. Like my daddy always told me, 'Fate don't negotiate.' Fate always does the right thing, and that's beautiful."

"One other thing, Gage…"

"Whatever you want."

"I returned to the hotel to find you, and they had no record of a Gage Dolon. Do I have your correct name?"

"Oh, that. I booked my room with my corporate credit card under the company name D. Counseling, LLC. I like to keep my personal information, well, personal. That's why my check has no address. I'm so sorry. I should have explained that."

"Thank you for clearing that up. Okay then, I'll see you in a couple of hours at Shiney's?"

"You betcha. I'll be there at three o'clock sharp. I can't wait to see you again."

When Hailey hung up, the women looked at one another and together said, "Wow."

"Fate always does the right thing? Hale, that was creepy," Felicia said. "You've found a bona fide weirdo. I think he's totally insane."

"I'm not so sure. He's very intelligent."

"You're defending him? He's got your ring, and he's talking about fate and 'meant to be' and stuff like that. You gotta be careful here, Hale. Next thing you know, he'll be stalking you."

"I'm aware of that." The phone call hadn't been comfortable for Hailey, but she couldn't afford to freak out about Gage until that ring was back on her finger.

"Are you going to coach him?"

"Only until I get my ring back."

"That's smart." Felicia stood up. "Do you want me to go with you?"

"I do, but it will probably be best if I'm alone."

"You're probably right, and I completely understand."

"I'm sorry, Felly. Maybe we can have dinner when everything is better."

"Hey, that sounds like a country song title," Felicia laughed. "I'm going to take off. I figure you'll be wound up pretty tight until three o'clock."

"You know me. I'll go through those resumes. Thanks again for that."

"Anything for my girl," Felicia said as she left the office.

Eleven

GAGE ADJUSTED HIS headphones. The microphone embedded in the *Compliment Generator* on the corner of Hailey's desk worked beautifully. He replayed the entire audio of the conversation between Hailey and Felicia he had captured during the last half hour. Hailey may think their next get-together would be his coaching session, but that was something she'd have to take up with fate. He was pleased she hadn't done something as stupid and futile as to get the police involved.

As he saved the recording on his laptop, he laughed at Felicia's assessment of him. Of course, he wasn't insane, and Hailey had *not* agreed with Felicia about that, thank God. In fact, Hailey claiming he was intelligent was his favorite part.

Though Felicia hadn't done any apparent harm in that conversation, the way she constantly questioned his motives and spewed such crap to Hailey during the last couple of days was disappointing, to say the least. He logged onto a website, paying $69 for a complete background report on Felicia Blakner. The results came back quickly, giving him a couple of hours to review it.

He raised his binoculars, honing in on Hailey's office window. It was the time of day when the sun's glare obscured it. He tossed the binoculars aside, kicked off his shoes, and crossed his feet on the dashboard. He settled in to people-watch and read more about "Felly" while waiting for an audience with the best person of all.

He knew Hailey would be on time. In fact, she'd be early for this meeting, that's for damned sure. He knew exactly how the scenario would play out. She'd walk out of her building and probably jaywalk from the Handel Towers entrance to Shiney's instead of using the crosswalk. He'd shoot a frontal video view of Hailey walking toward him—a rarity so far. If she hurried across the street, her breasts would bustle nicely. His dash-cam was set and trained on the Handel Tower Building's front doors.

He imagined Hailey entering Shiney's to find him missing. After freaking out for ten minutes, searching for him inside and outside of Shiney's, she'd call the only phone number she had for him and get no answer. The moment before Hailey reached the point of total despair, he'd enter Shiney's and satisfy her intense longing for him. She'd be so excited she'd call out to him if not run into his arms.

· · ·

Hailey paced in her office, starting several emails she hadn't finished. She found it impossible to concentrate on anything while waiting to meet Gage. She switched tasks to reviewing the resumes Felicia had delivered and soon pushed them aside, too. She shuffled some paperwork, only able to focus on her meeting with Gage and getting the damned ring back.

She opened an archived email folder on her computer and scanned the email messages she had sent to her parents after Mason had proposed. She found the email she was searching for, and it displayed photos of the ring from several angles. She considered having a replica created on the fly at her own expense. That could take too many days if not weeks. Mason would notice the missing ring within hours. The perfect conclusion to her dilemma was to meet Gage, get the ring, cancel their coaching, and put this awful two-day chapter of her life behind her.

She checked the clock while the minutes dragged. She decided to go to Shiney's early and wait. It was 2:45 p.m. If Gage showed up early, that would be wonderful.

When she exited the elevator in the lobby, she arced around the Echelonian booth to avoid Isaac, as it would be a poor time for him to approach her. Fortunately, he and his partner were preoccupied with other passers-by engaged in their pitch.

Outside on the street, she hesitated at the curb. Traffic was moderate since rush hour hadn't begun, so she opted to jaywalk straight to Shiney's instead of using the crosswalk. When she stepped off the curb, the traffic signal turned green. She jogged to hurry across the street.

Inside, the savory aroma of Shiney's Shrimp Shack's grilled specials greeted her. She had no appetite. Midway between lunch and dinner, the bistro wasn't crowded. Hailey had scoped out all the tables in less than a minute and didn't see Gage. As her anxiety rose, she returned to the entryway and looked out the glass front door, watching people walk by. *Please be early,* she thought.

"Can I seat you?" asked a young woman behind her. She had an embroidered Shiney's patch on her overalls.

"Thank you. Not yet. I'm waiting for someone," Hailey answered.

The minutes ticked by. At 3:05, Gage still had not walked through the door. She checked her phone to ensure it hadn't accidentally turned off and its signal strength was good. Coverage was never a problem here. She called her office and remotely checked her voicemail.

You have no new messages. Please press pound for more options.

Dammit. Hailey stepped away from the window and leaned against the wall. She ordered a glass of water and paced along the front window. If he didn't show, Hailey knew Felicia's suggestion to call the police would be the only logical option left.

At 3:16PM, Gage strolled into Shiney's Shrimp Shack. He wore the same sports jacket he had worn at dinner last night. Before the door could close behind him, Hailey said, "Gage! You made it! Oh, thank God!" She hurried to him.

"Wow! What a greeting!" Gage said, grinning. He opened his arms for her. Hailey stopped and looked at each outspread hand for the ring. He tried to hug her. Hailey's stiffness resulted in an awkward embrace that Gage enjoyed anyway.

He held her arm's length and said, "You look so worried—I hate seeing you this way!"

"I *am* worried," she replied. "Obviously, I'm incredibly distracted. Where is it?"

"I need to talk to you about that. Let's get a table," Gage said.

"Wait, I would rather…"

Gage stepped away and raised two fingers for the host, who grabbed two menus and asked them to follow her. Gage said, "This will be quick. Come along."

Gage followed the woman, and Hailey said, "Hold on!" She touched his shoulder to stop him, and when he didn't, she tried to walk beside him through the narrow aisle between tables. "What do you mean we need to talk about it?" Hailey said, trying to keep her voice steady. "Where is the ring?"

"Not to worry. Everything is fine," Gage said.

"This is feeling like a game now, Gage and I have to be honest, I don't like it," Hailey said.

The host stopped beside a booth, and Gage slid into his seat, smiling slightly. He pulled out his sanitizing wipes and began wiping down the menu and the table's edge.

Before Hailey sat, the host began explaining the day's special. Hailey stopped her by holding up her hand. "Can you give us a minute, please?"

"Certainly, ma'am," the host said and left them.

Gage said, "Please, Hailey. Have a seat." He pointed to her side of the booth.

"Are you even listening to me?" Hailey asked as she scooted into her side of the booth.

"Hailey, everything here is going to happen exactly as it should. There's no reason for you to be upset."

Hailey seethed at Gage's aloofness about her crisis. She took a deep breath.

"That's better," Gage said. He reached for Hailey's menu to clean it, and she pulled it away. "I don't need my menu cleaned. I need my ring."

"Fine," Gage said. "If you'll remember, in your presentation, you talked about under-promising and over-delivering to enhance loyalty among work peers."

Hailey's jaw clenched. She folded her hands on the table to contain her anger.

"I came here prepared to solve one problem for you. But as fate would have it, I will solve two problems."

"I'm listening," Hailey said, motioning for him to get to it.

"I must first tell you that I owe you an apology because I haven't been completely honest with you, and I'm in agony about it."

Hailey's anger subsided as worry flooded her. Her heart began thumping. Was Gage about to ask forgiveness for having taken advantage of her? "What is it?"

Gage removed a phone from his inside jacket pocket, pressed a button on its side, and turned the screen toward her. He swiped the screen with his finger several times, scrolling photos of both Hailey's car and the truck she had collided with the night of her accident.

"It's funny," Gage said, enlarging a close-up of a dent in the truck's bumper. "Damage I couldn't see that night in person is clearly visible in these photographs."

Hailey studied the photos, confused. "I'm sorry, I don't understand what this means. Did you take these pictures?"

Gage turned off the phone, returned it to his pocket, and grinned at her, shaking his head. "I told you not to worry about that pissed-off truck driver, and that remains sound advice. I apologize for not sharing the most important reason with you. He's phoneless."

"You *stole* the man's phone?" Hailey said, cocking her head in disbelief.

"Stole?" Gage drummed his fingers and said, "The word 'stole' would only apply if I didn't return the phone—which I plan to. The man's address is on it, and he'll have his phone. In a fortunate twist of fate, some of his photos of your damage will have been erased." Gage winked at her.

Hailey gaped at Gage. "How did you..." she scratched her head, "...get this man's phone?"

Gage's face filled with pride. "It was simple. During our little roadside tussle, some useful sleight-of-hand I learned back in college kicked in."

"Gage, what you've done is not only unethical, it is illegal. This is awful. You may have put me in a terrible legal position. How could you do this?"

"Now, now... Wait, Hailey," he said, motioning for her to slow down. "Remember I did all this to protect you, and I will not let him harm you."

Hailey sighed and tilted her head back. Her eyes closed, she said, "Gage, I have plenty of money and could easily have paid any damages. You have made this situation much worse."

"I'm sorry you feel that way. After what I did, I know one thing for sure: you are safe from that guy. I thought you'd be excited."

"Excited?" Hailey crossed her arms. "Gage, it would be best if you just gave me my ring, and I'll go. Where is it?"

"Let's talk about that."

"I don't want to talk anymore. Please, just give me my ring." Hailey's eyes drilled him.

"You've brought us to my second apology. Hailey, in my excitement to see you, I rushed from my office in Denburg and left your ring behind."

"You what?" Angry red flowed onto Hailey's face. Two of Shiney's employees appeared from around the corner to investigate the outburst. Gage waved them away.

"I don't want you to make a scene," Gage said as he reached for her arm. She pulled away.

Through clenched teeth, Hailey leaned on the table and said, "My ring was the entire purpose of this meeting, and you promised…"

"I'm so sorry. Can you forgive me? I can turn this into a positive!" Gage added.

Hailey covered her face with her hands and exhaled through her fingers, shaking her head. She wanted to curse, scream at him, and hit him. Gage's cheery demeanor amidst her crisis felt strange and scared her. She focused on remaining calm. Convincing Gage to simply hand her the ring was the easiest way to get it back. She didn't want to ruin that possibility by angering him.

"Fine, Gage. I'll go along. How are you going to turn this into a positive experience?"

Gage smiled. "I did promise to return your ring. And because of my oversight, I'm indebted to you. I'm going to return it with benefits!"

"I don't understand."

"I want you to come to Denburg. You'll see my office and my home. You'll learn so much about me that will be useful for the professional coaching you're giving me. Best of all, your ring is there. I'll slide it back onto your finger myself."

Hailey stared at Gage, unable to believe what she was hearing. She remembered she needed to be careful. "Gage, I cannot drive to Denburg today."

"Oh, of course not. You won't drive. I'll drive you. We already know we'll have a wonderful time if it's anything like last night. I'll have you back by morning."

"Morning?" Hailey looked around the restaurant. Everything would make sense at this moment if a television crew revealed themselves and announced she had been pranked on a hidden camera show.

"Yes, I'll have you back by morning," Gage assured her. "I've proven I'm a perfect gentleman. You woke up in my hotel room completely dressed, for goodness' sake! C'mon, let's go!"

"Gage, my husband wouldn't approve of me taking off to spend a night with you." Hailey smiled, hoping Gage would understand the moral problem with his suggestion.

"You mean *another* night," he said. "Maybe Mason would like to come?"

"No, I can guarantee you he won't. Listen, Gage, I have an enormous problem. I cannot go with you, and I desperately need my ring. Can you think of another solution to help me solve my problem?"

"Gosh, Hailey, coming home with me will be the quickest way to satisfy you." He shrugged, picked up his menu, and began reading it as though the conversation had concluded.

Hailey felt her anger about to explode with a vengeance. She took a deep breath and said, "I'll tell you what. I know we have an agreement that I will coach you—"

"More than an agreement," Gage interrupted without looking up from his menu. "We have a contract. And I'm so grateful you fully agreed to it and accepted my pre-payment."

"Right." Hailey paused. "Gage, let me explain it like this… My missing ring has ruined my ability to help you because I find its loss so distracting that I can't function as I should. I'm afraid more coaching can only happen if I get my ring back. Do you understand? I hate to draw a hard line, but this issue is so serious I have no choice."

Gage nodded and looked up from his menu. He slammed it shut and slapped it onto the table. "Hailey, is a little extra time with me a cost or a benefit to you?"

Hailey stared at him, stunned by the question. It was clear Gage required a correct answer. His eyes narrowed, and Hailey detected anger in them for the first time.

She cleared her throat and said, "I have enjoyed your company. It would be nice to share one another's company again at some point. I hope you can understand the awkward position I'm in."

"Then let's get rid of the awkwardness. We'll go to my place!"

Hailey jumped to her feet. "Gage, I can't!"

"Sweetheart, please sit down," he answered calmly.

Hailey held up her finger. "You have my property. I want it back. I'm finished playing games. You have refused to return my ring, leaving me no choice except to file a police report." She turned, walking away.

Gage called out, "Maybe Mason should help us look for it."

Hailey stopped. When she looked back, Gage was reading his menu again. He whistled a tune. He tapped the corner of his menu on her side of the table and said, "Sit."

Hailey came back and slowly sat.

Gage smiled and put the menu aside. "Now, then. I can get you what you want if you remember I want things, too. Healthy relationships are mutually beneficial."

Hailey leaned close to him and said, "You son-of-a-bitch. How dare you try to blackmail me?" She got up and ran for the front door.

Gage remained in his seat and shouted, "I want you to be happy, Hailey, and you're not. I can fix that. You need to trust me."

• • •

Hailey exited Shiney's Shrimp Shack, sobbing. She jaywalked, running back to her lobby entrance after barely a glance at the traffic. A car honked and slowed to avoid hitting her.

In the lobby, Isaac called out, "Ms. Vaughan?" He approached her from a new, full booth in the lobby. An Echelonian banner on it had the words *Truth and Justice*.

"No! Back off!" Hailey said, swatting her hand at him. She saw an elevator door closing and ran, catching it just in time. In her office suite, she stuffed her resumes into her satchel and sorted other paperwork to take home. Her cell phone rang. Prickles shot up her back. Gage couldn't be calling. He wouldn't dare. She exhaled when the caller ID read *Home*.

She cleared her throat and answered, "Hi."

"Hi. When are you getting home today?" Mason asked.

Hailey sighed, tears welling up. "Early. It's been a rough day."

"Then maybe my timing is good. Can you arrange to hold off getting here until after five o'clock?"

"Sure. Anything you want."

"That was easy. Why do you sound so defeated?"

"I'm exhausted." More than ever, she wished she could open up to Mason and tell him everything, but she couldn't handle the fallout the truth would cause. Exhausted was a good enough explanation for Mason now.

"I have a little surprise for you," Mason said.

"Really?"

"Yes, really. Now you sound surprised."

"I am—it's a good surprise." She dabbed her nose with a tissue to keep from sniffling.

"So you promise not to show up until after five o'clock?"

"It's a deal."

"Great, see you then."

Hailey's stomach knotted, and her lips were salty from tears. Her chances of getting the ring from Gage were slim to none. Going to the police about it seemed futile. Gage could simply deny having the ring, which he probably certainly would after she had screamed at him at Shiney's.

She decided to work out to burn off the tension that filled her. Some time at the gym would delay her long enough to satisfy Mason's surprise. The exercise was her bliss, and right now, she needed as much bliss as possible.

She slipped through the lobby and into the parking garage without interruption by Isaac or his partner, who were preoccupied with their new Echelonian booth.

On the drive to Fit Performance Gym, her spirits sank further. She couldn't remember the last time Mason had surprised her with anything. What if Mason's surprise was a genuine effort to resuscitate their marriage? If so, she felt unworthy of it. And how could she possibly come clean at this point? *By the way, Honey, I spent the night in a hotel room with a virtual stranger. I'm not sure if we had sex, and I'm still hoping he'll return the wedding ring you worked an entire year to buy for me.* Enjoying the whole evening while hiding her left hand would be impossible. Hailey parked in the gym parking lot and got out of her car, disgusted with herself.

Megan was on duty at the fitness center front desk when she entered. When Hailey waved on her way by, Megan said, "You don't look like yourself, darling."

"Rough day," Hailey replied, avoiding eye contact. She went straight to the locker room to change. She worked out harder than she had in a long time while trying to visualize her life after her ring and Gage dilemmas were resolved. Drenched after exercising for an hour and fifteen minutes, she showered and returned to her car. If she drove slowly, her timing would be just right for Mason's surprise.

As she drove out of the parking lot, her angst over Gage's behavior enveloped her again. It seemed to come in waves. His extreme enthusiasm about her conference presentation had turned a corner onto a bad road.

His attempt to blackmail her, using time together in exchange for a hollow promise to return the ring, infuriated her. She wondered if there was a way to use his fixation to her advantage in getting the ring back.

A more immediate problem was handling Mason when she got home. While stopped at a red light, she considered bandaging her hand and claiming an injury. Mason might buy that for a few days—not long enough to have a replica made.

She drove by the guard gate of Turlock Heights Estates a few minutes before 5:00PM, so she pulled over a short distance from her house. While she waited, she called Felicia and told her about her frustrating episode with Gage.

"He didn't forget the ring, he's a crazy asshole, Hale!" Felicia yelled.

"Yes, it was a shitty thing to do."

"Shitty thing? Hailey, this guy is unstable. He should be committed. Cut your losses, be rid of him, and forget about getting the ring back."

"I can't do that. Mason will be crushed, and I won't let this guy win. It goes against my principles."

"I'm thinking you aren't going to solve this on your own, Hale. Maybe it's time you got Mason involved. This guy probably has a criminal record. Have you checked?"

"No. Turns out I don't even have Gage's real name."

"I swear, if he lifts a finger to you, I'll make him wish he hadn't. You might still need to call the police, Hale."

"I hear you. Listen, I have to get home. Mason says he has a surprise for me. I think he's making dinner or something."

"Nice. What brought that on?"

"I'm not sure. Great timing, right?"

"Try to enjoy it, Hale. Things can't get any worse."

· · ·

Hailey hung up and continued driving to her house while rehearsing possible ways to tell Mason about the ring. At 5:15PM, she pulled into her driveway instead of parking in the garage. She called the house number, and when Mason answered, Hailey said, "Are you ready for me to come in?"

"Yes. Use the front door, not the garage door."

"Okay," Hailey hung up. She felt both excited and worried. At the front door, she rang the doorbell. Mason answered, wearing an apron and an oven mitt. He bowed slowly and said, "Dinner is served, my lady!" He held his arm out for her to take it.

Hailey burst into tears. She covered her face with her right arm, keeping her left hand behind her back.

"Hale, what's wrong?" Mason asked. He embraced her and then held her shoulders at arm's length. "Tell me why you are crying," he said. "Are you still upset about Robert?"

Although desperate to fix the missing ring dilemma without Mason learning the truth of it, she longed to be honest.

"I lost my ring ... again," she cried, unable to look at him. She squeezed her eyes shut, waiting for Mason's wrath to ignite.

"Hey, hey, hey! Take it easy," Mason said. He gently guided her to the living room sofa.

"Mason, I'm so sorry," Hailey said, holding her hand to him. She expected him to be screaming by now.

Mason squatted and took her hand in his. "How did it happen?" he asked. It was the question Hailey feared most. Why did he have to ask it? Mason's gentle understanding brought her such intense shame that she suddenly couldn't bear to hurt him the way honesty demanded. She hadn't been prepared for him to accept her explanation and now had no time to think of a good one.

She stammered and said, "I spent an hour at the St. Julia shelter this morning. We were kneading bread, and someone suggested I remove my ring. You would think I had learned my lesson after the meatloaf faux pas. I was certain I put the ring in my purse, and then after we finished the lunch service, the ring was missing."

Mason listened attentively, and then anger filled his face. His lips tightened like they did before each of their fights. He stood up, his fists balled up at his sides. "You try to do something good for poor people, and some thief goes into your purse and steals your damned ring."

Hailey watched him in disbelief at the clemency a little white lie had bought. Her story might have been the perfect misdirection with no identifiable person to blame and resolving her problem without suffering Mason's fury.

"Let's go," Mason said, tugging her hand. "We'll get to the bottom of this."

"What do you mean? What are you talking about?"

"I'm driving us back there. We'll search for it."

"Mason, the other volunteers, and I, we looked everywhere. It's gone."

"Well, I want to talk to the director. Did you file a police report?"

"Of course I did," Hailey lied again. "Mason, you've done something special for me here tonight, and I want to enjoy it. Please, let's allow the police to do their job. I love the ring you chose for me, and even though it is missing, its meaning hasn't changed."

Mason walked around the coffee table with his arms folded. "I appreciate that, Hale," he said as his face relaxed. "I know last time I was a complete jerk about your ring. I'm trying very hard to handle these issues better than I have in the past."

"That means a lot to me," Hailey said. "And you're doing well."

Mason relaxed more. "I agree the meaning of the ring is most important. So if we don't get it back, I promise to get you another one."

Hailey got up and hugged him. The phone rang. "I'll get it," Mason said. He went to the kitchen. He was making a real effort to control his anger, and she had never seen his temper subside so quickly. She reconsidered whether Mason could handle the truth about her experience with Gage and then promptly changed her mind. Loose lips sink ships. What had happened with Gage was a mistake that would never happen again.

Mason returned from the kitchen. "Did you get any phone hang-ups yesterday or today?" he asked.

"No."

Mason scratched his neck, puzzled. "I just got the third one this afternoon. I answer and hear only silence. No caller ID."

Hailey's throat tightened even though their home number was unlisted, thank God.

Mason took off his apron, sat down with her, and said, "Remember our first apartment when we had a phone number that was one digit off from the movie theater's number?"

"Of course," Hailey said, completely distracted by the phantom calls.

"And remember how we gave up and pretended to be the theater?" Mason pretended to hold a phone receiver and altered his voice. "Thank you for calling. Top Gun will show at 1:15, 3:40, 6:15, and 9 o'clock." He laughed. "I later felt bad about doing that prank, but those callers should have been more careful!"

"That was something," Hailey barely whispered.

"Cheer up," Mason said. "Are you ready for your surprise?"

"Yes. Yes, of course."

Mason stood and led her by the hand down the hallway, through the kitchen, and to their dining room table. It was set for two with two long candles. He pulled out a chair for her. A lump instantly formed in her throat. After she sat, he lit the candles and used some mini-speakers connected to an iPad to play *One More Night*, by Phil Collins, a song they had both loved while dating.

"Mason, this is all so wonderful. I can't believe you did this."

"I've done a lot of thinking about us lately, especially after the Robert situation. I figure the best way to start trusting you more is to treat you like you are trustworthy."

It was one of the sweetest things Hailey could remember Mason saying to her. His overture drenched her in shame.

Mason made several trips to the kitchen, bringing out an entrée of roasted chicken alongside a freshly tossed salad and bread he had kept warm in the oven. He wasn't a chef, so his effort wasn't lost on Hailey.

They talked, ate, and laughed in a romantic setting Hailey wished she could fully enjoy. After dinner, she decided to make an announcement she hoped would thrill Mason.

"Honey, I have to ask you a favor," she said.

"Sure," Mason said, pouring himself a glass of wine.

"After I fired Robert, Felicia ran an employment ad for me. She found many qualified candidates, and I wonder if you would screen the first-round picks for me."

Mason froze, blinking. "You're going to let *me* select your new assistant?"

"I'll choose the final, but they won't even reach me unless they get a thumbs up from you."

She expected Mason to agree immediately. Instead, he just stared at her. His smile disappeared, and he clucked his teeth a few times.

"What's wrong?" Hailey asked. "I thought you'd be thrilled."

"Nothing's wrong. You know the type of power you're giving me gets me really hot," Mason said. He burst into laughter, and Hailey joined in.

She slapped his shoulder and said, "Don't scare me like that!"

The phone rang. Hailey wanted to answer, but Mason was closer, and running for the phone would be odd.

"I'm going to get the resumes. I left them in the car," she said.

She heard Mason say, "Hello," as she went out through the kitchen door to the garage. She retrieved her satchel from the trunk, and when she came back in, Mason held the phone out to her.

"It's for you."

"Who is it?" she whispered.

Mason shrugged. "Says he's a client."

"Hello?" she answered.

"Hailey, it's Gage."

The words sliced through her as Mason stepped a few feet away to begin clearing the table. He'd hear everything. She had to think quickly.

"What is this regarding?"

"It's regarding my forgiveness for your rude outburst at the restaurant," Gage said. "Don't worry. I don't need an apology. I almost asked Mason to bring you to Denburg for me, and then I realized you might not have told him about me, and he might find our relationship confusing."

"Yes, that would be correct," Hailey said.

"See? I'm right again. And I was considerate enough not to blow your cover. However, I need to arrange to return your ring to you. Are you sure this isn't an awkward time to discuss it?"

"No, it's actually not a good time."

Mason mouthed, "Who is it?" Hailey shook her head and turned her head away.

"Then I'll be brief. You don't need to come to Denburg. I'll bring your ring to you. However, I expect you to keep your end of our coaching agreement."

"I'm not interested at this time."

Mason frowned and whispered, "If it's a telemarketer, hang up on their ass." Hailey held up a finger for him to wait.

Gage said, "Hailey, we had such a good time together. I have a hard time believing you want your last memory of us to be our last interaction. I always advise my clients to be honest, and if I'm honest, then I have to say my feelings were hurt when you raised your voice to me at Shiney's."

"You understood me correctly. I absolutely want to cancel my subscription, and please don't call again." Hailey hung up.

Mason looked at her for an explanation.

"It was *City Fitness Magazine* asking me to renew. God, they are so aggressive."

"You wasted a lot more breath than I would have," Mason said as he loaded dishes into the dishwasher.

Hailey said, "Honey, you cooked, so let me finish cleaning up. Go relax a while."

"Are the resumes in there?" Mason asked, pointing to the satchel she had placed on the island counter.

"Oh, yes. Thanks," Hailey said. She pulled out the stack and gave it to him.

"If I hurry, I'll have time to play with my new toy in the bedroom."

"What toy?"

As Mason left the room, he said, "You don't want to know."

Hailey leaned toward the doorway and yelled, "Is it a gun?"

"I'm not allowed to have those in the bedroom. My wife won't let me."

Hailey laughed and hollered, "She sounds strict."

After Mason had disappeared upstairs, Hailey pulled the home telephone manual from a drawer and found the call forwarding code. She forwarded all their landline calls to her mobile phone. She had done this before when her father had surgery and didn't want to miss any news of his condition. Besides, she and Mason rarely used their landline, each preferring their mobile phones.

Gage's call to their unlisted phone number disturbed her. Until she could resolve that, forwarding the calls would ensure Gage would speak only to her if he called again.

While she cleaned off the countertops in the kitchen, a new concern came to mind. If Gage had acquired their phone number, did he know her home address, too? It shouldn't matter, considering the 24-hour manned guard station. Still, the idea that Gage possibly knew where they lived was unsettling. She went to the bottom of the staircase and looked up to ensure Mason was still in their room. She then went to the kitchen and dialed security on their landline.

"Guard gate, may I help you?" a male voice asked.

"Howard?"

"Yes, Ms. Vaughan," Howard said, seeing her name and house number on his computer.

"Hi, I wanted to let you know we are not expecting any visitors whatsoever, so please ensure that no one is allowed entry without ID and a confirmation call to us, okay?"

"Yes, ma'am. That's the policy. Is everything okay, Ms. Vaughan?"

"Yes, we've gotten some strange phone hang-ups. Naturally, we're concerned. We want to be cautious."

"Certainly, I understand, ma'am. I'll make a note of your request."

Hailey finished putting away the food and made her way upstairs. When she entered the master bedroom, she found Mason on his knees on their bed, leaning over two stacks of sorted resumes.

"How's it going?" she asked.

"I'm done," Mason replied. He picked up the smaller stack and handed it to her.

"That was fast," Hailey said. She sat on the bed beside him and flipped each resume over, examining the names of each.

"Any of these applicants are fine with me," he said, tapping the stack. "I'll have to play with my new toy tomorrow." He went to his closet and pulled out a suit for work.

Hailey laughed as she flipped the final resume. "All women."

"Hey! You told me to make my selections!"

"I'm not upset," Hailey said. "I won't say a word to the EEOC about your gender discrimination."

They laughed.

Hailey sensed a dramatic change in Mason this evening. He really seemed to be trying. Had the awful experience with Gage somehow erased flaws in Mason that would typically bother her? Maybe the episode with Gage would be the best thing that happened to her and Mason if only she could unhook Gage from their lives.

She went to Mason, still dressing in his closet. She put her arms around him from behind as he fixed his tie in the mirror. Resting her chin on his shoulder, she said, "Let's go away."

"What are you talking about?"

"Let's take a trip. We had talked about it a week or two ago."

"I'd love that," Mason said. "Where to?"

"I had done a little research on Cancun. I found some great packages."

"Sounds great," Mason said, slipping on his jacket.

"Remember when we used to take road trips on a whim?" Hailey squeezed him tighter and kissed his neck. "Let's do that again. Why not?"

"I like it," Mason said. "And I've got more vacation time than I can use. Let's do it."

"How about we leave Tuesday and stay through the weekend?"

Mason looked at her momentarily as though he didn't recognize her.

"You sure you can give up that many days? This isn't like you."

"My priorities have gone off track. This will be a good way to fix them." She kissed him.

"A little dinner is all it takes? I gotta cook more often!" Mason said as he left the bedroom.

"I'm going to book it. I'll buy tickets tomorrow!" Hailey said. Tuesday couldn't come fast enough.

Twelve

HAILEY ARRIVED AT work and rode the garage elevator up to the lobby. When the doors opened, Isaac, the Echelonian, stood there as if he had been waiting for her.

"I met with your master, and I'm afraid we won't be working together," Hailey said as she brushed by him.

"Yes, I know. Still, we want to invite you to discover truth and justice. It will change your life forever, and Master knows you need it."

"The only thing I need is a new assistant, and I don't think you all supply those, do you?" Hailey said as she crossed the corridor and pressed the button for the upper-floor elevators.

"When you live a life of truth, anything you desire becomes yours."

"What the hell does that mean?" Hailey said, scowling at him.

"It means the answer to everything you need is through our truth. We want another opportunity to share how we can help you achieve the fullness of life that we have."

The elevator opened. As Hailey stepped in, she said, "No. The answer is no."

Isaac smiled at her and said, "The truth never changes. We'll be ready for you when you are ready for us."

She dropped her satchel on a chair in her office and immediately retrieved her voicemail messages.

The first message played:

Ms. Vaughan, this is Lance Ramsey's office calling, and we are ready to reschedule our meeting regarding some consulting services with you. You may call us back at your convenience.

Hailey put the back of her hand to her forehead and said, "Whew!" relieved the Ramsey account wasn't lost after all.

The following voicemail message interrupted her moment of celebration when Gage's voice said:

Hello, Hailey. I want to apologize for calling your home last night. I should have timed it better. If you want to talk to me about our ring, do give me a call. I hope we can put our awkward exchange last night behind us. You have my number.

Our ring? She listened to the third message.

Hello, Hailey. I hope I haven't scared you off. I hate it when that happens! I apologize for any discomfort I've caused you, and I'd like to take you to lunch to make things right between us—my treat. I'm waiting to hear from you.

The messages had been recorded less than five minutes apart. She immediately called Jonah and told him to alert security to check all visitor IDs and to follow protocol in always calling her before allowing anyone to visit her suite. When Jonah asked if there was anything, in particular, he should be on the lookout for, she said, "I'm dealing with a crisis, and I just want to make sure my suite is secure."

After reassurances from Jonah, she tried to put Gage out of her mind and went to work responding to the resumes Mason had selected. She emailed sixteen candidates and requested they contact her to schedule interview appointments.

Hailey's dad called, as he often did, to check on how she was doing. She told him she had lost her ring, and he promptly offered to replace it with a perfect replica if she could send him the photos. Because Mason knew the ring was gone, rushing a replica was unnecessary. She politely passed on her father's offer. The sacrifice required to get the ring was part of its significance to Mason, and having her father write a check was something Mason would never go for.

"Fair enough. That's my girl," her dad said. "Honest and proper to a fault!"

After saying goodbye to her dad, Hailey got on her computer and made travel arrangements for her and Mason to go to Cancun. The idea of flying away was beautiful, and the excursion would be a welcome escape that couldn't come at a better time.

Less than an hour later, she had booked several interviews in the early afternoon for her assistant position. The possibility of hiring someone before her trip made her happy. The person could log and manage Gage's attempts to communicate with her, and she could once again avoid having to answer her work phone.

When the first two applicants showed up after lunch, Hailey cut their interviews short. The first woman chewed and popped her gum while answering her questions, and the second began the interview by asking how much vacation time she'd get during the first year.

She heard the elevator door open and checked the clock. The third applicant was right on time. "One moment," Hailey said as she left her desk. She entered the reception area and was surprised to see a thin, clean-cut man. He had blond hair and was dressed in a suit and tie.

"May I help you?" Hailey asked.

"I'm here to interview for the administrative assistant position."

"What's your name?"

"Peyton—Peyton Bredlin. It's a pleasure to meet you, Ms. Vaughan."

"You're Peyton?" Hailey asked.

"My whole life, ma'am."

Hailey laughed. "Come on in." She smiled as she led him into her office because she knew Mason thought he had screened out all the men. He had passed on some resumes with gender-ambiguous names like Casey, Kelley, and Pat. Peyton Bredlin must have flown in under Mason's radar. Hailey offered Peyton the chair facing her desk.

So far, Peyton was already ahead of the other candidates in terms of professionalism. The interview had progressed comfortably with Peyton when her office phone rang. Caller ID showed *UNKNOWN*. She remembered Lance Ramsey's office could call back and this might be them. She put her hand on the handset and said, "Can you pardon me a moment?"

"Would you like me to step outside?" Peyton asked.

Hailey loved his courtesy. "No. That's unnecessary. This call might be important and should take only a moment."

"Hello?"

"Hailey, thank God you answered. Are you okay? I've been worried about you," Gage said. Hailey's disappointment the call wasn't from Lance Ramsey's office changed to anger that it was Gage. "Leave me alone, and do not call back again," she said. She slammed the phone down harder than she had meant to in front of Peyton, who kept his eyes down.

"I'm sorry about that," she said. "There's this guy who won't leave me alone."

"I'm sorry to hear that, Ms. Vaughan."

Hailey resumed the interview. Peyton shared more of his background and work history with her. He was witty, charming, and obviously polite. Though Peyton would be an excellent hire, Hailey worried Mason would think she took advantage of his oversight in including a male candidate. After her wonderful evening with Mason the previous night, she didn't want to ruin their streak of good vibes right before their trip to Cancun. The best professional decision for her was the worst for her marriage, which was too bad because Peyton was ideal.

At the end of the interview, Hailey complimented him and explained she'd be making a hiring decision by the next morning. She promised to call him either way.

"I look forward to hearing from you," Peyton said.

He stood and reached across the desk to shake Hailey's hand. Hailey noticed a figure appear in the doorway behind him. It was a man wearing a baseball cap—a familiar baseball cap.

• • •

"Oh, my God!" Hailey shrieked. Peyton flinched as though something might fall on his head. "What the hell are you doing here?" Hailey shouted.

Gage stepped into the office. "You won't take my calls. You've left me no choice. I needed to see you. I want to spend another night with you at the Marriott. I have a new room."

Peyton said, "Excuse me, I can see myself out." He walked toward Gage.

"Don't go, Peyton," Hailey said. He stopped. The men stood side by side.

"I want nothing more to do with you," Hailey said.

"I've paid you. You owe me the time. Otherwise, you've breached your agreement to fulfill the coaching I've already paid you for."

Hailey picked up her purse from the floor and dumped it on her desk. She opened her wallet, pulled out Gage's check, and ripped it up. "We're done. Our professional relationship is over, and I certainly don't want a personal relationship," she said.

"Let me buy you lunch," Gage said. "Give me one more chance. You've misunderstood me, and we can make all of this right."

"I want you out of this office. I'm calling security." She picked up the phone handset.

Gage walked to her desk. Hailey yelled, "Stay away from me."

Gage pressed the phone hook down and said, "Hailey, please, let's not fight anymore..."

Hailey pushed his hand from the phone and yelled, "Get out," pointing to the door.

"Why won't you give me a chance?"

"I think you should leave," Peyton said. He had moved directly behind Gage.

Gage turned. "Oh? What do we have here?" He looked at Hailey and thumbed over his shoulder at Peyton. "Does Mason know about him?"

"Ms. Vaughan would like you to leave," Peyton said. "I suggest you do so." He had his mobile phone out and ready to dial.

Gage smiled and took a step back from Peyton. "My relationship with this woman is none of your business. She's not allowed to hire you anyway." He turned to Hailey. "Do you honestly think Mason will approve of another male assistant?"

Hailey stood stunned.

Gage smiled.

"I want you out of my office," Hailey said.

They heard Peyton's voice. "Yes, officer, I'm reporting a trespasser in our office, and he refuses to leave." He pressed his mobile phone to his ear, his eyes trained on Gage. "I'm in the Handel Towers Building. The office belongs to Hailey Vaughan, V-A-U-G-H-A-N. We're on the sixth floor. Please come quickly."

Gage strolled out of the office. "You ought not to trifle with fate, Peyton," he said, disappearing into the reception area. Hailey and Peyton went to her office doorway to ensure Gage had left on the elevator.

Hailey held out her hands. They were trembling. "Peyton, could you please stay a few minutes longer?" she asked.

"Absolutely."

Hailey went to her desk and called Jonah. "You have no idea how much stress I've been under since the Robert incident. How can a total stranger just waltz into my office?"

"I'm so sorry, Ms. Vaughan. I will talk to all the guards again. Let me assure you it won't happen again, Ms. Vaughan."

"Thank you, Jonah. I really need you to understand how important the security of this building is." She ended the call and took a deep breath. "Peyton, how can I thank you for helping me. You really didn't have to get involved. It seems I can't get rid of him."

"Ex-lovers are the worst."

"Oh, this guy is *not* an ex," Hailey said.

Peyton seemed surprised. "He talked to you as though you were."

"I know. It's awful. That man attended a conference where I made a presentation and developed... a fixation, I guess. Before I realized how obsessed he was, he convinced me to begin coaching him. I've only met him twice, and now he's apparently stalking me."

"I'm sorry this happened to you. My sister was the victim of a stalker. I've seen what she experienced, and it was awful," Peyton said. "I know of some resources that might be helpful to you."

"I would so appreciate that." Hailey sat and said, "Maybe this situation has given you an unfair advantage, but I have a strong feeling about this decision. You've presented yourself so professionally that I want to hire you—if you are still interested in the position after everything you saw here today!"

Peyton laughed. "I'm not intimidated at all, and I'd be honored. Thank you so much for the opportunity, Ms. Vaughan!"

"Great. Can you start tomorrow?"

"I can start now if you prefer."

Hailey came around her desk and shook Peyton's hand, amazed at her good fortune. "Consider yourself hired. You can set up your desk the way you want it. Your first task will be to contact and cancel the remaining interviews I had for your position this afternoon." Hailey pulled some resumes from her desk and handed them to him.

"So, you're asking me to eliminate my competition?"

"Yes."

"It would be my pleasure," Peyton said in a ghoulish voice. He twiddled his fingertips together. They laughed.

"I love the sense of humor!" Hailey said.

"By the way," Peyton said. "You should block his number on your cell phone."

"How do you do that?"

"Would you like me to help you?" Peyton said, holding out his hand.

"By all means."

He took her phone and installed a call-blocking app, then showed her how to enter a number.

Hailey was thrilled about this added bit of control. She felt fortunate to have had Mason's inadvertent permission to hire Peyton.

Peyton went out to the reception desk, opened each drawer, and began familiarizing himself with the contents of a nearby filing cabinet.

Hailey appeared in his doorway. "There's something else I need to tell you," she said.

"Sure," Peyton said.

"My husband might call the office, and he'll be surprised to hear your voice answer because he won't know you have been hired so quickly. I would prefer he doesn't know about the incident with Gage. Are you okay with not mentioning it?"

"You have my word," Peyton said, raising his right hand. "You are the boss. I do as you say."

"Thank you. My husband and I are going away for a few days, and I'll tell him then. He has felt threatened by my previous male assistants, and it's caused some friction between us."

"I can handle that situation. Your husband has nothing to worry about."

"You've experienced this problem before?"

"No, I'm gay."

"That's absolutely wonderful," Hailey said, grinning. "I mean— forgive me! I didn't mean to make it sound like an accomplishment!"

Peyton laughed. "I understand!"

"You are the right choice for so many reasons. I'm thrilled!" Hailey said as she went back into her office. She called Felicia and thanked her for the resumes and the great find in Peyton. She also updated her on the Gage drama.

"I feel better that Peyton's there. I hope he works out for you," Felicia said.

"Me too. I have a good feeling about him."

. . .

Hailey exited the elevator in the lobby on her way home for the day. Jonah talked with the Echelonians at their kiosk nearby. When he saw Hailey, he ended his conversation and hurried toward her, saying, "Ms. Vaughan, I need to talk to you. Have you heard? It's great news. Your problem is gone."

"What problem?"

"Please come to my office."

Hailey followed him. What problem of hers could Jonah know about? Not Gage. Maybe Echelonians were being booted from the lobby.

When they arrived at Jonah's office, he rotated a newspaper on his desk so Hailey could read it. He tapped his finger on a headline: *Wife Discovers Husband Bludgeoned.* Hailey picked up the paper, and when she read the story's first line, she clapped her hand over her mouth. She slowly sank into the chair by Jonah's desk.

The subject of the article was Robert Molam, her former assistant. His wife arrived home yesterday to find him dead in their entryway. The article included a statement by a sergeant saying he hadn't witnessed a more gruesome scene in over eighteen years on the force.

"This is horrible. How is this great news?" Hailey said, disgusted.

Jonah stammered and then said, "I'm sorry. I didn't say that the best way."

Hailey shoved the newspaper away. "Thank you for informing me," she said, leaving the office. Robert had been dishonest with her and stolen her property. Despite those facts, his untimely death brought Hailey no comfort or satisfaction.

On her way home, she turned off the radio and drove silently. She wondered if the circumstances of Robert's death involved his criminal past. Obviously, he had been the victim of a rage-filled homicide. Mason was the only person she knew who had a problem with Robert, but suspecting Mason was absurd.

At home, Hailey went into their kitchen and saw Mason napping on the sofa in the den. The TV was on. When he heard Hailey's shoes on the tile floor, he sat up and said, "Oh, hi."

"Honey, I have some news," Hailey said, leaning against the sink.

"What is it?" Mason said, rubbing his eyes.

"Robert's dead."

Mason stood up. "What?"

"He was murdered. His wife found him bludgeoned in the entryway of their house."

Mason turned off the TV and came to her, "Do they know who did it?"

"Not yet. Jonah showed me a newspaper story. It will probably be on the news tonight."

"Karma."

"Oh, Mason, for goodness sake! He didn't deserve *that*."

On his way to the stairs, Mason passed by Hailey and said, "I'm just saying… People try to be sneaky and get away with their dirt, and it always comes back to them."

Hailey followed him upstairs to change out of her work clothes. Mason's words looped in her head. She tried to dismiss them, reminding herself that she hadn't done anything wrong.

• • •

On Friday morning, Hailey met Peyton at the office, and they walked to Hot Perks. She didn't mention Robert's death. So far, Peyton was doing fine, and she didn't need to distract him with news about her previous assistant.

As they entered the coffee shop, Peyton commented on the poster taped to the glass door featuring the missing woman, Marissa Swenker.

"I'm still heartbroken about that," Hailey said as they got in line. "I knew her. She was always so cheerful and such a nice girl. I hope they find her."

They ordered their drinks to go, and when they returned to the office, Hailey spent much of the morning acclimating Peyton to the tasks of his job description. They reviewed client files and Hailey's calendar. Peyton was a pro, quickly learning Hailey's preferences and approach to her clients.

She took him to the management office and arranged for a key card so Peyton could access the suite whenever necessary.

Throughout the day, Peyton didn't mention the incident with Gage. He waited for Hailey to bring Gage up and then produced some printouts he had prepared the night before. They included precautions for stalking victims she could take and study.

Hailey asked him to arrange for a private investigator so they could obtain more information about Gage and to be prepared in case they needed to report him to the police. She was surprised when Peyton produced a list of three P.I. service companies they could choose from.

"Do you want to call them yourself?" he asked.

Hailey flipped through the pages and replied, "No. You've had some experience with this, so I'd like you to screen and hire the one you think is best."

Hailey's life was coming together. Peyton's introduction to her couldn't have come at a better time. He was intelligent, competent, and sympathetic to her problem with Gage. And maybe she was finally rid of Gage. He hadn't contacted her all day. Hailey went home that afternoon feeling relieved.

Over the weekend, she and Mason were in good spirits as they anticipated their time away together. Hailey kept her mobile phone close, ready to handle Gage if he called the home number again. That call never came. In fact, as the weekend progressed, Hailey felt more relief than she had in days. With Mason fully aware her ring was missing and Gage not calling, her life was getting back on track just in time for a fabulous vacation.

Thirteen

ON MONDAY MORNING, Hailey arrived at the office and was surprised to find Peyton already there. He handed her a medium half-caf, no-foam, non-fat, vanilla soy latte.

Hailey sipped and said, "How did you know my drink."

"I try to pay attention," he said with a grin.

"Nothing escapes you, does it?"

"Rarely." He laughed.

When Hailey headed for her office, Peyton said, "Ms. Vaughan, one other thing… I had an interesting conversation with those gentlemen with a lobby booth."

"Are they harassing you, too?" Hailey said, putting a hand on her hip.

"No, it was a pleasant conversation. While talking to them, an idea struck me. They are constantly there. What if we were to ask them to help us? They could watch for Gage and might do a better job than security."

Hailey came back to Peyton's desk. "They've been trying to convert me, and I find them a nuisance. I met with their leader, some guru in a warehouse across town, and you wouldn't believe how arrogant and presumptuous he was with me."

"Wow, I guess that wasn't the best idea," Peyton said.

"Don't get me wrong, I love your initiative. I just don't want to feel indebted to them after accepting a favor from them."

"I understand," Peyton said. He returned to his seat.

Hailey went to her office, closed the door, and called Felicia. "Thank you again for helping me get those resumes. Peyton has been great so far. He's a quick study, and the timing of his hire couldn't be better because Mason and I are going out of town tomorrow."

"Are you kidding me? Where to?"

"Cancun, through next weekend. I have got to get away so my life can cool down and regain some sanity."

"That's so wonderful, Hale. It will be good for you. I have a feeling, Mason, and you are turning a new leaf!"

"As long as Gage doesn't screw it up. You'll love this—I forwarded my home phone calls to my mobile phone."

"That's so convenient. How did you do it?"

"It's totally easy. We just dial *72 on our phone and then the number we want to forward to."

"I'm going to try it. You better hope Mason doesn't miss a call because of that."

"He won't. We hardly ever get calls on our home phone anymore."

"Has creepy Gage called again?"

"No, thank God. I hope the trip will let him cool off even more."

"Let's hope so. Do you need me to do anything at the house? Mail? Anything?"

"No, Dora cleans on Friday. If I need you to go by, your name is on the list at the gate. Don't forget there's a key in the knothole on the backside of the porch pillar."

"That key is still there? Good thing you live in a private community." Hailey laughed.

"If I don't see you before you go, have a great time, and call me when you get back."

"Thank you so much, Felly."

• • •

That evening, Hailey and Mason enjoyed dinner together, and Dora stayed late to help them pack for their trip. In a giddy mood, Mason made Hailey laugh, practicing Spanish phrases he knew were incorrect. The anticipation of their trip had already closed some of the emotional distance between them.

Hailey had kept her mobile phone handy, even at the dinner table, in case Gage tried to call the house. If he called from a new number, she wanted to log and block it, but there were no calls that evening. Hailey went to bed, hoping Gage had finally given up and that his absence would be permanent.

They drove to the airport the following day shortly after dawn. Their conversation flowed easily on the flight to Mexico, and their moods were great. The pleasant flight was a nice appetizer for the time they'd have to relax and unravel from their concerns.

Hailey rested her head against her window, watching the clouds float by under her. She smiled at the idea of being unreachable by anyone except Peyton, who'd agreed to contact her only via the hotel front desk. He had also promised to log any contact Gage attempted during her absence.

Their plane landed at Cancun International Airport. After a short cab ride, they stepped into the hand-tiled entryway of the Hacienda Escapar Resort. The tropical sun streamed into an ornate courtyard as the hotel staff offered warm greetings and took their bags.

Mason went to the front desk to check in while Hailey waited outside to enjoy the sun, checking her email and voicemail for what she hoped would be the last time for six days. She turned off her phone and slipped it into her handbag.

Their room was appointed with a mini-bar, king bed, and beautiful modern art coordinated with the linens and wispy window coverings. Off to one side, a separate reading nook had a private patio door that opened to a panoramic view of a sandy beach dotted with umbrella sun loungers.

Mason slid the door open, and a warm breeze flowed through the room. He excused himself to the bathroom while Hailey sat and fell back onto the bed with her arms spread. She took a big breath and exhaled, watching the ceiling fan turn.

Mason emerged from the bathroom. When Hailey saw him, she burst into hysterical laughter. Mason wore only his black socks and a tattered baby-blue terrycloth bathrobe that was too short. It was the same robe he had worn for Hailey on their honeymoon—when she had laughed as hard.

"You look stunning," she said.

"I feel stunning!"

"Come here, you stud!" She stood up, pulled him close, and they kissed. Mason gently pushed her back onto the bed. While she unbuttoned her blouse, all the stresses of work seemed to vanish for Hailey. And for Mason, knowing he had Hailey's exclusive attention, isolated far from any other men who knew her, made him feel euphoric. Cancun would launch their marriage on a solid recovery path. Everything about this place, the escape, the lovemaking, and their future felt right.

· · ·

While Hailey and Mason had been sailing through the sky to Cancun, Gage drove up to the guardhouse of Turlock Heights Estates. The guard closed the gate after Gage's Blazer went inside.

Getting past the guard had been easy with a letter on HOA letterhead, buckets of paint on his passenger seat, and a magnetic sign on the side of his Blazer that read *Gustoso Lot Striping.*

Driving toward Hailey and Mason's home, he rolled down the window, pulled the magnetic sign from his door, and threw it into the back seat.

Finding Hailey's house was easy, too. Google's satellite imagery had presented Gage with a clear view of the house's rough layout, the driveway, and the backyard. He parked at the curb and then carried a small work bag and a foot ladder to the front door, where he rang the bell.

An older woman wearing a hairnet and apron opened the door a few inches.

"Hello, are you Dora?"

"Yes," she said. "How can I help you?"

"I'm here to replace the smoke detectors."

"I'm sorry. I don't know anything about that," she replied.

"Of course, you don't. All of the homes are required to have their detectors checked and replaced this year. The owners, Hailey and Mason, contacted me and asked me to check theirs. I'm doing it for free."

"I'm sorry. I must call them before I can let you in," Dora said.

"Oh, absolutely," Gage said. "Hailey knew you would say that, so she gave me this note." He gave it to Dora. Written on Hailey's business stationery.

Dear Dora,

Please allow the inspector to check and replace the smoke detectors while we are on vacation. He is doing us a huge favor at no charge.

Thank you! See you soon.

Hailey Vaughan

While Dora read the note, Gage said, "Hailey mentioned something about being on vacation in Cancun and that she would likely be on the beach most of the day without her phone, and she didn't want to miss our free installation. She seemed really anxious for me to get it done for her, and I won't be able to return for a couple of weeks if I don't get it done today."

Dora recognized the signature she saw at the bottom of her paychecks. Gage seemed to know where they were vacationing, and Hailey's warning that she might be unreachable wasn't the sort of information a stranger would know.

Dora opened the door, and Gage came in. He took a small toolbox to the center of the living room and spread a towel on the floor beneath the smoke detector. He climbed the stepladder and examined the detector while Dora put Hailey's permission note in a basket they kept by the front door for mail, car keys, and other miscellaneous items. As she passed by him, Gage said, "Dora, I'm going to need to cut power to this room, so I don't electrocute myself. Can you tell me where the circuit breakers are?"

Dora led him through the kitchen to the inside garage door. She opened it and pointed to the gray panel on the wall.

"Perfect. You are wonderful," Gage said.

Dora went back into the kitchen to continue her work.

Gage found the breaker to the kitchen, living room, and master bedroom and switched off power to both. Within minutes, he removed the old smoke detector and installed a new, slightly larger one with wider venting around its perimeter. He went to the kitchen where Dora worked and replaced the detector there, too.

"Can you direct me to the master bedroom?" he asked. "Hailey said there was a smoke detector there too."

Dora wiped her hands on a towel, led Gage up the stairs, and opened the master suite's double doors.

"Thank you," Gage said. "I'll only be a few minutes." Dora lingered in the doorway for a few minutes, watching Gage set up, then left. Gage got to the critical work of upgrading the smoke detector. When he finished, he went to the garage and restored power to all the rooms except the foyer.

He took his laptop upstairs to the master bedroom and connected it to the home's Wi-Fi network using the password Robert had supplied. He launched an app that brought up four video feeds on his laptop's screen. In one, he saw footage of himself standing with the laptop in Hailey's bedroom. The sunlight that drenched the bedroom produced a crystal clear image as he walked to different parts of the bedroom. He clicked the arrow key on his laptop, and the camera inside the detector panned. He scanned and zoomed in on the bedroom, including the king-sized bed. He snapped his finger, and a sound indicator on the screen showed a solid audio spike.

He went to Hailey's bedside table. After checking for a dial tone, he picked up the phone handset, pressed *72, and entered a new forwarding number. He took a disposable phone from his pocket and dialed Hailey's home number. The phone in his other pocket vibrated. He hung up and grinned. He'd be sure to tell Hailey if any calls came in on the home line.

After using his laptop to verify the other cameras in the house, Gage smiled as he cleaned up his ladder and towel. He whispered, "Just like magic." He heard Dora in the laundry room at the end of the upstairs hallway. He went softly down the stairs to the foyer, took Hailey's permission letter back from the basket, and folded and stuffed it into his pocket.

He went to the alarm keypad by the front door. It was a wireless system familiar to him. The LED was off. He opened the alarm cover and removed the main control panel from its hinge. He let it hang by its wires while he pulled a pair of needle-nose pliers from his pocket. He cut the wires and spliced in a radio-controlled relay switch before snapping the cover back in place.

He went to the garage, restored power to the foyer, and hurried back inside. The alarm system beeped five times throughout the house, indicating a reset.

Dora heard the alarm beeps and came to the top of the stairs. On the landing below, Gage looked up and said, "I've restored the power and tested the detectors. You can rest easy. You are all much safer now."

"Thank you," Dora said. She came down the stairs and walked Gage to the front door.

Fourteen

IT WAS THEIR last day in Cancun. Hailey and Mason's getaway had been everything she had hoped for. They were tanned, Hailey catching rays while catching up on a backlog of books she had wanted to read for months. Mason tried his hand at surfing and took to it like a teenager. Keeping her phone off-limits allowed Hailey to decompress, releasing the tension that had built up before the trip.

After a delicious surf and turf lunch delivered to their cabana, they relaxed together on the beach. Hailey laid face down on an oversized beach towel for a nap.

Mason stood and slapped sand from his legs. "I'm going to use the bathroom."

"I'll save your spot," Hailey joked, keeping her eyes closed.

Mason stopped in the lobby to buy a magazine before going to their room. He swiped his key, and when he opened the door, he saw a beautiful bouquet on the credenza. A generous assortment of flowers funneled into a decorative green and orange hand-painted vase.

When he walked to it, he smelled its sweet, tropical fragrance. Water droplets still speckled some of the petals. He noticed a miniature envelope clipped to a support stick that protruded from the center. He opened the card and read it.

Be careful... your beauty might wither these flowers with jealousy. Enjoy your last day.

I miss you.

The back of Mason's neck prickled, and he gritted his teeth. The card had no other identifying information.

He went to the room phone and called the front desk, demanding to know who had delivered them. When they told him the flower delivery was a service fulfilled by a local shop, not the resort, and identifying the sender wasn't possible, he slammed the phone down.

Mason stomped back to the cabana, kicking sand on his way to where Hailey sat in a beach chair.

"I need you to come with me, Hailey," he said.

She turned her head and slowly opened her eyes to look up from under a wide-brimmed hat. "What is it, Honey?"

"Just come with me. It's important." Mason left her and headed to the hotel.

Hailey got up. "Should we take our things?" she hollered to him.

"I don't know yet," Mason snapped. "Just come on."

"Mason, what's happened? You're scaring me," Hailey said as she jogged to catch him.

When he swiped his key card again and shoved the hotel room open, Hailey saw the bouquet. At first, she looked confused. Then she hugged Mason around the neck and kissed him, saying, "Oh, sweetheart, they're beautiful."

When Mason didn't return the hug, she let go of him. "What's wrong?"

"Read the card." Mason pointed to it. He had clipped it back in place.

As Hailey walked toward the bouquet, panic set in. *There is no way... It isn't possible...*

She opened the card and read it. "Oh, my God," she said, stepping back. The message sent prickles up her back. She flipped the card several times, looking for the sender's ID, just as Mason had.

"Who is he?" Mason asked.

Hailey's mouth opened, but no words came out as she tossed the card onto the credenza.

"Answer me!" Mason yelled.

"Mason, relax. This is obviously a mistake," she said. "These flowers must have been delivered to the wrong room."

"Then why did you say, 'Oh, my God' the way you did?"

Hailey knew precisely who had sent the flowers. Gage's reference to "wither with jealousy" in the card might as well have been a written signature.

"What can I tell you, Mason? Some lucky woman is missing her flowers. I'll take them to the front desk and ask." Hailey reached to pick up the vase.

"I already asked them. They know nothing about these flowers."

"That's ridiculous! How would the flowers get in the room?" Hailey asked.

"That's a good question," Mason said. He walked to the patio door and pulled the handle. It slid open. "Unlocked. Maybe one of your 'clients' followed us, broke into the room, and left you flowers."

"You're being impossible," Hailey said. "We've done so well. Can we please not fight?" She went to him with her arms open. She tried to embrace him. Mason didn't return the hug, standing stiff with an icy expression. When Hailey let go, Mason left the room and slammed the door behind him.

A new fear gripped Hailey. Was Gage in Cancun? Had he copied their room key? She locked the patio door, grabbed her suitcase, and threw it onto the bed. All her clothing and other belongings seemed to be untouched. She searched the bathroom and then examined every corner of their hotel room. Nothing seemed out of place except the gorgeous bouquet that had ruined their vacation.

She got her phone from her purse. After she looked under the bed, half expecting Gage to peer out from under, she remained on her knees and called Peyton.

"Hello, Vaughan Consulting."

"Thank God you answered!" Hailey said.

"What's the matter, Ms. Vaughan?"

Hailey explained the flowers to Peyton and asked if anyone had called the office for her Cancun information.

"No one has called about that, ma'am."

"Peyton, if you told anyone my whereabouts, please say so. I won't be angry. I would rather understand how it happened than be in the dark."

"Ms. Vaughan, I swear no one called about that."

"Peyton, I think this is Gage's work, and I really need to know how he found me 2,400 miles away and managed to place a bouquet on a table in our locked room without my husband or me knowing about it."

Hailey heard Mason's key swipe at the door and then the click of the lock. She hung up on Peyton and tossed her phone back into her purse. She stood and braced for more of Mason's irrational anger.

He approached her, pushed her suitcase aside, and sat on the bed. He patted his hand for her to sit by him. "I'm sorry," he said. "I should have believed you. My reaction wasn't fair. There's no reason you would know who the flowers were from. The sender didn't write your name on the card, so it isn't fair for me to blame you. I was an idiot."

Mason's apology enveloped Hailey in the most excruciating shame she had felt yet. His request that she forgive him sliced through her. She deserved Mason's fury for her dishonesty. If he had berated her, at least she would be getting what she deserved.

"Please don't apologize," Hailey said. "I don't want the flowers. The only flowers that would interest me would come from you."

Mason embraced and kissed her. Hailey felt her eyes welling up and her throat tightened. She pulled away from the kiss and burst into tears.

"Hey, hey, hey," Mason said, lifting her chin with his finger. "What's this about?"

Hailey wrapped her arms around him and buried her face in his shoulder, sobbing as her whole body shook. She held him, hiding her face until she could compose herself enough to talk. "There's something I need to tell you."

Mason gently held her away to see her face, then stood and stepped back. "What is it?"

"Mason, I promise nothing has happened, but…" she hesitated when Mason crossed his arms. "…a new client seems fixated on me and may have sent the flowers. I'm not working with him anymore—at all. I've told him I never want to work with him again. I've told him I'm married to you. I've mentioned you by name several times. I don't want anything to do with him, but he's pursuing me, and now I'm afraid."

Mason walked to the patio window, looked out at the ocean, and returned to her. "Why didn't you tell me?"

"Sweetheart, please let me tell you… I'm so grateful you are giving me a chance to explain. First, you always worried that I was having an affair with Robert. That never *ever* happened. This other man saw one of my presentations and contacted me for professional coaching. After meeting him twice, I wasn't comfortable and canceled all future work with him. He's still been calling and won't leave me alone. I wanted to tell you sooner but feared you would accuse me again." Hailey's voice wobbled, and she paused to steady it. "I took a horrible gamble that I could make him go away alone without my having to upset you. Mason, I'm really sorry, and I'm afraid at this point. I don't know what to do."

Mason had listened intently to Hailey, giving her tiny nods from a stern face as she explained her dilemma.

"How would he know you are here in Cancun?" he asked.

"I don't know." Hailey shrugged and widened her eyes. "I really don't."

Mason went to the opposite side of the bed, sat down, and let his head fall against the headboard. Hailey kept her eyes locked on him. He hadn't exploded. She knew that was a good thing. He drew his tongue back and forth across his top teeth like he always did before a blow-up. He looked down and, studying his thumbnail, said, "Are you gonna say you won't give me his address?"

"I don't have it."

Mason looked at her. "Then how were you planning to bill him?"

"He gave me a retainer—by check. It had no address. I suppose that should have been a clue. Anyway, I didn't cash the check, and I've since ripped it up."

Mason slowly nodded with his tongue poked into his cheek. He got up from the bed and said, "I need to walk. I'll be back in a while." As he opened the door, Hailey said, "Mason…"

He stopped.

"Thank you," Hailey said.

"Thank you, too." He left the room.

Hailey went to the door and locked the deadbolt. When Mason returned, he'd understand why. She wiped her face with a tissue and then called Peyton again. "I'm sorry I had to hang up on you. Gage has found me. I need you to research restraining orders," she said.

"You got it," Peyton said. "I'll have everything ready for you when you return. Before you hang up, Ms. Vaughan, I have some other important information for you."

"Oh?"

"I didn't want to interrupt your vacation, so I was going to wait until you were back in town, but because of what's happened, I think it would be best to tell you as soon as possible."

"Yes. What is it?"

"As you requested, I hired a private investigator who has already provided us with more information about Gage."

Hailey felt her heart begin to pound. She took a deep breath and said, "Okay, tell me."

"Gage's last name, Dolon, is fake. And his first name isn't Gage—that's his middle name. His first name is John. So he's John Gage Mauldin. He's an electrician."

"Electrician? He told me he was a marriage and family therapist."

"Not even close. I have filed all this information for you."

"Thank you. I can't tell you how grateful I am for your assistance. This is disturbing and yet so important to know."

"There's more," Peyton said. "The investigator discovered a previous connection between you and Gage. It turns out John Mauldin did some electrical work a few months ago for the Handel Towers Building. He won a bid for new smoke detector installations, and that work required him to visit every office in the building, including yours."

"You're saying I've met him before?"

"Apparently," Peyton said. "I called Jonah to ask about him, of course, not mentioning your situation, and he said John Mauldin has worked in the building numerous times. The investigator said he'll need a few more days to complete his work. I will give you the report when you come in. He has found no criminal record."

"Thank you, Peyton. Thank you so much."

"You're welcome, Ms. Vaughan."

"Please research what is needed for a restraining order."

"Will do. I'll see you soon."

Hailey flopped onto the bed and sighed. Her vacation had suddenly taken a wrong turn, and she felt her anxiety returning with a vengeance.

She put in earbuds and launched her phone's music player to try to relax. After a few minutes, she heard a loud knock at the door.

She turned off the music and hurried to the door. "Who is it?"

"It's your stalker, and I'm obsessed with you."

Hailey flung the door open and said, "Mason, that's not funny!" As she stood in the doorway pouting, Mason picked her up by the waist and carried her inside so he could close the door.

"I've cooled down enough to hear his name."

Hailey worried Mason would take matters into his own hands. With Gage having such a short fuse, any encounter between the men would be a disaster. "His name is Gage," she said.

"Last name?"

"Mason, I think we should let the police handle him."

"Just tell me, please."

"Dolon, D-O-L-O-N"

"Thanks. By the way, here's a replacement for you." Mason pulled a new room key card from his pocket and handed it to her. "The front desk changed it for me on the computer."

"Do you think he delivered the flowers himself?" Hailey asked.

"I don't know." Mason opened his suitcase on the luggage rack and slipped his hands under his clothes, feeling around. "But if he tries to deliver anything else to this room, it will be a poor decision on his part."

• • •

After an exhausting evening of trying to keep Gage out of her head, a tense dinner, and walking on the beach with Mason, they went to bed. She spent most of the sleepless night tossing and turning, trying to jog her memory of the previous encounter with Gage months ago. She vaguely recalled a contractor visiting her office to do smoke detector work. She had paid little attention to the contractor at the time. She remembered a man with a ladder. She also recalled being annoyed by the laughter between the guy and Robert during her phone conversations with clients. She had told them several times to quiet down.

A few days later, a guy named John called and asked her to go out with him. After telling him she was married, he called two more times, unfazed by her mention of Mason. The calls had ended.

Hailey's excellent memory of names and faces couldn't link John and Gage as the same person. She wished she had paid closer attention to his appearance while he had been in her office.

After a continental breakfast brought to their room, they were on their way back to the airport.

"You okay?" Mason asked in the cab.

"Yes. My work is flooding back into my mind, that's all," Hailey said through a yawn.

At the airport, she constantly scanned everyone near them as they checked in and went through security. At their boarding gate, she coaxed Mason to sit in a row of seats with their back to the wall.

"Your stalker couldn't have booked himself on our flight. Relax," he said. Hailey couldn't. She studied the waiting passengers. Mason shrugged and turned his attention to his phone.

Hailey was as tense during the first part of their flight as she had been for the last twenty-four hours. She walked to the lavatory twice, looking at each passenger. After feeling certain Gage wasn't on board, she relaxed for the remainder of the flight.

She looked out the window, letting her eyes lose focus on the slight curve of the horizon beyond the plane's wing. Mason's mood had soured, and Hailey presumed it was because of her preoccupation with Gage.

Mason pulled a baseball cap from his carry-on bag, reclined his seat, and pulled the brim down for a nap. Hailey put her head on his shoulder.

After landing, they stayed in their seats, waiting out the predictable rush of passengers that jammed the aisle to exit the plane. When most had left, Hailey and Mason got up and went to the baggage claim. They found the conveyor belt for their flight had already begun serving luggage, and many passengers had already retrieved their bags and were gone.

After waiting fifteen minutes, new luggage stopped appearing from behind the leather flaps of the conveyor belt's door. Soon, the only remaining piece of luggage still circling was a badly damaged pink suitcase strapped shut with duct tape.

"Don't tell me our bags are lost," Mason said. He moved where he could see through the flaps where the bags came out.

"How could it be lost?" Hailey asked. "We had no layovers. We were on time." She went to Mason and stroked his back, knowing how easily he got worked up over travel frustrations. "Let's report it lost and get out of here," she said. "At least I have my overnight bag and purse. I can replace the clothes. I want to be home."

Mason went into a nearby office to file a claim for the luggage. He had taken the inconvenience surprisingly well.

As they drove home, Hailey's phone rang. It was Peyton.

"Hey, Peyton. What's up?"

"Ms. Vaughan, welcome back."

"Thank you. Any news?"

"Yes, Lance Ramsey's office called for you. I'm not sure why they keep going back and forth on this. They want to rebook that meeting with you to discuss their upcoming retreat next week."

"That's great news. They can go back and forth as much as they want to as long as they end on 'forth!' What did you tell them?"

"I scheduled a call for you to review their requirements at ten o'clock tomorrow. Is that okay?"

"Perfect. Thank you so much."

"You're coming into the office in the morning, right?"

"Absolutely. I'll see you then. Thanks, Peyton."

When Hailey hung up, Mason said, "Who is Peyton?"

Hailey's new assistant would be revealed sooner or later, so Hailey decided now was as good a time as any. "Peyton is my new assistant. I chose from the resumes you gave me."

"Congratulations! You didn't tell me you hired her already. Did I choose a winner?"

"I sure hope so."

"I've always loved the name Peyton," Mason said. "I remember in sixth grade, Peyton was the cutest girl in class."

Hailey wondered if she needed to come completely clean with Mason about Peyton's gender. Mason might laugh at his own oversight. Or he might accuse her of hiring Peyton simply because he was a man, launching a new jealousy bent. She decided she had shocked Mason enough. He didn't need to know yet. She ended the conversation, pretending to be interested in the opening of a shopping center they passed.

They arrived at the Turlock Heights Estates gate at 5:40 p.m. When the guard recognized their car, he stepped out and flagged them to stop. "I have a package for you," he said.

The guard handed Mason a box the size of a Rubik's Cube addressed to Hailey Vaughan. Mason placed it on her lap. She hadn't ordered anything for delivery to her house. She got a chill when she realized it could be her ring. The thought made her both happy and worried. The fancy box was wrapped in semi-translucent parchment paper, and her name was written in calligraphy. If Gage had returned the ring and included a note with his name, Mason would blow a gasket and never trust her again. It would also expose her teensy lie about losing the ring at the shelter.

"Have a good night, folks," the guard said, waving them through.

As Mason pulled through the gate, Hailey tried to tuck the box into her purse, but it wouldn't fit, so she held it on her lap. Mason looked at it several times and said, "What's Corigon Vintage Specialties?"

"It's probably some work supplies I bought."

Mason whistled and said, "Fancy. What does that mean? *As unique as your face. No two alike?*" He pointed to the side of the box.

"You know me, I'm a sucker for personalized office supplies," Hailey said.

"Well, aren't you going to open it?" Mason seemed more curious than usual.

"I'll wait until I get to the house. I have scissors there."

"Look, the box has a pull tab right there." Mason pointed to it.

Hailey realized that being secretive about the box's contents did more damage than good.

"Oh, I didn't see that," she said. She pulled the tab, ripping a line around the box's edge. Her heart pounded. Packing popcorn swelled from inside the box when she opened it. Mason slowed the car, dividing his attention between the road and Hailey as though she were unwrapping a Christmas present he had given her. Hailey's mouth felt dry, and her hands were sweaty as she reached in and felt something much larger than a ring. It was smooth and cold. She pulled out a painted head vase.

Relief swept over her. Days ago, her ring would have been the only thing she wanted to see. Now would have been a horrible moment for it to be returned.

When she looked closer at the vase, she noticed it was a near-perfect replica of her head. Her facial features, hair length, and color were all recreated with uncanny accuracy. Hailey looked at Mason, who drove with the corners of his mouth down, impressed. "Wow. Now *that's* amazing," he said.

"Yes, it is."

"You ordered that for yourself?" Mason asked.

"No."

Hailey saw a small card pressed to the edge of the box. She didn't take it out. She squeezed the box lid back on and set it on the floor.

"Who's it from?" Mason asked.

"It's from a client who knows I collect head vases."

"You don't seem very happy about it. You sure it's not your loverboy?"

"Mason, *please!*" Hailey shouted. "Don't make light of the problem. It's not funny. It's serious."

"Oh, calm down, would you? I think that vase looks amazing," Mason said. "Maybe get the name of whoever did it and have one made of me, so we have a set!"

"That's an idea," Hailey said in barely a whisper.

Mason drove the car into the garage. With no suitcases to unload, he got their overnight bags and went straight into the house, using the kitchen entrance. Hailey remembered the key she had hidden for Felicia and went outside to the front porch. She didn't feel a key when she put her finger into the knothole on the pillar. There was a cool, smooth object. She pulled out a foil-wrapped Godiva milk chocolate caramel. It was her favorite flavor, and Felicia knew it. "I love that girl," she said under her breath as she continued to search the hole for her key. It was missing.

She went into the house through the front door. On the way to her study, she opened the chocolate and bit the corner. Best friends were awesome, and the delicious flavor of the chocolate made her smile. She could always count on Felicia's thoughtfulness.

She placed the Corigon Vintage Specialties box on her study's desk and pulled out the card.

Dear Gorgeous Hailey,

You are officially collectible!

Best…

She left the vase in the box. She didn't want to see it. The thought of Gage handling it and rubbing his fingers all over it disgusted her.

She turned on her desktop computer and looked for a Corigon Vintage Specialties phone number. It was a few minutes before six o'clock, and as she dialed, Hailey wondered if the business would be closed. She was relieved when a woman answered.

"Yes, I'm calling about a piece you recently made, and I'm wondering if you can give me more information about it?" Hailey said, closing the door to her study.

Hailey described the head vase, giving its dimensions and her facial characteristics.

"Yes, I do remember that piece well. We finished it last week. Why do you ask?"

"Well, I happened to be the model for the piece."

"You're the fabulous Hailey? What a pleasure!"

"I beg your pardon…"

"I'm sorry, Hailey," the woman said. "It's just that your husband is so in love with you it warmed my heart to work on your piece. Every woman should be so lucky."

Hailey sat down at her desk, blinking while she processed the words.

"Hailey?" the woman said.

"Yes—I'm sorry."

"How did you like it? Were you surprised?"

"Yes. More than you can imagine."

"Your husband was so excited we had to ask him to stop calling about our progress."

"That's very flattering." Hailey's voice had gone flat.

"We've never had a customer who was more prepared than he was. He came in with a life-sized bust of your head and photographs from every angle. If anything wasn't to spec, it was certainly our fault!"

"Could you do me a favor and describe my husband?"

"Sure, I suppose..." the woman's voice became suspicious.

"Never mind," Hailey said. "I have a different question. I'd like to surprise my husband like he's surprised me. Could you create a matching head vase for him and not include the scar by his nose? He's very self-conscious about it."

"You know, I did notice that little mark, and omitting it will be no problem."

"Thank you, you've been accommodating. I'll be in touch." Hailey ended the call, having learned precisely what she needed to do.

She returned to the kitchen and set her satchel on the table. She pulled out paperwork to catch up on overdue client billing and plan for the Ramsey phone call the next morning. Before she began, though, she made coffee because she wanted to get caught up on her backlog of work.

Mason came downstairs after changing into a suit. "Coffee smells good," he said. He kissed her as he walked by on his way to the garage with a long, zipped duffle bag. Hailey knew what was inside. After being without his guns for almost a week, he no doubt wanted time to clean them for target practice at the range the next day.

"I'll be in the garage for about an hour before I take off for work a little early tonight. I'll see you in the morning," he said. "Thanks again for a great time in Cancun. We should get away more often."

"I agree," Hailey said. "Have a good shift." She blew him another kiss as he exited. She then made herself a sandwich to go with her coffee and dove into her work, trying to keep Gage from crashing into her thoughts. Letting Mason in on the basics of her Gage dilemma had been a relief. Threatening to reveal himself to Mason was no longer a tool Gage could use to blackmail her.

• • •

Gage's yellow Blazer pulled up to the entrance of Turlock Heights Estates. The guard came to the guardhouse doorway and said, "Pull up a bit more. The camera isn't reading your license plate."

"Don't have plates yet. I just bought her used less than an hour ago."

"No problem, sir. Let me have your ID."

"Absolutely." After Gage searched his wallet, he said, "I'll be damned if I didn't leave my driver's license at the dealer when I signed the paperwork. Is that going to be a problem?"

"Gotta have some ID," the guard said. "Who are you here to visit?"

"Mason Barger. He's my brother."

"No kidding? We love Mason. Nicest gun freak you have ever met. It's a pleasure to meet you, Mr. Barger! Bear with me while I do my job and give him a call. I'll have you on your way in no time."

Gage tipped his cap and rolled up the window. He held his mobile phone face-up between his leg and the driver's door to keep it hidden. It vibrated. He answered and put the phone on speaker.

"Mr. Barger, I have a man at the gate claiming to be your brother. Can I trust him?" The guard chuckled.

Gage shielded his mouth with his hand and said, "Do me a favor and tell him I don't have a brother, and then let him in."

"You got it, sir."

Gage hung up and opened the window again.

The guard leaned back and said, "Mason said he doesn't have a brother."

Gage played confused. "That bastard…"

The guard laughed and opened the gate. "Mason made me say that. You have a good one, my friend!"

Gage mimed wiping sweat from his forehead. "If you don't see Mason for a long time, it's probably because I killed him."

The guard laughed harder as Gage drove into the private, guarded, and gated community.

Fifteen

AFTER A FEW hours, travel fatigue set in, and Hailey's eyes felt too dry and heavy to continue. She looked at the digital clock on the microwave and opened and closed her eyes several times until it came into focus. 2:11 a.m.

She started to clean up her work and then left it out so she could continue early in the morning. She trudged up the stairs and set her phone on her nightstand. She stripped to her bra and panties and then went to her closet and grabbed her favorite silk nightgown. She sat on the bed, draping the nightie beside her. She was relieved to be home and thankful her home had such phenomenal security. She fell to her back and exhaled deeply. Her own bed felt terrific. She had every intention of brushing her teeth and putting on her nightgown before going to sleep, but when her eyes opened again, it was 8:15 a.m.

She heard footsteps climbing the staircase. She sat up quickly and said, "Who is it?" When no one answered, she said it louder. "Who's there?"

She side-stepped toward the bathroom for a better angle to the top of the staircase.

"Just me," Dora said, coming into view.

"My God, you scared me," Hailey said, clutching her chest.

"I apologize, Ms. Hailey. I will try to walk louder."

"No, it's okay," Hailey said. "I'm on edge today. You don't have to walk harder. That will scare me more!"

Dora laughed and said, "I came upstairs to tell you I'm here and also to say welcome back."

"Thank you, that's so nice of you."

"You're welcome. And, Ms. Hailey, I also want to ask if I can have Friday off to be with my grandson at his graduation."

"Of course you can. I wouldn't allow you to miss it! I think Mason and I can survive without your help until Monday. Even so, you might want to come in early to check on us!" They laughed. Dora headed downstairs.

Hailey looked down and realized she was still in her underwear. The bedspread was wrinkled where she had lain on it. She went into the bathroom, turned on the shower, and opened her medicine cabinet to get her toothbrush. It was missing. She searched the bathroom for the small overnight bag she had taken on the Cancun trip. It contained her hairbrush, deodorant, lotions, and other toiletries. Mason would have left it on her bathroom counter. He wouldn't have unpacked any of those items for her because he wouldn't know where to put them. She searched the bathroom and then the master bedroom. It, too, had vanished.

She hollered at the top of the stairs, "Dora, have you seen my overnight bag anywhere down there?"

"No, ma'am," Dora's voice echoed from the kitchen.

Hailey called Mason's cell phone. "Where's my overnight bag? I can't find it," she said.

"I left it by your sink in the bathroom."

"Well, it's not there."

"Hale, I don't know what to tell you. That's where I put it. I'll be home shortly to help you look for it."

Hailey showered quickly, puzzled by her missing items. She dressed and went downstairs with plenty of time to get to the office before her ten o'clock meeting.

As she came into the kitchen, she stopped. A bouquet of vibrant purple peonies in a decorative vase sat on the table. Hailey's paperwork had been moved from the table, many of her papers stacked and pushed to one side.

"Dora, please come here!" she hollered.

She heard Dora's footsteps approaching from the far end of the hall. "Yes, ma'am," Dora said as she entered the kitchen. She looked concerned.

"Dora, while I really appreciate the beautiful flowers, I have to remind you that you are never, ever to touch my work. This is important, and I hate to be so strict about it. My paperwork may look disorganized, but it isn't. This is critical for me. Do you understand?"

"I'm sorry, Ms. Hailey. I did not bring the flowers and have not touched your papers."

"How could that be?" Hailey asked. Dora raised her shoulders and offered a sympathetic expression. Hailey had seen Mason leave for work last night. It is possible the flower incident in Cancun gave him the idea of getting her flowers. The problem was that he wouldn't have had time to do so. "Are you sure?" she asked.

Dora nodded. "I promise I did not touch any of your papers. You told me never to do that on my first day, and I never have."

"I apologize, Dora. Please forgive me." Hailey walked around the table, staring at the flowers and paperwork as though examining a crime scene. Her mind raced for an explanation.

"May I go?" Dora asked.

"Oh, I'm sorry. Yes," Hailey said, having forgotten Dora's presence.

Her stomach felt queasy. She needed some food to settle it. She went into the walk-in pantry and got a couple of pieces of bread. When she came out, she noticed the toaster missing from the countertop.

"Dora!"

Dora returned. "Yes, Ms. Hailey?"

"Where is the toaster?"

Dora looked at the space on the countertop where it had been. She was as confused as Hailey.

"I'm sorry. I have not seen it. Maybe it broke and Mr. Mason took it to the garage to fix it."

Hailey went to the garage door and opened it. She checked Mason's workbench. It was bare. She returned to the kitchen and raised her arms, saying, "Am I dreaming? What's going on in my house?"

"I'm sorry, ma'am. I wish I could tell you where it is."

"It's not your fault. Don't worry about it. Thank you," Hailey said. Dora disappeared down the hallway.

Hailey took a closer look at the vase. It was a beautiful glazed green amphora with handles, much like the vase Gage had obtained from the Marriott restaurant at their second dinner. This one had a different pattern. She parted the flowers for a card or label—or anything. The bouquet had nothing that linked it to any sender.

Hailey refused to believe her suspicion. It was too horrifying. At this point, she couldn't ask Mason if the arrangement was from him because if they weren't, he'd go ballistic.

The flowers looked familiar. She leaned against the kitchen island and tapped her finger against her cheek, thinking. She walked out her front door to the front lawn. The gardener had planted similar peonies in a flower bed that spanned the front of their house and flanked the front sidewalk. The peonies in her manicured flowerbed were the same color as those in the vase. She went to them and parted some of the plants. She saw cut stems randomly protruding from the dirt. The severed stems were spaced evenly and impossible to see without moving other vegetation that concealed them.

Panic set in. The only possible explanation for all the oddities she had experienced this morning was one she couldn't accept. The thought that Gage may have been in her house brought a wave of nausea, and she leaned onto her knees, taking deep breaths until it passed.

As she returned inside, she tried to imagine how Gage could be responsible. She and Mason enjoyed multiple layers of security for their home. The Turlock Heights Estates community was entirely enclosed by high ivy-covered brick walls monitored by cameras 24/7. With the only entrance gated, it would be virtually impossible for a vehicle to sneak in or out undetected. And their home had an alarm system. Anyone gaining access to her house was supposed to be impossible.

She closed the front door behind her and was about to go check all the downstairs windows and doors when she froze. Something was wrong. The silence. The open-door alarm had not chirped. She looked at the alarm panel on the nearby wall. The display was off.

She pressed a button on the keypad and heard a series of chirps throughout the house as the alarm system came to life. Dora leaned out into the hallway from the laundry room.

"Dora, did you turn off the alarm when you came in earlier?"

"No, ma'am. I knew you were home, so I didn't touch it."

"Was the front door unlocked when you came in?"

"I'm sorry, Ms. Hailey, I don't know because I always use my key no matter what. Is everything okay?"

"No—no, it isn't." She stared at Dora, who hurried toward her, ready to answer more questions. "May I please see your house key?" Hailey asked.

"Sure." Dora pulled it from the front pocket of her apron. Hailey examined it. She recognized the appearance of every spare key she had made. Dora had once lost a key while still a relatively new employee and had come to Hailey in tears. She offered to pay for having the house re-keyed. Hailey had refused, explaining that accidents happen and there was no need to worry since they lived in a protected community. She had replaced Dora's key with a customized orange one that had a smiley face on the head.

After confirming Dora still had the unique key, Hailey handed it back to her. Dora noticed Hailey's hand was trembling. "Ms. Hailey, you seem upset. Is there anything I can do?"

"No," Hailey said, going to the kitchen table, where she picked up her phone. She called Mason.

He answered his phone, saying, "I'll be home in less than an hour. Did you find your things?"

"No, I didn't. But listen. Do you know what happened to the toaster?" She held her breath for his answer.

"No. What are you talking about? Hale, listen, I'm trying to close up the club, and then I'm on my way home. Can we talk then?"

"Fine," Hailey said, even though it wasn't fine. Her mouth had gone dry. She took the vase and flower arrangement outside and dumped them in the large garbage bin beside the house. She then picked up her purse and dug through it for her keys as she hurried to the garage door. Over her shoulder, she said, "I'm leaving, Dora."

"Yes, ma'am," Dora called from the back of the house.

Hailey got in her car and began backing out before the garage door had fully opened, almost scraping the roof of her Lexus. She speed-dialed Felicia and chirped her tires as she accelerated away from her house.

Her fear of Gage was giving way to anger. His manipulative game of hide and seek had become dangerous and had to end. If she told Mason about this, God help Gage. Everything would come out about the ring, and it wasn't hard to imagine Mason facing a homicide charge.

When Felicia answered, she said, "Did you have a fantabulous trip? Tell me *everything!*"

"Please tell me you left me some chocolate in our hiding place for the key."

"I left you some chocolate. Now, why did I say that?" Felicia laughed.

"The Godiva milk chocolate caramel piece. Tell me you left it and that you have our house key?"

"Hale, what are you talking about? I didn't go to your house. You said I didn't need to, remember? Would you tell me what's going on? You're freaking me out."

"Oh my God, Felly! I think Gage broke into the house while I was sleeping."

"No!"

"I wish I was kidding." Hailey pulled off to the side of the road near the guard gate. "I have to call you back."

"Hale! Wait!" Felicia said. "Does Mason know?"

"No. I just discovered it."

"Tell him. He'll protect you. You need to tell Mason."

"I can't. Mason will kill Gage—and I mean that literally. It will lead to a bigger disaster."

"What if this guy breaks in again and kills Mason? Mason is well-armed. At least let him protect himself. This is too big for you, Hailey. You need help."

"I hear you," Hailey said, refusing to commit. "I've got to go now. I'll call you later." She got out of her car and ran to the guardhouse. She recognized Howard Logan on duty, one of the friendliest guards. He stepped out to meet her.

"Top of the morning to you, Ms. Vaughan," he said.

"Howard, I desperately need your help," Hailey said. She eased by Howard to enter the guardhouse.

"Whoa!" Howard said, surprised at her assertiveness. "What's the matter? You're pale as paper."

"I need to see the entrance log from last night or whatever you keep records on. I may have been the victim of a burglary."

"I can call the police for you to report it right away," Howard said.

Hailey took his arm. "No! Wait," she said. "Before you do that, tell me what information you take on guests who enter."

"Well, Ms. Vaughan, you know the association's rules: No vehicles enter without an owner's permission. That's in stone. After permission is granted, we manually log license plates and keep 90 days of video footage."

"Great. Show me the footage from last night."

Howard hesitated and then said, "I suppose. Why don't you have a seat?" Howard pointed to a second chair. His wooden desk spanned the width of the small structure. He sat beside her. The cozy guardhouse comfortably fit three or four people. Rarely did it contain more than one guard on duty. A small television on the corner of the desk was tuned to a 24-hour news station.

A computer and monitor were centered on the desk. Howard clicked a mouse, and the monitor showed a split-screen of multiple video feeds from around the perimeter of Turlock Heights Estates. He enlarged the one for the entry gate.

"What time are you concerned about?"

"This morning between 2:30 and 8:00."

As Howard clicked and dragged the video slider, slowing to pause on each vehicle, Hailey looked out the window and saw Mason's car turning from the main road toward the gate. She ducked under the desk, tucking herself out of sight on her hands and knees. She whispered, "Howard, don't tell him I'm here."

Howard, confused, did as she requested. "Yes, ma'am."

He stood, and his legs blocked the side door as Mason's car approached. Howard raised his hand and saluted as Mason's car passed. Through his teeth, he said, "Hold on, Ms. Vaughan, he's slowing down by your car."

Hailey squeezed her eyes shut.

"Hold on ... hold on ... okay. He's gone through the gate," Howard said.

When Howard turned back inside, Hailey emerged from the desk, her face slightly red. "Thank you," she said. "I just—"

Howard raised his hand and said, "No need to explain, ma'am. The only information I need from anyone is a name, license plate, and who they are here to see."

They resumed reviewing the video footage. Between 1:30AM and 7:00AM, only six vehicles had entered. Howard recited the first and last names of each driver and most of the passengers, all residents.

"We had no guests during that time."

Hailey checked her watch. Spending more time here would push her ETA for the Ramsey phone call, but she knew the crisis Gage had created was much more serious. The video Howard had shown her so far had not satisfied her. "Go back. Can you go back earlier in the evening?"

"Sure." Rather than using the slider, Howard rewound to 6:00PM the previous evening. The feed showed the long shadows of dusk stretching from inbound cars, and then they arrived with headlights on. Howard continued naming all drivers, proud of his knowledge. Hailey ignored his voice, focusing entirely on the make and model of cars. At 8:46PM, she saw a vehicle that made her gasp. It was a yellow Chevy Blazer.

Oh God. "That one!" Hailey pointed at the screen.

Howard paused the video.

"Get the license plate."

Howard backed up a few frames and then zoomed in on the image. The Blazer had no license plates.

"That's impossible!" Hailey shouted. "How did he get in with no plates?"

"Hold on, Ms. Vaughan. Let me check the log."

Hailey folded her hands to keep them from shaking. She focused on not hyperventilating.

Howard had pressed a phone between his shoulder and ear and said, "This log entry is just scribble. I'm calling Milton. He was on duty last night."

Hailey was surprised by the clarity of the video images. When the image froze, she saw scratches and smudges where the license plate on the Blazer should have been. She leaned closer to the screen to see the driver. His face was shadowed.

While Howard talked to Milton, he waved several residents through the gate. He said, "I'm putting you on speaker so you can tell her yourself." He pressed a button, and the other guard's voice squawked through.

"Yes, that SUV was Mason's brother, Ms. Vaughan."

"Mason doesn't have a brother," Hailey said.

"Well, that's how he introduced himself. When I called your house, Mason told me to give him a hard time and send him in, so I did."

"But that's impossible. Mason was already gone for work, and our phone didn't ring."

"I wish I had an answer for you about that. Has there been a problem?"

"Yes, there's been a problem." Hailey closed her eyes and rubbed her temples, unable to believe what she heard. "What kind of identification did you get?"

"He had just bought the car. It didn't have plates, and he said he left his driver's license at the dealer. When your husband vouched for him, I let him in."

"I don't know what happened, but my husband did not vouch for him. You let a stranger who carried no identification whatsoever into our property. That is against association rules. You could lose your job for this."

"I understand, ma'am," Milton said, his voice subdued.

Howard agreed to call Milton back if they needed anything else from him and then ended the call.

"Your husband is home. Why don't we ask him right now?"

"No," Hailey said. "I can't tell him yet. He won't be able to handle it, and it will make this problem bigger."

Howard sat by Hailey, and together, they fast-forwarded, reviewing the next four hours of footage. They didn't see the yellow Blazer exit. With traffic more sparse after midnight, they could scan the video quicker, racing through several hours in less than a minute.

"He was in a very long time," Howard stated the obvious. Hailey didn't respond.

Finally, at 4:16AM, Hailey saw it. The exit camera showed the yellow Blazer drive slowly out of the gate. "That's it," Hailey said. "That's him."

"I'll file a police report," Howard said. He opened a drawer and pulled out a pad and pen.

"No," Hailey said. "Howard, I need to take care of this myself."

"Well, if there's been a security breach, we must report it. Like you said, I could lose my job."

"I promise you won't lose your job over this. Please assure me you will let me handle this. If you can keep this under your hat, I'll make sure you get the credit for having cracked it."

Howard gave her a slight nod, still seeming uneasy about an apparent crime Hailey had asked him to ignore. She took his hand and shook it, clasping it between hers. "Hold on a minute," she said.

She ran to her car and checked her wallet. There were six twenty-dollar bills she hadn't used in Cancun. She pulled five of them and went back to the guardhouse. Howard sat at the desk, still apprehensive.

"Please take this for your trouble," she said. She pressed the folded bills into his palm.

"Oh, I couldn't—"

"I insist, Howard. This is incredibly important to me, and I want you to know your help is appreciated."

Howard smiled as he tucked the cash into his pocket. "I'm going to work with you," he said.

Comfortable that Howard was now on board, Hailey needed another favor. If she had a copy of the video footage as proof, Gage couldn't refute it, and she could hit him with a believable threat to prosecute. Perhaps her wedding ring would make a reasonable settlement.

"Howard, is there a way I could get a copy of this videotape?"

Howard whistled and said, "Gosh." He thought for a moment. "I don't know, Ms. Vaughan. I'm not good with computers, and I wouldn't know the first thing about how to get the video to you."

"Then, if you can bring up the vehicle footage, I'll take a few snapshots of the screen with my phone."

"I suppose that'd be okay." Howard took the computer mouse, and while he reset the video back to the beginning, Hailey opened her phone's camera app to take photos. She saw the thumbnail images of her most recent photos lined up at the bottom of the phone's screen. She had taken some gorgeous photos in Cancun, including brilliant sunsets, yet the most recent images showed up as black boxes. She tapped one and enlarged it. Completely black. She scrolled to the next one. It was black too. Had she lost all of her Cancun photos? After scrolling through six photos, Hailey found one that first confused her. The image showed a silhouette of a person lying on a bed beside the outline of a small table. She swiped her finger for the next photo. It had better lighting.

Hailey gasped and said, "No, no, no, no!" The phone trembled in her hand.

"Ms. Vaughan, what is it?" Howard asked.

Hailey didn't hear him. She saw herself lying face up on her bed. The photo was taken in her bedroom, dimly lit by light from the hallway. In the photo, she lay asleep in her bra and panties. Her head was turned to the side, and her mouth hung open.

"Oh, my God!" she screamed, jumping. She dropped the phone on the desk and clapped her hands over her mouth.

"Whoa, whoa, hold on," Howard said. "Take it easy." He touched her shoulder. She shook it off, grabbed the phone, and bolted from the guardhouse.

Howard yelled, "Ms. Vaughan, is there anything I can do?"

"Yes! Do not say a word!"

Hailey drove out of the gate while Howard stood at the guardhouse door, watching her. The life of security and control she had created for herself had proven insignificant to Gage, who had once again enjoyed unfettered access to her. And what did he want from her? If he were going to kidnap or otherwise harm her, he had plenty of time and opportunity to do so.

Her phone vibrated. She jumped. It was Peyton.

She cleared her throat and took a big breath. "Hello."

"Ms. Vaughan, it's Peyton checking on your ETA for this morning's call with the Ramsey people."

Hailey tried to reply as her throat tightened, and the tears streamed down her face.

"Ms. Vaughan, are you there?"

She blurted out, "Yes."

"Has something happened?"

"Peyton, I'm in a horrible mess," she sobbed.

"I'm sorry, Ms. Vaughan. I'd like to help you. I'll bet I can."

Hailey laughed through her tears. "You're good, but I don't think you're that good—no offense!"

"None taken," Peyton said. "Please don't worry. You hired me to help you. Can you tell me what happened?"

"It's him again. It's Gage. I can't..."

"Where are you now?"

"Driving. I'm on ... I don't know."

"Let me reschedule your meeting."

"I'm sure they'll cancel my consultation. That will have to be okay... I have a much bigger problem. I'll talk to you when I get there."

"Ms. Vaughan, please do come to the office. I want to show you I'm worth my pay."

• • •

When Hailey exited the garage elevator, she scanned the lobby, worried Gage might be lurking. She saw no security guards on duty, and it angered her.

Sitting at the Echelonian kiosk, Isaac jumped up from his chair and hurried toward her. "Ms. Vaughan?" he said.

Hailey saw him, and her shoulders sagged. She had no energy for an Echelonian confrontation.

When Isaac reached her, he said, "I have a message from Master," he said.

"What is it?"

"You look worried about something. Our truth is what you need. Accept it, and you'll be rescued from any problem your life presents.

Again, he extends his offer to you. Becoming one of us will be the best thing for you."

"How dare you tell me what is best for me," Hailey said.

"Our truth and justice always make people what they should be. In your case, Master knows you should join us."

"Tell your master he's not my master."

"We want to urge you to reconsider."

"I'm not interested."

Isaac's face became serious. He stepped closer and said, "Your face is filled with need. We know you are searching for something."

"Yes, I'm searching for the security guard supposed to be on duty here. Have you seen him?"

Isaac ignored her question. "If you join us, you can die to your past and gain a new future."

Hailey walked away, saying, "I'm done. I've heard enough of your gibberish."

Isaac followed her to the elevator. "You need our help as much as we expect yours."

"Expect? Where do you people get off? I *don't* need you. Leave me alone, or I'll remove you from the building."

"That would be unfortunate for both of us."

"Oh? Are you threatening me?" Hailey said as she stepped into the elevator.

"Master said you'll come to us soon. He dreamt of your arrival to our cause, and his dreams always come true. And on that day, our message of truth will change you forever."

Hailey rolled her eyes and said, "Back off." Isaac stopped following her.

Before taking the elevator to her suite, she went around the corner to discuss the lax security with Jonah. The door to the management office was open. Inside, she saw the security guard sitting in a new chair. The small office had been completely remodeled, the walls painted, and new carpet installed. Jonah sat behind a beautiful polished wooden desk that held a new computer. In each corner of the ceiling, speakers aimed downward, playing music. The smell of new upholstery and carpet hit Hailey when she entered.

"What happened in here?" Hailey asked.

"We've done a few upgrades," Jonah said, beaming.

"A few?" Hailey said, drawing her finger across the new desk. She straightened a newly mounted painting on the wall by the door.

"We have a very generous donor," he said, smiling at the security guard on duty, who chuckled.

"Who?"

"Them." Jonah pointed to the lobby. "The 'higher level' people."

"The Echelonians?" Hailey asked.

"Money. They are dripping with money," the guard said.

"Why aren't you on watchout in the lobby?" Hailey asked the guard. "I came in. You were nowhere to be found. Lack of security has already put me at risk too many times."

Jonah motioned with his head for the guard to leave. The guard obeyed.

"So, is this why they have a booth in our lobby? This is some nice mutual back-scratching," Hailey said as she looked around the office.

"Ms. Vaughan, it's not like that…"

"But I think it is," Hailey said. She stepped outside the door and said, "I'll contact the owner myself if you aren't willing to keep security on their post."

• • •

In the elevator, Hailey checked her phone. Felicia had called three times since Hailey had abruptly ended their phone call on the way to the guardhouse. She'd call Felicia back from the privacy of her office.

When the elevator opened, Peyton stood by his desk, waiting for her. "Welcome, Ms. Vaughan!" He handed her a half-caf, no-foam, non-fat, vanilla soy latte from Hot Perks.

"Thank you, Peyton. I wish I could say it's good to be back."

"I have good news for you."

"Please!" she replied.

"I was able to reschedule the Ramsey meeting for tomorrow."

"That's fantastic!"

"It was easier than I thought it would be, and I was able to tell them the truth—that you had an emergency that was completely out of your control," Peyton said. "They weren't upset. They had double-booked this morning's phone meeting with another appointment in their calendar, so they were happy to reschedule."

"I can't thank you enough," Hailey said. She wished she felt more excited about it. Anxiety about Gage tempered her enthusiasm over the potential new client.

"I also have several ideas on how to deal with your stalker. Please don't worry. You may have more options than you think."

Hailey let Peyton's words of encouragement soak in. She felt tears welling up. Peyton pulled a tissue from a box on his desk and brought it to her. He offered a hug she accepted. Though she hardly knew Peyton, he seemed dialed into her needs. Felicia was her best friend, but ending up in this situation after consistently going against Felicia's advice made Hailey feel ashamed. If Gage would simply give up, it would fix so many problems.

"I'm glad you have a plan," she sniffled. "Because I can't tell you how desperate I am becoming. Come into my office, and let's review your plan." Peyton collected some notes from his desk and followed her. She closed them in.

"I've contacted the hotel where you stayed in Cancun. They explained your rooms are numbered in the interior hallways and exterior patios. Some local flower shops will deliver arrangements to the outdoor patio table. Perhaps your sliding door was open, and an overeager delivery person put it in your room."

Hailey wished that explanation was viable. "Peyton, that may be true, but I know the flowers were from Gage. The language in the note was unmistakable. It was him."

Hailey's declaration drained some of the excitement from Peyton's face. "Okay, scratch that. Let's move on," he said. "Ms. Vaughan, I have to ask if your husband knows about Gage yet, because that will affect our plans."

Hailey sighed as she collapsed onto her desk chair. "He knows only that Gage is pursuing me. He doesn't know the specifics, and I'd like to keep it that way. Mason is volatile. I don't want to alarm him if it isn't necessary."

"I ask because I've contacted a security company who can assign personnel to protect you when you are out and about. Their rates are reasonable, and my sister used them." He handed Hailey a printout of their brochure. "I also printed out the state's anti-stalking laws. We can file a protective order. If this guy violates it, the protective order will convert the stalking charge from a misdemeanor to a felony. You told me you never dated this Gage, right?"

"No, absolutely not."

"Then it might be worthwhile to get your husband's support. That would make things easier."

Hailey shifted in her chair. She wished she had a stronger reason that telling Mason wasn't appropriate. If Mason found out about her night with Gage at the hotel and Gage's possession of the ring, it would be a death blow to their marriage.

"Peyton, I'm thrilled you did all this research, and I'm sure it will be useful, but my relationship with my husband is incredibly tenuous right now. I think involving him with the details of Gage and hiring a security person Mason doesn't know to escort me around town will cause a bigger problem for me. Mason already wants me to carry a gun, and if he found Gage, he'd kill him."

"I understand," Peyton said. He crossed two more lines off his list.

"I brought a device that will allow us to record any phone calls from Gage on the office line. With your permission, I can connect it to my office phone since I answer calls, and it will serve as a log of his harassment if he calls again."

"Yes. Do it," Hailey said.

"Finally, for now," Peyton said, "I talked to Jonah in the management office. He said he keeps video recordings of the lobby for at least six months. Without mentioning any specifics of your situation, I asked if he would make this video resource available to law enforcement if needed. He agreed. We can already prosecute Gage for trespassing, and I'll begin that process if you want me to. If the complaint comes from your business, then the paperwork wouldn't need to include your husband, and perhaps you could keep him from knowing."

Hailey leaned back in her chair and looked at Peyton as if he were a hero. "I'm so grateful for all the help you are giving me. I want to think about all of these options. Gage has made my life hell. If I press charges, I'll have to be even more involved with him—perhaps face-to-face in court. It will make him come after me more. If I can escape him without pressing charges, I want to take that route first."

Peyton's face became somber. "Ms. Vaughan, many stalking victims don't prosecute because they worry it will provoke worse behavior in the stalker. The truth is there are many classifications of stalkers. For some, the threat of prosecution stops their pursuit. For others, their behavior escalates no matter what the victim does."

"I know," Hailey said. "I realize the risk. It's not an easy decision for me, but that's what I want to do."

"You know, there's something else you might consider."

"What's that?"

"Those Echelonians downstairs. I talked to one of the guys who mentioned they provide shelter and protection to their members who are battered spouses or have suffered from what the Echelonians call behavior that is 'unjust.' I'm unsure if what Gage is doing to you falls into that category, but it could be worth a shot if you were to talk to them. You'd be in good hands if they care for members as effectively as they recruit them."

"Funny you should mention that. I told you I've met with their leader, Eusebio something-or-other, and he claims I belong with them and joining them and believing as they do is my destiny based on some dream he had. His minions downstairs constantly pester me. To be honest, I think they'd be more annoying than helpful to me. Why can't they just let people live their lives in peace?"

"I understand what you are saying. I'm just trying to present you with the best options."

"And I appreciate that, Peyton. I really do."

Sixteen

AS HAILEY DROVE home, the thought of being alone in the house after Mason left for work terrified her. Given Gage's successful security breach, her 24-hour guard gate and house alarm had never seemed more inadequate. With the guards on high alert, there should be virtually no chance of an unauthorized vehicle entering the community. If Gage succeeded in getting to her house again, she'd be completely vulnerable without Mason at home. She couldn't allow that.

She had an idea and decided she was ready to turn a new leaf with Mason. The Cancun trip had brought them closer together, and it was time she demonstrated her trust in him.

When she entered the house, she found Mason on his hands and knees in the kitchen, scrubbing the floor with a brush.

"What happened?" Hailey asked.

"Damned coffee maker. I dropped it while I was cleaning it. I want to make sure these grounds don't soak into the tile." He resumed scrubbing.

"Can I help?" Hailey asked.

"No, I've got it."

He seemed tenser than she would expect him to be after simply dropping a coffee maker. She went to the fridge and got out a bottle of water.

"Why was your car parked at the gate this morning?" Mason asked.

She had known something was bothering him, and now it made sense.

"I went out for a run."

"You always start your runs from the house." Mason dipped the brush into the soapy water in the sink and scrubbed harder.

"Well, today I tried something different," she said.

Mason stopped and looked up at her, clearly unsatisfied with her vague answer.

Hailey added, "I've tightened my training and want an exact mile count. If I start at the gate, it reduces my distance nearly a quarter of a mile each way." Hailey knew Mason probably wouldn't buy that explanation.

Mason tossed the brush into the sink and stood to rinse a scouring pad. "Okay," he said. He snatched a towel from the oven handle and dried his hands.

"Mason, let's go sit down," Hailey said. "I want to talk to you about something important."

Mason tossed the towel onto the countertop and said, "Did the guy contact you again?"

"No." She took his hand and led him to the den. She sat first and gave his hand a gentle tug to sit beside her. She recognized Mason's flat demeanor as one he always wore when he had talked himself into a jealous fit.

Hailey took a big breath and said, "I want to go out on a limb and ask you to help me with something that may shock you."

"After Cancun, I don't need any more shocks. Tell me what the hell is going on, Hailey," Mason said, folding his hands.

"After much thought, I think I've convinced myself that I want you to show me how to use a gun."

Disbelief dissolved into a smile on Mason's face. "What?" he said.

"I'm serious," Hailey said.

Mason laughed. "Who are you, and what did you do with my wife?"

Hailey joined him, laughing. Seeing Mason swell with excitement felt good to Hailey. The truth was there was never a better time to open her mind a little concerning Mason's guns. It could improve their marriage while providing a way for her to protect herself from Gage when Mason wasn't around.

"What brought this on?" he asked.

"I've done a lot of thinking about what you said about Robert. And now, with this client I told you about in Cancun, I stopped being so helpless."

The corners of Mason's mouth went down. "I'm impressed," he said. "What did you have in mind, exactly?"

"I'm open to anything. I don't have to tell you that simply holding a gun would be a big step for me."

"You can say that again," Mason said. He thought for a moment. "We'll take it slow. Are you ready to hold one now?"

"I think so." Hailey raised her shoulders in a playful grimace to show her trepidation.

"I'll tell you what. I will go to the garage and bring in a handgun we can start with. It will be unloaded. Are you okay with that?" Hailey appreciated Mason's abundance of caution as he over-explained every step he would take. She nodded, sat back on the sofa, and folded her hands on her lap.

As Mason left the den, Hailey heard him say, "Wow." She heard the kitchen door to the garage open and close. A few moments later, Mason returned, carrying a handgun wrapped in a towel. He set it on the coffee table in front of them and unwrapped it. Like all of Mason's guns, it was pristine, shining as if it had never been used, although Hailey knew better.

Mason said, "I want to remind you this gun is unloaded. Still, you never want to point it at anyone you don't intend to shoot."

"Don't worry," Hailey said. "What type of gun is it?"

"This is a Sig Sauer P220 combat pistol. It's one of my favorites, and it's incredibly accurate."

"Is this 'Cocky?'" Hailey asked.

Mason looked stunned. "How did you know that?"

"I've heard you talk about 'Cocky' on the phone before."

Mason laughed. "Yes, this is 'Cocky.' Are you willing to hold my 'Cocky'?"

Hailey swatted his arm and laughed. After taking a deep breath, she sighed and held out her hand. Mason held the gun firmly by the slide and wrapped Hailey's fingers around the grip.

"Wow, it's heavier than I expected," Hailey said.

"Now, let me ask you something," Mason said.

"Sure. Anything."

"Did he hurt you?" Mason asked.

Hailey looked at him. Mason's face was serious. Had he learned about Gage's break-in? Did Gage contact Mason? "What do you mean?" Hailey asked, her pulse raced.

"Cocky... has he hurt you yet? You've touched a real gun now. Has anything horrible happened to you?"

"Ha, ha, hilarious," Hailey said as relief rushed over her. She returned to the gun and said, "So what steps do I need to take to shoot this?"

"Whoa, hold on. First things first. Holding this gun was a big step, and I think that's enough for a first training session. We'll shoot it soon. The last thing I want to do is scare you off," Mason said.

"I won't be afraid."

"Hailey, you don't expect to shoot it here, do you? We've got to go to the range—which we can do—just not this minute." He held out his hand, and Hailey gave him the gun. She knew she couldn't push him to show her how to shoot the gun without generating the suspicion that always led to awful interrogations.

He wrapped the gun in the cloth. Hailey followed him into the kitchen, and before he went into the garage, she said, "Where do you keep them?"

She knew Mason hid his guns out of caution and courtesy to her. Until now, she had never cared where they were.

He stopped and said, "I keep most of them locked in a gun vault."

"Hmph. I've never seen a vault anywhere. Where is it?"

He cocked his head and smirked at her. Hailey shrugged and said, "I'm only curious, sweetheart."

"In the bottom drawer of my workbench."

"Is it a key lock?" Hailey immediately sensed she had pushed too far when Mason put the wrapped handgun on the counter and turned to her.

His face filled with suspicion, and he said, "The vault has a combination and is also biometric. My handprint opens it. Does that make you feel better? Why are you asking me these questions? Is that guy freaking you out? I still want his address."

"I'm sorry for all the questions. I'm only trying to show that I'm growing and genuinely interested in your hobby. I didn't mean to make you uncomfortable."

"I'm not uncomfortable, just surprised you came home today converted into a gun enthusiast," Mason said. He held up Cocky and said, "I don't lock him up. He's hidden."

"Where?"

"You promise not to freak out?"

Hailey raised her right hand and said, "I swear."

"Let's just say the passenger headrest in my car has a Velcro flap."

"You're kidding me!"

Mason nodded and grinned.

"You mean I've slept against your ... Cocky?"

They laughed, and then, as Mason rested his hand on the doorknob, he said, "If you seriously want to learn about guns, then we need to go to the range where you can learn more about safety and take some shots."

"Okay. Let's do it," Hailey said. "Tomorrow afternoon? When I get home, okay? I'll come home from work on time, I promise."

"Consider it booked," Mason said. As he disappeared into the garage, he shook his head and said, "Unbelievable."

Hailey wanted access to a gun tonight, whether or not she knew how to fire it. She wasn't staying home alone without at least the ability to brandish a weapon. She needed the combination to the gun vault, but it was too soon to ask Mason.

Mason returned from the garage. As he passed her, he said, "I've got to get ready for work." He gave her a quick peck on the lips and headed upstairs to change into his suit.

She remembered she had yet to return Felicia's call. She would love Felicia's company tonight and decided to call her after Mason left. She took out flour, butter, chocolate chips, and a cookie pan to stage the kitchen to make cookies. When Mason came downstairs, he smiled when he saw the ingredients and Hailey measuring them. He kissed her goodbye.

When she heard his car pull out of the driveway, she went to the living room window, watched him drive away, and then went to the garage. She opened the bottom drawer of Mason's workbench. The gun vault had the outline of a hand on it. She placed her hand on it. A red light flashed, and the vault beeped. It had a number keypad for the combination. Hailey tried the numbers that comprised Mason's birthday and social security number, the only numbers she knew Mason probably had memorized. None worked. Accessing the gun vault was not an option.

She went back inside and called Felicia.

"Do I know you?" Felicia answered sarcastically.

"I'm so sorry I didn't call you back earlier today, Felly. You won't believe all the things that have happened."

"Don't ever hang up on me and scare me like that again," Felicia scolded.

"Forgive me. I'll make it up to you. Is there any way I can crash with you tonight?"

"Like, stay over?"

"Yes. It's Gage. He's out of control. I'm afraid he might return, and I don't want to be alone here. I don't feel safe. I'll tell you everything."

"That bastard. Yes, you'll come here tonight."

"Thank you so much," Hailey said as she put the cookie pan and ingredients away.

"Hale, I might drag you to the police station before it's too late. You didn't nip this prick in the bud like you should have. The only thing he will understand is a serious smackdown."

"I asked Mason to teach me about guns."

"*You?*"

"I know. Unbelievable, right? You'll understand when I explain what has happened."

"So, does this mean you told Mason about Gage?"

"A little—sort of. I asked Mason to introduce me to guns. I'm still terrified of them, but I'd rather know how to use one if needed. I'll tell you more when I see you. I don't enjoy being here alone. Is it okay to come over now?"

"Sure. I'm here. Get here. I've missed you. I will show you how to bring this slimebag to his knees. I've got a gun you can use."

"What? Why didn't I know that?"

"Yes, I pack heat. I just don't say much about it. I'll be glad to loan it to you if it keeps my best friend safe."

"You never cease to amaze me. I'll see you in about twenty minutes.

I gotta get out of here."

• • •

Gage knew Hailey and Felicia had been friends for at least fifteen years. He had more than once heard them in conversation, reminiscing about partying in college.

Sitting on the shoulder of the road in his Blazer a short distance from the guard gate of Turlock Heights Estates, he replayed the audio of the phone call on his laptop. As he listened to Felicia blasting him and offering Hailey a gun, Gage ground his thumbnail into his index finger. He swung his arm into the passenger seat with the butt of his hand and screamed, "Fucking bitch!" He clutched the steering wheel and exhaled.

Felicia's influence on Hailey had been of only moderate concern to Gage until now. This last chit-chat, however, was regrettable. He could no longer ignore Felicia's trifling. She couldn't be allowed to knock fate off course. He relaxed and then laughed at temporarily forgetting things were destined to work out. They had to.

He pulled up Felicia's home address from the background check he had purchased. After typing it into his GPS unit, he set the laptop aside and pulled into traffic en route to Medlyn, a suburb directly south of Wenshire Harbor. The timing should be perfect. He'd arrive well before Hailey did.

During his drive, he was pleased to see Hailey's car, represented by a moving green arrow on the map, confirming he had the correct destination.

When he arrived on Felicia's street, he drove by her house slowly. She lived in a two-story townhome with an attached garage in a new development tract.

He made a U-turn and parked half a block away behind a pickup truck. His position let him remain inconspicuous while he enjoyed a clear view of any car that entered or exited Felicia's driveway.

He reclined his seat slightly and saw Hailey pull into the driveway in less than ten minutes. She exited her car door carrying a small bag and walked to Felicia's front door. Gage sucked his teeth and shook his head at her. His meticulous electronic handiwork in recent months had allowed him to listen to Hailey at any time while she was at home, at the office, in her car, or on her mobile phone. Now Felicia Blakner's house was about to mute Hailey's beautiful voice for an entire evening and night.

"Be careful, lover," he said as he watched her ring the doorbell. "She's no good for you." Gage breathed hard and felt sweaty as his world was about to go silent. He plugged his laptop into the cigarette lighter to recharge the low battery and then studied the recording program on the screen, cued for her mobile phone calls. He longed for Hailey to use her phone. *Call someone-anyone.* God, he missed her voice.

He took a tissue from a box under his seat and wiped his hands and forehead while Felicia greeted Hailey with a hug at her door. Felicia took Hailey's bag and pulled her inside by the hand. *Don't rush her, you bitch.* Hailey was gone, the window curtains were drawn, and Gage was in exile. Only once during the night did he glimpse her—when two silhouettes crossed one another in the upper room.

He pulled up some footage of Hailey, recorded courtesy of her and Mason's fancy new smoke detectors. The clips he enjoyed most showed her dressing and undressing in the master bedroom. A couple of the clips featured Hailey singing, which was a bonus. She had spoiled him with her visual treats. He loved how she never pulled her panties straight down, instead hooking her thumbs under the elastic and wiggling her hips to slide them off—teasing him. There was no way she didn't know he loved that. Sometimes, Gage would swear that Hailey played to the camera, turning her body just right for him to see her goodies.

He chose a ten-second video clip of Hailey toweling off in the bedroom after a shower. The arch of her back was just so delicious he set the clip in a non-stop loop on one side of his laptop screen. On the other, he opened a list of his favorite recordings and scrolled through hundreds of hours of Hailey's voice and footage. With this treasure, Hailey performed for him whenever he wanted her to. He could see her in any mood he preferred her to be in. His robust library had become an embarrassment of riches, and the thought of his wealth made him grin and calmed him. Masturbating to release his excitement from her video teasings satisfied him for only moments.

Shortly after 1:00AM, the upper room light in Felicia's house turned off. Now that he was reasonably sure Hailey was tucked in and not going anywhere until morning, Gage needed to run an errand across town. He zipped up his pants, and as he drove by, he rolled down the window and blew a kiss to the house, saying, "Sleep tight. I'll be back soon, lover!"

Gage drove to Club Parlay, located on the outskirts of Wenshire Harbor. He parked on the street and walked through the well-lit parking lot for guests. As he passed the front door, he heard the pounding of bass and the sounds of late-night partiers inside. He tipped his hat to the bouncer and walked around to the back of the club, where he found Mason's car. Parking was cramped, and the silver Mustang was blocked with six others in the poorly lit employee parking area at the rear entrance.

Gage pulled a suction cup from his jacket pocket, licked it, and pressed it to Mason's car window. Then, with a pen-like glass cutter, he traced an oval around the suction cup and removed the glass piece.

His mission was accomplished in less than a minute, and he was returning to his car. It shouldn't have been that easy. It wouldn't have been if fate wasn't on his side.

Seventeen

"THANK YOU SO much, Felly," Hailey said as they walked from Felicia's front door to her car in the driveway. She opened the car door and placed her bag inside. Neither woman noticed Gage watching them from half a block away.

Felicia mimed holding a gun and said, "Remember to disengage the safety, keep your wrist firm, aim, hold your breath, and then serve it up!" She squatted in a firing stance.

"I think I've got it," Hailey said. "If I'm lucky, I won't have to use it."

"But if you do, you'll be glad you have it. If it's you or him, make damned sure it's him."

They hugged. Hailey backed her red Lexus out of the driveway. Felicia waited to wave goodbye before going into her house. She worried about her friend. Despite the hours of talking and little sleep last night, Felicia hadn't convinced Hailey to involve the police in her dilemma. At least she had agreed to take the gun. It was a Ruger LC9, a special gun with sentimental value given to Felicia by her father before he passed.

Felicia went upstairs to her bedroom and slipped out of her sweats and into her work clothes. She turned on her favorite country station and sang along to *You're Going to Ruin My Bad Reputation* while she got ready for work.

She heard a heavy thud. She muted the radio and listened, wondering if something had fallen downstairs. The house was quiet. She unmuted the radio and turned the volume lower.

She went to the door and called, "Hailey, did you come back?"

No answer.

Felicia shrugged. After getting ready in her master bathroom, she returned to the bedroom, brushing her hair. Then she heard something like a fork or spoon falling into the kitchen sink downstairs.

As Murphy's Law would have it, the day she loaned out her gun was when she wanted to have it in hand to investigate the noise. She got a broom from the upstairs closet and slowly descended the steps. At the bottom of the landing, she hissed, "Sssssss," to see if she might startle some creature that had invaded her home. Last year, she had needed to call animal control to remove a raccoon that had found its way into her kitchen.

Her hiss flushed out nothing. When she reached the bottom landing, she looked down the hallway to the kitchen. There was a green blanket spread out on the floor. What the hell was going on? She walked to the kitchen.

When she stepped through the doorway, two arms dropped around her neck and jerked a tight wire. It happened too fast for her to scream. Gage forced her onto the floor and flipped her to her back, mounting her to stop her from bucking. He was several days unshaven, his lips pulled back in a snarl like a mad dog, and his eyes filled with contempt. He twisted the wire, tightening it until it disappeared between the folds of her neck. She clawed at it, unable to grip it. Her fingernails scraped her neck. She swung at Gage, landing useless blows to his shoulder and torso.

Gage held the wire behind her neck with one hand and used his other to rip a strip of duct tape. He taped her mouth shut and released the wire. Felicia coughed through her nose and sucked in a massive breath of air. Gage flipped her to her stomach and bound her wrists and feet.

"This was so unnecessary," he said. Felicia shook her head, trying to talk through the duct tape.

"I took care of that naughty mouth, didn't I?" Gage said. He wrapped her in the blanket and dragged her by the feet through her house to the garage's inside door. He pressed the wall button to open the door and backed his Blazer into the space beside Felicia's car. When he got out, he saw Felicia had wiggled partially out of the blanket and was trying to stand. Gage laid her back down while she throat-screamed under the duct tape. He re-wrapped her and loaded her up into the back of his Blazer. Fate was back on course.

$$\bullet \ \bullet \ \bullet$$

Hailey drove to the Turlock Heights Estates gate, hoping Mason hadn't left for work yet. Despite being armed with Felicia's gun, she was still terrified to enter her home alone.

Howard was on duty in the guardhouse. He waved for her to stop. "Are you doing better today, Ms. Vaughan?" he asked.

"Yes, thank you."

"I just wanted to say I told all the other guards we need to be extra vigilant. I didn't tell them why," he said with a smile.

"Have any unusual visitors been trying to get in?" she asked.

"No, ma'am."

"Thank you, Howard. Please call me at the house immediately if anyone asks to visit us."

"Will do." Howard saluted.

When Hailey pulled into her driveway, she pressed the garage door opener on her visor, half expecting to see Gage standing inside, waiting for her. The garage was empty. Mason wasn't home from work yet. It was Dora's day off.

With its strap slung over her shoulder, she slipped her hand inside her purse, gripping Felicia's Ruger.

Instead of entering the house through the garage, she went to the front door. She jiggled the knob and felt relieved it was locked. She checked in the pillar's knothole to see if Gage had left any more unwelcome gifts for her. When she found it empty, she used her key to open the front door and was relieved to hear the shrill tone of the security system. She keyed in the code, and the house went quiet.

She no longer trusted the alarm. Still unsure of how Gage had so successfully bypassed their alarm system and entered their house before, there was no reason he couldn't do it again if he made it past the guard gate. She pulled the gun out of her purse and held it in front of her as she went room to room downstairs, looking for signs of Gage. Before she rounded the doorway of each room, she announced, "I have a gun. I will shoot you."

Meanwhile, across town, Gage listened to live audio of Hailey's house through his phone's speaker on the seat beside him. He turned the volume as high as it would go. He laughed harder with each room she cleared. "Do you hear my wife?" he hollered over his shoulder to Felicia, still bound in the back. "You've got her all worked up and paranoid."

When he heard Hailey yell, "I know you're in here. Come out with your hands up," Gage laughed so hard his Blazer swerved on the road. "You've got me!" he said. "I give up, don't shoot!"

He couldn't wait to get home and enjoy the complete smoke detector video footage when he wasn't driving. He'd make popcorn. Maybe he would have Felicia watch it with him. He could explain to her the real passion Hailey had for him and how it only needed a few more tweaks and a little more time for her to accept their destiny.

After Hailey cleared the lower floor of her home, she felt confident Gage wasn't downstairs. She went to the kitchen and picked up the phone. She dialed the code to turn off call forwarding. If Howard called to warn her of anything unusual, the ringer on the house phone was easier to hear than her cell phone.

She climbed the stairs, repeating her armed check of each room. She tucked the gun back into her purse when all rooms were clear. Verifying she was alone in the house should have relieved her, but it didn't, which frustrated her.

She trained executives to stay focused, avoid distractions, and become impervious to anything that kept them from their goals. She hated that Gage had affected her this way. The resentment she felt for having to carry a gun was beginning to feel like a reasonable price for safety. Gage had disappeared for extended periods before, and she couldn't know when he'd show up again—inside her house. She took a run. She hadn't exercised for days, and doing so would help her release some of her tension. She called Peyton and left a message that she would be a little late. If traffic was light, she would still make it in plenty of time for the Ramsey phone call.

She wanted to take Felicia's Ruger on her run and tried to figure out a comfortable way to carry it.

She got some shorts and a shirt from a drawer and was about to put them on when she heard something. She went to the bedroom door and listened. It was the garage door motor humming. It *should* be Mason, but paranoia set in. She took the Ruger from the bed and hid behind the bedroom door. The kitchen door to the garage opened. She heard someone come in.

"Mason, is that you?" she hollered.

"Yes. Can you come down here? I want to talk to you about something."

"Sure. Give me a minute," she answered. Thank God it was Mason. She tucked the gun inside her purse and zipped it shut. If Mason saw her with a loaded Ruger, he'd be shocked and envious of anyone who had convinced her to carry it. She quickly changed, grabbed her purse, and went downstairs. Mason sat on a barstool at the kitchen island. He motioned for her to come closer and said, "I have good and bad news. Which first?"

"Bad."

"While I was at work last night, someone broke into my car."

"Oh, no!" Hailey said, pulling a stool to sit by him.

Mason nodded. "It was an odd break-in. An almost perfect circle cut in the glass without shattering the window."

"Did your car have something valuable in view?" Hailey asked.

"No, but Cocky is gone."

"What? I thought you kept that gun hidden."

Mason shrugged. "For the life of me, I can't figure out how anyone would know about Cocky. Last night, you were the first person I've ever told about the headrest. Did you happen to mention it to anyone since then?"

"Absolutely not. Who would I tell?"

"I figured that. Anyway, I gotta replace my passenger window. I found a mobile glass repair guy who will do the repair here."

"I'm so sorry that happened, Mason."

"Yeah, well, nobody died, I suppose."

"Please don't tell me that's the good news," Hailey said.

"Now, here's the good news." He pulled a small box from his coat pocket and handed it to her.

She opened the box and found a diamond ring. It was smaller and unlike her missing wedding ring.

"Oh, Mason," she said, covering her mouth.

He took her hand and slid the ring onto her finger. "I know it isn't the original, but I felt so bad about some thief having it. I wanted to get you a new one as soon as possible. This is the best I can do at the moment. I'd like to replace the original someday. That ring meant a lot to me."

Hailey's eyes welled up. Mason wiped a tear away with his thumb and embraced her.

"What's wrong? I wanted this to be a happy moment," he said.

"Oh, it is a happy moment. I'm okay," Hailey said. "I'm just so touched." She felt awful. Mason didn't make anywhere close to the money she did, and although they did commingle funds in a joint account, Mason had obviously purchased the replacement ring through his own account. With all his faults, he was trying.

"This ring is wonderful. I'm grateful for your thoughtfulness." They kissed.

"I'm going to bed," Mason said, leaving the kitchen.

"Get some rest, Honey. You'll probably be asleep when I get back, right?"

"If I'm lucky."

She heard Mason's tired footsteps climbing the stairs.

Hailey said, "By the way, I want you to know I'm leaving on my run from our house and not the guard gate today."

"Fine, Dear," Mason said, intent on getting into bed.

Hailey had no intention of leaving Felicia's gun behind and didn't want to run while carrying a purse. She went to the pantry and pulled a runner's hydration pack from the shelf she hadn't used for a long time. She removed the rubber bladder to make room to tuck the Ruger inside. The pack slung comfortably over her shoulder. She zipped it up and took off for her run.

Hailey ran from her home past the guard gate and waved to Howard, who gave her his predicable salute. She hadn't been to Fit Performance Gym since before her trip to Cancun. The exercise felt good and grounded her. She found it easiest to think through and resolve her life's challenges during her workouts.

She checked every car she passed and every vehicle that passed her, on the lookout for Gage's Blazer. She turned onto Center Street and then took the path that brought her through the woods onto the wide-open lawn surrounding Fit Performance Gym. Something didn't look right. The fitness center's large glass front was dark. Hailey checked her pulse as she jogged up to the front door. A laminated sign was taped inside the window.

Fit Performance Gym has been closed. Welcome to the future site of the Echelon Truth and Justice Pavilion. Visit any recruitment center for membership details. Join us and find truth and justice.

Hailey pulled the locked door's handle and said, "No! Please!" Her favorite escape had been taken over by the Echelonians. She felt another part of her world collapsing.

She jogged back home, fueled by frustration, as she lamented the loss of her gym. When she passed the Turlock Heights Estates gate, she waved to Howard and called Peyton during the last quarter mile of her run. "It's Hailey. Are we still on for eleven o'clock with the Ramsey people?"

"Absolutely," Peyton said. "His assistant called to confirm about thirty minutes ago. Everything is set."

"Great. I'll be in shortly."

• • •

Hailey entered her house quietly to avoid waking Mason. The hydration pack concealed Felicia's gun so well and was so comfortable she decided to keep it when she left for work. She removed her keys before placing them on the table by the front door.

As she climbed the stairs, she was surprised to hear sounds from the kitchen and saw the light on. "Hi, Dear. I'm surprised you're still up!" she called to him.

"Let's talk about surprises for a minute, shall we," Mason's voice echoed.

Hailey stopped. "Excuse me?"

"Get in here, now," Mason yelled. *What now?* Hailey thought. She could judge Mason's anger level by his tone, and this one sounded terrible. She descended the stairs and went into the kitchen. On the island countertop, Mason had spread out handguns and rifles on white towels, taking up every inch of space. Empty guncases on the floor were opened, their foam lining showing the hollow shape of the guns they had contained. His sleeves were rolled up, and he leaned with his arms spread on the island countertop. His dominant stance with the weapons created the image of a gun ad. His bloodshot eyes sent a chill through Hailey. She fought the urge to run, trying to mask her fear.

"Why do you have the guns out, sweetheart? I'm interested in learning about them, but isn't this a bit much?" Hailey said, positioning herself on the opposite side of the island.

"You want to talk to me about an agreement?" Mason said through clenched teeth. He thumbed at himself and said, "I have trust issues. We both know that. Even though I sometimes blame you, the truth is I've always considered it to be *my* problem. Deep down, I never believed I had a right to mistrust you. Until today."

"Mason, what are you talking about?" Hailey asked.

He turned away from her and pressed a button on their home phone. When Hailey heard her own voice from the speaker, panic shot through her.

Hi, Gage. This is Hailey. Thank you for a great time last night. You slept so peacefully this morning, so I slipped out without waking you. Listen, I have a bit of a dilemma; I must have misplaced my wedding ring last night, and I'm wondering if you've found it in the hotel room. If so, can you call me or leave me a message on my cell phone? Thanks so much. Bye.

Mason turned back to her. He wiped his face on his sleeve and said, "What the hell did we just listen to?"

Hailey held up her hand to calm him. "Mason, I know that sounds horrible, and I know it is totally cliché to say it isn't what it seems, but I need you to understand that it isn't what it seems."

"I would love to hear you explain this," Mason sneered. He folded his hands on the countertop and flashed a fake smile at her.

"Nothing happened between us. Mason, it was a business meeting, and I think he may have drugged me to get the ring."

Mason quoted Hailey's voicemail, counting off her sentences on his fingers. "You looked so peaceful sleeping this morning ... I slipped out without waking you ... Leave me a message on my cell phone?"

Hailey interrupted. "I did *not* have an affair. It's not what it sounds like."

"And now you want me to ignore my lying ears?" Mason laughed sarcastically.

"Yes—I mean, no," Hailey stammered. "Will you please let me explain?"

"What else is there to explain? You took off your wedding ring during a hotel sleepover with a stranger and asked him to call you back if he found it," Mason said. He poked his tongue in his cheek while shaking his head.

"I don't care about that ring anymore. In fact, get my second mistake off your finger, slut!" he screamed.

She had never seen Mason this furious. She was afraid to approach him. "Nothing happened between us," Hailey said, "but I didn't think you would believe me. I didn't want to upset you." She pulled the ring from her finger, put it on the countertop, and slid it toward him. Mason slapped his hand onto it, snatched it up, and put it into his pocket.

"So you kept your affair a secret for my benefit?"

"No, it wasn't an affair. I wanted to tell you all the details of the weird, innocent meeting with this guy, but I was afraid." Hailey's words dissolved into sobs.

"Why the tears?" he asked. "Is it painful to be caught? Does it hurt that my hunch about your cheating was correct all along?" He kicked the cabinet hard enough to crack its wooden door, and Hailey's shoulders jumped as the sound echoed through the house. The image of Mason's red face and disheveled hair framed above the guns spread out on the kitchen island terrified her.

He picked up a Browning Hi-Power 9mm pistol and drew his thumb across the engraved manufacturer's stamp on its side. "When?" he asked.

"It happened just over a week ago."

"Where?"

"We met at the Marriott's restaurant."

Mason blew a disgusted breath through his nose.

"Mason, he was a new coaching client. We reviewed his goals and hobbies as part of my normal profile for a new coaching client. He said he baked baklava. I said I loved baklava. He said he had some in his room and wanted to give me a sample. I went, tasted it, felt light-headed, and don't remember much more."

"He said, 'I have candy in my room for you, little girl,' and you fell for that? That's a lame-ass kidnapper trick, Hailey! What's wrong with you?"

Hailey yelled, "I know it was really stupid of me! I woke up fully dressed, and nothing happened."

"That's what he told you? Unbelievable..." Mason crossed his arms, the gun barrel protruding from the back of his armpit.

"Mason, can we go somewhere else to talk, or you put the guns away? They're making me very ... uncomfortable."

"Maybe feeling uncomfortable is what you deserve."

"My God, are you threatening me?" she said, hoping that going on the offensive might level her disadvantage. In a normal state of mind, Mason would never physically hurt her, but he wasn't in a normal state of mind.

Mason ignored her accusation. "Did you ever meet him again after that?"

Hailey hesitated. Her mouth had gone dry.

"It's not a difficult question, Hailey." Mason put down the Browning pistol and picked up a Heckler & Koch Mark 23. He knew this was a gun whose appearance would be the most offensive and intimidating to Hailey. He was correct.

She took a step back from him. She couldn't imagine Mason aiming any gun at her. She had never seen him this angry. She felt an unfamiliar urge. She wished she had kept the hydration pack handy. She knew she was no match for a gun enthusiast with a gun in hand, but he might faint from shock if she pulled the Ruger on him.

Hailey said, "Yes, I met him again to get the ring back, and then he claimed to have forgotten it."

Mason's jaw clenched, making his temples flare. "Mind if I talk to him?" He aimed the handgun at the sink and closed one eye to check the sight.

The number Hailey thought was Gage's mobile number had stopped working long ago. Mason wouldn't believe that. "I can't. I don't have his number," she said.

"Oh, come on, Hailey! Now you're being pathetic."

"I—I," she stammered again.

Mason laughed and shrugged. "Come here."

"Mason, you're scaring me."

"Now!"

Hailey came around the island, stepping as close to him as she dared, staying out of arm's reach.

"Let me tell you something," Mason said. He lowered his chin and stared into her eyes. "I want you to be absolutely sure I will get every single answer you're trying to hide from me. Know that."

"Mason, I'm telling you—"

"Shut up! Your lame excuses reek of bullshit, and I'm done hearing them. You should leave now." He flicked the gun barrel toward the door and lowered it to his side. His finger looked like it was on the trigger.

"Sweetheart, you're scaring me. Please don't do anything rash," she said.

"Me? Rash? Get out!" he shouted.

Hailey backed to the garage door, keeping her eyes on him. She had never seen Mason more disgusted or angry. She reached back and felt her for the door handle behind her and then disappeared into the garage.

• • •

Hailey drove to her office wearing her workout clothes. She didn't care. At this point, her safety trumped all other concerns. Gage had become a big reason to be afraid while home alone. Now Mason had just given her a reason to be scared to go home. She wished she could prove to Mason that her encounter with Gage was innocent, yet she couldn't even prove it to herself. The devil was in the details, and the voicemail message Mason had listened to revealed details she never intended Mason to know.

She called Felicia at home. After the phone rang four times, the call went to voicemail. She called her mobile phone. Again, voicemail. *Where are you? Answer!* Hailey called her house again and left a message, saying, "Felly, I'm in big trouble. I need you. I'm ready to accept your offer to smuggle me out of town. Please, *please* call me back as soon as you get this."

As she pulled into the parking garage at the office, she clapped her hand on her forehead. She had forgotten the hydration pack with Felicia's Ruger tucked inside. As if describing the innocence of her encounter with Gage wasn't hard enough, Mason's mind would be blown if he looked inside the pack.

She called Felicia again. No answer on her home or mobile phones. Felicia had no qualms about taking every call she got, even in places Hailey felt it was rude. For her not to answer for over an hour was unusual.

When Hailey got to her office, it was 10:57 a.m. Peyton jumped up from his chair and said, "Whew! You made it!" He handed her a cold, medium half-caf, no-foam, non-fat, vanilla soy latte from Hot Perks.

Hailey took the drink and whispered, "Thanks."

"You're welcome, Ms. Vaughan. I'm so relieved you'll make the meeting. I'm sure the Ramsey people will be, too."

Hailey only sighed.

"You seem exhausted."

"I am."

"I've prepared your desk for the call."

In her office, Hailey found an empty notepad and pen on her desk. Beside them were Peyton's notes from his conversation with Lance Ramsey's assistant about the meeting. A yellow sticky note stuck to the top read:

Mr. Ramsey's Assistant's name is Suri.

"This is wonderful, Peyton. Thank you."

"Do you need me to sit in?"

"Please do."

"Let me turn on voicemail for the main line," he said. He went to his desk and returned moments later with his notepad.

The phone meeting ended up not being with Lance Ramsey himself. His assistant, Suri, facilitated the call. She indicated the Ramsey executives needed Hailey's assessment of their role descriptions. They had heard of Hailey's popular hat-swapping workshop, where executives acted out scenarios while playing one another's roles to clarify coworker perceptions. With the number of executives at the Ramsey Company, they would need to divide into groups to complete a consultation. That could take an entire week. They discussed Hailey's weekly fee of fifteen thousand dollars, which Suri said was not a problem. She added if Hailey was immediately available, they would arrange for her to conduct her workshop during their executive retreat on the island of Kauai. The only stipulation was that she needed to leave tomorrow.

Peyton had managed the office well during her vacation to Cancun. After seeing his competence firsthand, Hailey felt safe leaving the office for a week with him at the helm. Boarding a plane to escape her personal problems sounded great. "Your retreat schedule fits mine perfectly. I can leave tomorrow," she told Suri.

"Fantastic. We'll arrange a car to the airport for you."

"Thanks, and thank you for your patience in finalizing this."

"Our pleasure. Safe travels."

They ended the call. Peyton smiled while busily jotting notes. Hailey was thrilled. She would return refreshed and prepared to run the damage control her life needed.

Peyton returned to his desk, and Hailey called Felicia again. No answer. She left a threatening message, saying, "You said you were going to call the police on my behalf, but it looks like I might be calling the police for *you*! C'mon, where the hell are you? Call me back. I'm going to Hawaii and need to talk to you."

"Bingo," she heard Peyton say outside her door.

"What is it?" Hailey asked.

Peyton stepped into her doorway. "We have our first recording."

Hailey went out to his desk. He pressed the speakerphone and played the message.

"Hailey, you poor thing. Sometimes, I press buttons on my phone and don't know if I'm rewinding, forwarding, or recording. I think I accidentally forwarded your voicemail to your house. I'm so sorry. Can you forgive me? I can make it right, but we'll need to talk. You ought to take my call next time."

"Bastard! That wasn't an accident!" Hailey screamed at the phone. Peyton gently hung up the receiver.

"You can save that recording, right?" Hailey asked.

"Yes, except he didn't identify himself," Peyton said.

"Are you kidding? That is him. That is Gage whatever-the-hell his last name is."

The fax machine rang and then spit out two sheets of paper. They contained the agenda for the Ramsey retreat in Kauai.

"Perhaps it's time for additional security," Peyton said.

"At this point, I'm ready to do that."

"Ms. Vaughan, may I ask you a personal question?" Peyton said, scratching his neck. Hailey had never seen Peyton nervous, even when Gage was in their office.

"You said nothing happened between you and Gage. So, may I ask why we can't get the assistance of your husband?"

Hailey sighed. "Peyton, it's complicated. I did meet with Gage without Mason knowing about it. I have since told Mason about that. I also told him I had dinner with Gage. I think that was about as much information as Mason could take. Mason doesn't know Gage was limping on an injured leg that evening. After dinner, I helped him to his hotel room. He asked me to try a dessert he made, and I passed out. I woke up completely clothed, and nothing happened. You'll have to trust me when I tell you dropping all these unfortunate but innocent details on Mason will create a bigger problem for me. Mason would be too blinded by jealousy to accept that I might be innocent."

Peyton had listened intently. "It's a tragedy when someone won't accept the truth," he said.

"I agree. And I've never been stuck in a situation with a more damning appearance. I am innocent. In any case, Mason is aware of Gage now, and he's furious with me. The last thing Mason wants to do is to be wrong about his hunch."

"I'm so sorry," Peyton said. "That doesn't seem fair."

"You're right. It's not fair." Hailey shrugged. "I'll tell you what … when I return from Hawaii, we'll get the police involved if Gage is still a problem." She went back into her office to book her flight to Kauai. Suri, Ramsey's assistant, offered to make all of Hailey's travel arrangements. Hailey insisted on doing it herself. Before paying the fare, she logged onto her joint checking account to verify the funds. She saw a withdrawal of $7,000 was posted less than two hours ago. She clicked the transaction for details, revealing it was a wire transfer to Mason's private checking account. They usually would have discussed any financial transaction of that size in advance.

She was tempted to send him an email notifying him of her smaller withdrawal for travel expenses. Doing this would only annoy him. Anything she did at the moment would upset him. And he'd presume her trip, to wherever he imagined, was with Gage.

She needed to pack and wished she could safely go home for her clothes. However, she wanted to avoid Mason at all costs. She imagined Mason having grown angrier after she left, lying in wait for her, maybe in a closet or behind a shower curtain. More than her clothes, she wanted to get Felicia's gun. There was a chance Mason hadn't looked in the pack. For all his jealousy, he never went through her personal belongings—that she knew of.

She called the guard gate and recognized the voice that answered.

"Hi Howard, it's Ms. Vaughan. I need you to do me a favor."

"Certainly. Anything you need, ma'am."

"I have a surprise for my husband. I know he's at the house now. Can you please call me immediately if he leaves? I will rush over and set up some things at the house. He'll be so tickled."

"You got it, Ms. Vaughan."

After she hung up, Peyton hollered, "I have Toby Blakner on line one."

"Oh, I'll take it, that's important." Toby was Felicia's mother.

"Mrs. Blakner?"

"Yes, Hailey, have you, by any chance, heard from Felicia today?"

"Yes, I stayed at her place last night and saw her this morning, but she hasn't returned any of my calls all day."

"Me either, and it's terribly unusual for me not to be able to get a hold of her."

Hailey said, "I'm leaving the office in a few minutes. I'll go to her house."

"Thank you so much, Dear. Can you call me and let me know she's okay?"

"Of course."

Peyton handed Hailey a printout of a private security company's brochure. "They offer armed security and could provide protection for you as long as you need it," he said. "They referred me to two stalker victims they've helped. I called and got nothing except high praise for the service."

Hailey looked at the numbers. "Can they start today?"

"That's the thing," Peyton said. "The soonest they can have someone available for you is tomorrow. They also need a $1,500 deposit."

"Do it. I'll take the protection for tomorrow before my flight," Hailey said. If Mason could spitefully pillage their joint checking account, she could protect her life with the remainder of the money.

Eighteen

HAILEY LEFT THE office to check on Felicia. On her way out of the building, Isaac caught up to her and said, "We have what you seek. Are you ready to be saved by accepting our truth?"

Hailey waved him away and said, "Not now, Isaac!"

"As you wish," Isaac replied, continuing to follow her. "We also want to invite you to tour our new facility."

Hailey stopped and turned to him. "It was my gym. It was my escape. You people have stolen it. Tell that to your master."

"The escape we offer is much better than a gymnasium."

Hailey sucked her teeth and continued walking to the elevator. "I need to escape you."

"We apologize for the inconvenience, but our presence at the new Truth and Justice Pavilion will provide what you and many others need. It is wonderful news that truth and justice now have a beautiful new home." Isaac grinned as though Hailey should celebrate.

She squinted at him. "You people are insane." She left him, taking the stairwell to her car instead of waiting for the garage elevator. One of the first tasks of her new personal security guard would be to keep the Echelonians away from her.

Hailey drove from the Handel Towers Building garage looking for Gage's Blazer. She saw no sign of him.

Her concern about Felicia intensified. Had she been injured or fallen too ill to answer her phone? They had left on beautiful terms this morning, so they had no personal issue.

She drove to Felicia's house and parked in the driveway. She looked through the crack in the side of the garage door. It was too dark inside to see if her car was there. She rang the doorbell. No answer. She knocked, waited, and knocked again.

Hailey went around the back and checked the kitchen door. It was unlocked. She peered in and shouted, "Felly? Are you home?" There was no answer. The only thing that appeared out of place in the kitchen was Felicia's hairbrush lying on the floor beside the table that had been moved off-center. She stepped inside and slowly went upstairs, calling out for Felicia. In the master bedroom, Felicia's sweat clothes were on her bed, and her makeup bag opened on her sink.

A scratching noise came from the hallway. "Felly?" she said. Felicia's cat, Hamlet, pranced in the door and pressed against her leg.

"Where's your mama?" Hailey asked. Hamlet purred and flicked his tail.

Hailey went back downstairs and out to her car. She scrolled through her phone, found the number to Felicia's sales office, and called it. Felicia had not shown up for work, and none of her coworkers had seen her since yesterday. Hailey was about to call Felicia's mom with the uncomfortable news Felicia was missing when an email chimed on Hailey's phone. It was from Felicia.

I'm fine. I just need a few days away. Sorry I didn't tell you.

The signature at the bottom of the message said, *Sent from my mobile phone.*

Hailey replied:

Good for you, but where did you go? Why didn't you tell me? Call! Your mom is worried.

After a brief wait, a reply came.

I need to be alone. Please tell my mother I'll be in touch.

Hailey stared at the words. Felicia never needed to be alone. And she never referred to her mother as "my mother." She always called her mother "mama," even to Hailey. She would have said, "Tell Mama I'll call." Hailey had hundreds of emails from Felicia to prove it. Hailey immediately called the police, giving them Felicia's age, address, and other information to complete a missing person's report. Calling the police for Felicia was an easy decision that carried none of the complications Hailey envisioned if she had called them for herself.

Hailey sat stunned after she hung up. Felicia was always accessible to her and one of her most predictable friends. Her phone chimed with a new email. When she opened her Inbox, she saw an email from Gage.

I wanted to show you how good we look together. Please don't share these gems with Mason. He's not ready for them yet, and they certainly won't help his jealousy problem.

Several photos were attached. In the first, she lay naked on a bed facing away from the camera. Her red and blue tattoo of a hummingbird was clearly visible on her lower back. A naked man stood over her, his hand resting on her curvaceous hip. The photo cut him off at the neck. In other photos, the man held Hailey's body in various poses of lovemaking. In a second email, a video attachment showed Hailey and the man from the neck down, again naked, lying side by side. He spread his fingers on her stomach and caressed it while his other hand cupped her breast.

Neither the man's face nor Hailey's was visible in any of the photos, but given her telltale tattoo, they were nonetheless damning.

Hailey recognized the side table with the phone and ashtray. A towel draped on the bed featured the Marriott logo. A glimpse at the truth of what had happened in the hotel room brought on nausea, and she opened the car door to vomit, only gagging and coughing.

She hyperventilated with panic. "Oh, God, oh, God, oh, God!" She couldn't fathom what Mason would do when he saw this image. She was thankful they were not together right now. This morning, Mason looked at her as though he wanted to kill her after hearing her voicemail to Gage about the ring. Now, after she had beseeched him to believe her behavior wasn't as it seemed, the photography was damning beyond any hope of recovery.

Her phone rang. Mason's mobile number showed on the caller ID. Hailey's stomach was already knotted as she tried to catch her breath. She tried to press the phone's screen to answer the call. It slipped from her sweaty fingers. She answered. "Hello?"

"Hale, it's me," Mason said.

"Oh, hi," Hailey said, pretending to be surprised. She braced herself for his tantrum.

"Listen, I want to apologize about this morning."

"You do?" Hailey frowned. There's no way Mason would be saying this if he had seen the photographs.

"Yes. I've been thinking," Mason continued. "My reaction to your voicemail this morning was unfair. I want to be fair to you."

Hailey listened, trying to comprehend the sudden clemency Mason offered. His calmness was scarier than a death threat.

"I appreciate that," she said.

"Oh, and another thing... I'm standing here looking at some photographs you may not have wanted me to see."

The words took Hailey's breath. Here it is. She braced herself and said, "Oh?"

"Yes. There are six photos here in front of me."

"Mason, I don't know what you are looking at, but—"

"Calm down, Hailey. I just want to know why you didn't tell me you were involved in an auto accident."

"I was, uh..." Hailey's mind raced to reconcile what was happening. She remembered Gage's promise he had protected her by taking the phone and the photos no longer existed. "That happened a while back. There was no damage."

"Apparently, it happened a couple of weeks ago, and the photo shows damage to the rear bumper of a pickup truck. A nasty letter from the driver accuses you of leaving the scene."

Hailey couldn't answer, so Mason continued. "I gotta tell you, Hale, all these secrets you're keeping to protect my feelings are beginning to hurt."

"Mason, I'm so sorry. It was *not* a hit-and-run. What does the driver want? There was no damage, so we dropped it."

"Okay, let me read you something." She heard Mason fumble with paper. "Wow. Fancy attorney letterhead," he said. "I don't understand all the legalese, but I think it describes a payment demand to avoid the risk of indictment on a hit-and-run charge. There's a police report included."

"A police report? That's impossible!" Hailey yelled.

"Hale, I have an idea. Why don't you come home, and we'll talk this over? Listen. I'm not mad, Sweetie. I want to get beyond this."

"I'm amazed and grateful for your attitude about this. What did you do with my husband?" Hailey joked.

Mason didn't laugh. "I'm sorry for frightening you, and after you left, I realized acting on my temper doesn't get us anywhere. Why don't you come home so we can discuss this?"

Hailey considered Mason's proposal. He'd never let a mistake as serious as a car accident go this easily. He also never showed this sort of urgency to meet with her. The last time he called her 'Sweetie' was probably their wedding night.

"Uh, I'm trying to tie up some loose ends at the office. Let's just finish this talk right now, okay?" Hailey said.

"I feel sorry for my blow-up this morning. I simply want to see my wife. Why don't you take the afternoon off? Maybe we'll go do that shooting you've wanted to try."

"After you were so angry this morning, I wonder if that's such a good idea," Hailey said.

"Don't be silly. Now you're just being irrational," he said. "I want to see you."

She cleared her throat, braced herself, and said, "I took a job out of town for a week," she said. "They want me to leave immediately, so I'm afraid I need to pack and run today."

"Okay, I understand. What time will you be home to pack?"

"I'll be home at the usual time, probably about 5:30 or so."

"Okay, then. I'll see you around 5:30. Bye-bye, Sweetie."

After the call, Hailey sat still, contemplating the bizarre change in Mason's emotional state. If Gage had also sent the hotel photos, Mason's forgiveness and invitation had to be a deadly lure. She rested her forehead on the steering wheel.

Less than five minutes after her call with Mason, her phone rang again. It was the Turlock Heights Estates guard gate.

"Hello, Ms. Vaughan. Just thought you'd like to know your husband just exited. You might want to get your surprise shindig set up."

"Thank you so much," Hailey said. "I'm on my way, and please call me if he returns before I arrive."

"Will do, ma'am."

• • •

Hailey sped home, stretching two yellow lights and only slowing for two stop signs. She knew her opportunity to get the Ruger would be short. As she came to the gate, Howard tried to wave her through. Hailey stopped and rolled down her window.

"If he shows up, *please* call me, okay?"

"You got it," Howard said. He flashed an okay sign.

Hailey pulled her Lexus into the garage and left the door open because she planned to be in the house for only a few minutes. Inside the house, she found the hydration pack right where she had left it. She grabbed it, disabled the alarm, and went to the kitchen. Several guns remained on the island countertop, and the lights were on. Mason would be back soon.

Hailey put her phone and keys down and picked up a revolver. It was fat with a snub nose. Felicia's felt better. She kept her finger far from the trigger, and after being unable to determine if it was loaded, she gently placed it down.

She tucked her keys and phone into the hydration pack and slung it over her shoulder. She ran upstairs to put some clothes together for her trip. When she entered their master bedroom, she heard the hum of the garage door motor and the chirp of tires in the driveway. It had to be Mason. Why hadn't Howard warned her?

She ran down the stairs, almost falling, and out to the backyard, closing the door behind her. She went to the side of the house and squatted by the backyard gate beside some trash bins. Through the fence's wood slats, she saw Mason's Mustang parked diagonally in the driveway, blocking her car from backing out of the garage.

She held her breath and listened, expecting to hear the garage door to the kitchen close. It didn't. She unzipped the pack, confirmed she had a key to Mason's car on her key ring, and then clasped it in her hand. When she heard Mason calling her inside the house, she unlatched the gate and sprinted. She reached Mason's car and pulled the driver's door handle. In a stroke of luck, it was unlocked. She flung the pack on the seat, and when she tried to insert the key, she found Mason's key still in the ignition. She turned it and, when she looked up, saw Mason sprinting toward her from inside the garage. She screamed and tried to put the car in reverse while she slapped at the buttons on the armrest, trying to lock the doors. The door lock clicked the instant before Mason reached the handle. He pulled it so hard the car swayed.

"Get out, whore!" Mason shouted. He slapped the window with his palm. His eyes were maniacal.

Hailey got the car into reverse and accelerated back out of the driveway. Mason ran after the car, and before Hailey could put it in drive, he leaped onto the hood. "Stop! Get out *now!*" When she slammed the brakes, he slid off the hood, jumped to his feet, and rushed the car again.

Mason pulled his shoe off and tried to smash the driver's window while screaming at her. Neighbors came out to their yards to investigate the commotion. They saw Hailey tear away in Mason's car, wheels smoking as she floored the Mustang, reaching the end of the block in only seconds. She saw Mason in her rearview mirror standing in the street before he ran back toward their house.

Hailey closed in on the Turlock Heights Estates exit. Howard saw Mason's car speeding in his direction and stepped out of the guard gate. He motioned for her to slow down, but Hailey raced by his outstretched hands, nearly clipping him.

Hailey knew Mason would do whatever it took to get to her. Since he didn't have his keys, he might call the police, get a taxi, or even ask to borrow a neighbor's car. She made a sharp right turn onto the first street and wound her way through the neighborhood adjacent to Turlock Heights Estates, taking side streets back toward Wenshire Harbor.

While stopped at a traffic light, she heard a ringtone. She opened the car's armrest and found Mason's cell phone. In another beautiful stroke of luck, he had not removed it from the car when he had parked so hurriedly in the driveway. The caller ID showed an unfamiliar number. She sent the call to voicemail and tapped the screen to listen to Mason's messages. Any hint of information about his plans would be helpful. The most recent message was recorded five minutes earlier.

Hi, Mason, it's Howard at the gate. Your wife just drove through to your house, just like you suspected. If she tries to leave before you get back, I'll try to stall her for you. Bye.

"Two-timing asshole," Hailey said. She wondered how much Mason had paid him.

• • •

Hailey drove to Skeflan Point, about twenty miles away from her home. She had never been to the town and hoped it would provide an obscure enough location to remain hidden from Mason while she gathered her thoughts. She needed to go to her office eventually but knew it would be foolish to go now. It would be the first place Mason would go. Gage would look for her there, too. She needed a covert place to stay the night. Gage's knowledge of her whereabouts had been uncanny, and she longed to be invisible.

She drove to the Skeflan Point police station and parked on the street outside of their small lot. She checked to make sure her doors were locked. The well-lit location and frequent activity of officers coming and going provided some comfort. She took the Ruger from the pack and placed it between her legs on the seat.

She might not get a sound night of sleep, but she'd wake up tomorrow, and that wasn't guaranteed if she went home or to the office.

Hailey's phone rang. It was Peyton. Relieved to hear from him, she quickly answered.

"Peyton, thank God."

"Ms. Vaughan, can you please call me back on a phone other than your cell phone?"

"Why?"

"I can't discuss that now. Please call me back on my cell phone as soon as possible."

"Sure," Hailey said. She hung up. The solution was easy—she had Mason's phone. She dialed her office, and Peyton answered.

"Ms. Vaughan, I have some information to share that might disturb you. I want you to know I've already taken measures for you."

"What? What is it?"

"The private investigator just did a bug sweep of your office and uncovered fourteen listening devices."

"How is that possible? Where?" Hailey asked.

The investigator said, "They were installed in the phone handsets, magnetically to the door hinges, on the ceiling tiles above your desk, and several other places. One was built into that 'Compliment Generator' you keep on your desk. Unfortunately, technology has made these devices incredibly discreet."

"That son-of-a-bitch," Hailey said.

"We've removed them. I'm calling you from outside the office, and my phone is clean. Are you talking to me from your car?"

"Yes, I mean, no, I'm in Mason's."

"Good. The investigator says it is crucial he sweeps your car, too."

"Okay, but I don't know when that will be possible. I don't have access to my car at the moment. Peyton, I want you to call the security firm you were investigating. I need them to start immediately."

"I've already contacted them and paid the deposit like you requested. I'm waiting for a callback to schedule a start time."

"Use the credit card in my top desk drawer to get them to help me ASAP."

"Okay, I'll call them again. We are after hours," Peyton said. "They may have an emergency rate. I'll leave an urgent message if I can't get through."

"Please make it happen, Peyton." Hailey didn't care about the cost.

"Will do, Ms. Vaughan. In the meantime, I wouldn't go to the office if I were you. We think we've found all the bugs, but it is better to be cautious. Do you need a place to stay?"

"No. I think I'll be okay until morning. After what you told me about the bugs, I don't want to say where I am even though my phone is completely turned off."

"Ms. Vaughan, you might consider talking to the Echelonians. I had a conversation with Isaac in the lobby on my way to lunch. I described a hypothetical situation that parallels yours, and he told me they have provided safe harbor for many battered women."

"Peyton, I'm okay. I'm sick of them. I don't need them. Just work on the private security guard."

"I understand. Call me if there is anything else I can do for you."

• • •

Except for a walk across the street to a hamburger restaurant to use the restroom and get some food, Hailey stayed in the car, reclined in the driver's seat, determined not to leave the police station's proximity until she got word from Peyton about the security arrangements. Mason's phone vibrated six times that evening, three times showing their home number on the screen. She sent every call to voicemail.

A few minutes after 10:00 p.m., Mason's phone rang. The caller ID read *Club Parlay*. Hailey answered, "Hello."

"Yes, uh," a male caller seemed surprised. "Is this Mason's phone?"

"Yes, it is."

"Well, can I talk to him?"

"Mason isn't available. Why are you calling?"

"I'm calling to find out if he's coming in."

"This is his wife. I was going to ask you the same question."

"No, we haven't seen or heard from him."

"He's having some car trouble," Hailey said. "I'll tell him to call you back ASAP."

"Okay, thanks."

Mason never missed work. He was never late. He probably had a rental car by now.

Hailey spent the night drifting in and out of unsatisfying sleep. Several times she woke with her heart pounding as images of Mason and Gage collided in her dreams.

At 5:40AM, Mason's phone vibrated, jolting her awake. It was Peyton.

"Hello, Peyton," Hailey answered, yawning.

"Good morning, Ms. Vaughan. An armed bodyguard will be waiting for you at the garage entrance to Handel Towers at 7:00 a.m."

The words felt like medicine to her. "Thank you so much," she replied.

"The security company didn't answer last night. I got through a few minutes ago. The guard is on his way. He asked for your Handel Towers parking space number."

"That's fantastic. I'll be in soon."

"Me too. I'll see you at the office."

She drove from the police station and stopped at a McDonald's, where she used the restroom and got coffee. She couldn't wait for her trip to Kauai in the afternoon, where she'd enjoy a reprieve from her stress for at least a week at the Ramsey retreat.

When she drove into the garage at Handel Towers and rounded the corner to her parking level, a man with a crew cut, arms crossed, wearing a suit and tie, stood beside her parking spot. A white wire coiled from his ear to a place under his collar. He motioned for her to pull forward and opened the door.

"Ms. Vaughan?"

"Yes," Hailey said, taking his hand to get out.

"I'm Wilson Harper, here to protect you."

Here to protect you. The words were a salve to her anxiety. "Thank you. I can't tell you how grateful I am for your service."

"I was told you drive a Lexus," Wilson said, walking around the Mustang.

"This is my husband's car," Hailey said.

Wilson went to the car's rear, spoke the license plate number into his phone, and then took several photos of the car. Wilson scanned the garage as they walked toward the elevator, examining the cars and a few nearby people.

He pressed the elevator button and motioned for her to move to one side while they waited. "We don't allow opening elevator doors to surprise us," he said. He faced away from the elevator, on the lookout for anyone who might approach. His presence felt wonderful, and Hailey felt safe for the first time in days. So far, the steep fee was worth it. If Gage or Mason showed up now, Hailey wouldn't be helpless.

"My job is to be paranoid on your behalf," Wilson said. "My goal is to remain inconspicuous while thwarting anything that might cause you harm."

"That sounds more wonderful than you can imagine."

"Good. We'll reach our goals if you work with me and follow my procedures."

"I will follow your instructions," Hailey said, smiling. They got onto the elevator.

"Now, if you can tell me your public stops in advance, it will make my job easier."

"For today, I'll remain in the building. I leave for the airport this afternoon."

"Do you need an escort on the trip?"

"No, once I'm out of town, I'll be okay."

When they entered the lobby, Isaac saw Hailey from the Echelonian booth and walked toward her. Hailey whispered, "They're trying to convert me to their religion, and they make me uncomfortable. Could you..."

"Leave it to me," Wilson said. He stepped between her and the approaching Isaac, raised his hand, and said, "Please stand back, sir. Ms. Vaughan isn't available at the moment."

Isaac looked confused and said, "Ms. Vaughan, our leader has a new offer for you. He wishes to speak to you at the Truth and Justice Pavilion. You should bring some spare clothing. If you are as enthused as we are about what you'll see, you'll certainly want to stay awhile."

Hailey laughed. "Are you serious?"

Isaac nodded, smiling.

"Give your master a message for me. Tell him the truth is I'm not interested in talking to him, and if he wants to be 'just,' he'll stop pestering me and let me live my life as I wish."

Hailey and Wilson stepped into the elevator. Isaac stood outside, wearing an expression of regret as the doors slid closed, separating them from him.

"Thank you, that was fantastic," Hailey said. As they rode up to her office, she explained her disdain for the need to transfer elevators to reach the upper floors.

"Your assistant provided some information about an aggressor. Is this the man?" He held out his phone that displayed a headshot of Gage.

"Yes, how did you get that photo?"

"Identification is fundamental to our business, and we have great resources. It's important for me to know of any other specific threats to your safety, so are there any other individuals we should know about?"

"Yes ... As of yesterday, my husband."

When they entered the office, Hailey introduced Wilson to Peyton, who stood to shake hands. Hailey then showed Wilson around her private office. He took some phone photos, checked the edges of each window, and used binoculars to check out the nearby buildings and visible portions of the street below. He stood on her desk to push up a ceiling tile, checked the space above with a flashlight, and then examined the door locks. After several laps around Hailey's private office, he sat on one of Hailey's guest chairs and typed some notes on his phone.

"Ms. Vaughan, the Ramsey people offered a limousine," Peyton said, entering her office. "In fact, they insisted on providing one, but I didn't feel comfortable with any transportation we didn't arrange ourselves."

"Good call," Wilson said.

Peyton grinned. "I contacted a separate car service, and they will pick you up between 2:00 and 2:15 this afternoon to catch your 4:45 flight."

"I feel so protected," Hailey said. "Thank you!"

Wilson excused himself to wait out in Peyton's area.

Hailey said, "Peyton, I can't thank you enough for your quick thinking and persistence in protecting me."

"My pleasure," Peyton said. "Speaking of persistence, Isaac the Echelonian caught up to me when I was going for coffee this morning..."

"Have they been harassing you?" Hailey asked, picking up her office phone.

"No, not at all," Peyton said. He motioned for her to put the phone down. "They're really fond of you. He asked me what it would take to get you to meet with their leader again."

"I appreciate that, Peyton, really. For now, I'm completely disinterested. Now, I have an unusual request."

"Anything."

"I haven't packed and can't go home, so I need you to purchase a few outfits and odds and ends for my trip. Are you comfortable doing this?"

"Absolutely. Whatever you need, Ms. Vaughan."

Hailey wrote down her sizes and some suggested outfits and accessories that would be comfortable in Hawaii to cover her week of consulting there. Peyton departed, leaving her in Wilson's care.

Her mobile phone vibrated. It was her home phone number. She sent it to voicemail.

A couple of hours later, Peyton returned with a new suitcase containing Hailey's new clothes and offered to review the outfits with her. "I hope I've matched your style," he said.

"Everything here looks great, and these will be perfect for travel. I'll keep on my running shoes for the flight," Hailey said, lifting a pair of jeans and a melon-colored silk blouse from the suitcase.

The office phone rang. Peyton went to his desk to answer it.

While alone in her office, Hailey pulled her hydration pack from her satchel and tucked it under the new clothes in her suitcase. She planned to declare the gun and check her suitcase for her flight. At this point, she put nothing past Gage—including finding her in Hawaii.

"Ms. Vaughan, I have Felicia on line 1," Peyton called out.

"Oh, thank God!" Hailey said. "I'll take it." She picked up and said, "Hey, lady, where on earth have you been? I've been worried sick about you!"

"Hailey, I'm hurting without you!" Gage's voice shot through her. "Please don't hang up," he said.

"No! Leave me alone!" Hailey screamed, slamming the handset down. Both Peyton and Wilson raced into her office. Hailey stood beside her desk, staring at the phone. "He got through," she said.

"I'm so sorry, ma'am," Peyton said, approaching her. Wilson stayed by the door. "The caller said she was Felicia. It was a female's voice."

"He couldn't have imitated a woman's voice that well," Hailey said.

Peyton held his hand and said, "I swear to you."

Hailey thought momentarily and then said, "How would he know Felicia? I never told him about her."

"Ms. Vaughan, I don't want to scare you, but he probably knows much more than you think. He may have heard every word spoken in this office for weeks."

"Oh, my God! He's involved with her disappearance—I know it," Hailey said. "He's got her."

"Do you want me to call the police?" Peyton asked.

"I've already filed a missing person's report without mentioning Gage. Call the police. Tell them we suspect Gage."

"We have recordings of his incoming calls," Peyton said, "but none have anything to do with Felicia."

"Say whatever you need to say to get them on the case."

"Right away," Peyton hurried to his desk.

• • •

Peyton ordered Chinese food delivered for lunch, and despite Hailey's insistence she had no appetite, he ordered enough for her, too. Her limousine would arrive soon. The only thing on her mind at this point was getting out of town.

Wilson joined them, and they ate in her office. Hailey picked through some Kung Pao chicken and rice, taking only a few bites before setting it aside.

At 1:45 p.m., the phone rang. Peyton answered Hailey's desk phone. "Great, thanks," he said before hanging up. "It's the car service. They're ready for you downstairs."

Hailey checked her watch. "A few minutes early. Perfect. Get me out of here."

Wilson pulled her suitcase and led her to the elevator. "Ms. Vaughan, wait here while I scout the lobby and check in with your driver. I'll return for you in less than two minutes."

"Wait!" Hailey said. Wilson stopped. "I've rejected calls from my husband last night and this morning. I want to remind you to look out for him as well..."

"Of course," Wilson said before leaving.

While they waited, Hailey reviewed some last-minute instructions with Peyton for the following week. "I have my husband's car. Here are the keys and his cell phone. If he shows up here, just give them to him." Hailey handed them over. Peyton tucked them in his top desk drawer.

Wilson returned and said, "We're ready." He picked up Hailey's suitcase and held the elevator door open for her.

Peyton said, "Have a safe trip, Ms. Vaughan. I'll be here or on my cell phone if you need anything."

"Thank you, Peyton. You've been wonderful. I'll call you after I land."

Wilson and Hailey rode to the lobby and stepped out. Isaac and another Echelonian watched her. They stayed at their booth as Wilson carried her suitcase to the large glass doors of Handel Towers.

The stretch limo was parked in the loading zone, hazard lights blinking and the trunk open to receive Hailey's luggage. A uniformed driver with an Elite Star Limo patch on his lapel stood beside the opened back door.

Wilson scanned the street and sidewalk. He held his hand out, stopping Hailey before she stepped out of the building. During a break in the foot traffic, he took her arm and escorted her to the limo's open door. He handed the driver Hailey's suitcase and helped Hailey get inside the car. Before closing her in, he said, "If you want to extend my service by a couple of hours, I can accompany you to the airport."

"No, I'm fine from here. I won't set foot outside the limo until I'm at the airport. Thanks."

"You have my phone number. I'll work with Peyton to greet you at the airport security checkpoint when you return," he said.

"Thanks," Hailey said, anxious to begin her Hawaiian escape.

After the driver loaded Hailey's suitcase, she felt the limo's trunk slam shut. Wilson closed her door and stepped back, still studying nearby pedestrians and the lobby doors. Hailey waved from behind the tinted window. Wilson couldn't see her.

The limo pulled away. She was on her way. Thank God.

Nineteen

THE DRIVER PARTITION slid down a few inches. "We're right on time," the driver said.

"Thank you," Hailey replied. It was the perfect time to refocus her mind and reduce her anxiety with some preparation for the week. Hailey pulled out her laptop to prepare for her retreat on the hour-long drive to the airport.

After she had typed up some new notes for her opening presentation, she looked out the window and noticed they were not traveling on Highway 73 in the direction of the airport. Instead, they were traveling east on the interstate. Hailey set her laptop aside and knelt for a better view through the window. "Hello, driver!" she called out. The partition had slid back up. The driver didn't answer.

She pulled her phone from her bag to call Peyton but had no signal. She couldn't remember the last time her phone had dropped a call. The signal on her mobile phone was never a problem.

She crawled to the partition and knocked on it, saying, "Hello? *Hello?*" No reply.

Her heart pounded, and she banged on the partition harder, yelling, "You're going the wrong way! I need to get to the airport. Pull over, or I'm calling the police." The limo slowed, but Hailey soon realized it wasn't because of her threat. They were turning off the highway onto Meadowbrook Way, a small service road used only by customers of a small camping area seventeen miles from Wenshire Harbor.

Panicked, she jumped out the moment the car slowed enough. She tucked her laptop into her satchel and slung it over her shoulder. The ride got bumpier as the road narrowed and degraded into disintegrating pavement.

The limo slowed for a curve, and she reached for the door handle. It was missing. She tried to roll down the window. The button did nothing.

They passed an abandoned campground with RV slabs and hookups overgrown with weeds. The road got bumpier. Hailey saw trees and foliage whisking past the window. She rechecked her phone. Still no signal. Still, she tried 911. The screen only showed a *No Service* message.

She hadn't seen if the limo driver had a passenger. If so, it had to be one of two people. She screamed, "Gage! Mason! Who is up there?" She pounded on the partition, begging the driver to stop the car. There was no answer, and the limo continued racing deeper into a thicker wooded area where some of the foliage brushed and scraped against the window.

After driving miles from the interstate into what looked like a forest, the limo slowed. Hailey got on her back and kicked the window as hard as possible. The glass was too thick. She swung her purse at it and screamed, "Let me out! Open the door! Please!" at the top of her lungs. The bumps swayed her head as she tried to note any landmarks. She only saw trees occasionally separated by small clearings that whizzed past the window.

The limo came to a stop. Hailey began another frantic attempt to kick out the window, failing again. She pressed her face against the glass, trying to see toward the front of the car. As dust swirled and settled, she saw the edge of a rusty chain stretched across the road.

The driver's partition slid down two inches. Hailey rushed to it. The opening wasn't large enough for her to reach through, but provided a clear view of the driver's cabin.

Hailey first saw a hat, sunglasses, a fake mustache, and a toupee in a pile on the passenger seat.

In the driver's seat, Gage grinned at her in the rearview mirror. His face was thick with makeup. He looked over his shoulder and said, "Hello there, lover."

• • •

Wilson returned to the office and reported Hailey was safely on her way, and then he left. Peyton forwarded the office calls to his mobile phone and prepared to leave the office for the day. He was excited to take the helm at Hailey's office for a week.

The phone rang as he was pushing his chair in at 2:10 p.m. He answered on the first ring. "Vaughan Consulting, may I help you?"

"Peyton, we've been waiting at the curb for ten minutes. Where is Ms. Vaughan?"

"You picked her up almost a half-hour ago. Wilson took her down. Is this a joke?"

"It's no joke. We're sitting here in an empty car."

"Wilson just left. He said he delivered her."

"Well, he didn't. She's not in or near the lobby. Nobody outside either."

"Hold on. I'm calling Wilson."

"Hurry up. We'll keep the car running."

Peyton put the office phone on hold and dialed on his mobile phone.

"What's up?" Wilson answered.

"Where the hell is Hailey?"

"What are you talking about? I loaded her into the car."

"Then why are they calling me from the curb downstairs saying they can't find her? You saw her get into the Escalade?"

Wilson went silent on the line.

"Hello?" Peyton said.

"It wasn't an Escalade," Wilson said. "I'm on my way back."

Peyton hung up, took the office phone off hold, and explained Hailey had been picked up by the wrong car.

He then dialed Hailey's mobile phone. Her voicemail picked up on the first ring. He tried again, this time leaving a message. "Ms. Vaughan, please call me back at the office as soon as possible. Apparently, there's been some confusion about your ride."

Peyton locked the office and rushed to the lobby. There was no guard in sight when he exited the elevator, contrary to Jonah's assurances a few minutes ago. He ran around the corner and found Jonah's office closed and the door locked. No wonder Hailey had been so upset about the lax security.

He crossed the lobby to the front doors and stopped. The Escalade had left. He looked outside at the curb where Hailey would have entered it. Mid-afternoon foot traffic on a sunny day was always heavy, and the sidewalk was busy.

He walked to the Echelonian booth. When Isaac saw him approaching, he stood and said, "Brother, I died on May 4, 2007."

Peyton replied, "I died on January 18, 2010." The men shook hands and then embraced.

"She's missing," Peyton said.

Isaac's expression became serious. "How?" The other Echelonian joined them.

"I have no idea," Peyton said. He nibbled his cheek as he continued to scan the lobby. "Master sent one of our cars to bring her to us for her best good. Now the driver has called, claiming she never got into it. How could you not see something, Isaac?"

"Hold on! You're blaming me?" Isaac looked at his partner and then back to Peyton.

"Look, she didn't vaporize. She got into a car other than ours. How could you miss that?"

"A stretch limo showed up. The time was right. I wasn't given a vehicle description!"

Peyton shrugged. "You need to call Master. Tell him the truth—that we both failed."

"But that's not the truth," Isaac said. "This was your mission."

"We both failed, and that *is* the truth!" Peyton yelled. People passing in the lobby turned to watch.

Isaac lowered his voice and said, "Are you sure she didn't just run?"

Peyton shook his head. "Impossible. She was clueless. I think her stalker got her."

Isaac turned to his partner and said, "Call Master." The man pulled a phone from his pocket.

Peyton leaned on the booth beside a stand of Echelonian flyers. "Everything was perfect," he said. "Vaughan is a prize for our cause I don't want to forfeit."

"I don't blame you," Isaac said. "She carries the Master's highest reward. Her joining our truth would have locked you in as vice deacon."

"There's still time," Peyton said. "She's been gone less than an hour. I want to believe there's a simple explanation. Something that will fix everything. We will have her."

"We should have just taken her last week," Isaac said.

"No. She wasn't desperate enough to receive and accept the message of truth. Today was the perfect day."

Isaac's partner hung up his phone and said, "Master is ordering an alert texted to all members immediately. The first member to locate and reveal her whereabouts to him will be raised a level in rank with a month of full pavilion privileges."

Peyton let his arms flop to his sides. As he left the men, he shook his head and took the elevator back to Hailey's office.

Back at his desk, he dialed 911 and then repeatedly called Hailey's mobile phone over the next hour. He got no answer. He had carefully followed email and text messages from fellow Echelonians seeking information on Hailey's disappearance. So far, his brothers and sisters had failed to yield solid leads.

The phone rang. The caller ID showed Mason and Hailey's home number. Before she left, Hailey had given Peyton strict instructions to send all calls from their home number to voicemail. This time, Peyton picked up.

"Hello, Ms. Vaughan's office," he answered. The line was quiet. "Ms. Vaughan's office," he repeated.

"Who is this?" Mason said.

"Mr. Barger, my name is Peyton Bredlin. I'm your wife's assistant."

"Where's my wife?"

"I'm sorry, I can't—"

"Put her on the phone *now*. This is important. I need my car."

"Sir, your wife left your keys and mobile phone in the office. I will leave them with security in the lobby if you want to stop by for them at your convenience."

Mason laughed. "How am I supposed to drive there without a car, Peyton? I have to talk to her as soon as possible, so tell her to call me."

"Mr. Barger, I'm trying to tell you your wife is missing."

"I'm sure she is. Hailey, if you're listening on the other line, I'm not in the mood to play hide-and-seek with you."

"Please, Mr. Barger, listen to me. She's not listening. I arranged a car to take her to the airport. Wilson escorted her to the limo, and then the limo company called, saying they had not picked her up. She's gone."

"Who's Wilson?"

"Her private security guard."

"What the hell are you talking about?"

"Sir, are you aware a man has been stalking your wife?"

"Is that what she's calling it?"

"Mr. Barger, I've seen him."

"You talking about that guy—Gage?"

"Yes, so you do know about him?"

"I know enough."

"Sir, Gage is real, and your wife could be in serious danger. She's been terrified, and now I cannot reach her."

"Let me tell you something, Peyton. If she has a problem with this guy, it is because she's in a hell of her own making after fucking around on me."

"Mr. Barger, I may have been placed into your wife's life to reveal the truth to you, and the truth is she's not having an affair and—"

"Whatever bonus she paid you to say that, I'll double it if you tell me where she is."

"Sir, I don't lie. I never lie. Your wife told me the truth with nothing to gain by lying to me. She has not cheated on you."

Mason paused and said, "You think this Gage guy has her?"

"I hope not, but nothing else adds up. What should I do?"

"Call the police."

"I did."

"Do you have this Gage's address?"

"His last address was in Denburg. A private investigator told us the address was an abandoned lot. We don't have an updated address or phone number."

"You hired a private investigator?"

"Yes, your wife insisted."

"I thought you said he's been stalking her. Doesn't he call?"

"Yes, but he uses disposable phones. All we have are some recordings of his voice. If you have any suggestions, I'd love to hear them."

"The only thing effective with an asshole like this is brute force."

"I'm sorry, sir, that isn't an option if we can't find him," Peyton said. "But Mr. Barger, I want to emphasize your wife told me in confidence that she never cheated with Gage, and I believe her. She obviously loves you."

"Peyton, let me give you something to think about. What if I'm right? What if Hailey has run off with this man? I mean ... if I'm not the lunatic she's made me out to be, she may have roped you into assisting her to do something awful. Just think about that."

"Mr. Barger, I have the utmost trust in your wife. Besides, she seems genuinely afraid of Gage."

Peyton heard a click. The phone went dead. He had not yet logged onto Hailey's computer. He had considered Hailey's information private, and breaching it went against the core Echelonian credo. However, if someone other than an Echelonian brother or sister had taken her, she may have lost her opportunity to accept the truth and be saved. She was a victim of an injustice, and violating her privacy to protect her might be appropriate. Peyton's rationale strengthened. Hailey's disappearance had also jeopardized his promotion to Echelonian vice deacon.

He went into Hailey's office and turned on the light. Her desk was clean. Her computer turned off just as she had left it. He sat in her chair and turned on her computer. A search for all email messages to or from Gage brought up only two results. He clicked on the first one and gasped when he saw its contents—a series of photo attachments that appeared to be Hailey's naked body poised in sexual positions with a naked man. One of the attachments was a video. When Peyton saw it, he pushed back from the keyboard and stood. He watched the man stroking Hailey's skin and caressing her everywhere.

Peyton interlocked his fingers on his head and closed his eyes while he waited for the shock to wear off. He shook his head as he looked at the images and said, "You lied to me. After all I did for you, you *lied* to me."

Peyton's anger turned to disappointment and pity. Though he and the other Echelonian followers had presented Hailey with every opportunity to accept their truth, she had rejected it. Without accepting the Echelonian message, she was doomed to live far below her potential and would certainly lose her salvation.

• • •

Hailey stared in horror as Gage grinned at her.

"Don't be scared," Gage said. "Everything's happening exactly as it should."

"You bastard, let me out of this car!"

"You're fighting something you can't fight. Fate's scary when it's … unexpected. I want you to relax."

Hailey shouted, "Let me out, you son-of-a-bitch!" She pounded the partition again. Gage got out of the car. Hailey crawled to the door, but Gage wasn't headed there. Instead, he went to the front of the limo. Hailey crawled back and peered through the crack in the partition. She saw Gage take several steps up a road that had degraded to nothing more than two dirt wheel tracks separated by a strip of grass. He unlocked a rusty padlock and unhooked a chain strung across the road. He tossed the chain to the ground.

Hailey tried to shove her hand into the driver's compartment. The opening was too narrow. She slammed it with her shoulder twice. It wouldn't break. Gage looked back when he heard the commotion. He pulled the chain across the road, hand over hand, while smiling and shaking his head. Hailey dropped to her back and kicked the partition, but it was too solid to break.

Gage wrapped the chain neatly around a post on one side and then returned to the car. He returned to the driver's seat and said, "I reckon this car is damn-near as strong as our bond. Built to last, for sure."

"We have no bond," Hailey said, and then she beat the partition harder until she slumped down to the floor and wept.

Gage accelerated. The limo swayed and bumped. "I love your fire, and you're gonna love mine," he said. "We were meant for each other. I'm only helping the inevitable. Our love is patient. It is kind. Our love does not envy, it does not boast, it is not proud. It is not easily angered, and it keeps no record of wrongs. Our love does not delight in evil but rejoices with the truth. It always protects, always trusts, always hopes, and always perseveres. Our love will never fail." Hailey watched Gage smile in the rearview mirror, contented after his recital.

She rechecked her phone. Still no signal. The trees became thicker as they drove deeper into the woods. Occasionally, a swath of branches scraped the roof or windows. They rounded more corners, crossed a creek, and turned into a large clearing of manicured lawn split by a gravel driveway that arced to a large log cabin atop a hill.

Halfway up the driveway, Gage stopped the limo beside a shed. He lowered Hailey's rear window by an inch. She heard the muffled sounds of deep barks. Gage got out, went to the shed, and swung open two wooden doors, revealing a chain-link cage as tall as a man. Inside, two enormous

Caucasian Shepherd dogs leaped high, again and again, their muzzles nearly touching the roof of their cage. When the doors opened, their barks grew so loud Hailey could feel their vibration in her chest.

Gage came to Hailey's window and shouted, "I don't want to see you get hurt, Love, so I'm making this introduction to warn you. Maxi and Mum love to gnaw, especially things that move and produce blood. Be sure you tell me if you decide to take an unscheduled walk outside our home because if they get loose, they'll—well, let's say they don't share my affection for you."

Gage whistled. The dogs began spinning in circles. Their barks rose in pitch, and saliva flung from their mouths. He closed the shed doors, partially muting the barks, and returned to the driver's seat. Hailey's window slid up, and the limo drove to the top of the hill, parking outside the cabin's front door. The cabin was bigger than it had looked from the bottom of the hill, and the front had a wide porch with wooden pillars. To the rear and sides, the dense vegetation had been cleared to a hundred feet away.

Gage got out and went into the cabin. Hailey kept checking her phone for a signal. There was none. She frantically searched the limo for a weapon. The only loose items except her laptop and bag were some brochures, wine glasses, and an ice tray in the refrigerator.

Gage returned a minute later wearing latex gloves and holding a small cloth bag. He went to the limo's rear door and rested his hand on the handle. Despite the closed window, Hailey heard him say, "Now, don't be afraid."

Her adrenaline surged, and she positioned herself to rush the door when it opened. If she could get loose, she could run, and she was sure Gage would have no chance of catching her on foot.

Gage opened the door. She tried to lunge through the opening. Gage's hand grabbed her neck, and he shoved her back inside. He jumped in and slammed the door behind him. He threw the bag on the seat beside him. Hailey attacked, kicking and screaming, "No! No! No!" She swung her fists, landing blows to his shoulders. He covered his head with his hands and took a few blows before he tackled her to the floor face-down and mounted her. When Hailey realized her offensive had no effect, she stopped. Gage rose on his knees to keep from putting his full weight on her.

"Gage, listen, please. If you let me go, you can have the ring, and no one needs to know this happened. We can forget it. Let's not make things any worse than they are."

"Things aren't that bad. Certainly not for me!" Gage said. "As for your bargain, you'd better be careful, or you might bargain yourself right out of our happily ever after." He picked up the bag and slid his hand inside, feeling its contents. "Right now, we need to take care of a little something. I'm going to restrain you for your own safety. I don't want you to bruise your gorgeous skin before you recognize the silliness of fighting. Do you understand?"

"Gage, please…" Hailey's eyes were wide as she tried to turn her head to look up at him. Her whole body trembled.

Gage removed a pair of flex cuffs and pinched them between his teeth. Hailey saw them and bucked and writhed to escape from under him, but he was too heavy and held her fast. He reached down, and after laughing for a moment at how deftly Hailey moved her wrists to keep them from his grip, he pulled them behind her back, securing them.

Gage's hand returned to the bag and pulled out a pair of pliers and a silver chain with a large heart-shaped locket the size of a padlock. He wrapped the chain around Hailey's neck. His face turned red, and he growled as he squeezed the pliers with both hands, closing an open link that connected the chain.

"lover, your new necklace is locked as securely as our love," he said, pausing momentarily to pant. "One more small bit of business, and then we can get you inside." He put the pliers back into the bag and pulled out something he kept hidden in the palm of his hand.

"What are you doing?" Hailey asked. She struggled to see behind her. Gage gently pressed the side of her face back to the floor. "Shhhh," he said. "You're going to feel a little prick. I promise it will be quick."

"No! What are you doing?" Hailey tried to twist under him. He tightened his legs. A tiny plastic cup dropped beside Hailey's face.

Gage used his teeth to tear the paper wrapper from a sterile lance and then pinched it between his lips while taking a firm hold of Hailey's hands. She writhed under him and screamed, "Nooo!" Gage squeezed her finger, and when Hailey felt the puncture, she screamed louder and thrust her hips, nearly bucking him off. He grabbed the plastic cup, put her finger into it, and milked several drops of blood from it. He put a cap on the cup, set it aside, and tried to soothe her, saying, "All done, there we go, all done, there we go." He wrapped an adhesive bandage around her finger and stroked the sweaty hair from her forehead, saying, "Calm down, that's it, calm down."

When he dismounted her, Hailey flipped over and used her legs to shove herself away from him until her back was against the driver's partition.

Gage chuckled as he retrieved a screwdriver from the bag. He slipped it into the hole where the door handle should have been, and after jabbing it in a few times, it clicked. He pushed the door open.

Hailey wanted to run, but if Gage had so easily stopped her while her hands were free, trying to escape cuffed would be a wasted attempt. She needed to get out of the car.

Gage used both hands to grab the bottom of the limo's rear seats. He heaved upward and pulled the seats off, revealing a storage compartment under them. After setting the seats on the floor, he reached into the compartment and raised a man's foot and leg by the ankle while fishing something with the other. Hailey screamed. Gage tried and failed to shush her. Eventually, he pulled out a handgun and dropped the leg back inside, pushing it down to return the seats to their position.

"I tried to explain to the driver that the customer is always right. When he refused to let me borrow the limo, I was forced to give him some negative feedback. I'm sorry you had to see that, lover."

Gage carefully picked up the gun with his gloved fingertips. Hailey recognized the gun. It was Cocky.

"Even though you hate guns, I'm still grateful you didn't find this pew-pew device during our drive. I asked fate to give me a sign. If you found Cocky on our way home, I'd know I was wrong about our fate. On the other hand, if you behaved like I thought you would, then I'd know I'm right."

He dipped his gloved finger in Hailey's blood, flicked it onto the door's armrest, and smeared some onto the door jamb with his foot. He wiped some blood onto the floor mat and used the last little bit to wipe onto Cocky's stock, trigger, and around the tip of the muzzle. He placed the gun on the rear limo seat and motioned to Hailey, saying, "Come with me, lover."

Hailey stayed curled up in the corner of the limo, her wrists bound behind her and legs retracted, ready to kick.

Gage said, "You're going to find that everything we are about to experience together will be much more comfortable for you if you don't fight it."

"Go to hell. That's your fate," Hailey replied, her voice shaking.

"Wow," Gage smirked. "Your fire is one of the things I love most about you! That will come in handy later."

He crawled to her and reached for her leg. Hailey tried to kick his hand. He avoided it and eventually grabbed her ankles. He pulled her legs straight and flipped her to her stomach again.

Hailey sobbed. She turned her head to the side, looking over her shoulder at him, and said, "Why are you doing this?"

Gage dragged her to the door by her ankles, careful not to carpet-burn her pristine skin. He scooped her under the knees and neck and picked her up. He carried her up the steps to the cabin's porch and set her down on her feet, resting one hand on her shoulder. He reached into his pocket for the door key.

Hailey bent over and said, "I'm going to be sick."

"No, not here!" Gage said. "Hold on, use this…" He ran to a waste can on the porch a few feet away.

Hailey turned and ran, jumping from the porch and easily clearing the four steps.

Gage yelled, "No! Stop!" as Hailey leaned forward, sprinting down the driveway toward the dirt road. Though her wrists were bound behind her, she had good control of her speed and was fueled by more than enough adrenaline. She glanced back. Gage was running after her with his eyes wide as he shouted for her to stop, his face red, his arms pumping high.

When Hailey passed the dogs' cage, their barks rose to a new level of excitement. Their fangs flashed, and saliva twirled from their mouths as they spun and clawed at the fence. The thought that Gage might release the dogs terrified her. She extended her lead on him until she rounded the corner from the driveway and onto the dirt road, where she continued running in the direction they had come in the limo.

She looked back and saw Gage slow to a jog before he stopped at the driveway entrance. He leaned onto his knees, his head bowed in the middle of the road. She heard his faint yell, "See you in a few minutes, lover. Stop fighting it."

Hailey ran until the road's curve took Gage completely out of sight. She remembered her phone was still in her pocket, so she stopped and pulled her bound hands to her side to take it out. The phone had no signal, and her battery was at seventeen percent. She turned it off to save the remaining battery life.

She continued running to a bend where she saw a bridge about a quarter-mile ahead. As she approached it, she tried to sort out her options. Why would Gage say he'd see her in a few minutes?

A slanted sign punctured with bullet holes read Townsend River at the bridge. She remembered passing it on the drive to the cabin. She froze, listening for what she thought was an approaching vehicle. She heard only water cascading over the rocks in the river below. To be safe, she abandoned the road and jogged into the woods until she felt far enough from the road to avoid detection. She knew Townsend River was the same river she crossed in the woods on the way to Fit Performance Gym. Gage had driven the limo east for at least twenty minutes from town, and at the turn, they had turned south before the road wound. Based on their travel time, Hailey didn't think they were more than twenty miles from town. She decided following the river west would be a safer route back to town than taking a road Gage was sure to scour.

Hailey squatted and fell to her side to get her cuffed hands from behind her to her front. Though she was winded, she held her breath, pulled her knees nearly to her chin, and pulled her body through her bound wrists. She got up, jogged through the trees, and descended an embankment to the river's edge. She found a tree stump protruding from the riverbank and wrapped her arms around it. The flex cuffs had little slack between them but enough to rub the connecting section against the stump. She rubbed hard and succeeded only in scraping bark from the stump and dirtying the unforgiving plastic. She jogged further and found a boulder protruding a few feet from the shore. It had a jagged edge and was about the size of a briefcase. The results were more promising when she scrapped the cuffs along the edge. The cuffs scratched. Hailey rubbed harder, pulling her wrists apart with as much force as possible. The friction warmed the cuffs, but they didn't break before she needed a rest. Sitting by the rock, she shooed away some mosquitos and noticed the sun had slightly changed position, making the west more distinct. If she could free her wrists and run without being hindered, she felt confident she could follow the river and reach town by dusk. Even if she didn't get her wrists free, she'd have to keep going.

She got her second wind and pressed the cuffs against the edge of the rock. She rubbed with a vengeance, using as much of her weight as possible. The skin on her wrist burned. She rubbed harder. When the cuffs snapped loose, she gasped and fell to her back, panting and smiling. One of the flex cuffs had broken, leaving the other as a bracelet she could deal with later.

Hailey got up and resumed her run. The river's slither took her through beautiful acreage and sometimes tricky terrain that buttressed the shore with steep bluffs. She ran inland in these places, hurdling fallen trees and sometimes slowing to ease through briars.

The necklace Gage had put on her bounced with her strides, the big locket thumping against her neck and seeming heavier with each mile. Its chain was too strong to break, so she tried pulling it over her head. It was too snug to pass her chin. She couldn't feel a latch and remembered Gage had locked it onto her neck with pliers.

After a couple of hours of running, the sun grew as it approached the horizon. Hailey's feet and ankles were covered with mud from running through swampland. She had become desperately thirsty. She saw something familiar as she came to a high-point of the terrain. Recognition swept over her, and she yelled, "Yes!" Scary Church stood in the distance. Its disintegrating structure and steeple were a welcome sight. To the right, she saw the woods through which she ran to what used to be Fit Performance Gym.

She ran with renewed enthusiasm and pulled her phone from her pocket. She realized she had forgotten to turn it off the last time she checked it a few miles ago. She pulled it out and saw that the signal strength alternated between two and three bars, and her battery had depleted to eight percent. She called Peyton.

"Hello?" Peyton answered.

"Yes, Peyton, it's me. Thank God you picked up. My phone battery is almost dead."

Peyton didn't respond.

Hailey said, "I've been abducted by Gage."

"I know."

"You do?"

"Yes."

"Have you called the police?"

"I have."

"Thank you. I've escaped. Please hurry and come pick me up. I'm running along the Townsend River into Henderton. I can see Center Street in the distance. I'm still wearing the outfit you picked for me. You'll see me ... Peyton? Are you there?"

"Why did you lie to me?"

Stunned, Hailey slowed her jog. "What are you talking about?"

"I saw the photos of you and Gage on your computer. You told me you were a victim."

"I *am* a victim! Peyton, I'm telling you those photos aren't what they seem. And what were you doing on my computer?"

"You were in trouble. I was trying to save you. It was the right thing to do."

"Peyton, this is a horrible time to discuss the photos. I need you or the police to pick me up in Henderton."

"Ms. Vaughan, I'm afraid I cannot support you given the betrayal and the lifestyle you've chosen."

"Peyton, listen to me. I'm trying to escape. I—need—help."

"The consequences you've chosen are inescapable."

"Unbelievable! What has gotten into you?"

"The truth has gotten into me. Ms. Vaughan, you can run from the truth, but the truth will always find you, and until you embrace it, it can never set you free."

"You're one of them? You're an Echelonian? You hid that from me?"

"Ms. Vaughan, you might have heard the saying, 'There is none so blind as he who won't see.' If you had opened your mind to the truth, you wouldn't feel blind."

"You're fired. Get the hell out of my office!"

"Jonah already has my key. When you are ready to embrace it, the truth will still be there for you."

The line went dead, and the phone chirped. She pulled it from her ear to check the screen.

Low Battery. Connect charger.

She stared at the message in disbelief. She dialed 911. The phone chirped again, and the message blinked. She pocketed the phone and resumed her run along the final stretch to the safety of Henderton.

An old truss bridge spanned the river about a quarter-mile ahead. As she neared, she saw no traffic on it. She climbed the embankment with the hope of catching a passing vehicle. A ride for the last leg of her journey would be a godsend.

At the top, she saw that the bridge connected a single-lane road that curved out of sight in both directions. Since the road didn't look well-traveled, waiting for a passing car wasn't reasonable. Hailey headed off for her final trek to Henderton. Sand and rocks slid from her feet as she descended the opposite embankment to the river. The foliage and trees were flush to the river's edge, so she ran in the water, splashing in the shallows.

She returned to the riverbank when it widened and soon found footprints in the mud. They looked fresh. She wondered if some fishermen or campers might be nearby. She had slowed to examine them when something struck her thigh. She felt a searing pain after an impact strong enough to throw her off balance. She shrieked and grabbed her leg, where a dart protruded from her jeans. She quickly snatched it out. A drop of liquid oozed from a needle connected to an empty syringe barrel.

Gage stepped out from a thicket in the distance ahead of her. He lowered the barrel of a scoped rifle and blew her a kiss.

Hailey screamed and fled in the direction she had come. She slipped on the mud twice before she leaped into the shallows, her feet splashing as she high-stepped toward the bridge.

Gage cupped his hands around his mouth and shouted, "You got two more minutes for recess, lover. Then I'm gonna have to take you home where you belong." He loaded another dart into the rifle as he walked in her direction.

Hailey reached the base of the bridge and climbed the embankment. She felt her heart pounding and the thick chain necklace thumping against her throat. She ran down the road, desperately hoping to find a passing vehicle or pedestrian—anyone. After a minute, the only effect she felt from the dart was pain in her leg at the injection site. She tried to run faster. If Gage had tranquilized her, she knew her time was limited. She wondered if hiding from him while it wore off would be possible. All she could do at this point was hope Gage had under-dosed her or that her surge of adrenaline would somehow defeat any anesthetic.

The road turned, and she saw a black limousine parked on the shoulder. She knew Gage wasn't in it and continued running toward it. She decided to try the limo in case Gage had left the keys in it, even though it was probably absurd. He would never have made such a mistake.

Before she could reach the limo, she felt her feet becoming heavy and warmth spreading all over her body. "No!" she yelled. She tried to force her feet to continue. Each stride became heavier. She wasn't going to make it. She headed for the woods, staggering to the side of the road. Her knees buckled. She crawled on the shoulder until she collapsed. She tried to reach for her phone, but her arm flopped to the ground with her thumb hooked in her pocket.

As she lay there with her face pressed to the dirt, the last thing Hailey saw was Gage in the distance, walking toward her. His hands were tucked in his pockets as he strolled with the air rifle pinched under one arm.

Twenty

PEYTON PARKED IN the newly paved lot of the Truth and Justice Pavilion. Visits to the Echelonian headquarters always excited him, especially since they had moved into their luxurious new facility. Any evidence of its former use as a gym had long vanished.

Eusebio Xismanchitl had summoned him for an in-person accounting of Hailey's disappearance. Two guards wearing suits blocked the front door. When Peyton neared them, one man recognized him and said, "Greetings, Brother Bredlin. I died on April 3, 2008."

Peyton replied, "I died on January 18, 2010." The men shook hands and then embraced. The other guard opened the door for him and said, "Master Eusebio is waiting for you."

Peyton entered the spacious lobby. The scent of new carpet and freshly painted walls greeted him. To his left was a soundproof mother's lounge enclosed in glass with tiered seating. Six double doors opened to the empty auditorium, where workers cleaned pews and tested the sound system for this evening's presentation. To his right, a row of chairs lined a wall with hundreds of brochures and pamphlets for members to use to save non-believers and bring them to the truth.

Master Eusebio stood near one of the auditorium entrances. As usual, he was flanked by his aides—several suited Echelonian men. He talked with a couple that appeared to be guests—perhaps taking a tour of the new facility. One was a gorgeous dark-haired woman who stood taller than Eusebio and any of his men. The other was an older gentleman who looked like he could be the woman's father.

One of the aides saw Peyton approaching and held up his finger. He whispered something to Eusebio, who nodded. The man motioned for Peyton to come.

Eusebio held out his hand for Peyton, who took it and kissed it. He bowed his head and said, "Greetings, Master. I died on January 18, 2010. I come to you bearing and upholding our truth and justice at all costs."

Eusebio embraced him and then pointed to the guests. "Peyton, I want to introduce you to two special people. This is Aldred Hurd and Morana Mahker, visiting from Los Angeles. They are planning a mission to bring our truth to the public and our justice to the impoverished at any cost."

Morana extended her hand and said, "I've heard you're a hard worker and quite the chameleon for the cause, Peyton. Good work."

"Thank you. I try to be worthy."

Aldred said, "If you're looking for work in LA, we'd be honored to have you, brother."

Eusebio said, "You can hear more about their plans at their presentation tonight in the auditorium, Peyton. Meanwhile, I need to speak to Peyton privately in my office. Will you excuse us?"

Eusebio and his aides led Peyton through a side door and down a long hallway to a private suite whose door was guarded by two more Echelonians. They opened the doors and stepped aside for the entourage to enter.

The suite was a large rectangular room with all the studio apartment amenities. A fruit basket sat by a sink, and a large window looked out over the manicured front lawn. The framed quotes and art decorating the walls of his old office had migrated and were supplemented with new pieces.

Eusebio pointed to one of two oversized chairs that faced his desk. Peyton sat.

"I want to know what happened," Eusebio said, going around to sit in his throne-like chair.

"Master, I bring you some uncomfortable truth."

"Time is scarce, Peyton. Be as succinct as you can." One of the aides came and poured water into a glass for Eusebio.

"Master, Hailey Vaughan was not who we thought she was."

"Oh?" Eusebio said.

"I've discovered she was dishonest on a matter of morality."

"So, did you *let* her escape?"

"No, of course not. Her stalker reached her before we did."

Eusebio took a drink and said, "That's what I heard. It's unfortunate. Had you acquired Vaughan, we could have impressed the truth upon her without the distractions of her work or this … stalker."

"Yes, Master. But now that we know she wasn't worthy—"

Eusebio held up his hand. "Not too fast. Her sin does not erase your oversight. I expected you to deliver her to us today. You had a mission to fulfill, and you failed."

"Yes, Master." Peyton thought momentarily and then said, "Is it possible I could still become a vice deacon?"

Eusebio shook his head. "Your promotion was contingent on acquiring Vaughan and her acceptance of our message." He shrugged. "Is there anything else, Peyton?"

"No. Not at all."

• • •

Hailey's eyes opened halfway and closed again. She knew she was on her back. She felt like she had slept for a week, yet instead of waking refreshed, she was drained. Her thoughts seemed to move in slow motion. She sensed music playing. It was a song too faint to recognize.

When she fully opened her eyes, she saw a wood beam spanning the ceiling. A notepad paper sign tacked there faced down and read:

Welcome Home, lover!

A short distance from the beam was a round, recessed ceiling light.

She fought through the fogginess to determine her whereabouts. Slowly, her memory assembled the pieces of her limo ride from the office, her flight from Gage's property, and running in the woods along a river. She raised her head, and the room spun. She squeezed her eyes shut until it passed. She looked at her feet and saw that she lay on a double bed in the center of a small room with a hardwood floor. The wall to her left had a full-length mirror mounted to it. The opposite wall had a polished three-drawer bureau with a table lamp and two lit candles. They filled the air with the aroma of cinnamon. Until that moment, cinnamon had been Hailey's favorite scent. She saw her overnight bag, missing since Cancun, between the candles.

At first, she was relieved she still wore her jeans and shirt. Then, she saw they were spotless, not caked in the mud and briars she had collected on her run. Her shoes had been removed. The bedspread under her looked familiar. It had an identical pattern to her bedspread at home.

She tried to sit up and discovered her wrists were restrained by padded flex cuffs connected to chains that went down either side of the bed and locked on the metal frame. Her hands had a decent range of motion. She could touch her face with either hand if she leaned but couldn't bring her hands together. The ceiling light had turned on for no apparent reason. The only other light source was a single window on the wall above her head. Its curtains were drawn—curtains matching those in Hailey's bedroom in Turlock Heights Estates.

She raised her feet. They, too, were cuffed to the foot of the bed frame. She yanked her foot hard against the cuffs. The thick chain was far too strong to break.

She rested her head again and saw shelves high on the walls around the entire perimeter of the room, exactly like her home study. Each shelf was lined with ornate head vases, some replicas of those Hailey owned. Two slightly larger head vases sat on a special shelf centered above the door. One vase was a likeness of her head and the other of Gage's. They were connected at the lips, frozen in a ceramic kiss that turned Hailey's stomach. A music player on a small bedside table quietly played Sade's *Hang On To Your Love*. The song looped repeatedly.

Hailey pulled her feet against the flex cuffs and snapped her arms toward one another, trying to break the cuffs. "Dammit," she said and slammed her feet onto the bed.

The sound triggered footsteps outside her room, and the door opened. Gage peered in and smiled. "Hello there, lover."

Hailey stared at him with no expression.

"You may not feel like yourself for a little bit longer," Gage said, stepping through the door. He carried a large water bottle with a bendable straw. "The sleepy juice I used to slow you down this afternoon might create hallucinations. If you're having any, I hope they aren't scary." He came to her bedside and checked the snugness of her left wrist restraint. He slipped his hand under her head and raised it while positioning the straw for her to drink.

Hailey was so thirsty she didn't resist and took long swigs of the water until Gage pulled the straw out. Hailey coughed and then, groggy, said, "Gage, please take the cuffs off. They hurt. They're useless. I'm exhausted."

He laughed as he went around to the right side of the bed. "I want to trust you, and I will—soon. You must realize our relationship is like a tiny baby, and you're asking me to treat it as if it's all grown up." He pulled on the other wrist, testing its snugness. "We're going to incubate our relationship so it will survive and grow strong."

Hailey tried to touch her hands together over her stomach. They stopped inches apart. She pulled the restraints harder and strained.

"Oh, it's secure," Gage said. "Don't strain or fight it. I sure don't want you to pull a muscle. That would be awful for you."

Hailey dropped her arms back to the bed and focused on the ceiling, seething.

"Can you touch your face?" Gage asked.

Hailey pulled her head to one side and touched her cheek with her fingertips. "I want you to be able to touch your hand to your face. There's nothing I hate worse than an itch I can't scratch on my face." He went to the foot of the bed, lifted her ankles against the restraints, and then gently set them down. "There we go. Snug as a bug," he said. "I've got to run an errand, which will give you more recovery time from all our excitement!" He grinned and winked at her before leaving. Before the door clicked shut, Gage leaned back in and said, "I almost forgot something incredibly important. Do you need to use the bathroom?"

Hailey recognized it as an opportunity to learn what was outside her room. Knowing the layout of whatever building she was in would be vital to escaping.

"Yes," she said.

Gage came back to her bedside and bent down. "No problem, lover." He pulled a metal bedpan from under her bed. "I'm going to lift your tush so you can get it over the potty."

Hailey stared at him, unable to believe what she was hearing.

"No. I need a bathroom, not a pan," she said.

"And you have your very own bathroom outside. For now, though, I think using the portable potty is best. After all, you're still woozy, and I'd hate for you to get up from the bed and take a fall that could damage that gorgeous mug." He gently pinched her chin and opened the zipper flap on her jeans to unzip them.

"No!" Hailey said, twisting her hips away.

"Are we being shy?" Gage asked. "Now, don't be self-conscious. I've already seen everything the good lord gave you." He tried to scoop his hands under her hips to lift her.

She stiffened her body and said, "Gage, never mind. I can wait."

Gage put his hands on his hips as he looked down at her. "Suit yourself. You'll have to urinate soon, and if I'm not here to help you, we might have an accident."

"Then untie me, and we won't have an accident," Hailey snapped.

Gage dropped the empty bedpan on the bed beside her. "I'll tell you what," he said. "This might be my chance to show you my unconditional love for every aspect of you. If you have a problem using the pan, just let your bladder go. I won't be gone long. I'll give you a good scrubbing when I get back, and that'll be an activity you are sure to enjoy."

Hailey turned away.

Gage went to the digital music player and pressed a button before he left the room.

At first, the room fell quiet until she could isolate the faint sound of a voice speaking through the tiny speakers on the side table. The voice was so soft she held her breath to listen, trying to understand the words. She soon recognized it was her own voice.

I'm happy to be yours, Gage. Our bond is unbreakable, Gage. I love you, Gage.

The word Gage was clearly spliced in because its tone and pitch differed from the rest of the phrase, but all the words were definitely spoken by her. After ten seconds of silence, the recorded words played again.

I'm happy to be yours, Gage. Our bond is unbreakable, Gage. I love you, Gage.

She heard a door outside her room open and close. Then, through the windows, she heard a vehicle start and drive away.

I'm happy to be yours, Gage. Our bond is unbreakable, Gage. I love you, Gage.

• • •

After a half-hour drive, Gage arrived back in town with the limo. He drove into an alley behind Club Parlay, where Mason would soon arrive for work. Gage waited for an employee to dump two barrels of trash into the dumpster and disappear back inside before he pulled forward and parked adjacent to the rear employee lot. Dusk provided enough darkness for him to slip out of the car without being identifiable by the outdoor security cameras he had noted. He had already placed "Cocky," nicely splattered with Hailey's blood, on the floor by the passenger door.

So far, everything had gone as planned. Gage regretted he wouldn't be able to hear the less-than-convincing explanation Mason would give police about his non-involvement in Hailey's disappearance.

He pulled the brim of a baseball cap low and left the limo unlocked, walking three blocks to his Blazer parked around the corner from a donut shop. He went inside and ordered two donuts—a plain cake donut for himself and a Bavarian chocolate cream filled for Hailey. It was her favorite, and he couldn't wait to see her excitement when he gave it to her. He imagined them enjoying the donuts together this evening. He fantasized about Hailey breaking off a fluffy hunk of donut and popping it into his mouth before they kissed and licked the sugar off one another's lips. Of course, that would lead to abandoning the half-eaten donuts for the lovemaking Hailey would beg for.

With the evening's dessert taken care of, Gage smiled as he drove to pick up an extra-special to-go dinner he would enjoy with his wife, lover, and future mother of his many children. It would be a spectacular evening and the start of a beautiful new life. Sometimes fate sure takes her time, but she always comes around.

• • •

For two hours, Hailey alternated between lying on her back and turning on each side as far as she could. She discovered that the ceiling light turned on when she made any significant movement. If she kept still for ninety seconds, it turned off. She looked at her wrists for wires and could not see any motion detectors on the walls. Somehow, something in the room sensed her movement.

The water she had guzzled had passed through her system, and her bladder had become full to the point she had worried about. She shook her legs, tried to cross them, and writhed, twisting her body to control it. She knew using the bedpan was inevitable and didn't want to give Gage a reason to give her a hand-cleaning.

She shifted her waist toward her hand and unbuttoned and unzipped her jeans. After some struggle, she pulled her jeans and panties down a few inches on one side and shifted her hips toward the other side of the bed to do the same there. Eventually, she got them down to her knees. She arched her back and pulled the bedpan under her, sitting up as far as possible.

As she relieved herself, she saw the table lamp and wondered whether its base would shatter if she could get her hands on it. If so, a shard might provide a weapon if she could free herself.

When she finished, she dismounted the bedpan without spilling it and pushed it down by her knees. She pulled her pants up and was tempted to toss the bedpan to the floor, but doing so would only add the stench of urine to her problems.

She laid back and tried to block out her spoken mantra that had played through the music player hundreds of times. She focused on every other sound she could hear. The faint chirps of birds now and then and the winds rustling through the trees outside the window. Occasionally, the dogs barked themselves into a frenzy, although the sound was distant.

After being still for a while, she heard something she couldn't identify. It wasn't rhythmic and happened every few minutes. She heard a blunt thud she also felt through the bed. It came from the floor, and she wondered if someone was under the cabin. Soon, the sound stopped.

As evening set in, her room's interior dimmed. Hailey visualized every possible escape scenario she could fathom. She lifted her chin to see out the window above her head. The sky had darkened enough to see stars through a thin crack in the curtains. Then, there was a new sound—something closer. A slow creak of a floorboard outside her door. "Hello?" she called out. The cabin fell silent until she heard another, smaller creak a few moments later. Hailey raised her head as far as she could. The ceiling light blinked on. She watched the doorknob, waiting for it to turn. A moment later, she heard a click behind the wall that held the mirror. The ceiling light turned off. She pulled her arms against the cuffs, waving her hands to bring back the light. It stayed off. While her eyes adjusted to the darkness, she heard the doorknob jiggle, and the door slowly opened. Hailey said, "Who is it?" and bucked in another futile attempt to free herself. The chains on her cuffs clanked against the side of the bed. After a few moments, the door slowly closed again without a click. The night sky brought in enough light for Hailey to see a figure's silhouette standing before rushing toward her. Hailey screamed as a hand clapped over her mouth. She turned her head back and forth, trying to dislodge it, but it held on tight as a voice close to her ear said, "Shhhh."

Hailey calmed down, taking heavy breaths through her nose as the hand loosened. "Gage, please don't. Please!" she said.

The hand tightened again, and a voice whispered, "I'm not him. I won't hurt you." Hailey's eyes adjusted to the darkness more, and she recognized a thin woman standing beside her.

"Please help me!" Hailey said. "Free my hands!"

"Shhh!" the woman said and then whispered, "You must be quiet." She knelt beside Hailey's bed and took her hand.

"Please tell me what's happening," Hailey said.

The woman interlocked her fingers with Hailey's and said, "Listen carefully. We don't have much time. The cabin is wired to record video and audio, day and night. He watches every move you make."

"Then how did you—"

"Shhh! Please." The woman gently put her fingers to Hailey's lips. "I cut the electricity to this room, and I can only leave it off for a few minutes, or he will know."

"We've got to get out of here. Unlock my wrists," Hailey said.

The woman quietly laughed. "I wish it was that easy. He's more prepared than you can imagine."

"But who are you?" Hailey asked, her eyes wide as she tried to gather any details of the woman's face.

The woman jumped to her feet. She cocked her head and covered Hailey's mouth, listening for something. Hailey only heard the dogs barking.

The woman said, "Oh, my God. He's back early."

"I don't hear anything. Please don't leave me!" Hailey said, squeezing the woman's hand.

"The dogs—their bark is different when it's him. I promise I'll be back," the woman said. She ran to the door. Hailey craned her neck and saw the woman's silhouette on her hands and knees, opening the door slowly.

"Please tell me who you are!" Hailey said.

Before the woman crawled out, she paused and said, "I'm you."

Twenty-One

NEWS OF HAILEY'S disappearance had reached the media and was now the lead news story on local radio and television. At the Turlock Heights Estates guard gate, Howard was on duty, listening to the latest reports on the radio, when a blue Chevy Impala slowed to a stop at the gate.

The driver, a chubby man wearing round glasses, rolled down the window and said, "I'm here to visit Mason Barger."

Howard picked up the phone and said, "Gonna have to get Mr. Barger's permission. Name, please."

The man showed Howard a badge and said, "Police business."

"Private community, sir," Howard said. "Can't let you in without permission unless you have a warrant. Homeowners' association rules."

The man handed Howard a document and said, "Your HOA needs to update its facts."

Howard took the paper and saw California Code of Civil Procedure Section 415.21 printed on it, stating that any person shall be granted access to a gated community for a reasonable period of time to perform lawful service of process upon identification by displaying a badge.

"I'm a detective and need to speak with Mr. Barger. You might want to keep this in mind, too." He handed Howard another document containing California Penal Code 148(a), which defined the penalties for obstructing an officer.

Howard opened the gate. In his rearview mirror, the detective saw Howard put the phone to his ear.

When he arrived at the house, Mason stood on his porch by the front door.

The detective walked up the sidewalk carrying a large envelope and said, "Good evening. Are you Mr. Barger?"

"Yes."

"I'm Detective Loren Woods, assigned to your wife's case. Can we talk for a few minutes?"

Mason opened the front door for the detective to enter. They went to the living room and sat on facing sofas. Detective Woods said, "You know we're on a missing-person case involving your wife. I'm sure you understand why we need to ask some questions."

"Sure. Whatever you need," Mason said.

The detective placed the envelope on the table between them and said, "First of all, I have to commend you for filing a missing person's report so promptly."

"I'm not the one who filed it," Mason said.

The corners of the detective's mouth turned down. "You aren't?"

"No, that was her assistant, Peyton."

"So when exactly did you learn your wife was missing?"

"I called for her at her office, and her assistant told me."

"When was the last time you saw your wife?"

"Yesterday morning."

"Everything okay between you two? Any arguments?"

"We're fine." Mason's expression tightened.

"I apologize. I didn't mean to upset you."

"I'm not upset," Mason said. He swallowed and wrung his hands.

"Of course not. Was your wife at home last night?"

"I don't believe so."

"So you aren't sure if she was here last night?"

"I usually don't see her at night. That's when I work."

"So, you were at work last night, Mr. Barger?"

Mason hesitated. "No, I took the night off."

"So you were out searching for your wife?"

"No, well, sort of," Mason said. He crossed and uncrossed his legs, tapping the arm of the sofa with his fingertips. "I made some calls. Called her office. Called some friends."

"That's a start. Her assistant, Peyton, showed us a stack of flyers he printed out on her photocopy machine. When we talked to him, he said he planned to post them outside her building and on the doors of any business in her work neighborhood that would let him. Have you done anything … similar?"

"No, not yet."

The detective shook his head slightly and jotted something on a pad.

"Why are you shaking your head?" Mason asked.

"No reason, sir. We're almost finished. Have you talked to any neighbors here about her disappearance?" Detective Woods pointed his pen to the windows on either side of the room.

"No."

"Hmph," the detective said, nodding.

"What's that grunt supposed to mean?" Mason asked. "I found out about her disappearance late."

"Oh, please don't take offense, Mr. Barger. These questions are all standard." The detective picked up the envelope and slid a black and white photo from it, placing it on the table and rotating it to Mason.

"Do you recognize this vehicle?"

The grainy image showed a silver Mustang.

"Looks like my car."

"Right. It is your car—at least according to the license plate. This photo was taken in your wife's parking garage at the Handel Towers Building about an hour ago."

"So what?"

"Do you and your wife swap cars often?"

"I wouldn't say often, but it wouldn't be out of the question."

"Hmph," the detective said. "In this case, why was your wife driving your car before she disappeared?"

"What exactly are you getting at? I don't like the direction you're trying to pull me with these questions."

Detective Woods frowned and raised his hand. "Hold on, Mr. Barger. I'm not trying to pull you anywhere. I simply asked if you remember why you and your wife traded vehicles yesterday."

Mason sat back and crossed his arms. "No, I don't remember."

The detective slouched to one side, crossed his legs, and rested one arm on the sofa back. "Let me share some info that may or may not be relevant." He removed a few sheets of paper from the envelope and separated one. "According to a witness we interviewed, 'Mason jumped on the hood of the car, pounding on the windshield and was screaming at her. When he fell off, she raced away.' Does that quote from one of your neighbors trigger any recollection of trading cars with your wife, Mr. Barger?"

"Who said that?"

"That's an interesting answer to my question."

Mason's leg shook while he glared at Detective Woods.

"Mr. Barger, I'm sorry if I've upset you. It wasn't my intention. I do want to thank you for your patience as we try to bring your wife back to you safe and sound. Let's move on to something easier for you to recall… Your wife was on her way to the airport when she disappeared. Where was she flying?"

"I don't know."

"So, your wife was on her way out of town, and you have no idea where she was headed?"

"My wife travels often. She doesn't always tell me where she's going. This may seem strange to you, but it is normal for us."

"Fair enough. I'm just trying to make sense of all this. Let's move on. Can you tell me about the limousine rental?"

"What are you talking about?"

"You arranged for your wife to take a limousine to the airport for her trip, correct?"

"No, not correct. I did no such thing."

The detective produced a photocopy of a receipt from Elite Star Limos charged to Mason's credit card and signed with his signature.

"This is impossible," Mason said, examining the receipt. His signature looked authentic.

"Listen, Mr. Barger. I know this is a tough time for you," Detective Woods said. "But let's look at this from my perspective. You and your wife seem to be working through some issues in your relationship. A neighbor sees you screaming at your wife while you jump onto and off the hood of a car she's driving. Then she apparently goes unannounced to the airport in a limo you rented just before she goes missing on a day you took off from work. I'm certain you understand why I have to ask these questions, right?"

"My wife's odd behavior, her secrecy, and all this crap you are trying to tie to me have a straightforward explanation."

The detective pressed a pen to the envelope and looked at Mason, waiting to jot down the exonerating puzzle piece.

Mason stood and went to the window. "Listen, uh, detective. My wife and I have been going through a tough time recently. The truth is my wife is having an affair." Mason returned to the sofa. "She and her boyfriend have set me up. I don't believe she's really missing. They must have set me up."

"Her boyfriend? Who is that?"

"His name is Gage. I don't know anything more about him except he's the one you need to investigate, not me."

"Pardon me, Mr. Barger. That seems like a very convenient answer."

"It's not convenient. It's the truth."

The detective wrote some notes and said, "Please bear with me, Mr. Barger. We're almost finished … Do you happen to be a gun owner?"

"Yes."

"Are all your weapons registered?" the detective asked, pulling a photo from the envelope.

"Yes." Mason scooted to the edge of his seat, his hands clasped. He wanted to force the detective to leave but knew doing so would only fan suspicion.

The detective placed a photo on the table and spun it to Mason. The color image showed "Cocky" resting on what looked like the floor mat of an automobile. Blood was clearly visible on several parts of the gun. "Does this gun look familiar?"

Mason hesitated and then said, "That looks like one I owned. I don't have it anymore. It was stolen from me."

"Did you file a report?"

"No, it just happened a couple of days ago."

"So you didn't file a report?"

"Did you hear me? I said no," Mason snapped. "What does a gun have to do with my wife?"

"There was a homicide in the limousine you rented for your wife."

"I didn't rent a limousine."

Detective Woods tapped his finger on the limo receipt.

"I never signed that. It's a forgery!" Mason stood.

"Okay, take it easy, Mr. Barger," Detective Woods said, motioning for Mason to have a seat. "We'll sort that out later. I have a bigger problem." He scratched his head.

"What?" Mason asked.

"The limo driver is dead. And this gun," the detective tapped on the photo, "was discovered in the back. Your wife's blood is on it, your fingerprints are on it, and, as it turns out, the gun doesn't just look like your gun; it is registered to you."

• • •

Shortly after the mystery woman had left her room, Hailey moved her arm, and the ceiling light blinked on. She heard a distant vehicle. The engine grew louder until it stopped directly outside the cabin. Hailey shifted in her bed and sighed, trying to keep calm. Despite the padding on the cuffs, her wrists and ankles ached.

A car door slammed, followed by the cabin door opening and closing. The crack around her door lit up, and footsteps approached.

The door opened, and Gage peered in. Hailey raised her head. Gage sighed as though he had been holding his breath. "Even though I see you there, I still can't believe you're here, lover!" He flipped a switch on the wall.

The table lamp came on. He came to her side and said, "How are you feeling?"

"Like a prisoner."

"Not for long."

"Does that mean you're releasing me?"

Gage laughed. "It means soon your time with me won't be against your will. Trust me. You'll see." He drew his finger across her forehead, moving hair from her eyes. Hailey turned her head away and resisted the urge to head-butt his hand.

Gage picked up the bedpan and swirled the urine around. "Good girl. I see you've used the facilities."

Hailey swung her knee as hard as she could, landing a blow to the bottom of the bedpan. Urine splattered on Gage. He dropped the bedpan to the floor and gasped, holding his arms stiff as his spread fingers dripped. Hailey glared at him, bracing for his rage.

Gage wiped his mouth on his sleeve and said, "Ah, there's more of that fire I love." He wiped his hands and wrists on the bedspread, picked up the bedpan, and took it to the bureau, sidestepping the spill. He hummed a tune as he walked and removed a small box from his shirt pocket. He slid out a paper-sealed container the size of a pen and ripped the tip with his teeth. "Thank God you saved me a couple of teaspoons," he said, tilting the bedpan. He dipped a stick inside and shook it before setting it aside on the bureau.

He turned to Hailey and noticed her staring wide-eyed at him. "You look so afraid," he said. "Forgive me—where are my manners?" He picked up the box and brought it to her, holding it closer to her face than necessary for her to read it.

Ovulation and Fertility Test Kit (30 Stick Pack)

Gage grinned at her and said, "I bought this brand because it was the only one with a little smiley face that turns blue when you're ready to be impregnated. I knew you'd love the little smiley face considering all the cutesy things you keep on your desk at your home and work offices."

"You bastard," Hailey said. She launched a new frantic battle with her restraints, flopping and twisting on the bed. She kicked her legs and yanked her arms, clanking the chains. Gage set aside the ovulation kit and pressed her to the bed until she was still. He tried to clear her hair from her face again. She jerked her head away to avoid his touch.

He stepped back and watched her momentarily while she trembled with anger. "Relax," he said. "We're going to have the family you've always wanted, lover! And, by the way, I completely agreed with you in your last spat with Mason about this ... Your biological clock is absolutely ticking." He put his hand on her stomach and said, "We've got to get these eggs some of my wigglers, and that needs to happen sooner rather than later. In fact, you'd have plenty of kids already if Mason could have delivered the goods. Don't worry..." he tapped his finger against his zipper, "I'm not firing blanks, that's for damned sure. You'll see. How about some food?"

Hailey squeezed her eyes shut, too angry to speak.

Gage stroked the side of her face. "I brought you a dinner I know you'll enjoy. First, it looks like you've given me some cleaning to do." He left the room and returned with towels draped over his shoulder a few minutes later. He wore bright yellow rubber gloves and carried a bucket of water and a mop. He hummed and whistled while he worked. Hailey stared straight up at the ceiling. Soon, the room smelled like disinfectant, and Gage exited.

A few minutes later, he returned having changed his clothes. He carried a paper sack with a Concetta of Italy logo. "When was the last time Mason brought you your favorite dinner?" he asked. "Of course, you have no answer because he doesn't do that." Gage put the sack on the bureau, slid out a to-go tray, and brought her a serving of chicken marsala, the same dish she had ordered at the Marriott. He put his nose close to it and waved the aroma with his hand. Some mushrooms and sauce had spilled into an adjacent container compartment, drenching the mixed vegetables.

"Oh my! We've experienced some shifting during flight," he said. "I know you hate a hot entree that's gone cold, so hold on, I can make it perfect." He left the room, carefully carrying the container. Hailey heard the sounds of a drawer and utensils, then a beep followed by a microwave humming. Gage returned. The elements of her entree had been repositioned back into their respective compartments in the plastic container. A smear of sauce showed where Gage had rearranged it.

"Hungry?" he asked.

Hailey looked at the food and then turned away. "That's okay," Gage said as he closed the container. "I don't want you to go hungry, so you just call if you need food. I have plenty of your favorites." He stared at Hailey for a moment. She wouldn't look at him, turning her head toward the wall. "It's okay to be angry," Gage said. "I have been angry at fate a million times. Somehow, she always brings what's best."

Gage decided to leave her for a bit. There was plenty of time for her to come around. He went out the door, and as he pulled it closed, Hailey said, "Gage, I want to stand up. I feel so claustrophobic. Would you let me walk outside this room a little? You can leave my wrists tied." Hailey forced the anger away from her face while waiting for his answer.

"You don't suffer from claustrophobia," Gage said.

"I feel it now," Hailey replied.

Gage studied her and said, "Soon. You will get everything you want soon." He pulled a second bedpan from under the bed and placed it beside her. "I want you to try to get some more rest. All of this excitement can't be good for your hormonal balance. You'll thank me when you wake up feeling great tomorrow." He turned off the light and closed the door.

Hailey heard water running and then the clank of dishes in the next room. Then, she was surprised to hear a female speaking. She couldn't make out their words, but Gage was interacting with a woman Hailey presumed was the one who had visited her. For over an hour, the hum of their conversation continued until she heard Gage yell, "Useless bitch! Now!" followed by a slap. Something metal crashed to the floor. The sound made Hailey jump. There was a beat of silence, and then she heard Gage's voice again, quieter. The only other sound Hailey heard that night was a heavy door closing in another part of the cabin. Hailey fought sleep. Her ordeal and the residual effects of having been tranquilized had left her exhausted. She dozed off.

• • •

When Hailey woke, the curtains of her window were illuminated by morning sunlight. A steamer hissed in the kitchen, and she heard voices rise over the sound. The smell of toast and coffee seeped into her room.

She rose up onto her elbows and immediately needed the bedpan. After struggling to position it, she used it and lay back, staring at the *Welcome Home* note on the ceiling. During the hours she had spent cuffed to the bed, she realized any chance of escape required convincing Gage to trust her. He had used a remote location and restraints to keep her captive indefinitely if he chose to. Her tantrums and pleas to him had been useless and probably caused him to tighten his grip. She needed a new tactic. She decided to say whatever was necessary to disarm Gage's suspicion and put herself in a position to escape.

A knock at the door jolted her from her scheming. "Yes?" she said. In her helpless position, granting permission for entry felt absurd. The knob turned.

Gage peered in. "Good morning!" he said, smiling.

"Good morning." Hailey raised her head and forced herself to smile.

Gage pushed the door open with his shoulder and stepped in with a food tray.

"I see some sleep has improved your mood."

"It always does. What is that?" Hailey tried to see what was on the tray.

Gage placed it on her lap and tucked a couple of pillows under her torso so she was nearly sitting up.

Breakfast consisted of oatmeal sprinkled with brown sugar, topped with sliced strawberries, a sliced banana, a thick, lightly toasted slice of sourdough with canola margarine and fresh-squeezed orange juice. On the corner of the tray sat a medium half-caf, no-foam, non-fat, vanilla soy latte in a paper Hot Perks Coffee Shop cup. Hailey slowly looked at each item on the tray while Gage watched. They were all of Hailey's favorite breakfast items. In fact, this was a breakfast she enjoyed whenever she had the time. The banana was sliced first lengthwise to make smaller segments to add to her oatmeal. The similarity to the way she would have prepared it was unnerving.

Gage removed the bedpan and set it beside the door before hurrying back to her side. "Well?" he said, prodding her.

"It has all my favorites," Hailey said. "I can't remember the last time I enjoyed breakfast in bed." She forced herself to look up at him and smile again.

"You're most welcome, lover. And you can't remember the last time you were treated to breakfast in bed because Mason doesn't bring you breakfast, does he?"

Hailey resisted a rebuttal. She had issues with how Mason treated her, but given Gage's offenses, criticism of Mason annoyed her. "No, you're correct. He doesn't bring me breakfast."

"And I do. It's how I care for you. You and I are not in inner space like you and Mason were. Go ahead and taste it!" He pointed close to the toast. She picked up the spoon and scooped a bite of oatmeal, moving her head toward her shackled hand to get the bite into her mouth. It was delicious.

She bit the corner of the toast. Gage knelt beside the bed and watched her chew. "Toasted at level 6. Not too dark, yet still with plenty of crispiness," he said.

Hailey nodded and drank some orange juice while Gage watched. His eyes were full of the enthusiasm she had noticed during their first meetings at the Marriott. The enthusiasm didn't strike her as happy enthusiasm now. It was an irrational glee of insanity.

He went to the music player and turned it on. Sade's *Hang On To Your Love* played again.

"That song never gets old," Hailey said, wiping a crumb from her mouth.

Gage stopped and looked over his shoulder at her as though he hadn't heard her correctly. Hailey added, "I feel like it was written for us."

Gage stroked her forehead with the backs of his fingers, grinning. "You'll call me when you finish. Eat up, lover. We have a big day."

"Thank you again for this wonderful breakfast. I couldn't have made it better myself."

Gage picked up the bedpan and paused on the way to the door without looking back at her. "My pleasure. It is all my pleasure."

With nothing except plastic utensils, a paper plate, and a flimsy tray,

Hailey had nothing ready-made to use as a weapon or tool for escape. She knew she needed to keep up her strength if she wanted to have any hope of escape, so she finished all the food.

She heard a conversation between Gage and a woman outside her door and then a few dishes clanging, followed by the hum of a small motor. She finished her breakfast and, while trying to put the large tray off to one side, it slid off the bed and fell to the floor, crashing.

Gage burst through the door and slammed it shut behind him. "What have you done?" he asked, staring at the toppled tray. A few pieces of strawberry and some sticky chunks of oatmeal lay beside it. The alarm on his face subsided fast.

"I'm sorry," Hailey said. "But it's hard to be careful when I'm restrained."

Gage left, closing the door behind him. Moments later, he returned with a bucket and washcloth. He wore the yellow gloves and knelt beside the bed to clean up the mess.

"You know I forgive you," he said.

"I appreciate that."

Gage stood, his face red from the exertion while bent over. He took his cleaning supplies from the room and returned, holding a new pair of flex cuffs. He came to her side and said, "I have someone very special who would like to meet you."

"I would love that," Hailey said. She felt her cheek muscles tiring from her insincere smiles.

"But for your safety, I must put these on your hands only, lover."

Hailey raised her wrist as far as it would go. Gage cuffed her in front with the new cuffs and removed the restraints on her feet. It seemed Gage was going to remove her from the room. She knew nothing about the space outside her door and desperately wanted to see the cabin's layout.

Gage helped Hailey to her feet and guided her to the door, where he stopped. Before he opened it, he said, "I hope what you are about to see will cement in your mind how much I love you."

"Gage, what a beautiful thing to say," Hailey said, projecting as much sincerity as possible.

Gage rubbed his hands together, turned the doorknob, and pushed the door open, revealing a sight that stunned Hailey. The cabin's main living area was immaculate, clean to a sterile level, and had the sparse appearance of an art gallery. An open kitchen had a single spotless counter divided by a sink below a small window. The interior had none of the rustic characteristics of the exterior she had seen outside the cabin. Off to one side, a small dining room table was decorated with a small floral bouquet centerpiece on a tablecloth identical to Hailey's dining room at home.

A sofa faced a fireplace above which hung a bookcase. Off in a corner, a stool and pottery wheel sat on a plastic tarp. A table beside them was covered with newspapers, paintbrushes, some wooden tools, and a book opened to pages of colored pottery.

To her right was a wall with two doors. Gage watched Hailey carefully as she took in the scene. He seemed giddy. "Well, what do you think?" he asked. "We've placed no less than one hundred objects in this room that will make you feel at home."

"I can't believe you did this for me. You've really made it into such a lovely space," Hailey said.

Gage clapped his hands and said, "I *knew* you would think so. I just knew it! Like me, you hate clutter."

He guided Hailey to the kitchen and opened the cupboards. They were full of familiar items. The cereals, the bread, and the canned goods were all brands and flavors found in Hailey's home cupboard. Another familiar object caught her attention on the counter below. It was her toaster. The one that had gone missing from her house. She pointed to it and said, "Does that belong to me?"

"Oh, yes," Gage said. "It always has. Did you enjoy your breakfast toast? I popped it up early after only ninety seconds, just like you do."

"How do you know that?"

"All your questions will be answered soon, lover. What's important is I did know that, right?"

"I appreciate everything you have prepared for me. But since our relationship is still a tiny baby, could you hold off on calling me 'lover'?"

Gage reached up and cupped her cheek in the palm of his hand. Hailey squeezed her fists to allow his touch. "But we *are* lovers, and you are about to see the extent of my preparation for you," Gage said.

Hailey looked over her shoulder to another part of the cabin to get her cheek away from his touch.

Gage shouted, "Suri!" startling Hailey. A few feet away, a rectangular door in the wooden floor raised up, pushed open by a young woman. She locked the door open with a support stick and then climbed from darkness up the narrow steps. She stood before them wearing a green sundress. She pivoted and smiled with her arms at her sides. Hailey gaped in disbelief. The woman's hair was auburn and cut just below the shoulder, precisely to Hailey's length and style. She wore replicas of Hailey's Oakley sunglasses and Burberry Herringbone watch. She even sported Hailey's favorite shade of lipstick. The green sundress was one Hailey remembered having taken to Cancun. The woman wore the identical chain necklace and oversized locket Gage had locked onto Hailey's neck, and on her finger was Hailey's gorgeous wedding ring she hadn't seen since the night she had spent with Gage at the Marriott.

"What do we say, Suri?" Gage asked.

The woman tilted her head and said, "Hello. My name is Hailey Vaughan. I'm a business consultant."

Gage giggled and stepped to a place where he could see both women's faces. Hailey was too mesmerized by the woman to notice him move away from her.

Gage went to the woman and put his arm around her. "We've been waiting for you, lover!" he said to Hailey. He pointed to the woman and added, "I've been practicing for your arrival with this one for a long time. And now, my practice and visualization have resulted in the manifestation of the real you! An imitation meets its original for the first time!" He beamed and shook his head like a proud contractor, examining the perfect completion of a challenging project. "I have chills, and I think this occasion calls for a drink!"

The woman said, "May I serve you, lover?" Gage flicked his hand to her, and she ran to the kitchen, opened an upper cupboard, and pulled out a bottle of wine and three glasses.

"I don't care for any alcohol, thank you," Hailey said.

Gage said, "Did you hear that, Suri?"

"Yes, I heard her, lover," the woman said.

"Why did she say that?" Gage asked.

The woman put the glasses down, faced him, and said, "Hailey rarely drinks alcohol, lover. If she chooses to drink, she does so sparingly and only then on special occasions."

Gage raised his eyebrows at Hailey, coaxing her to be impressed. Hailey's eyes were locked on the woman.

"So, what drink will you make for your original?" Gage asked the woman.

She removed the sunglasses and said, "I'm preparing a medium, half-caf, no-foam, non-fat, vanilla soy latte."

The sentence brought an odd feeling to Hailey—a familiarity with the woman she couldn't pin down. The woman watched Hailey, and her eyes seemed to plead while Gage could hardly stand still with excitement. Hailey tried to cut through the woman's likeness of her, trying to gain some recognition.

"Is that the drink you prefer?" Gage asked Hailey.

The woman's face became concerned. While Gage wasn't looking at her, she mouthed, "Please..."

"Yes. That's my drink. Thank you," Hailey said, her voice trailing off to a whisper.

The woman smiled and started preparing coffee in a new coffee maker beside a milk steamer.

Recognition registered, and Hailey lost her breath for a moment. The woman was Marissa Swenker from Hot Perks Coffee Shop, who had gone missing months ago.

Hailey's face had gone flush. Gage led her to the sofa and pointed to where he wanted her to sit.

"You don't look well, lover," he said.

"I ... uh ... I'm overwhelmed by everything you have done. This is all so new to me."

"Yes, and get used to it," Gage said. He sat by her and shifted to face her. "It's new to you because *he* never cared for you like I do. In fact, I don't know if any other man has gone to the lengths for his woman I have for you."

Hailey's mind raced to make sense of Marissa's presence in the cabin. She was positive of her identity and wondered how Gage would react if he knew that.

"What is your name?" Hailey asked her.

Marissa looked at Gage, who answered for her. "For all intents and purposes, her name was Hailey Vaughan—until you arrived. There won't be a reason for the two of you to talk. If you *do* need to address her, call her Suri."

"It's nice to meet you, Suri," Hailey said.

The woman smiled. Gage said, "Shouldn't you say, 'It's nice to meet me,' Suri?" He laughed.

The women didn't.

Realizing Marissa had been held captive faded Hailey's concern for herself. Her plan to escape now had to include a rescue. There was no way she would leave Marissa behind. Marissa had promised to revisit her room, but knowing when Gage would leave the cabin was impossible. He seemed so tickled to have "his woman" and her look-alike alone that he might be content to stay there for days.

They heard the steamer, and Marissa soon brought Hailey's coffee in a ceramic mug that had an image of two hands clasped together above the inscription *Love Never Dies*. She placed the mug on a saucer on the coffee table in front of Hailey and said, "Careful, it's hot." Marissa had always said this when she slid Hailey her drink at Hot Perks.

Marissa returned to the kitchen with two glasses of equal portions of wine, handing one to Gage. They toasted one another and then lifted their glasses in a toast to Hailey. She raised her cuffed hands with the mug and said, "To the best welcome and hospitality a girl could ask for."

"Bravo!" Gage said, clapping.

Hailey took a sip and smiled. The coffee was perfect, and the fact it was once again served by Marissa made Hailey's eyes well up. She blinked back the tears.

Gage said. "Now we have something of a show for you." He scooted closer to Hailey and put his arm around her as if they were settling in to watch a romantic movie together. Gage took Hailey's coffee mug she had held with both hands and set it on the coffee table. He then took Hailey's hand, intertwining his fingers with hers. His hand had begun to sweat and felt clammy. He pressed his thigh against hers and motioned with his other hand for Marissa to begin.

She took a moment with her eyes closed, then opened them and said, "Hello, my name is Hailey Vaughan. I specialize in professional coaching and business consulting, emphasizing management development and strategic processes that maximize productivity. I have an established list of clients and can provide references if needed. I'm booked for two months. If you would like, we can schedule what I call 'client discovery,' where we meet at your office to develop a company profile to hit the ground running when my consultation begins."

Marissa had scarcely spoken the last words when Gage jumped up from the couch, clapping and cheering. "I love that part—'hit the ground running,'" he said. He looked down at Hailey while he clapped and asked, "Would you hire her? She's a hot ticket. Two-month waiting list!"

Hailey gave a slight nod, unable to peel her eyes off Marissa. Not only was Marissa physically impersonating her to a tee, but she had also recited Hailey's new-prospect pitch verbatim. "How did you learn that so well?" Hailey asked.

"I have the best teacher in the whole wide world," Marissa said, pointing to Gage. "I was born to play you. You're my ultimate role. It feels so natural, and I become more like you daily."

Gage nodded and tapped his watch. "That's enough, Suri."

"If you'll pardon me," Marissa said, "I really need to get back to my preparation for an upcoming business consultation."

"Of course," Gage said.

"It's good to finally be together," she said to Hailey.

"It sure is," Gage answered for Hailey.

Hailey's cheek muscles quivered, and she could not hide the bewilderment on her face. Marissa politely bowed and climbed down the narrow staircase from which she had emerged. Hailey watched the door swing down and lock into the floor, leaving hardly a seam.

Gage said, "We're making good progress." He leaned to Hailey's neck and sniffed her. "Are you ready for a shower, lover?"

Hailey wondered if he meant alone or with him. She raised her cuffed hands and said, "That will be difficult with these on. Can you remove them?"

"Soon. In the meantime, I'll wash you. You'll see how gentle and thorough I can be. Did Mason ever wash you?"

Hailey hesitated and then said, "No."

"And that's a shame. I would think it is a squandered honor to never wash my wife."

"Listen, Gage," Hailey said. "I was never hurt by the fact Mason didn't wash me, and I don't want to put you through the trouble."

"Oh, it's no trouble at all. I know your routine. Other than size, you will find little difference between your bathroom here and where you used to live."

"Gage, I appreciate the offer. And everything you've done for me has been incredibly generous. But I think I'd prefer to shower later, perhaps before bed like I sometimes do," Hailey said.

"It's rare for you to do that. You love your morning showers. They seem to perk you up like nothing else except your fancy coffee drink from Hot Perks." He raised his arm and put it around her. His shirt had a sweat stain, and he squeezed her shoulder into his armpit. She smelled the spicy scent of his deodorant that failed to mask his odor. "I'll give you a couple of options. You tell me which appeals most to you, lover. Number one," Gage held up a finger. "We wait until tonight when we can shower together in the en suite of our private quarters." He motioned toward one of the doors. "Or, number two, we give you a little scrub-a-dub now in the guest bathroom so a shower tonight won't be needed, and we can get right to… you know, business. Now, which option does my lady prefer?"

Hailey thought carefully. The first option potentially delayed time alone with him until evening, but the shared shower was inevitable in that case. As she considered option two, Gage said, "Tough choice?"

Hailey said, "I think I'll take the second option. A few minutes to freshen up right now would be good. Mason loves it when I surprise him after I'm clean."

Gage pulled his arm from her shoulder and shouted in her face, "Mason is over! He was *not* for you. You do *not* do things for him anymore!"

"I'm sorry," Hailey said, her eyes wide.

"I am, too," Gage said as he calmed. He folded his hands. "I'm just sick and tired of you playing pretend wife with him when what we have is real. I had hoped to have seen more progress from you by now."

"May I ask what progress?" Hailey asked. Figuring out Gage's bizarre expectations was proving to be more of a challenge than she expected.

Gage's eyes narrowed. "You may not understand this, but I don't want to force you to do anything. I can feel your desire for me growing like the pre-eruption rumblings of a volcano, ready to burst forth at any moment. I know beyond the shadow of any doubt it will happen. Fate only needed the opportunity to play out as it should. Fate is smiling because I've given her the opportunity she's been waiting for. Even so, I sense something isn't right with you yet."

"I feel like our relationship is growing," Hailey said. "Sometimes fate needs just a little more time."

"I thought my intricate, uncompromising preparations," Gage swept his finger around the cabin, "would have helped you see what you mean to me. Your life with me won't compare to your existence with Mason. This should have become more obvious to you by now."

Hailey reached out and took his hand. "I am so amazed and thrilled by what you've done," she said. She looked around the place, nodding and smiling.

Gage watched her silently and said, "It's a good thing I'm so patient, lover. A less patient man would have pushed fate harder, forcing the inevitable to happen sooner. Do you realize how patient I've been with you?"

"Oh, yes. And, believe me, I appreciate it," Hailey said, looking into his eyes for emphasis.

"I don't think you realize how much restraint I've exercised with you."

"Yes, I do," Hailey argued.

"I don't think you realize how much preparation and sweat I've put into our future."

"Yes, I do! I really do," Hailey said louder. "Thank you."

"It's been harder work than you can imagine. It just seems by now, fate would show mercy—I mean, I've eaten all my vegetables, so you'd think I could enjoy some fucking dessert!"

Hailey looked down at her hands and froze, not wanting to further provoke him.

Gage's face had reddened again, and he took a big breath, exhaling upward. "I could have rescued you from him and brought you here so many times. I could have rescued you beside the road at the scene of your accident. Believe me, I was tempted. I could have rescued you from the dark parking lot after our first meeting at the Marriott. That was tempting, too. I could have rescued you the night you willingly came to my hotel room and laid yourself before me. That was such a delicious sample—the first night of thousands we'll spend side-by-side, holding one another in bed. I could have rescued you from the house you share with the man who believes he's your husband. That would have been easiest. Instead, I postponed your rescue. I let you sleep. I waited. I've paid a debt to patience, and patience owes me—soon."

"Thank you for waiting," Hailey said. "I'm so sorry if I've disappointed you," she said. "I certainly don't want to do that. In fact, now that you've explained my good fortune and all you've done for me, I'm feeling closer to you." Hailey raised her cuffed hand, placed it on Gage's knee, and rubbed it, cringing inside.

"It's a nice try, lover," Gage said. He flicked her hand away and cracked his knuckles. The sound sent a shiver through Hailey.

"I beg your pardon?"

He moved and sat on the coffee table to face her. He looked into her eyes. "You and I are both aware of the game you're trying to pull on me, aren't we?"

"Oh no, I'm not playing games!" Hailey stammered. "You are opening my eyes and teaching me there have been feelings between us for much longer than I've realized."

Gage pinched the tip of his pinky in her face and said, "I'm this close to believing you." One corner of his mouth went up, making a crooked smile. "This close."

"Gage, I can't believe how stubborn I've been. Thank God you stuck with me until I could see the obvious! You have made me aware of things Mason didn't do."

Gage clapped his hands over his ears and shouted, "Stop it!"

Hailey jumped.

"I think you're pretending," he said.

"Of course not!" Hailey laughed as though it were absurd. "Gage, I'm trying, I'm really trying to learn what you are teaching me, and I feel like it is coming to me. Please forgive me if I seem a bit awkward at first. I'll grow into our relationship quickly."

Gage patted her on the cheek. "For the sake of our future, I hope so. Fight fate and you'll fail. Follow fate, and it's fine. Remember that."

Hailey nodded. "I will."

"Up you go," Gage said. He took Hailey's arm and helped her to her feet.

"To the guest bathroom?" she asked.

"No. We're going to your bedroom."

• • •

Mason knew he had scared Hailey. Even after their most heated arguments, her absence for over a day without so much as a phone call was unusual. Clearly, she no longer trusted him and had chosen to run off with her new man.

After he met with the detective, Mason called Howard, the guard, and asked him for a ride to Wenshire Harbor. Howard was off-duty and, with minimal prodding by Mason, agreed to do the favor—hoping it would either ensure or enhance a Christmas bonus. He drove Mason to the parking garage at Hailey's office. As Peyton had promised, building security returned his phone and the keys to his Mustang. The phone battery was drained, and Hailey must have taken the charger because it was missing from the car.

After he thanked Howard with a couple of twenty-dollar bills, he drove home. When he arrived at the house, he had again worked himself into a frenzy. He slammed the front door as he entered the house and went straight to the garage. Hailey's car was still there. "You back yet?" he yelled down the hall. *Of course, she isn't back.*

He plugged his phone into a charger in the den and then went to Hailey's study. He rifled through her desk drawers, flinging papers to the floor as he searched for any information about Gage and any document she might have signed as Mason Barger. It had to be Hailey who had forged his name for the limo because how could Gage possibly know his signature? Hailey sure as hell wasn't a victim of foul play.

After fifteen useless minutes searching through Hailey's office, he took a break and leaned against the door frame. The only reason to doubt Hailey was framing him was that the detective claimed to have found her blood and Cocky in the limo. Hailey hated needles so much she avoided shots. She also hated the sight of blood, nearly fainting when Mason had accidentally sliced his thumb in the kitchen a few months ago. However, at this point, if Hailey's infatuation with Gage exceeded her fear of Mason, who knows what she would be willing to do? And she was the only person in the universe with whom he had shared Cocky's secret location. Was it coincidental that one day after telling her this secret, Cocky disappeared? In the smash and grab of his car, the only thing grabbed had been Cocky.

Mason left Hailey's study and walked to the kitchen. As he passed the den, he heard his revived phone chiming as it retrieved the messages he had missed while it was off.

It rang when he reached for it.

The caller ID showed Benny Mullins, a coworker from Club Parlay. Mason and Hailey occasionally hung out with Benny and his wife.

"Hello."

"Hey, Mason, is everything okay with you and Hailey?"

"Why?"

"I just saw the email. I'm sorry, man. I'll delete it right away."

"What email? I haven't had my phone."

"Man, you better go take a look. Hailey might have pocket-sent a message she didn't mean to."

"Thanks. I will," Mason said. He hung up and scrolled his email messages and saw multiple messages forwarded to him with the same subject:

FW: If you cooked at home, I wouldn't eat out.

As Mason read through the emails from family and friends, most expressed the same confusion.

"Why did you send this? Is that you?"

"Is this how you're moonlighting? LOL!"

"Was this an accident? Call me."

"I think Hailey's email got hacked."

Mason found the original message sent from Hailey at the bottom of the list. It had a paper clip indicating attachments. He opened the message and saw several color photos. The first showed Hailey naked, lying on a bed facing away, her hummingbird tattoo clearly visible. Behind her, a naked man cropped at the shoulders stood over her and gave a thumbs-up sign beside his erection.

The home phone rang. Mason didn't acknowledge it, completely fixated on what he was seeing. He scrolled to the next photo that showed the same man lying on top of Hailey with her legs wrapped around him.

Hailey's face was obscured. Mason took a deep breath as his chest thumped from a rage-fueled surge of adrenaline.

His phone vibrated. A caller ID box appeared over the photo. *E. Vaughan,* Hailey's dad. Mason sent it to voicemail and scrolled to the last photo—one that almost made his legs collapse. It featured Gage wearing Mason's baby-blue honeymoon bathrobe opened in the front, his hand showing an A-OK sign.

The only text in the email was an auto-signature below the last image.

Sent from my phone. Please forgive my typos.

He scrolled back up to the top of the message, where something else caught his eye. The *To* and *cc* fields were full of email addresses.

He fell back onto the sofa and tossed the phone down beside him. Until now, he had not seen actual evidence Hailey had cheated. After all the years of irrational jealousy, absolute proof of Hailey's infidelity hurt far more than his suspicion ever had. He stood and grabbed his hair as he circled the den, consciously breathing to slow the fuse that had been lit in him.

The house phone rang again. He went to it and saw *E. Vaughan* there, too. He unplugged it from the wall and headed upstairs.

Hailey's attempt to hide the affair was pathetic, and rubbing it in his face was a new low for her. How could she think she could get away with taunting him this way? *She ought to have known better.*

In the master bedroom, he pulled out his laptop from under the side of the bed and opened his email program. His temples flared while he fought to control his emotions. He opened Hailey's damning email message and printed a copy of each photo. Then he flung back the comforter and sheet on Hailey's side of the bed and spread the photos out there. He went to the garage and returned to the bedroom carrying a Beretta 92FS with a silencer. He stood over the bed and fired fifteen rounds into the photos, obliterating the images of Hailey's body and Gage's genitals. He placed the empty gun on one of the photos and carefully made the bed again, concealing the Beretta's lump as well as possible.

He returned to the garage, grabbed a crowbar, and smashed out the driver's window in Hailey's Lexus. The alarm sounded. Mason didn't care. He popped open the trunk and threw Hailey's gym bag and some paperwork to the ground.

He stormed back into the house and kicked the kitchen island cabinet as he passed by. He went to Hailey's study and dragged the crowbar's hook along her shelves of head vases that wrapped the room. The vases that didn't break on impact shattered when they crashed to the floor. He smashed her computer monitor, toppled her chair, and shoved all the paperwork off her desk. He returned to their master bathroom, swept all the items in her medicine cabinet, and threw them to the sink and floor.

For the next hour, Mason went through each room of their house, destroying every material thing Hailey valued. When he finished, he went to the garage and returned with a black Remington tactical shotgun. He rested it on his shoulder while circling the kitchen island and then carried it throughout the house, imagining walking in on Hailey and Gage as he entered each room.

Eventually, he went to the foyer and leaned the gun against the wall by the door. He looked outside. The evening had settled in, and the street light out front had flickered on. He went out to his car, drove it a block away, and parked around the corner. He walked back to the house and locked himself inside. He turned off the kitchen lights and returned to the living room with his shotgun. He sat in the recliner nearest the front door and turned off the table lamp beside it. The house was dark and quiet.

Hailey had not only made one of his worst nightmares come true, but she had also rubbed it in his face and publicized it to everyone they knew. He didn't know when she would return, only that she would. No wait was too long. He sat in the quiet darkness, holding the 12-gauge ready for when Hailey showed—preferably with her lover.

Twenty-Two

AS GAGE LED Hailey by the hand toward her room, he said, "Lunch will be served at noon, your favorite time to have it." She noticed a floor mat outside the door that said, *Welcome!* Gage held the door while she entered, and then he followed her inside, locking them in with a keyed deadbolt. Gage had not used the deadbolt on her door before. He slid the key into his pocket. Hailey's heart pounded.

Hailey expected Gage to make her lay on the bed so he could cuff her to it. Instead, he removed the cuffs. Her hands were free. She instinctively stepped away from him.

"I want you to note the trust I'm putting in you," he said. The absurdity of the statement almost brought out a sarcastic laugh from Hailey she stifled. She rubbed her wrists and said, "Thank you." She sat on the bed and folded her hands, trying to appear contented.

"Oh, you're welcome, lover. Your trust in me will only grow. You'll see." He went to each side of the bed and removed the connecting cuffs attached to the bed frame. He looped them around his hand, and then, to Hailey's relief, he unlocked the door's deadbolt. Before he exited, he rested his hand on the knob and gazed back at her. Hailey felt like she was an exotic new car he had just purchased, and he couldn't resist peeking into the garage whenever he remembered he owned it.

"Today, you've shown me some true progress, even if some of it was for show," he said. "You gotta love progress."

Hailey smiled back and covered her heart with her hand. "I do."

"And I love it when you say, 'I do'!" Gage said. His smile grew. "You rest for a while, and I'll have a surprise for lunch. You'll love it. I know it!" He pulled the door closed. She heard the key slide in and the deadbolt lock.

For the first time, Hailey walked freely around the room. She parted the window curtains, and her heart sank when she saw white decorative iron bars mounted to it. The bars couldn't be there to keep people out.

She searched the bureau drawers and found many pieces of her old clothing. She went through her overnight bag containing her toothbrush, deodorant, and other items that had gone missing after Cancun. Other than those items, the room was bare and empty of tools that could be useful in breaking out.

The faint sound of her voice came through the speakers again. She went to the music player and tried to turn it off. It would not stop playing. The *Stop* button didn't work. She put her pillow over it to stop the chanting of her synthesized affection for Gage.

She spent the rest of the morning memorizing every square inch of the room. The door was a heavy, solid fire door, so trying to kick or otherwise ram it open was futile. She pressed her face to the floor to look under the door crack. The welcome mat blocked the narrow field of view.

She saw a row of trees a short distance from the window. They were thick enough to block her view of anything beyond them and marked the edge of a narrow, clear-cut space around the side and rear of the cabin. The view was gorgeous and ruined by the iron bars. When she pressed her cheek to the window, she saw a narrow slice of blue sky above.

The ceiling was drywall supported by the solid wood beam that transected it. Hailey stood on her bed, pressing it in several places. It had no soft spots, not even a ventilation duct. She searched for the cameras and couldn't find anything that resembled one. Every crack in her room was sealed so tightly an insect couldn't breach the caulked floorboard.

A few minutes before noon, she heard a commotion outside her door. Water was running in the kitchen with the sounds of chopping and Gage and Marissa talking. Soon, the aroma of sautéed vegetables and steak crept under her door. She heard the key slide into the deadbolt and quickly sat on the bed. Gage entered carrying a lunch tray. Vegetables, steak, and rice with a side of Caesar salad and crusty bread. A mineral water bottle and a couple of chocolate mints completed the tray. It was one of Hailey's favorite meals she often prepared for Mason.

"Bon appétit, lover. Knock when you are finished," Gage said. As he went for the door, he stopped and returned to the opposite side of the bed. He removed the pillow from the music player, tucked it back on the bed without saying a word, and left.

Anxiety had zapped Hailey's appetite. She knew she needed to eat to maintain her strength, so she forced down most of the food. The steak was seared to a perfect medium, and the salad was crisp and chilled. Gage had provided delicious fuel she intended to use against him when the time was right. Knowing the Townsend River would take her back to town, she focused on how to get there. This time, she was prepared for Gage to hunt her. After finishing the food, she put her tray by the door and used the bedpan. She placed it by her empty food tray and knocked on the door. Gage opened it with the key and said, "Can I get you seconds, lover?"

"No, thank you," Hailey said.

"How are you feeling?" he asked.

"Thank you for the delicious food. I want to walk outside. May I?"

Gage smiled and said, "Soon. I want you to rest and consider everything I've arranged for your happiness so far."

"Okay, I can wait," Hailey answered with a smile.

Gage pulled the door closed, and the deadbolt locked.

Hailey rested face up on her bed. She examined the ceiling and walls of the room, wondering if Gage himself had constructed it with no seams or cracks.

A sound caught her attention. Faint at first, it was a woman's voice—Marissa's voice. It sounded like a moan and grew louder. The sound was rhythmic, with moans punctuated by a thump after each. Soon, she heard words with the moaning. Hailey went to the door and pressed her ear to it. She heard:

"Give it, baby! Give it, baby! Give it, baby!"

A chill shot through her.

She heard Gage say, "Louder!"

Marissa obeyed, yelling, "Almost, baby... almost, baby... almost, baby! Yes! Yes! Yes!"

Hailey stood frozen. She listened more closely. She heard Marissa yell, "That's how you like it ... That's how you like it ... That's how you like it ... Take it, baby—take it *all*."

Gage's voice rose, joining Marissa's, saying, "Oh, Hailey ... Oh, Hailey ... Yes, lover ... Yes, Hailey!"

Hailey ran to the bedpan and fell to her knees, gagging, but only a string of saliva stretched from her mouth. She spit and panted, waiting for the nausea to pass.

After twenty minutes of hearing Marissa pretending to be her and precisely calling out the intimate phrases Hailey shared with Mason, the cabin fell silent. Hailey went to the corner of the room and slid down to the floor. She wondered what more Gage could possibly take from her.

• • •

Marissa laid face-up, looking at the crack of light that lined the only way out of her makeshift dungeon Gage referred to as "below."

She swept her hand along the wall, found the short bead chain, and pulled it. A tiny light bulb illuminated the narrow, rectangular space where she spent most of her time when not tending to Gage's whims.

All four wood-plank walls were backed by solid earth. The room seemed like an afterthought. Given the secrecy of the door that rose into the living room, Marissa wondered if Gage intended the space to be his hiding place.

She turned her head, listening to Gage plodding around the bedroom's hardwood floor where she had given him her best sexual performance of Hailey in bed. Gage's footsteps moved to the floor of his master bathroom. She knew he'd be in the shower for at least ten minutes.

She turned the light bulb off. She had grown fond of darkness and become adept at working in it. It had become her only source of privacy after the introduction of the camera Gage had mounted.

She felt for and lifted a towel that served as a carpet, pulling a bent butter knife from under it. She felt along the wall and used the knife to pry out a wooden plank. She reached into a space she had hollowed out in the dirt behind it and pulled out a plastic grocery bag. After untying its top, she dumped several items onto her lap. The first was a penlight Gage had dropped while working on mounting a corner camera in her virtual prison cell a month earlier. She thought he had intentionally dropped the penlight to test her, so she had left it untouched on the towel for over a week.

Days later, Gage emptied a toolbox on the kitchen table in search of something. She had heard him mumble, "Where is that penlight?" before retrieving a more powerful baton flashlight from under the sink. The penlight became hers.

The other two items were a syringe vial and a tranquilizer dart. She picked up the towel from the floor and moved to the corner under the camera. While doing her cleaning chores in the cabin, she passed by and looked over Gage's shoulder at the camera feed on his laptop. She had discovered the camera mounted in her space didn't record the area directly below its lens. That's where she now squatted, draping the towel over her head to seal in any light the camera might catch. She turned on the penlight and rotated the vial to read the label.

Ketamine Hydrochloride Injection, USP 500mg/5mL For Slow Intravenous or Intramuscular Use. Store at controlled room temperature.

Though the rubber seal had been punctured, the vial was still two-thirds full. Marissa didn't know what ketamine was, but she, unfortunately, knew what it did. Two weeks ago, Gage had ordered her to change into shorts and a new pair of running shoes he gave her. He pulled a hummingbird feeder from a bag and ordered her to take it to the edge of the lawn and hang it on a branch he had marked with a ribbon.

The bizarre request had terrified Marissa, and she cried, begging him not to let the dogs out of their cages. Gage slapped her and then pushed her out onto the porch before slamming the door. Marissa slowly approached the tree, hesitating several times, keeping an eye on the dog pens halfway down the hill by the driveway. Looking over her shoulder, she saw Gage watching her from the open kitchen window. He had motioned for her to continue, shouting, "Don't mind me. Get it hung."

Marissa knew there must be more to the odd chore than there seemed. The only place Gage had ever allowed her to walk outside was to and from the locked dog pens with dog food. He had set her up for a dog mauling or some other sick game. For a moment, she had thought he was daring her to escape. She wasn't about to take that bait, knowing the beating that failure would guarantee.

When she raised the feeder to hook it onto the branch, she heard the pop an instant before she felt the stinging impact on her bare thigh. She shrieked, dropped the feeder, and fell. A rifle barrel disappeared from between the iron bars of the kitchen window. She pulled a dart syringe from her leg. A few drops of clear liquid oozed from the needle, and the syringe chamber was almost empty. Marissa had stood and stumbled, fleeing for cover amongst the trees. The last thing she remembered about that afternoon was running, falling, and seeing the blurry image of Gage standing over her while the forest spun around her. She had awakened on her back in her under-floor space feeling sore. She remembered becoming nauseated when the light coming through the cracks of her door spun.

Gage said nothing of the incident, and Marissa knew better than to mention it. She had since watched him fill darts and practice loading them into his air rifle. One night, he darted an opossum on the lawn through the same window he had used to shoot her. He draped the critter on the porch and sat in a rocker with a glass of wine, waiting for it to wake, but it never did. Marissa performed her usual chores the next day, keeping the cabin spotless while Gage worked on his laptop. She noticed the spent opossum dart and vial in the waste bin.

That night, while Gage was in town, Marissa took her biggest risk yet. She had learned how to circumvent the camera-triggering motion detectors Gage had placed all over the cabin. If she moved slowly enough, the lights wouldn't come on, and the cameras wouldn't record. She had practiced slow crawling in her space for hours and was ready to test it. She slowly pushed up the door to her space, taking a full minute to open it wide enough to fit through. She inched across the floor to the trash, where she fished out the syringe and vial. On the way back across the floor, her heart pounded, knowing if she heard Gage's car, she'd need to hurry and risk activating the cameras. She inched back down into her space without a light turning on.

Now Marissa examined every detail of the syringe and vial. The dart was designed to inject its payload using impact and a steel ball. She wished she could inject Gage with the tranquilizer, but injection using the dart needle was impossible without a finger plunger. Gage never had his guns in sight unless one was in his hand, and he never allowed her to see him put the dart gun away.

Marissa had been cleaning the cabin when Gage first brought Hailey in. Marissa knew exactly what Gage had done when she saw him carry Hailey's limp body into the room. She'd cried herself to sleep that night and prayed Hailey would wake up.

Marissa heard Gage's footsteps above. She turned off the penlight, shoved the items back into the bag, and tucked it in the wall hole. She then quietly sealed it with the wooden plank.

Gage's footsteps got louder and stopped over her door. "Going out. Stay below. No talking. I'm listening."

"Yes, lover. Drive safely, lover," Marissa said.

Gage's footsteps went away. Marissa heard the front door open and close. Gage's Blazer started, and after the engine revved a couple of times, she heard him drive away.

For nearly two hours, she waited in silence for night to fall before she gently pushed the door in the floor open enough to peer out at the living room floor. When the door had lifted enough to get through, Marissa climbed out, moving as slowly as possible.

She heard pounding on Hailey's door when she got her torso out onto the living room floor.

"Is anybody there? Gage? … Please let me out … Hello?"

Marissa continued her slow creep across the floor like a caterpillar. She had to get to the circuit breaker as quickly and as slowly as possible, ignoring Hailey's pleas and pounding.

• • •

Hailey, too, had heard Gage's car leave. She couldn't see the driveway despite putting her cheek against the window. She moved back to the door and knocked. The cabin was silent. "Hello?" she yelled, pounding on the door. She put her ear to it and listened. Nothing.

She pressed her lips to the door's crack and said, "Is anybody there? Gage?" There was no answer. If Gage was home, he would have answered. He would have rushed to her. Maybe Marissa was out there. Hailey wanted to call out her name, but if Gage was somehow listening or watching her, she didn't want him to know she had recognized Marissa.

"Please talk to me! I know you're out there!" she hollered. She heard a thump, and then the cabin fell silent again. Hailey returned to her bed after a final bout of pounding on the door.

It had become dark outside. Hailey turned on the table lamp by the door. The cabin had been completely quiet for hours. The only sound was Hailey's faint voice under the pillow she had returned to the speakers.

I'm happy to be yours, Gage. Our bond is unbreakable, Gage. I love you, Gage.

She paced beside her bed and considered whether she could dismantle it and use part of the frame as a battering ram to break the door. She knew the odds of her being able to chop through or break the door alone were slim. If Gage returned while she was trying to do so, he'd lock her down tighter and probably resume using the flex cuffs. She went to the window to examine the bars for what seemed like the hundredth time when she heard a voice whisper something.

"Hello?" Hailey asked.

When there was no answer, Hailey went to the door. She heard a tap at the bottom of the door. She knelt and heard a faint whisper. She pressed her cheek to the floor. It was dark outside her door. The voice said, "Whisper. You have to whisper."

"Okay."

"Ms. Vaughan, go to your bed. Lie face-up. Keep still and wait for the lights to turn off."

"But we need to talk."

"We will. Please do what I say. We don't have much time."

Hailey obeyed, lying face up on the bed. She looked up at the ceiling, and the light blinked off sooner than it should have. Her eyes had just begun to adjust to the darkness when she heard a key slide into the deadbolt. The door opened with an eerie slowness that scared Hailey, even though she knew who was opening it. She remained still.

Looking past her feet, she saw Marissa's silhouette crawl into the room. The main room of the cabin was completely dark. Marissa gently closed the door behind her, holding the knob firmly to keep it quiet.

Safely inside, Marissa stood and ran to Hailey, who sat upright on the bed. She grabbed her in the desperate embrace of a long-lost family member. While they hugged, Marissa's upper body shook, and she sobbed into Hailey's shoulder.

"Shhh! It's okay," Hailey said, stroking her hair. "We're going to get out of here."

"My name is Marissa Swenker. I used to serve you coffee at Hot Perks Coffee Shop."

"I know exactly who you are," Hailey said. "I recognized you earlier today." She took Marissa's shoulders and said, "Sweetheart, the whole world is looking for you."

Marissa hugged Hailey again and whispered, "I'm sorry, Ms.

Vaughan. I'm so sorry this has happened to you."

Hailey cupped the back of Marissa's head and pulled it tight to her. "I can't believe you're concerned about me. You have endured so much more than I have. Take it easy. We'll be okay."

Marissa touched Hailey's lips and whispered, "Be quieter."

"Okay," Hailey whispered.

"I cut the power to this room again, so we may not have long to talk. If he tries to view your camera and can't while he's away, he'll freak out and rush back here. The dogs know his car. If they bark happy barks, I'll have to crawl out of here as fast as possible."

"Why do you crawl?" Hailey asked.

"The cabin is rigged with motion sensors. If I don't move slowly enough, lights come on, and cameras record. He'll get an alert on his phone and check the camera feed."

"Unbelievable," Hailey said.

"Believe it. I've triggered the cameras before. He punished me when he got home if he didn't like what he saw me doing."

"Punished?"

Marissa hiked her skirt to one side, took Hailey's hand, and drew her fingers across her thigh. Hailey felt the rough patches of scarred skin and gasped. "My God... We're getting out of here. We're going home," she said, trying to stand.

Marissa pulled her arm and said, "No."

"Why not?"

"You have no idea how prepared he is. Running away is what he expects."

"But we can't stay here. We *have* to get out."

"The moment we leave the cabin, he'll know and see every move we make."

"How?"

Marissa drew her hand along Hailey's neck until she found the necklace chain and slid her fingers down to the oversized heart-shaped locket. She pulled it a few inches from Hailey's chest and let it fall back. "That," she said. "It's not a keepsake. It's a GPS tracker. You probably saw I'm wearing an identical one."

"So that's how he did it," Hailey said.

"You ran, didn't you?"

"As far as I could."

"I heard the shouting when you got away. He came back winded and took one of his guns."

"What guns? Where are they," Hailey asked, squeezing Marissa's hand.

"I don't know. They're locked somewhere in his room. I've never been able to find the place. This whole cabin is a puzzle."

"Have you tried to get away?" Hailey asked.

"Yes, but he used GPS to track me just like he tracked you."

"Marissa, we need a plan. We *have* to get out. What is his weakness? He must have a weakness we can use against him. How do we disable the cameras? And what tools do we have?"

"Hold on, I'll tell you what I know."

"I'm sorry." Hailey gently squeezed Marissa's hand.

"His biggest weakness is *you*. The only time he doesn't seem smart is when he's talking about you. He stops making any sense."

"If I am a big enough distraction, he'll lower his guard, right? It's how we'll get out of here. I'm already making him think his plan is working. If I convince him I've fallen in love, he might drop his guard so we can—"

"No!" Marissa blurted. She covered her own mouth.

"What? What is it?"

"Please don't. He's already told me the day you make love to him is the day I become useless. He began digging a trough beside the cabin. He said it was for me."

"Listen to me," Hailey said. "That will not happen. I'm not going to make love to him."

"He believes you will. He thinks soon you'll want to. He talks about it all the time. He's been practicing for you."

Hailey didn't respond. She looked away.

"You heard it, didn't you?" Marissa said.

Hailey nodded.

"If I tell you how much he knows about you, you won't believe me."

Hailey said, "I already know he bugged my office, he's been tracking my car, and he's been in my house…"

"There's so much more," Marissa said. "He tries to control you in every way. Remember how I'm the voice of Trace Ramsey's assistant? You were never on your way to Hawaii. One way or another, he was going to get you here."

The information took Hailey's breath away.

Marissa continued, "He knows *everything* you do. He has microphones in your car, and he attached another tracking thingy in the seam of your purse so he can know every place you visit. He can see into your office with binoculars from the street, and he can listen to you at the same time. I've seen him looking at his video recordings of you. He plays your voice constantly. He takes the recordings and makes you say things you've never said to him." Marissa's whisper became quieter, and she said, "I'm so sorry." She cried.

Hailey held her and said, "It's not your fault, sweetheart." She wiped Marissa's face and said, "If he wants me, then why is he doing this to you?"

Marissa sniffled. "You rejected him. When he couldn't have you, he made me his 'surrogate.' That's why he calls me 'Suri.' I'm practice."

Hailey cupped her hands over Marissa's cheeks and turned her face to hers. "We are going to get out of here."

"I wish that was true. He is so prepared."

"Stop doubting it. We will escape."

"I can't run like you, and he knows it."

"I don't care if I have to carry you on my back."

"If we make it off the property while he's gone, we will die."

"How?"

"The dogs. They'll kill us."

"That's not true. They didn't kill me when I ran."

"The dog cage door is automatic. He puts it on manual when he's here and keeps a remote control in his pocket. When he goes away, the cages open automatically with laser sensors he put around the edge of the lawn. The dogs are huge, much bigger than you and me, and they're so mean. I think even he's afraid of them. He uses a whistle to send them to their cages. I've never seen him pet them. When the cage opens, they know there's something to chase. Sometimes, I hear the cages spring open and awful sounds at night. The next morning, dead animals like opossums or coyotes are on the lawn. And he feeds the dogs just enough to keep them hungry. He whipped me for putting too much food in their tins. I saw..." Marissa stopped.

"What is it?" Hailey said.

"I saw them kill someone."

"My God," Hailey said.

"Yes. There was another woman. I thought he had finally caught you. He brought her in here, and she lasted only a day. She pretended she was still cuffed after she freed her wrists and ankles. The first time Gage opened the cabin's front door, she ran for it. I was in the kitchen. He must have opened the cages with the remote when she got halfway across the lawn. The woman tried to climb a tree at the edge of the lawn. She wasn't fast enough. The dogs jumped and pulled her down. I couldn't watch it, but I heard it. It was awful."

As Hailey listened, a horrifying thought struck her. "Marissa, what did the woman look like?" she asked.

"I knew she wasn't you because she was a brunette, a little heavy, and wore glasses."

Before Marissa finished her description, Hailey blurted, "Oh my God, no!"

Marissa put her finger to Hailey's lips to shush her. Hailey buried her face in the pillow and wept.

Marissa stroked her back and waited. When Hailey sat up, Marissa whispered, "You knew her?"

Hailey could only nod, tears streaming down her face. They held one another until Hailey was ready to speak again.

"She was my best friend," Hailey came up sobbing.

Marissa wiped Hailey's tears and then felt for the bedside stand. She opened a drawer and pulled out a box of tissue. "I'm so sorry," Marissa said. "I shouldn't have told you."

"Thank you," Hailey said, wiping her nose. "Absolutely nothing about this is your fault. He will pay."

Twenty-Three

THE NEXT MORNING Hailey woke to the aroma of a hot breakfast. She knocked on her door. Within moments, Gage opened it.

"Good morning, lover," he said. Hailey looked over his shoulder and saw Marissa working in the kitchen.

"Hello," Hailey answered. Gage cupped his hand to his ear and raised his eyebrows.

"lover," Hailey added with no conviction. Every fiber in her being rebelled against speaking to the murderer of her best friend. Playing along with his pet names was even more difficult. At this point, everything she did would be toward an end.

"Ahh. Sounds so sweet," Gage said, grinning. "Ready for some breakfast?"

Hailey nodded and said, "Thank you."

"And still so polite. Come with me." He led her by the hand to the table set formally for two people. Gage pulled a chair for her.

She sat.

The breakfast spread featured eggs, bacon, toast, oatmeal, a sliced fruit platter, and fresh-squeezed orange juice. Steam came from a medium Hot Perks paper cup. The initials TG were on the side of the cup. Hailey wished it actually meant to-go.

"How often did Mason prepare breakfast like this for you?"

"I have to say I can't remember," Hailey replied.

Gage looked at Marissa and said, "What type of coffee do we have today?"

"A medium, half-caf, no-foam, non-fat, vanilla soy latte, lover."

"I've never had a drink called a lover," Gage said, laughing and elbowing Hailey.

She smiled and said, "I have to thank you, lover."

"Oh?" Gage said as he scooped a generous helping of scrambled eggs onto her plate from a large bowl.

"Obviously, I've had a lot of time to think about everything. I have come to realize that as ironic as it might sound, I've experienced a type of freedom here I didn't enjoy before."

Gage put the bowl of eggs down and rubbed his hands together, eager for Hailey to explain more.

"With Mason, I was on such a tight leash," she said. Marissa shot Hailey a concerned look from the far end of the kitchen while Gage's attention was on the food.

"And don't I know it!" Gage said. "That pathological jealousy of his made you suffer so. I cringed every time I heard him raking you over the coals based on his own insecurities. How many times did he accuse you of shagging Robert at your office because you were late getting home? Ten? Twenty? So unfair." Gage served himself some eggs.

"Right," Hailey said, pulling a couple of bacon strips from the plate Gage held for her. She hadn't expected Gage to respond with such detail. She remembered Marissa's revelation about how completely Gage had recorded her life.

"Just out of curiosity, how did you come to know about that?" Hailey asked.

He bit into an apple and laughed. "That's the beautiful thing about our relationship! Lovers look after and protect one another no matter what it takes. I've been watching over you since long before you ever knew it. I've been determined to make sure our destiny is preserved!"

"I can't believe you looked out for me that way."

Gage grinned and slowly stood, coming around the table to her. He leaned in for a kiss. Hailey squeezed her fists under the table and puckered. Their lips met, and Gage sucked, exaggerating the sound of the kiss.

Marissa dropped a spoon, sending it clanging into the sink.

Gage spun to Marissa and yelled, "Dammit, Suri, you ruin a perfect moment?" He walked toward her.

"I'm so sorry, lover," Marissa said.

"Thank you!" Hailey said. Gage stopped. "Thank you for that perfect moment. I feel so taken care of."

"I do take care of you, don't I?" Gage came back.

"Of course you do, and it's sad it took so long for me to realize it."

Gage sat and folded his hands on the table. "You've grown to see who Mason really was, haven't you?"

Hailey nodded. "Being with you has taught me more about him."

"Do you see how self-destructive maintaining your relationship with Mason was?" Marissa got a towel and went to work scrubbing the kitchen counter in vigorous circles.

Hailey said, "Sometimes we don't see how damaging a relationship can be while we're stuck in it."

"Exactly!" Gage said. "You need the right person to come along and show you what you've been missing. Only then can you understand your relationship was shitty and you should kill it."

"Would Ms. Vaughan like more coffee?" Marissa said.

"No, thank you, M—" Hailey stopped short of saying Marissa's name. Gage stopped chewing, looked at each of them, and then resumed with a swig of orange juice. "No more interruptions, Suri."

"Yes, lover," Marissa replied.

"Like I was saying, sometimes you need a point of comparison, and I've told you that from the first time we met. A temporary surrogate can be eye-opening. Did Mason lift you up onto a pedestal the way I do?"

"No, he never treated me like you do. I can say that for certain."

"Damn right he didn't. You compromised your standards by being with him. You were not a proper match. How do you feel when you think of Mason at this moment?"

Hailey paused to put care into her answer. "I think all relationships could use improvement because—"

"NO!" Gage shouted, pounding his fist on the table. "That's bullshit! Some relationships need to be shot in the head, and I'm sick of tiptoeing around the truth—*our* truth."

Hailey's face went pale, and her eyes widened. "I'm sorry!" she said. "I meant some relationships shouldn't have existed…because they are completely destructive…and hurtful."

"Whose relationship is wrong?"

"Mine…"

Gage stopped chewing and leaned closer.

"With Mason," Hailey added.

The contortion drained from Gage's face, and he loosened his collar with his finger. "I'm sorry I startled you," he said as he dabbed the corners of his mouth with a napkin. "I just needed to hear you tell me the truth and it's taken so long I had begun to think you were deceiving me by telling me things you thought I wanted to hear."

The fear hadn't left Hailey's face when she said, "I can't believe you went through all that trouble for me. I feel closer to you than I ever have."

Gage took a big bite of toast and with a full mouth, said, "Are you ready to sleep with me?"

Behind him, Marissa stopped placing dishes into the cabinet and shot Hailey a warning look, mouthing, "No… Please…"

"Sleep?" Hailey asked.

Gage smiled and laughed through his nose. "Yes, there will be sleep involved at some point."

"Almost. I'm slowly getting more comfortable. I need just a little more time."

Gage looked at her for a long time and then said, "I was going to wait until your feelings came around a bit more. Now I'm sensing this might be a good time for us to take the next step in our relationship."

Hailey adjusted herself in her chair and folded her hands to keep them from shaking.

Gage got up and opened a cabinet over the stove and pulled out a fire extinguisher. He walked over to the front door and set it down on the floor.

He then came back to Hailey and extending his hand, said, "Come with me, lover."

"Gage, I really don't—"

"Come!" Gage barked.

Hailey took his hand, and he led her into the main room. He sat in the middle of the sofa giving Hailey no option except to sit right beside him.

"Suri!" Gage yelled. Marissa came running from the kitchen and stood by the sofa. "Sit," he said. She obeyed, sitting on his opposite side. From under the coffee table, he pulled out a laptop, opened and booted it. He logged on with a swipe of his finger on the fingerprint reader. The screen divided into quadrants, each quarter showing a different video feed. Gage pointed to one of them. "Who knows what that is?"

Hailey took a moment to study what appeared to be a live video feed of grass and a tree with a barrel beside it.

Marissa raised her hand.

"Go ahead, Suri," Gage said, like a schoolteacher.

"It's our front yard, lover."

"That's right." He tapped Hailey on the knee and pointed to the kitchen window. "Go look and see."

Hailey got up and went to the window. The leaves rustled on the trees as a breeze went through it. The mid-morning sun made it look so peaceful, Hailey wished she could go to it—and then run and run and run as far from this place as her legs would take her. Beside the tree, a brown barrel was sealed with a lid.

"Come back, lover," Gage said.

Hailey returned to her seat. Gage tapped his finger on the video feed showing the tree and barrel. On the screen below it was a green button. Gage maneuvered the mouse to the button and said, "Who wants to click it?"

When neither woman answered, he raised his hand high above the keyboard, his index finger pointed down. "One, two, three…" He pressed the return key. There was an enormous explosion outside that shook the cabin. Hailey jumped, and Marissa shrieked, covering her head.

Gage laughed. After a few moments, they heard the pinging sound of shrapnel hitting the cabin's roof. Gage went to the kitchen window and said, "My God, I underestimated the power."

He went to the front door, grabbed the extinguisher, and ran outside where he sprayed the remains of the barrel and the charred grass near it. He came back in and went to the kitchen. "Whoa! Looks like we need a new window," he pointed to a diagonal crack in the glass.

Hailey stole a look at Marissa, who stared at Gage with a disturbed expression.

Gage returned to his seat between them. He folded his hands and turned to Hailey. "You know, your pretend husband, Mason wants to kill you. Did you know that?"

"No," Hailey said softly.

"Oh, yes," Gage said, nodding. "He had plans for you. From what I could see, your next visit home would have been your last."

"What do you mean?" Hailey said, sniffling.

"Let me show you," Gage said. He clicked a few times on the laptop and brought up a clip showing Mason circling the kitchen island that was full of guns. The shotgun rested on his shoulder. His face looked full of contempt, and when he left the kitchen, the clip ended.

Hailey said, "How did you get this?" Her voice was angry, and Marissa sent her a warning look.

"I told you I look after you. There's more." Gage opened another clip that showed Mason sitting in the living room chair by the front door with the shotgun draped across his legs. When Mason turned off the light, the clip went to infrared video, giving Mason a more eerie, ghostly appearance. "He was waiting for you, oh, yes he was. If I hadn't rescued you—well let's just say the gun training he was planning to give you would have put you on the wrong side of the barrel."

Hailey felt the muscles in her face quivering as she fought to suppress her anger. She calmly said, "Then I suppose that is why it's so great you've rescued me from him."

Gage leaned to Marissa and thumbed toward Hailey. "Look at this one. Is it any wonder God wanted her for me?"

Marissa tried to smile. Gage sat back, and after a long pause, he said, "You are telling me all the right things, but your words aren't hitting me like they ought to. I can smell your dishonesty lover. We have to clean up that stench before our relationship can be what it ought to be."

"What do you mean?" Hailey asked. "I'm being honest with you."

"Did you mean it when you said Mason is harmful to you and he's never treated you the way I do?"

"Yes."

"Was your relationship with him destructive?"

"Yes."

"Are you better off without him?" Gage held up a finger. "Answer truthfully."

Hailey paused and then said, "Yes."

"It is good you recognize I've rescued you. It is good you recognize Mason's harm to your life. You're going to take care of your problem right now, lover."

Gage clicked on the laptop, changing the video. Hailey saw four new feeds of her home, labeled living room, kitchen, den, and master bedroom. Gage used his mouse to enlarge the view of kitchen feed. It showed Mason leaning against their island countertop, reading a paper. The guns were still there beside a cereal box and a half-cut cantaloupe.

"Doesn't look very concerned about you, does he?" Gage asked.

Hailey bit her lip and blinked back tears.

"Don't worry. We're going to fix everything right now," Gage said. He turned the laptop toward Hailey and said, "If you mean what you say, click on the green button."

"No, don't! It's a bomb!" Marissa blurted.

Gage slapped her with the back of his hand. She crumpled on the sofa, clutching her cheek.

Hailey grabbed Gage's arm and said, "Please don't hurt her. That doesn't make me want you."

Gage smiled and said, "That was the most honest thing you've said today." He stood and went to the middle of the floor and raised the door to Marissa's space. "Get below, Suri," he said. Marissa climbed down, and he slammed the door closed and then stomped his foot. He returned to the sofa and said, "Have you pressed the button yet?"

"No."

"He is not going to change, Hailey. He suffers from pathologic jealousy. So if you are truly as finished with him as you claim to be, then end him. On the other hand, if you still have feelings for him, then the most merciful act is to put him out of his misery."

"I can't," Hailey said. "This isn't going to solve anything, Gage."

He stood over her, his fists tightened. They were level with her face, and she closed her eyes, waiting for the blow. Instead she heard Gage press a key on the laptop. "No!" she cried. Nothing had happened on the screen. Gage looked confused. He turned the laptop toward him and clicked the mouse. Nothing.

"Dammit. The damned computer's frozen." He clicked the mouse repeatedly while glaring at the screen. Hailey stayed quiet, hoping he'd calm down as much as possible before drawing any of his attention.

He forced the video program to close, opened it, and tried again. The program froze again. He clicked through the video program's settings, trying to find the problem.

After ten minutes, he pounded the coffee table with enough force to make the laptop hop. "A trip. I've got to make a fucking trip," he said. He closed the laptop, stood, and looked at Hailey. The tension on his face faded into a smile. "But first, let's get you cleaned up."

"Pardon?" Hailey said.

"A shower. It's time we cleaned you up. You can't perform well if you don't feel clean. I've heard you say that to Mason, so I know it's true." He pointed to the bathroom door and reached down to take Hailey's hand.

"I don't need a shower yet," Hailey said. She pulled her hand away.

Gage took her arm again.

Hailey pulled against him. "Really, Gage, I'm okay. I don't want a shower."

"Come," Gage snapped.

Hailey's heart pounded as Gage pulled her across the floor into the bathroom. He went in with her and closed the door behind them. Hailey saw a small window the size of a briefcase on the far wall. It had bars on the outside. "Give me some privacy, please," she said.

"Undress, lover," Gage said, smiling.

"Gage, please don't," Hailey said. "Of all people, you know how I get when I'm tense." She stepped closer to him and touched one of his shirt buttons. "Can you just let me have a few minutes of privacy so I can clean up for you?"

A slow smile spread on Gage's face. "I like how you put that cute little 'for you' at the end. It makes it seem like you have some sort of surprise for me."

"As a matter of fact, I do," Hailey replied. The flirting sickened her, even though it distracted Gage nicely.

Gage caressed her cheek with the back of his fingers. Hailey forced herself to accept his touch.

"I like it," he said. He slid the shower door open and turned on the water, adjusting its temperature for her. "I know you like your showers hot." He shook the water off his hand and dried it on a towel by the sink. "You better hurry up, then. You've got me all excited." He rested his hand on the doorknob and then looked back at her. He smiled, his lips pressed tightly together while he shook his head in amazement at her. "I'll get the room ready."

As he pulled the door closed, Hailey said, "Wait! I have a request. Would you take off the necklace for a few minutes? As you know, I always take my necklaces off before I shower."

"That's a fair request," Gage said. "But the answer is no. The locket represents our bond, and our bond will never be broken. The locket should never leave your body, lover. Just as your wedding ring shouldn't have." He winked at her and exited, pulling the door closed behind him.

Hailey went to the door and checked the knob for a lock. It had none. She unbuttoned the blouse she had worn since she had left her office and took off her jeans, keeping her eyes on the door.

Before she removed her bra and panties, she pulled the door to make sure the latch had clicked. She placed her jeans with each pant leg opened on the floor outside the shower so she could quickly step into them and laid her blouse opened, too.

Gage had stocked the shower with her favorite shampoo and beauty bar in the soap tray. The opportunity to clean up should have refreshed her. She was too tense to enjoy it. She sprayed water into the locket, soaking it, hoping it would ruin whatever electronic tracking Gage had inserted. While she washed, she tried to think of an acceptable surprise to fulfill her promise to Gage. Steam filled the bathroom quickly, adding a welcome opaque layer of fog on the door. As Hailey scrubbed, she heard the bathroom door open, and she let out a short gasp.

"Don't worry, lover, it's just me," Gage said.

Hailey backed against the shower wall, crossed her arms over her breasts. "No peeking, now!"

"I promise. But you must know you'll only get me hotter with those little teases," Gage replied. "I brought you some fresh clothes. They're in the bag on the sink. Be sure you put on everything you find in the bag. You're going to love your outfit."

"Thank you," Hailey said. She saw Gage's outline through the fogged shower door. He bent down and scooped her old clothing before leaving.

• • •

After closing Hailey into the bathroom, Gage put her old clothes into a plastic bag and went back to the sofa. He sat and rebooted his laptop. He clicked the mouse a few times and shook his leg, willing the video program to launch quicker. One by one, the four quadrants of video feed popped onto the screen showing Hailey's house. He saw that Mason no longer stood by the stove. He had moved to a barstool where he read a newspaper. Gage preferred that Mason stand by the stove because that area would carry the main force of the explosion. Regardless, there was little chance anything within thirty feet of the island would be identifiable.

He watched Mason answer the phone. Gage was tempted to pull the audio feed to hear the conversation and then decided against it. At this point, Mason's words were of no consequence. Gage had placed himself in a satisfying position to assist fate's will. If it wasn't meant to be, he wouldn't succeed.

• • •

Mason dumped the cantaloupe rind in the garbage and tucked the cereal box back on the shelf in the pantry. As he returned to his newspaper, the phone rang. He was sick and tired of fielding the phone calls of curious and concerned friends who had received copies of Hailey's amateur porn with Gage. He had let the majority of them go to voicemail, which had reached capacity and no longer recorded new messages. This call was from a number he didn't recognize.

"Hello."

"Mr. Barger, this is Detective Woods. I have some more questions for you."

"I don't have anything else to say to you." Mason turned the newspaper page on the table in front of him.

"I certainly can't force you to talk to me, but I think cooperation would be in your best interest."

"Oh?" Before Mason could say another word, the explosion annihilated the kitchen, den and living room, blasting out all the windows of the home's lower floor.

"Mr. Barger? Mr. Barger?" After a crackle and then silence, Detective Woods pulled the handset from his ear, frowned at it and then hung up.

• • •

"Dammit!" Gage screamed. He had clicked the *Detonate* button on the laptop's screen while the cursor was an hourglass. When the laptop's processor caught up, the click registered and the bomb detonated.

The video feeds of Hailey and Mason's kitchen, and living room were black with a *No Signal* message. Gage saw smoke swirling to fill the master bedroom until that screen, too, went black.

He stood, put his hands on his hips, and looked down at the screen. From all appearances, the bomb had worked nicely. Finally Hailey's distraction had been eliminated. She was now better off. Soon she'd realize that.

He closed the laptop and went to his room to change into something special for her—something more comfortable. He had fantasized about wearing it a thousand times. Hailey would love it.

• • •

Hailey turned off the shower and, without drying herself, wrapped her body with a towel as tightly as possible. She slid the shower door open and saw the large, brown paper bag Gage had left for her beside the sink. She wondered if he had heard the running shower stop, so she listened for him. It was quiet.

She opened the bag and was horrified to find it only contained a bra and panties. She held up the bra to examine it. A 32C demi-bra, it matched those in her collection at home. The other item was a pair of pink panties with lace trim. When she unfolded them, she saw they were crotchless. She wadded them up and threw them back into the bag.

Gage knocked on the door. "Are you dressed, lover?"

"No, wait," Hailey said, pressing the door closed. "Gage I need more to wear than this. You're going to ruin the surprise."

Gage laughed a little and then laughed harder. "It's a joke, lover. Where's your sense of humor?"

Gage opened the door. Hailey shouted, "Wait!"

"Now, now, now," Gage replied. He handed another bag through the open door and then peeked around the edge. "Wow, you might set fire to that towel. You look hot!"

Hailey took the bag from him and closed the door against his push.

"Five minutes, lover," Gage said. "That's all you should need."

Hailey pulled a nightgown and real panties from the bag. All objects and surfaces had Gage's signature cleanliness. He had left only a soap tray, a flimsy toilet brush, hand towels and a bottle of mouthwash.

She opened the cabinet under the sink that held some perfectly folded and color-coordinated wash rags, towels, and toilet paper. The medicine cabinet over the sink had two more beauty bars on a lone shelf. Beside them, she saw something that sent shivers through her. Six ovulation and fertility test kits and six sealed pregnancy test kits. She closed the medicine cabinet when she heard footsteps approaching. The sharp knock on the door startled her even though she expected it. The door opened before she could answer it.

Hailey froze, her mouth hung open. Gage opened his arms and pivoted in a full circle to display his outfit. He wore Mason's blue terrycloth bathrobe, frayed at the bottom and the arms too short.

"Are you squeaky clean, lover?" he asked.

Hailey only stared at the robe, seeking some understanding as to how this could be happening.

"There's something I can't wait to show you," Gage asked. He pulled her toward her room.

Hailey resisted. Gage looked back at her and said, "Don't fight it. You won't be sorry."

At the door, Gage hooked his arm in hers. Before he pushed the door open, he said, "I'm so excited."

The door swung open. The walls of her room were purple, lit by filtered spotlights Gage had placed at the base of each wall.

Sade's, *Hang On To Your Love* was playing louder than ever. On the center of the bed sat a small plate of six cubes of baklava. On her pillow was a greeting card. In large red letters on its center was the word, *lover*.

"Come, lover," Gage said. He pulled her inside, grinning.

When Hailey stepped inside, Gage closed the door and locked the deadbolt with a key that had already been inserted into it. He pulled the key out and dropped it into his bathrobe pocket.

She saw a silver tray on the bureau. A lace doily centered on it held a tube of lubricant jelly. She took a deep breath and exhaled, fighting off panic.

"You sound excited. I can hear you breathing," Gage said as he tried to embrace her.

Hailey pushed him away. "Gage, can we... I mean, would it be okay to leave the door open? I've just been in here so much... and I just... my claustrophobia."

"I'll open it soon. First, we have some business to attend to." He sat on the bed and patted his hand on it for her to sit. His face had become stern. Hailey sat on the bed as far from him as possible. He took the card from the pillow and scooted closer. "Read your card."

Hailey opened it.

To Hailey, the true love of my life,

Today we come together as one to satisfy fate with our love. Unified in love, our love is deep and true. Our love never ends. Thank you for finally accepting my love.

I love you, lover.

Your fiancé.

Hailey looked up after she read the word fiancé.

Gage pulled his fist from behind his back and opened it, revealing her wedding ring. "Yes, we're finally going to be married." He took her hand and slipped the ring onto her finger. "Mason is gone, and he won't hurt you anymore."

"What do you mean?" Hailey said, pushing away from him on the bed.

"I mean the person you knew as your husband won't bother us anymore."

"Did you…"

"No, I didn't kill him."

"Then why are you saying these things about his not bothering us?"

"Because he's gone. He caused his own death. I'm sorry to be the one to tell you that."

"No! That's not true, he wouldn't. Where is my husband?"

"I'm right here."

"No!" Hailey jumped to her feet. Gage grabbed her arm and forced her back down to the bed. She fell to her back.

Hailey was finished trying to finesse Gage. She could no longer play along. She jumped to her feet and rushed him, leaping with the whole force of her body at him. He caught her and fell back into the door and then to the floor, pulling Hailey with him. Hailey swung her fists and kicked, trying to stop him—to destroy the monster. Gage's robe came untied. He was naked under it. Hailey screamed and tried to kick him in the groin. He flipped her face down and pulled her hands behind her back.

He mounted her and while he panted, said, "You're tricky, Wifey, yes, you are. You had me going there. I thought we had Mason out of your system." He pulled a pair of flex cuffs from his robe pocket and bound her wrists. "I didn't think I'd need these anymore, but all of a sudden you became so terribly naughty. That's not what fate wants."

Hailey sobbed, her cheek pressed to the floor.

"It's not your fault," Gage said. "You simply need more time to learn fighting fate is useless." He rose up onto his knees, still straddling her. "I'm going to stand up. I'll leave your ankles untied if you can be a good wifey and not do something that would set our relationship back."

"I promise," Hailey said.

"Atta girl," Gage said. He took hold of her upper arms and raised her to her feet. "I want you to lie down," he said. He guided her to the bed and Hailey lay down and then curled up into the fetal position.

"Please!" Hailey said. "Please, open the door. I feel too closed in."

"A Hailey who would attack me is a Hailey who would run, and that would seriously damage our relationship." He went to the bureau and picked up the lubricant jelly. He uncapped it and squeezed some onto his finger.

Hailey sat up on the bed. "Gage, what are you doing? No, no, don't!"

Gage came to her and forced her down onto the bed. Hailey drew her legs up and then kicked, landing the blow to his groin she had attempted earlier. Gage fell to the floor, clutching his crotch. Hailey jumped from the bed, her hands still cuffed behind her, and ran to the door and pounded on it screaming, "Marissa! Help! Do something—it's time!" Gage lunged toward her and swept his arm to grab her ankle. Hailey kicked his hand away and beat the door harder, begging Marissa for help.

A grin spread on Gage's face as he pushed himself up to stand. "She can't help you. It's time, Hailey."

Hailey tried to run around him. Gage caught her arm and dragged her to the bed. He threw her onto her back, this time careful to avoid her feet. He clapped his hand over her mouth to stop her screams, and she felt the slippery fingers of this other hand trying to part her legs. He shoved one of his legs between hers and then the other to separate her knees. With her hands bound, Hailey couldn't stop him. He was too strong. As he tore her panties, an enormous crash came from the main room.

Gage froze with Hailey pinned and trembling under him. A look of disbelief spread on his face. He stood and slowly walked to the door, his head cocked to one side, listening. He felt inside his pocket for the key. It was missing. He looked all around him on the floor. He came back to the bed and bent over to look beside and under it.

Hailey kept her eyes focused straight up on the ceiling, not making a move. Gage stared at her for a moment and then came back to her and took hold of her hip. He rolled her over and pried open one of her fists, removing the key from it. "That would have been a problem," he said.

He unlocked the deadbolt and leaned outside the room before he stepped out and pulled the door closed behind him. Hailey heard the lock turn, followed by Gage's heavy footsteps that faded to another part of the cabin.

A few moments later, she heard Marissa cry out as Gage whipped her with a belt, cursing her between blows. Hailey got up and ran to the door. She kicked it and beat it with her knee, screaming for Gage to stop. He ignored her. The beating lasted for two minutes until Marissa's screams had become hoarse. Hailey put her back against the door and slid to the floor.

Twenty minutes later, Hailey's eyes were red from crying. She heard a key slide into her deadbolt and scooted to the side. Gage came in. He did not smile or greet her. He grabbed her under her arms and lifted her to her feet. Gripping her wrist cuffs firmly with one hand, he guided her out of the room with the other resting on her shoulder. They walked to the middle of the main room where Marissa lay on the floor, bound hand and foot. Marissa wore shorts. The backs of her thighs were red with welts. She sniffled a few times, not looking at Hailey. Gage's laptop was on the coffee table beside her. Its screen was shattered, and the keyboard was dislodged and crooked.

"On your knees," Gage said. His voice had a tone Hailey had never heard. She complied and lay down beside Marissa. Gage bound Hailey's ankles to match Marissa's and then checked the tightness of the ties on both women.

He tinkered with the laptop for a few minutes while the women lay silently. When he couldn't get it to start, he slammed the lid shut, picked up the laptop and hurled it into the trash.

After staring at the women for a moment, he squatted by them and said, "Not a word." He went into his bedroom.

Hailey whispered, "Are you okay?"

Marissa moved her head to face the floor and whispered, "He's listening."

After a few minutes, Gage came out wearing overalls and boots that clomped on the wooden floor. "I know every move you make," he said, and then went out the front door closing it behind him.

They heard shoveling outside. Slow, steady digs, sometimes accompanied by grunts.

"You stopped him, didn't you?" Hailey asked. Marissa didn't answer. Hailey added, "Thank you," and then sobbed into the floor.

Marissa shifted her legs to touch Hailey's and whispered, "I told you I'm useless after he has sex with you. He's finishing the grave."

Hailey said, "That will not happen, Marissa. We have to make a move now."

The shoveling had stopped. The front door flew open, startling them. Gage leaned in. His face was sweaty, and he wiped it on his sleeve. He said, "Good. Not a damned word out of either of you." He closed the door. Moments later, the shoveling resumed.

"I'm not going to lay here helpless," Hailey said. "We have to do something."

"Keep your voice down," Marissa whispered. "I'm afraid. He's angrier than I've ever seen him."

Hailey rolled to her side and pulled her knees up. She rolled onto them and sat up. In one fluid move, she was on her feet.

"What are you doing?" Marissa said. "Stop! Get down. He'll see you."

Hailey wondered if some alarm would send Gage running into the cabin. The shoveling continued outside. She hopped as quietly as possible to the kitchen and used her mouth to pull a steak knife from a knife block.

She hopped back to Marissa and dropped the knife on the floor. She sat and scooted to it, picking it up behind her. She pulled her hands to one side. "Raise your wrists as far as you can."

She sawed the flex cuffs that bound Marissa's wrists, freeing them. Marissa took the knife and quickly severed both their ankle cuffs and Hailey's wrist cuffs.

Hailey ran to the front door. It had a double key deadbolt like her bedroom's lock. Marissa grabbed keys from the coffee table and ran to her. "He left his keys," she said. Hailey stepped aside, and Marissa quickly isolated the deadbolt key from the rest.

The women held their breath while Marissa slid it into the lock. The deadbolt turned and clicked into place. They froze until they heard the shoveling continue.

"Marissa, we need weapons. Are you sure you don't know where his guns are?"

"He never shows me. He always makes me go below before he takes them out or puts them away."

"If he is able to break-in, we're going to have to run for it."

A new fear-filled Marissa's face. "He'll catch me. I can't run like you. I won't have a chance. I'm so sorry."

"Don't apologize, sweetheart. Listen to me. We're both getting out of here one way or another. Look! His car key is here." Hailey peeled the Chevy key away from the others.

"It won't start the car. He told me it has a hidden kill switch. He said I could save myself a beating by not trying and failing to steal it. If we make it to the car and it won't start, he'll have us."

Hailey thought for a moment and then said, "We need weapons. We have to be able to defend ourselves. Go look in his room for the guns. And please bring me some clothes. I'll keep watch. Hurry!"

Marissa went to Gage's bedroom door and hesitated before willfully breaking Gage's rule by entering without permission.

Hailey stayed by the door, listening to the shoveling and expecting it to stop at any time. She wasn't sure what she would do when Gage came back.

Marissa stayed in Gage's room for what seemed too long to Hailey. When she reappeared, she walked slower and carried a laundry bag and Hailey's running shoes. She had changed into jeans and a t-shirt. Something about her looked different.

"What happened in there?" Hailey asked.

"I found my things. He had them in a box." She tugged on her shirt and raised her wrist to show a bracelet. "This is what I was wearing when he took me."

"And you'll be wearing them when you escape, too," Hailey said.

Marissa thought for a moment and then said, "You need to go get us help by yourself." Her voice was calm, and all panic had vanished from her face.

"What's gotten into you?" Hailey asked.

"I've decided I will only slow you down if I try to run with you. You need to go alone. I will be fine. Don't worry about me. He won't kill me as long as he doesn't have you."

"Don't be absurd!" Hailey said. "I'm not going to leave you here with that monster."

"If you don't go, we will both die. If you do go, you will live. Then you can send help, and maybe we'll both live. These are your clothes. Your running shoes, too."

Marissa held the bag open while Hailey pawed through its contents. She recognized more of her own clothes. She looked for her mobile phone. It wasn't in the bag.

Hailey stopped when she saw Marissa wipe a tear. Hailey hugged her and said, "I don't want to leave you here."

"Please don't argue with me," Marissa replied. "I'm not wrong about this."

Hailey rushed to put on a t-shirt, jeans, and her running shoes. Marissa walked to the kitchen and stood far enough from the window to see outside without being seen by Gage. "He's in that trench at the edge of the lawn. He's digging. It's a grave. It's *my* grave—unless you go." She went to a table lamp in the main room, lifted it and removed a folded piece of paper from its hollowed-out base and unfolded as she went to Hailey. "We're twenty-two miles east of Wenshire Harbor. He printed this from his laptop a few weeks ago. I got it from the trash while he was away."

"Yes, I know. I ran the river the first time and had the town in view when he tranquilized me," Hailey said. She tugged on her necklace and said, "I have to get this off, or he'll track me again."

"Not without that," Marissa said, pointing to the broken laptop.

"But his phone…" Hailey said.

"Oh, my God," Marissa said. She ran to the coffee table and picked up Gage's phone. "It looks like he won't be able to track you at all."

"Call! Call! Call!" Hailey said.

Marissa had already pressed buttons to turn on the phone and then turned the screen toward Hailey. It showed a prompt for a security code. "I don't know the code," Marissa said.

"Hit *Emergency Call*," Hailey said.

"I did! There's no signal. I think his phone connected through his laptop."

The doorknob jiggled, stopped, and then jiggled again. They heard three firm knocks and then Gage's voice scream, "Open this fucking door, *NOW!*"

Hailey shrieked. Marissa dropped Gage's phone and hid behind Hailey. Gage pounded and kicked the door. He shouted, "Open the door, or I'll break it, and then, you."

"The door is solid," Marissa said. "He told me a horse couldn't kick it down."

"Let's hope not," Hailey said. She looked through the peephole. Gage's disheveled hair made him look as insane as his behavior. He tapped the door with the shovel handle and then stepped back and took a full swing, landing the shovel's blade in its center. Hailey and Marissa felt the impact through the floor.

"Hailey? Hailey?" Gage called. They heard the panic in his voice. "Why are you doing this, lover? If you deny fate, then fate will make you sorry."

"I have your gun. Don't make me shoot," Hailey said.

Gage exaggerated a laugh. "You wouldn't know which end to hold. Enough with the games. It's time to open the door, lover."

Hailey didn't answer. Marissa had watched the exchange wide-eyed.

Gage took another swing with the shovel. The handle cracked sending the blade skipping off the porch.

Hailey checked the peephole again. "I can't see him anymore," Hailey said.

"Where did he go?" Marissa asked.

"I don't know."

Marissa ran to the kitchen window in time to see Gage disappear around the corner of the cabin. "He's going to the back," she said.

"What's there?" Hailey asked.

"A tool shed. I don't know what's inside it. Also, his bedroom window."

"Can he get in through it?"

"It's barred like the rest."

"Help me barricade the door," Hailey said.

They slid the furniture across the floor pushing the sofa against the front door and then stacked books, table chairs, and every other heavy object they could find against it. They heard Gage's footsteps again.

The women had climbed onto the blockade when they heard the scream of a circular saw. The motor revved to full speed and then labored as its teeth chewed through the door, spraying sawdust all over them and the furniture. A horizontal line grew from left to right in the door as the blade devoured the wood.

Hailey grabbed Marissa's arm and shouted, "Cut the power! The electricity!"

Marissa ran to the closet, opened the circuit panel, and flipped all the breakers. The saw's motor stopped, and the blade jammed, its teeth locked in the door. The kitchen ceiling light went off and the microwave's digital time readout vanished.

Gage tugged on the saw several times, freeing the blade and then dropped the saw onto the porch.

They heard his footsteps running and then a crash of glass from the kitchen. Gage's face appeared in the broken kitchen window. The bars prevented his face from getting close to the window's opening. He shielded his eyes from the sun to peer in, but the cabin's interior was too dark. Hailey and Marissa kept still.

"Open the door, or you both die," Gage yelled. Hailey put her finger to her lips. Marissa nodded.

Gage swung a claw hammer at the window's bars. After beating them for over a minute, the bars held fast with barely a dent. He disappeared from the window. His own security had created a fortress.

They heard him shouting from the opposite side of the cabin. He repeated, "Open the door... open the door ... open the door." His voice moved. They heard another crash of glass from Hailey's room and then footsteps outside the front door again as he circled. He yelled into the kitchen window, "The longer you make me wait, the bigger your punishment, lovers." He resumed beating the bars with his hammer.

"We can't hold him off forever," Hailey said. "He'll break through the bars eventually."

"We *have* to find his guns," Marissa said. "I'll look again." She ran toward Gage's bedroom door. A moment later she came out and said, "The window isn't bright enough. I need the lights in there." She ran to the front closet and found the circuit breaker labeled *MASTER BDRM* and flipped it on.

Gage's pounding continued at the kitchen window where he had resumed work on the bars.

"I'll help you search," Hailey said. They ran to Gage's bedroom. When Hailey entered, she was unprepared for what she saw—and heard. The room was a veritable shrine to her. Every inch of the ceiling and walls were covered with photographs of Hailey. On the center of the dresser, Mason was cut out of their wedding photo, and an image of Gage taped where Mason had been. Beside the photo was a head vase identical to the one Gage had sent her.

On an adjacent wall, a bookcase contained two shelves loaded with books about business-consulting practices Gage had forced Marissa to study. A third shelf was dedicated to replicas of awards Hailey had won, going back to high school.

An armoire, also covered with photographs, had speakers on it that played Hailey's voice the way it had in her room, except louder. While Marissa pulled items out of dresser drawers, Hailey paused and listened. The audio was choppy as Gage had spliced Hailey's words into phrases of his choosing.

"Good morning, Gage … Let's have breakfast, Gage … I missed you, Gage … I will wait for you, Gage … Let's have lunch, Gage … We will be together, Gage … I'm hot, Gage … I love you, Gage… Let's have dinner, Gage… Don't leave me, Gage…"

She opened the armoire and discovered more photos taped inside. There were also clothes that belonged to her along with perfumes, lotions, and a tall stack of handouts from her corporate presentations that must have spanned over a year. She saw her old laptop and iPad that had gone missing from her office months ago. On a shelf above these items, a stereo system had stacks of CD's and USB thumb drives piled on it—so many they fell off the side onto Hailey's other items.

Marissa paused her search and looked up. "All of it is you." She pointed her finger all around the room. "I know it is shocking, but please help me look for his guns, Ms. Vaughan. He's going to get in soon."

"Wait!" Hailey said. Marissa stopped. Hailey held up her finger. "We have to do more than just keep him from getting in. We need a better plan."

Hailey insisted Marissa try to escape in the Blazer on the chance it would start with the key. When the front porch was clear, Hailey would run across the lawn, drawing Gage to follow her into the woods. Meanwhile, Marissa would try to start the Blazer. If she succeeded, Hailey could easily ditch Gage on foot and meet Marissa, who would be waiting for her in the Blazer at the Townsend River Bridge a short distance from the property. If that plan failed, and Gage had, indeed, installed a kill switch in the Blazer, then Hailey was to run along the Townsend River to town, this time without the risk of Gage being able to track her by phone or laptop. She expected the run to take about three hours. Hailey was relieved Gage had fed her well. She felt ready to run.

Twenty-Four

THEIR PLAN IN place, Hailey guzzled a bottle of water, draining it empty. She felt her pocket to make sure it contained Gage's phone. "His next pass around the cabin, I'm running," she said. "Are you sure about the dogs?"

"One of the circuit breakers is for their cage door," Marissa said. "He'd have to run down and open them manually, and trust me, he doesn't want them to get you."

Hailey rested her hand on the doorknob. She hugged Marissa and pushed her to arm's length. "If this works, we'll be free, and you'll be home tonight."

Marissa held up her crossed fingers and said, "Yes, but if it doesn't work, please don't come back. I know you'll send help."

After a brief silence, they heard a crash from the back of the house as Gage made a new attempt to break the bars of his bedroom window.

Hailey said, "Here I go." She turned the deadbolt key, opened the door, and ran outside. Marissa pulled the door shut and locked it.

Hailey had imagined her escape to be an all-out adrenaline-fueled sprint. Before she reached the middle of the yard, she was surprised by her own sense of calm. She saw a small opening in a bank of large trees and headed for it. She knew the river would be a short distance on the other side. She saw the enclosed dog pens halfway down the long driveway to her left. The dogs had already been barking from Gage's yelling and pounding, so Hailey's flight across the lawn barely changed their tone and excitement.

She ran for the row of trees that bordered the lawn. Some had low-hanging branches to which she could jump and climb if she heard the dog cages open. She darted through an opening and stopped in the shadows. Through the branches, she saw the dog cages hadn't opened. The entire cabin was in view. Its rustic log-on-log design was inconsistent with the sterile, modern décor Gage had created inside.

She walked inside the edge of the trees while she watched the cabin. She had expected Gage to chase her. Instead, he was nowhere to be seen. Was it possible he hadn't noticed her escape? If only Marissa had come with her, they might potentially have had a head start of hours before Gage realized they weren't in the cabin. It didn't matter now. Their plan, if it succeeded, would be easier, safer for Marissa, and more effective.

She held her breath and listened. The thought Gage might have found a way into the cabin from the backside worried her. That's when she saw him. He appeared from the cabin's right side and stepped onto the porch. A sledgehammer rested on his shoulder, and he carried a heavy burlap bag. When he reached the front door, he dropped the bag, fished out a wedge from it, and inserted it between logs in the cabin wall, wiggling it into place. He swung with the sledgehammer, landing a blow to the wedge. The sharp clink of steel on steel echoed across the lawn.

Hailey blew on her hands and moved back to the opening. She studied Gage to assess whether he might have found a gun because that would change everything. She figured he would have shot the lock on the door if he was armed, so she stepped through the trees onto the lawn. His back was to her. He cupped his hands over his mouth and shouted at the cabin, "You've both been so incredibly naughty." He paused for a reply, wiped his face on his arm, and wound up for another swing.

Hailey knew that, if necessary, Gage would destroy the cabin log by log to get in. She took a big breath and shouted, "Hey, lover!"

Gage broke his swing. The hammer missed the wedge, hit the cabin wall, and fell to the ground. He spun to Hailey, confused. Watching her carefully, he reached for the doorknob and jiggled it. Hailey took a few steps closer. She saw Marissa peeking out the kitchen window.

Gage descended the porch steps and then slowly walked toward her. He shook his finger at her and said, "How did you get out here, lover? You're a slippery one, aren't you?"

Hailey's heart pounded as she resisted the urge to flee. "Why have you kept the most beautiful part of our home's property hidden from me? You must have known I would love it." She pointed back into the woods.

An incredulous smile spread on Gage's face as he stepped closer.

Hailey said, "I found the perfect place for us to camp. Want to come see?" She pointed back into the clearing through which she had stepped.

"Aww, you're up to something, aren't you, lover? Your daddy made you go camping when you were a little girl, and you hated it, remember?"

"Maybe I'll enjoy camping if I try it with you."

Gage laughed. "Do you honestly expect me to fly into such a dirty web?" He feigned sadness. "I don't know what you've got going on, but I forgive you for that adorable attempt to trick me. Now, come back inside where you belong." He held out his hand to her.

Hailey stepped back.

Gage stepped closer. He thumbed over his shoulder and said, "Suri ain't going anywhere—if that's your plan." He had reached the middle of the lawn. Hailey took another step back. She was only a couple of steps from the opening in the trees.

"Wait!" Gage said. He held his hand up for her to stop. "Don't go further, lover! The dogs!"

"You wouldn't let them hurt me, would you?"

"I won't be able to stop them," Gage said, looking from Hailey to the dog pens and back. "I'll give you anything you want. Just please, *please* don't go any further!"

Hailey had reached the edge of the lawn. Gage bolted for her, screaming, "No!"

Hailey disappeared into the woods. Behind her, she heard brush slapping against his legs as he raced after her. The woods had no trail, and the brush was thick in places. She wove between the densest vegetation and had just started up an incline when she grabbed her leg and screamed, "Ouch. Oh, my God!" She staggered and continued trying to run while clutching her upper thigh with both hands.

Gage saw Hailey almost fall, and he accelerated. "I won't hurt you, lover! Just stop! Don't fight fate." The distance between her and Gage had shrunk, and he was gaining on her. She leaped over a log and fell on the other side. Gage shouted, "See? You're gonna hurt yourself! Stop running!"

Hailey continued, limping. She ducked tree limbs and hurdled fallen branches and rocks as well as she could while holding her thigh.

After running nearly a half-mile into the woods, Gage's face was red, and his shirt was soaked with sweat. He was about to give up when Hailey stopped and leaned on her knees. "Please leave me," she called back to him as she panted. Gage stumbled toward her, holding up his hands for her to wait. He wheezed so heavily he could hardly speak. "Just … stay put …lover."

Hailey backed away, grimacing as she rubbed her leg.

Gage closed in to within ten feet of her. A smile of relief broke through the exhaustion on his face. "That's it … just wait a minute. Let me check your leg. I might need to carry you."

He leaned onto his knees, bowed his head, and paused his panting to swallow. His lungs burned. The excitement of potentially recapturing Hailey, who stood only a few feet away, brought a new surge of adrenaline.

Hailey watched him, also trying to catch her breath. "Let's talk," she said.

"Okay, okay…" Gage motioned with his hands to reassure her. He took a step toward her.

Hailey stepped back and said, "I have a question for you."

"Anything, lover. Ask me *anything.*"

Hailey pulled Gage's mobile phone from her pocket and held it up for him to see. "What's the screen lock code to your phone? I can't figure it out, and without the code, I can't turn off the tracking on this god-awful necklace I will destroy."

Gage gaped at her in disbelief.

Hailey said, "Was that a hard question, you son-of-a-bitch?"

"I can answer, but first I need—"

"The code is the only information I need from you," Hailey interrupted.

"One-seven-two-six."

Before she typed the code into the phone, she gave him a disgusted look. Her address in Turlock Heights Estates was 1726. She tried the code, but it didn't work. "Wrong," she said.

"You must have typed it wrong," Gage said. He lunged, charging her, his eyes wide. He dove for her ankles. Hailey dodged him. "And you want me to trust you?" she asked. She circled him as he looked up at her from the ground.

He got back on his feet and reached his hand out. "Help me, lover."

Hailey stopped and said, "For the first time in weeks, you aren't recording my words. And that's a shame because I wish you could record me saying you will never have Hailey Vaughan ... you will never have Hailey Vaughan ... you will never have Hailey Vaughan."

"Stop it!" Gage covered his ears.

Hailey ran, dropping the hurt leg act that had drawn Gage to where she wanted him. He ran a few steps after her and then stopped, realizing how futile catching her was.

Hailey's legs pumped in full strides as she dodged trees and hurdled brush like a gazelle.

"I'll have you, lover!" Gage yelled. He cupped his hands over his mouth and added, "Don't you remember what happened last time you ran? I didn't like having to do that, and now you are putting me in the position of having to do it again."

Hailey tucked Gage's phone in her pocket and ran faster. The wind in her face never smelled and felt so good. She heard his voice fading behind her. Each stride lowered the volume of his threats until he was completely muted and had disappeared from sight.

At the top of a hill, she saw the creek making a gentle turn toward the west. Through the trees, she saw the afternoon sun shimmering on it. She was free.

• • •

After Hailey had run from the front door, Marissa pulled the door closed and pushed the sofa back against it. She hurried to the kitchen, where she saw Hailey disappear from the lawn's edge into a clearing in the trees. She was puzzled Gage hadn't chased her. She heard him pounding on the back of the cabin and the tools clanking as he dug through the shed. She went to his bedroom and looked out the window without getting close to it. Gage had left the shed. She heard footsteps on the porch again and then a crash of something heavy falling. She went to the front door, climbed onto the sofa, and looked out the peephole. Gage stood outside, trying to push something into the outer wall. He stepped back and raised a hammer, swinging it so hard the wall shook. He was about to take his second swing when Marissa heard Hailey yell at him.

Marissa ran to see out the kitchen window again. After a moment, Gage stepped off the porch and moved slowly toward Hailey as they continued a conversation Marissa couldn't hear. Moments later, Hailey turned and ran. Gage chased her, and they disappeared into the trees.

Immediately, Marissa ran to the front door, unlocked it, and stepped onto the porch. A sledgehammer lay beside a burlap bag from which two smaller hammers, a chisel, and a handsaw had spilled out. A wedge was inserted between logs into the cabin wall beside the door lock. She threw the tools inside the cabin door and returned for the sledgehammer. She could hardly raise it to shoulder height but freed the wedge by hitting it on its side. She threw the sledgehammer and wedge into the cabin and then listened. She heard no sound or movement from the break in the trees. In fact, the entire cabin's surroundings were still and quiet. The dogs' barks were no longer manic. It seemed even the birds were silent.

Marissa pulled the keys from the deadbolt and leaped from the porch, running to Gage's Blazer. She checked the driver's door while watching the edge of the woods. It was unlocked. She got in and left the door open, ready to sprint to the cabin at any sign of Gage. She jabbed the key at the ignition, missing on the first try because her hand shook. When it slid in, the ignition only made a single click. The Blazer wouldn't start. Gage's kill switch wasn't a bluff. She swept her hand under the dashboard, under her seat, and on the side but felt nothing resembling a switch.

She had no way to know how long Gage would be gone. She had to assume he would give up the chase and return soon. He'd come back for his truck to cut Hailey off before she reached town like before.

Marissa pulled the key from the ignition, got out of the Blazer, and ran back inside the cabin. She locked the door.

While she watched the opening to the woods, Marissa wondered if the best thing would be for Gage to drive away in his Blazer. But if that happened, he'd have the opportunity to intercept Hailey near several Townsend River bridges before she reached town. In a worst-case scenario, Gage would escape only to come after them later. Ensuring he was caught had to be a priority.

Marissa remembered Gage's skill with electronics. If he could install a kill switch, surely he could start the Blazer without a key. She wondered how she might disable the Blazer—pull some wires under the hood. She didn't know how to drain or siphon the gas tank. Doing so would take too long, anyway. She got a bottle of drinking water from the refrigerator and uncapped it while she ran to the front door. It worked in the movies, so maybe her idea would work now. It had been almost five minutes since Gage and Hailey had disappeared. Gage could return at any moment. She checked the peephole and then unlocked the door. Two steps onto the porch, a sound came from the woods, sending prickles through her until she saw a crow flapping from the trees.

She ran to the Blazer, opened the fuel door, and shoved the bottle in. The water *glug glug glugged* into the fuel tank while she scanned the lawn's edge for movement.

For an instant, she contemplated running on the road from the cabin to the camping area, which she estimated to be about five or six miles away. For the first time since her abduction, she felt confident the dogs weren't a risk. But if she couldn't reach the camping area or if it was abandoned, she feared spending a night alone in the woods almost as much as she feared Gage and his beasts finding her. She decided to stay in the cabin and depend on Hailey's success in getting help.

She locked the door of the Blazer and then ran to the porch. She stopped at the front door and rested her hand on the knob. Gage hadn't returned, and there was no sign of him. She wondered if she should check the tool shed behind the house. It was a considerable risk that could make the difference in surviving Gage's attempts to breach the cabin.

She side-stepped along the cabin wall, watching the trees as she crept past the kitchen window. All was still, and she heard no footsteps. At the corner, she turned and did the same to the back of the house. She saw the tool shed about twenty feet away. Its door was raised, propped open with an old broom. As she took a step toward it, she heard the snap of a branch sound from trees around the corner. She ran to the corner of the cabin and saw Gage break from the woods at the edge of the lawn. He sprinted at full speed toward the cabin.

Marissa shrieked and raced around to the front. She had the distance advantage, but Gage was closing in fast. His eyes were wide. As Marissa jumped onto the porch, Gage screamed, "Suri, wait! I just want to talk!"

Marissa saw his gut and the flesh of his face bounce with each step as he closed in. The dogs launched into a new barking frenzy. Marissa reached the door as Gage reached the steps. She lunged inside, slammed the door, and turned the deadbolt an instant before Gage's body hit the door. "Dead meat! You are dead meat!" he screamed so hard his voice cracked.

Marissa sat on the floor behind the sofa and used her legs to push it against the door while Gage continued to cuss outside. She went to the kitchen window and saw him walking in a tight circle on the lawn, his hands on his hips and head tilted back as he tried to catch his breath.

When he walked toward the window, Marissa backed away. Gage took hold of the bars. He looked inside and said, "Let's make a deal, Suri."

Marissa didn't answer.

"Hailey's confused. She's sick and needs my help. She's gonna get hurt out there. There are bears, mountain lions—hell, if she twists her ankle way out in the middle of nowhere, she's gonna be a meal for some animal. Now, help me here. You do like her, don't you? You don't want to see her hurt or dead, right?"

Marissa moved back to the edge of the kitchen.

"Atta girl. Do the right thing," Gage coaxed.

"I want to go home," Marissa said.

The statement seemed to catch Gage by surprise. "Sure ... Okay. Whatever you want ... I can make that happen for you if I can get indoors to get a few things. I'm sorry for how I've treated you. All that is over now."

Marissa rocked left and right on her feet as she listened and stepped closer. "I don't want you to hurt me anymore."

"That's a deal," Gage said. "Like I just told you, all that is over with. Now, be a sweetheart and let me in to just gather my things." He tapped his watch. "The sooner you do that, the sooner you go home."

"Do you promise you won't hurt me?" Marissa asked.

Gage finger-combed his hair a few times. Marissa saw the fingers he tried to keep so pristine were caked with dirt. A smile spread on his sweaty face, and he held up one hand. "I swear on my mama's grave. Give me a chance to show you. Oh, yes, I do promise. Please, let's hurry."

"And you'll really take me back to Wenshire Harbor."

"I'll drive you wherever you want to go. I'm gonna go to the front door. You'll meet me there and open the door briefly, won't you?"

He left the window.

"Wait," Marissa said. He stopped. "I just don't feel like I can trust you yet."

Gage used his toothy smile to hide the anger that swelled in him.

"Listen, we don't have much time. I'll tell you what… I'm going to walk way over there by those trees," he pointed to the edge of the lawn, "and if you go to the front door, you'll see me through the peephole. Unlock the door, and then you'll be able to lock yourself in Hailey's room and keep that key. That way, you don't have to trust me because you'll be locked up safe. It's a perfect deal for both of us."

"I need to think about it," Marissa said.

"There's no time!" Gage shouted. "C'mon, Suri. Do what I'm telling you."

Marissa said, "Please don't raise your voice to me."

"Sorry."

Marissa opened a cabinet, took out a tall glass, and filled it with water. After she took a sip, she said, "If I let you in, you might starve me until I 'learn it right.' Or maybe you'll make me be Hailey in your bed. Or you might whip me because I looked at the wrong thing—or you might lock me below."

Gage screamed, "That's over with! Don't you get that?"

Marissa poured the rest of her water into the sink and threw the glass at him as hard as possible. It struck the bars. Gage ducked. Shattered glass sprayed all over him. "If I have to repeat myself, you've failed—isn't that what you say to me?" Marissa said.

He stood and tilted his head, finger-raking glass from his hair. "You are going to die today."

Marissa leaned with one arm on the counter and stared at him. She had committed to her mutiny, and her disgust for Gage had finally surpassed her fear of him. She walked away and said, "I died when you brought me here."

Gage kicked the side of the cabin and disappeared from the window. As Marissa walked back into the cabin's main room, she heard Gage on the porch. She went to the peephole and watched him leaning against a pillar.

Gage jumped off the porch and went to the Blazer. A chill shot through Marissa as she hoped her sabotage would succeed. He tried the driver's door. It was locked. He stepped back, confused momentarily, and then said, "Dammit."

After trying the passenger door, he took a large rock from the dirt near the porch's edge and smashed the driver's window. He unlocked the door and then popped the hood. After he worked for a few minutes under the hood, the Blazer's engine started. Gage closed the hood and climbed into the driver's seat. Marissa's heart sank.

Gage backed the Blazer up and then turned the wheels. He pulled forward, aiming for the front corner of the cabin. He tried to accelerate. The engine sputtered, and the Blazer shook hard to a stop. Marissa watched him study the instrument panel. He pounded the dashboard with his fist and came out with the rock he had used to break the window. He threw it at the cabin's front door and cursed at Marissa.

She heard him circling the cabin, calling out to her and trying to bargain. He offered her freedom, money, a ride to anywhere she chose, food, and anything he thought would cause Marissa to open the door.

Marissa picked up a hammer she had retrieved from the bag Gage had left on the porch. She dragged a kitchen chair to each corner of the cabin, where she stood on it to smash every tinted dome security camera she could find. Gage heard the sounds of destruction and ran from window to window, trying to see her.

"What are you doing? Why won't you make a deal?" he hollered. "I've offered you anything you want!"

Marissa ignored him. She moved the chair under a square panel in the ceiling. She pushed it open, reached inside, and pulled out a DVR that stored all the video Gage transmitted to his laptop and phone. She let it fall, and it jerked to a stop halfway to the floor, dangling by its cords. She took hold of the cords with both hands and pulled them down, crashing the unit to the floor. She beat it with the hammer. Pieces of plastic and circuit board flew from each blow.

Gage heard the commotion and moved to the front door, where he yelled, "I don't know what you're doing, but I will burn the whole cabin down if I have to. Now open the door!" He began kicking and slamming his shoulder into the door.

Marissa went to Gage's bedroom, retrieved a stack of Hailey's photos, and dropped them on the kitchen countertop. Next, she brought out a case full of USB flash drives containing videos of Hailey. She set them by the photos. She then brought some of Hailey's clothes Gage had forced her to wear. She went to the kitchen window with the items neatly stacked together and yelled, "I'm ready to talk!"

The pounding at the front door stopped. Marissa heard footsteps. She leaned toward the kitchen window and saw Gage come into view. He stepped off the porch and approached her. Marissa stayed in the window until he got a few feet away, and then she stepped back. "I'm ready to talk, too," Gage said. Then he took hold of the bars and examined the items Marissa had gathered inside. "What the hell are you doing, Suri?"

Marissa said, "You've lost the real Hailey. All your memories of her are in this cabin. You burn it, and you will never have it again. You won't even have me to play your sick Hailey charade anymore." She opened a lower cabinet, pulled out a can of lighter fluid, and pulled a box of matches from the top of the refrigerator.

Gage said, "Hold on, Suri—"

"My name is Marissa, you asshole."

"Of course—yes—Marissa, listen..." He raised his hands to calm her. "We need to talk this through carefully. I want something, and you want something. Why can't we both get what we want?"

"You've never cared about what I want."

"Of course I did. I was better to you than you think. Hell, I protected you in this wilderness. I gave you shelter and food. You would have died out here without me. Think about that, Suri. I taught you new skills— Hailey's— skills you can use after I take you back to town, and I'd do that if you would just let me in."

"You think you've done me a favor?"

"Look, Suri, what are you going to do? Stay inside there forever? I've got an idea you'll like." Gage disappeared around the corner of the cabin. Marissa ran to his bedroom, where she could see out to the back. She watched Gage go behind the tool shed, and a moment later, he reappeared, pushing her bicycle. Marissa felt a lump in her throat. He didn't see her in the window, so he wheeled it around to the front. Marissa returned to the kitchen, where she saw Gage standing outside, holding the bike with a smile as though he was presenting it as a prize.

"I'll tell you what..." he said. "I'm going into the woods. I'll go far. Then you can ride out. You know the truck's broken, and I sure as hell can't catch you on foot. Now, let's do this because it will get me what I want, and you get what you want. Deal?"

Marissa looked at the bike with its flat tires. She said, "I don't trust you."

Gage threw the bike to the ground and yelled, "Dammit, what the hell does it take with you?"

Marissa picked up an 8 x 10 photo of Hailey putting on lipstick. She held the photo to the window and said, "Don't ever raise your voice to me."

"No, no, no, no, no!" Gage shouted as he rushed to the window bars. Marissa ripped the photo in half and dropped it into the sink. Gage reached through the bars for the photo pieces. They were out of reach. Marissa squirted lighter fluid into the sink and struck a match. The burst of flame lit her face in orange for a moment, and then she put out the fire by turning on the water.

Gage's tone changed to one of pleading, saying, "Why won't you make a deal?"

"You are pathetic," Marissa said. "Every time you try to enter the cabin, I will destroy a piece of Hailey." She left the kitchen.

In Gage's bedroom, the wispy semi-transparent curtains moved in the breeze above the shattered window's glass. Marissa was more determined than ever to find Gage's guns. And when she did, she'd have no problem killing him. She looked under the bed. It was too dark to see. She reached under and felt emptiness. She swept her hand as far as she could and touched something flat and square beneath the headboard. She pulled out a long, narrow box. It was too light and small to be a gun safe. She rotated it and found it was locked with a small padlock. Her pulse quickened. She took it to the main room and pounded the lock with a hammer. She couldn't break it. She then used the hammer claw to pry one of the box's hinges off. She tilted it in the light and saw an odd-looking gun made of metal with a hollow stock so it looked more like a crutch. She wiggled the hammer claw into the crack and pried the case until both hinges popped loose. She recognized the gun as the air rifle Gage had used on the opossum and the one he had taken when he rushed from the cabin to catch Hailey after her first escape.

She pulled it out of the case and examined it. Under a black velvet flap in the case, she found a case of ten darts filled with clear liquid and an empty one. The gun looked complicated and menacing at first. She had watched Gage use it more than once. After working on it for a few minutes, she found the bolt, pulled it down and back, opening the loading port. She remembered Gage pumping it before he shot it, so she pulled the long lever under the barrel, opening it like a V. She loaded an empty dart, locked it in the chamber, and pumped the lever twice. Pumping it the second time was difficult and required her to use her upper body weight. She took the gun back into the bedroom. She placed a pillow over it and pulled the trigger. She felt the gun kick and heard a muffled pop. A dart stuck in the wall below the window. Marissa smiled.

She put a loaded dart into the air rifle and pumped it three times. She aimed the gun around the room, targeting objects, and then stopped to listen. Gage had fallen silent. She checked out the windows in the bathroom and in Hailey's room. Gage had vanished, and for the first time, Marissa would have very much liked to see him.

Twenty-Five

MARISSA WENT FROM window to window, hunting for Gage. She held the air rifle low and stayed more than an arm's reach from the windows in case Gage had hidden below one of them.

The eerie silence outside scared Marissa more than Gage's tirades. At least with his screaming assaults, she knew where he was. Now, every sound startled her.

Hailey had been gone for over an hour. It was almost two o'clock in the afternoon. If things went as planned, the police would arrive in less than two hours. Marissa had waited so long for rescue she couldn't believe it was finally possible. She wondered if she would hear helicopters or sirens first. How would Gage react? His only option for escape was on foot, and he wouldn't get far.

She sat facing the window in the bedroom and held the gun with both hands. The room had no attic opening. There was no apparent gun vault. Marissa put the rifle down and looked through all the dresser drawers again. There was nothing. She had just sat on the bed again when she heard a voice say, "Marissa." She picked up the air rifle, stood, and listened, unsure of the voice's direction.

"Marissa, hurry! Over here!" It was a loud whisper that sounded like it came from somewhere in the cabin. Marissa held the rifle ready to fire as she moved slowly to the door. She stepped into the main room and saw Hailey peering through the bars of the kitchen window.

"Marissa, he's down at the dog cage. Quick, let me in!" Hailey said.

Marissa dropped the gun and ran to the front door. She moved the sofa and unlocked the deadbolt. When she opened the door, Hailey rushed in. Marissa closed the door and locked the deadbolt. They hugged.

"What are you doing back here?" Marissa said.

"I circled back and watched from the woods and saw the Blazer was still here, and he was trying to break in. I couldn't leave you alone with him."

"But you were our best hope of getting help. Now, how are we ever going to get out of here?"

"Together," Hailey said.

Marissa hugged Hailey again.

"Look what I found," Marissa said. She picked up the air rifle from the floor. "It works, and he left us more darts."

Hailey experienced the bizarre sensation of being grateful to see a gun.

Marissa pulled a bundle of flex cuffs from her back pocket. "We have these too."

"Do you think you can shoot him?" Hailey asked.

"The only gun I've shot is my brother's BB gun. I was a decent aim. The only problem is I threatened to destroy all the Hailey Vaughan items in the cabin if he tried to break in. I burned a photo while he watched. I haven't heard or seen him since I found the gun, and now he won't come near the cabin."

"I saw him standing by the dog cage. I don't think he'll let them—"

"Marissa!" They heard Gage calling from the front. Marissa spun, aiming the gun at the front door. Hailey motioned for her to relax and then went to the peephole. She saw Gage sitting on the lawn about thirty feet from the cabin near the tree where he had blown up the barrel. "I see him," Hailey said. "You must have scared him good—he's keeping his distance. I'll try to draw him in. You try to take a shot."

"I'll try. Now I'm worried I might miss," Marissa said.

"I'll get him to the kitchen window. You stay down until he's there. He should be close." Hailey went into the kitchen and, without any hesitation, walked to the window.

"Hi, Gage," she called out.

Gage looked at her, to the woods, and then back again. He smiled as he pushed up to his feet. "You came back!"

"Yes, I did. Maybe it was fate."

Gage let out a short laugh and then cocked his head. "Don't tease me, lover."

Hailey motioned for him to approach. "I want to talk to you."

Gage didn't move. "Show me your hands, lover."

Holding the loaded air rifle, Marissa crawled along the kitchen counter and squatted beside Hailey's knees.

Hailey sighed and raised her palms high for him to inspect. "When will you trust me?" she asked.

Gage laughed. "You sound like *me*." He walked around Marissa's toppled bicycle and approached the window.

Hailey said, "If we're going to be together, then we have to stop scaring one another, right?"

Gage stood an arm's length from the bars on the window. "God, you look beautiful," he said, grinning at her. "I thought I had lost you, lover."

"Here I am."

Gage reached up to grasp the bars. "Where's Suri?"

Hailey nudged Marissa with her knee. Marissa stood with the rifle and aimed. For the first time, the women saw horror on Gage's face. He screamed, "No!" and turned to run. Marissa fired from less than ten feet. The dart found its mark on the left side of Gage's abdomen. He tried to swat it out quickly, but the barbed dart needle only flopped, so he stopped to pull it out. He looked at the dart and then to the women. His expression was one of having been betrayed.

Hailey said, "Load another dart, Marissa."

Gage turned and ran.

Hailey said, "We can't let him escape! Give me the cuffs."

Marissa handed her a bunch of cuffs and said, "Are you sure I hit him? What if it didn't work?"

"You got him just like he got me. He'll go down," Hailey said, running to the front of the cabin.

"Reload the gun and follow me."

"What if I can't keep up?"

"He won't get far. I'll holler for you." Hailey raced out the front door and jumped from the porch just as Gage crashed through the trees at the edge of the lawn. He hadn't even gone for the opening.

Hailey called out, "Hurry, Marissa!" and then ran through the trees where Gage had disappeared. She saw him climbing an incline, and she accelerated, quickly closing in to within a comfortable distance. Gage looked over his shoulder, his face full of panic.

Hailey cupped her hands over her mouth and shouted, "You got less than a minute for recess, lover, and then it'll be time to take you back home."

Gage didn't respond. Despite trying to speed up, his pace slowed as he became more winded.

Hailey heard Marissa calling out to her in the distance. While Hailey continued to follow Gage, she shouted, "I'm up on the ridge … Follow my voice … I'll keep yelling for you … It's over for Gage … He's going down, and when he wakes up, things are going to be very different for him … Can you hear me, Marissa?"

"Yes. I hear you," Marissa shouted. She had Hailey in sight.

Gage ran a few more paces before he started staggering as though he was suddenly dizzy. Hailey ran an arc around him and watched. He went down to one knee and looked at her. She gave him a thumbs-up sign and said, "Nighty, night." Gage fell onto his side and moved his arms in a failed attempt to continue his flight by crawling.

Hailey called out to Marissa, took out the flex cuffs, and circled closer to Gage. His eyes were half-open.

Marissa jogged to them and brought the gun barrel to within a foot of Gage's leg. "Let's shoot him again."

"No. Save the darts," Hailey said. She picked up a long stick and poked Gage's shoulder as if he might explode. When he didn't respond, she said, "But if he makes a move, let him have it." She used her foot to push him over to his back. His mouth fell open. One nostril was rimmed with dirt. Hailey crossed his wrists on his stomach and cuffed them. She sat on his shins and squeezed his ankles together, cuffing them tight.

When Hailey stood, Marissa stepped closer and kicked Gage in the ribs. She dropped the gun, fell to her knees, and began pounding on his chest and face with her fists, screaming, "You bastard! You bastard!"

Hailey wrestled her off and held her, saying, "It's over now. He can't hurt you."

Marissa calmed down as she continued to glare at Gage's limp body. "I think we should leave him out here," she said.

"We shouldn't. If he wakes and gets free, we've accomplished nothing. We need to keep an eye on him. We have to drag him."

Marissa leaned the gun against a tree and lifted Gage's legs by his ankles. Hailey took hold of his wrists. Although they couldn't lift him entirely off the ground, they were able to raise him enough to drag him over the leaves, down the incline, and onto the lawn. They worked for twenty minutes to get him to the base of the front stairs. They heaved him upward, one stairstep at a time, until he lay sprawled on the porch.

"I don't want him to be inside with us," Marissa said.

"Me either. Does he have any rope inside?"

"Plenty." Marissa disappeared into the cabin.

Hailey looked down at Gage. His backside was brown with ground-in dirt and grass stains, and his breathing was sloppy. Hailey took out another flex cuff and connected his bound wrists to the bottom of the porch railing. She did the same with his feet. Marissa returned with a long length of clothesline rope, and Hailey bound his neck, waist, wrists, knees, and ankles to the porch railing and to a wood beam under the steps.

When she finished, she tugged it. "He's not going anywhere."

"I'll go back for the gun," Marissa said. She dashed off across the lawn. Hailey looked at Gage one more time before she went into the cabin.

• • •

Hailey and Marissa had two options. The first was to leave Gage secured and hike for help. Marissa's concern about her stamina precluded her from running the Townsend River to town. Their other option was to discover a way to summon help from the cabin. This option looked daunting without Gage's laptop and far out of the range of any mobile phone service.

Hailey pulled the sofa back to its position on the floor and cleared the entryway, leaving the door open so she could listen for Gage's movement. A few minutes later, she heard Marissa's footsteps climbing the porch, then a thud and a grunt. Hailey ran to the door, and Marissa pivoted to her.

"Did you kick him?" Hailey asked.

"It was an accident."

Hailey led Marissa into the cabin. Marissa leaned the gun against the wall inside the door. Hailey said, "I hate his guts, too, but let's keep him alive so he can see us win. He'll get what he deserves."

Marissa nodded without conviction.

It was 4:45 p.m. The sun would set in less than an hour. They didn't want to travel after dark. If they could find an air pump on the property, they could inflate Marissa's bicycle tires and take the road to the highway in the morning. They decided the best plan, with Gage secured, was to wait the night and leave at daybreak unless they could find some way to communicate with the outside world before then.

They were hungry and had a refrigerator still stocked with many of Hailey's favorite ingredients. Marissa made a sandwich for each of them. At the same time, Hailey got to work overturning furniture, gutting the closets, and emptying drawers in search of something they could use for communication or escape. They soon heard Gage moan on the porch. They went out to investigate, and Marissa picked up the air rifle by the door. Gage had shifted slightly on his side. He was still tied and fastened from head to toe with flex cuffs and rope. When he saw them, he raised his head, yelled something unintelligible again, and struggled in his restraints.

"Let's shoot him again," Marissa said.

"No. Save the dart."

"Are we going to have to listen to him all night?"

Hailey stepped closer to Gage, and when he saw her movement, Gage screamed something unintelligible and fought against his restraints.

"Can we at least gag him?" Marissa asked. "I never want to hear his voice again." Gage turned his head and tried to spit on her.

Hailey nodded, and Marissa disappeared into the cabin and returned with a sock and more rope. She balled up the sock and forced it into Gage's mouth, ending his slurred curses. Hailey tied the rope around his head and pulled it between his teeth, holding the sock firmly in his mouth.

Marissa knelt beside him and said, "If I can hear you, you're too loud.

Sound familiar, asshole?"

Gage's eyes narrowed, and he laughed through the gag.

"Come on," Hailey said, tugging Marissa's arm. They returned to the cabin where Gage's yells were muted, and they heard only faint thumps from his struggle.

Hailey went to Gage's bedroom.

Marissa followed her.

They scoured the bedroom for a half-hour, looking for any guns, other phones, 2-way radios—or anything useful. When they finished, the room looked like it had been ransacked by an unrushed burglar. Hailey Vaughan's paraphernalia covered every inch of the floor. The dresser and armoire drawers were pulled out and stacked against the wall.

They stood, staring at one another, wondering where else they could look when Hailey had an idea. She went to bed and pulled off the bedspread and satin sheets that matched those at her house. She lifted the mattress. "Do you see anything hidden under there?" she asked.

"Nothing," Marissa said.

Hailey let the mattress flop down and then looked at the side of the box spring. An odd seam about the size of a coat hanger ran along the edge. She knelt and pressed the seam with her fingers. It separated. She slid her hand inside and felt the springs and a bigger, cold metal object. She pulled out a pistol.

Marissa said, "You found them!" She knelt beside Hailey.

They didn't know what kind of gun it was, but the most important thing was they had it, and Gage didn't. Hailey put it on the bed and reached in again. She pulled out four guns, including the Ruger LC9 Felicia had given her. Hailey released the magazine and checked it to make sure it was loaded. She then reinserted the magazine and checked the loaded chamber indicator to ensure a round was in the chamber, just like Felicia had taught her.

"It looks like you know how to use that," Marissa said.

After Hailey stared at the gun momentarily, her eyes welled up, and she said, "I do."

With the guns, they also found a cloth bag full of ammunition boxes, a set of keys, Marissa's pepper spray, and Hailey's phone.

They had begun spreading the guns and the other items on the bed when they heard the dogs. Something was different about the sound. Their barks had grown louder. "The dogs are loose!" Marissa said.

Hailey took Felicia's Ruger and ran out to close the front door.

Marissa grabbed a Glock and followed. When she exited the bedroom, she saw Hailey stop in the middle of the main room floor, looking at the closed front door.

"Marissa?" Hailey said.

"What?"

"Did you close the door?"

"No."

"The keys are missing." Hailey went to the door and tried to open it. The deadbolt was locked. She peered through the peephole. "Oh, my God!"

"What!" Marissa said.

"He's gone!"

They heard the dogs sniffing the bottom door crack, scratching the door, and growling.

Hailey and Marissa raised their guns and backed themselves against the wall. They scanned the cabin's interior. Hailey's bedroom and the bathroom doors were closed. "He can't be in here," Marissa said. "He would have come after us right away."

"I thought you said he was afraid of his own dogs. Why would he lock himself out of the cabin?" Hailey asked. "We're back at square one."

"Things are different now." Marissa held up her gun and pointed to the Ruger in Hailey's hand.

Hailey gave a slight nod.

"Don't shoot!" They heard Gage's voice. It was coming from inside the cabin. They couldn't see him. The closet door opened, and Gage stepped out with his hands up. Marissa screamed, and both spun, aiming their guns at him. Gage opened his hands to show them he had no weapon. "Take it easy. Nobody needs to get hurt," he said.

"Step closer, and I will kill you," Hailey said.

Gage smiled. "You can put the gun down, lover. If you were going to kill me, you would have already done it. You took care of me out there." He pointed to the front door. "You didn't leave me helpless in the woods. You wanted me real close—here with you on the porch so you could look after me." Gage took a step toward them.

Marissa pulled the trigger of her Glock. It clicked. She shook the gun and tried to pull the trigger again, but it was locked.

Gage smiled at her and said, "You're about as dumb as a bag of rocks, Suri. I guess all the make-believe you did paid off for me because now all you can do is pretend to shoot a gun." He laughed.

"Kill him, Ms. Vaughan! Do it *now!*" Marissa screamed. She moved to stand behind Hailey.

Gage looked at Hailey. "Can't you see, lover? If I was meant to die, Suri would have chosen a loaded gun. You hate guns, Hailey. You don't want to be a murderer, do you?" He stepped closer.

Hailey backed away and shouted, "Get out of this cabin, or I swear I will pull this trigger!" She held the gun steady, supporting her wrist, remembering what Felly had taught her.

Marissa yelled, "What are you waiting for? Shoot him, *please!*"

"She won't shoot me because fate won't let her, Suri." Gage kept his eyes trained on Hailey's. "Fate always has its way, lover."

"Don't!" Hailey shouted.

Gage held out his hand. "Give me the gun before you hurt yourself." He took another step. "You can't fight fate, lover."

"You're not part of our fate," Hailey said.

Gage lunged. Marissa screamed. Hailey fired five shots into Gage's torso. He crashed to his side at her feet, a pool of blood spread beneath his chest.

Hailey stood over him with the gun aimed, ready to unload the remaining rounds. She and Marissa looked at him in silence, wondering if it could really be over or if he might still come back to life and continue tormenting them.

They opened the trap door in the main room, dragged his body to it, and let it fall down the steps. Marissa closed and locked it.

The gunshots had scattered the dogs. It was quiet outside the cabin as the sky dimmed to dusk. Hailey and Marissa made plans to get back to town. With the sun sinking into the treetops, they decided to wait until morning when travel would be safer. Though the dogs had gone silent, they were still a threat.

The excitement of finally leaving the cabin kept them up most of the night, each of them only dozing a few minutes at a time. Hailey kept the Ruger on her lap. The dogs returned during the night and resumed scratching the door and occasionally barking on the porch. "We're going to have to kill them," Marissa said.

Hailey pointed to the air rifle on the bed. "No, we won't."

When daylight came, Marissa got some meat from the refrigerator and lured the dogs to a place outside the kitchen by throwing the meat out the window. She darted the first dog. It yelped, ran a short distance away, and stopped, looking back at her. It bit at the dart and eventually pulled it out, but the tranquilizer had done its work, and a few minutes later, it staggered and collapsed on the grass. The other dog met the same fate a few minutes later.

Marissa and Hailey used a wheelbarrow to load the dogs one at a time. They locked them in their cage.

Marissa found an air compressor in the tool shed and inflated her bicycle tires. After packing some water in a couple of bags, Marissa and Hailey set off on their road to town. Marissa rode her bike while Hailey jogged beside her. They took the road seven miles until they passed the old campground. It was still abandoned. They soon saw cross-traffic on the highway in the distance—beautiful traffic.

• • •

Hailey weathered the inevitable media storm in the days after her and Marissa's escape. Despite her need for time to mourn and recover from her ordeal's extreme emotional toll, she arranged a memorial service for Mason. She helped Felicia's mother with a service for Felicia. She also hired movers to store any salvageable items from their destroyed home.

She agreed to go back to Gage's cabin with investigators on the condition they did not force Marissa to join them. When they returned to the scene, she saw police tape spanning the cabin's driveway and lawn. She wondered why it was needed in such a remote location. She walked the property, answering questions for detectives while keeping her arms tightly folded. Electronic devices and sealed bags were stacked on the front porch. Detectives began loading them into the back of a police van.

She saw the broken glass below the windows and the long slit in the front door where Gage had sliced through with the saw. Everything she had arranged in her life to feel secure, Gage had violated.

Three weeks later, Hailey drove to her office for the first time. She had rented a condominium on the outskirts of Wenshire Harbor. She wondered if she could emotionally handle working in the office that had been such a part of her nightmare.

She parked, and before going up to her suite, she walked to Hot Perks. When she entered, one of the workers behind the counter recognized her and said, "Morning, Ms. Vaughan." All the other workers and some of the patrons stopped and applauded. In the corner of the shop, a wooden display case featured a poster that read, LOST AND FOUND. It contained a large photo of Marissa. All the yellow ribbons employees had worn in her absence were pinned around its edge.

Hailey pointed and said, "I love that," as she went to the order counter.

"And we're so glad you are safe, too," the male cashier said.

Hailey placed her drink order, and the cashier said, "Are you in touch with Marissa?"

"Yes. We talk every day."

"Please tell her we miss her."

"I will."

When Hailey entered the Handel Towers lobby, she noticed the Echelonian booth was gone. She smiled on her way to the elevator.

"Welcome back, Ms. Vaughan," a voice said. It was Jonah, standing off to the side, talking to a guard from a new security company who wore a different uniform.

"Thank you, Jonah," Hailey said. Before stepping onto the elevator, she pointed to where the Echelonian booth had been and said, "I love the improvement."

Jonah gave her a thumbs-up. A young man dressed in a suit stepped onto the elevator with Hailey. "What floor?" Hailey asked.

"Five, thanks," the man said.

The doors closed them in. When the elevator lifted, the man turned to Hailey and said, "I'm Ronald."

Hailey extended her hand. "Hailey Vaughan."

"I'm so excited, I can't quit smiling," the man said.

"Why?"

"We're going to be neighbors, and I've found something absolutely amazing I'd love to share with you." The elevator opened to the fifth-floor office. "Give me just ten minutes, and I can completely change your life."

The man stepped out and motioned for Hailey to follow him.

"Change my life in only ten minutes?" Hailey laughed. She didn't follow him but leaned out to see the layout of the new business that had moved one floor from hers.

The office had a large open floor plan full of cubicles. To the left, Hailey recognized Isaac, who sat in a glass-enclosed office. He was talking to a young couple. He noticed her and waved. Draped high on the far wall was a banner with bright red letters.

DON'T RUN FROM THE TRUTH!

It can't set you free if you don't accept it.

"No—just, no," Hailey said, pressing the *Close Door* button.

· · · · · ·

Reviews

Thank you for reading *Prey for Us.* Word-of-mouth is crucial for any author to succeed. If you enjoyed this book, please consider leaving a review at Amazon, even if it's only a line or two. It would make all the difference and would be very much appreciated:
https://gneil.co/wr-review

Free Bonus Chapter:

Stop by to see maps of Gage's property, the interior of his cabin, and a full-length unpublished chapter detailing Marissa's trip to Gage's cabin after her nasty bike spill and the horrifying way Gage came to own the cabin. Download the chapter as an ebook, or listen to the creepy audio version FREE

Visit: gneil.co/wantonextras

If you liked *Wanton Regard*, you'd probably like my newest novel, *Guile.* Here's a sample of Chapter 1 for you:

G u i l e (preview)

One

IF HE HAD known what was in store for him, Ian Shaw would have used the gun. A simple trigger-pull would have spared so much pain. The small bullet would have done the world a huge favor. His loved ones would forgive him. As awful as it sounds, they'd secretly be grateful.

Everybody's rock bottom looks different. At 28 years old, Ian's was a portrait of abject misery painted by a cascade of horrible decisions. This afternoon, his mobile home grew hot enough to bake him after a decision to max out his last credit card on beer instead of fixing his air conditioner. He stretched out in his underwear on a tattered recliner with a bottle of Pabst Blue Ribbon warming between his legs. The torn pieces of his overdrawn bank statement lay strewn over unopened bills and demand letters on the floor beside him. His eyes glazed over while he looked at the stack, each envelope a complete waste of postage.

Unemployed, broke, heartbroken, and lonely, Ian was due for some good luck—at least that's what the kinder people told him. "Hang in there, and life will get better," some said. "Good things are right around the corner," others promised. A few tried to cheer him up with tired expressions. *It's always darkest just before the dawn.* He hated that one most because he knew it was bullshit. After countless nights spent camping, he knew the pre-dawn sky was as dark as midnight, and his life felt blacker than both right now. Sure, his encouragers meant well, but he had no faith in their prophecies.

The closest thing to optimism Ian felt was that his life couldn't get any worse. That's where he was wrong. Like most people, he didn't know a deeper, insidious level of misery lurks beneath rock bottom. The poor souls who find it become trapped in the utmost agony and despair. Here, only death offers mercy, obscuring other exits, which is why visitors rarely survive. It's difficult to reach without a perfect combination of foolish decisions and terrible luck. Ian would unwittingly begin drilling down to this abysmal level in the following days, thanks to his penchant for unwise decisions. As for the awful luck, he was dripping with it.

His life's downward spiral became a plummet two months ago when Kate, the love of his life, dumped him after a five-year relationship. Her non-negotiable breakup devastated him. He withdrew from friends and family. He stopped shaving, stopped eating, stopped caring, and started drinking.

He and Kate had run a small sandwich shop for two years. Kate handled the books and operations while Ian managed inventory and fulfilled his dream of becoming the closest thing he'd ever been to a chef. Poor management and an inability to sustain enough operating capital caused the business's financial health to decline in lockstep with the health of their relationship.

Ian still kicked himself for letting Kate blindside him. Missing all the clues, slathered a thick layer of embarrassment on top of his heartbreak.

The first hint of trouble came six months ago when she announced she'd purchased a flight for a weekend trip to a self-improvement seminar. Early in their relationship, she and Ian regularly took out-of-town excursions together, so it was reasonable for Ian to assume he'd go with her.

"Where are we staying?" he asked.

"I'm sorry, I should have told you," Kate said, wincing to soften the blow. "It's a women's retreat."

"Good for you!" Ian said, forcing enthusiasm.

"I thought you'd be upset."

"Nah! Why would I be?" he said, feeling upset. "Going with girlfriends?"

"No. Solo."

"Fantastic!" The enthusiasm took more effort.

Kate kept the additional details of her trip under wraps. While out of town, she contacted Ian only once with an obligatory call to tell him she'd arrived safely. When she returned three days later, she found Ian in the back of their sandwich shop, stocking new deliveries. After a tepid hug and a few clichéd exchanges about her flights and the weather, Kate said, "I think we should try abstinence."

Ian laughed.

Kate didn't.

"Am I that horrible in bed?" Ian said.

"It has nothing to do with quality."

"Whew!" Ian wiped his brow. He went to her, put his hands on her waist, and pulled her close. "If we're starting a diet, shouldn't we enjoy a little bite to eat first?"

She gently pushed him back. "Stop, Ian. This is important."

"You're serious?" he said, still searching her face for any hint of a joke. "Abstinence, just like that?"

Kate nodded.

"Why?" He stepped away and picked up a case of sodas from the floor.

"For some couples, abstinence improves the relationship," Kate said. "It strengthens the emotional connection by detaching the physical. It's counterintuitive, but studies have supported it."

Ian went to a shelf and slid the case onto it. "Is this something they pushed on you at that seminar?"

"It was one topic, but that doesn't matter. What's important is that abstinence is a powerful investment that could pay off for our relationship, and I want us to try it."

He came back to her, this time giving her space. "Don't couples who choose abstinence agree to it from the get-go?"

"Not always."

"Who begins abstinence after the fact? If this is some moral thing, it's too late to save ourselves for marriage." He picked up another case and heaved it onto the first.

"It's not about morality," Kate said. "It's called PCA, Post-Consummation Abstinence. Many couples have dramatically enhanced their emotional connection by abstaining from intercourse."

"Sounds backward to me," Ian said. He picked up a mesh bag of cucumbers and plopped it beside the sink. His sex life with Kate was great by her own admission. Something had happened to her on that trip. She'd normally be nervous while talking to him about such a sensitive topic. But now she exuded an unsettling calmness while making an announcement she had to know would rattle him. "This doesn't seem like you," he said. He turned on the faucet and began scrubbing cucumbers.

She came to stand beside him. "If abstinence can reveal a deeper commitment to the relationship, we need that."

"How long?"

"The suggested first round is sixty days."

"First round?" Ian scrubbed harder, lips tight, teeth clenched.

Kate watched him, waiting.

Ian stopped. "So, is this a test for me?"

"It's a test for us," Kate said. "If it's any consolation, it will be difficult for me, too, but I want you to agree to try."

If Ian knew one thing about Kate, it was if she got some bizarre new idea like this in her head, her mind would not change until it played out. Veganism, yoga, multiple detox diets, and two new-age religions were among Kate's personal fads that had popped and fizzled. He knew abstinence was doomed, too, but having to tug out his sexual release for whatever number of days while Kate came to her senses was an annoying price he'd have to pay. He pulled a shriveled cucumber from the bag and slammed it into the trash bin. "Looks like I have no choice."

Kate flashed a frown. "Of course you do."

"Then, my answer is no."

"Okay," Kate said. She shrugged.

"Just like that, you're willing to skip this abstinence thing?"

"I respect your decision. Abstinence is a difficult investment that not all couples can make." She paused, sliding her thumbnail back and forth against her fingertip, a nervous tick Ian instantly recognized.

"Are you disappointed?" he asked.

Kate sighed. "Yes."

"Fine. We'll do the abstinence thing."

"No, we won't."

Ian slapped the faucet handle down to turn the water off. "Making love when I know you don't want to is a buzz-kill, babe."

"When we make love, it will be because I want to," she said.

Ian looked at her skeptically.

Kate raised her right hand.

· · ·

The next evening, Ian cleaned the back of the sandwich shop after another day of paltry business. Kate had gone home early after announcing she didn't feel well.

Ian's phone buzzed with her number. "Hey, babe."

"Are you still at the shop?" Kate asked.

"Yep."

"Can you stay there for a bit longer?"

"Sure. Why?"

Then came the words Ian had recently grown to despise.

"We need to talk," she said.

He briefly pulled the phone from his ear and rolled his eyes. "Sure, what about?"

"In person will be better." Her strange calmness was back.

"If it's about abstinence, I'm still willing to try it—for a while," Ian said.

Kate hesitated. "I'll see you soon."

When she entered the back of the shop wearing a taut expression, Ian got up from his chair. "Hey, what's wrong?" he said, going to her with open arms.

She held up her hand, snubbing his hug, then pointed her finger back and forth between them. "We aren't working out, and we both know it."

The words impaled Ian. He opened his mouth but couldn't speak for a noticeable moment. "If it's about the abstinence—"

"It's so much more than that," Kate said. "You know we have some big issues."

"Issues worth ending us? C'mon, Kate! You didn't want to get married. I went along with that. You didn't want to move in together. I went along with that, even though sharing a place would save money and give us more time together. What issues are you talking about?"

"Let's not argue. This was a difficult decision, and I'm sorry."

Her sympathetic expression showed the sensitivity he loved about her but also carried a chilly resolve he didn't recognize.

He tried joking to loosen her up. "Am I too horny for you?"

Kate fought the slightest smile that would typically have swelled into a laugh. "No."

"Then what is it?" he asked.

"Ian, you are probably the most resourceful person I know. And I know you'll desperately want to fix our situation. It'll be easiest if we agree nothing's broken. The parts just no longer fit."

"What parts? We fit fine! And we're business partners. What about the shop?"

Kate gave him a pitiful look. Ian hated that look because it gave him the sensation of shrinking.

"The business is dying on the vine," she said. "It's time to cut losses." She looked around their cramped back office. "We can decide which of us gets what from the shop. I won't fight you for anything important to you."

"You are important to me," Ian said.

Kate looked away.

Ian's heart skipped when he thought she might be hiding tears, but she turned back to him, eyes dry, voice steady, and said, "I'm sorry, Ian. I realize this is painful."

Ian covered his face and slid his fingers up through his hair. "If you're still frustrated with our sales, that's all about to change. I told you I'm on the verge of signing our first catering contracts—big ones. I've got verbal commitments. They're basically done deals. I swear."

"A couple of contracts can't fix us." Then Kate surprised him by taking his hand.

Normally, Ian would have loved her touch, but the sympathy coming through her fingers shrank him more. He pulled away. "Kate, don't make this rash decision. Let's sleep on it and decide tomorrow."

"Sleep hasn't changed my mind for many nights. I'm sorry to have to hurt you this way. But I know we'll look back someday and agree we made the best possible decision."

"We aren't making this decision, *you* are!" Ian said, anger rushing in to replace his shock.

"Please don't raise your voice to me. Let's not make this harder than it is."

Ian slowly shook his head, staring at her in disbelief. "What do you want me to say—that I'm fine with it?"

Kate looked down at her hand, working her thumbnail against her fingertip again. "I have a request I'm hoping you'll accommodate."

"Now what?" Ian crossed his arms.

Kate took a deep breath and said, "I think it would be easiest for both of us if we didn't see each other or communicate for a while."

Ian felt the urge to quickly agree to appear more decisive than he felt. But accepting these terms ruined any chance of negotiation.

Kate didn't wait for his agreement. She turned and headed through the door to the front of the shop.

Ian hurried after her, saying, "Why don't we just take a break? We'll give each other some space. Let's start with... maybe a week. I'll cover the shop."

"I'm not willing to prolong the inevitable," Kate said, navigating between dining tables.

"Inevitable? Why is this inevitable?" Ian tried to get in front of her to block her exit but couldn't before she pushed through the front door. Outside in the parking lot, he sidestepped beside her. "You've met someone new. You've cheated on me, haven't you?"

"Ian, don't even go there," she said, reaching for her car door handle.

Ian threw his hands up. "What am I supposed to think?"

"If I could control what you think, this breakup would have been easier," Kate said. "I knew it would get complicated." She got into the driver's seat.

Ian stepped closer, blocking her door. "What's gotten into you?"

Kate closed her eyes and held up her hand. "Enough."

Ian stepped back.

She pulled the door closed.

Ian's eyes welled up while he watched her drive from the parking lot. He took a few steps as if he might chase her on foot. His throat tightened when her car disappeared around the corner. "Goddammit, Kate." His voice cracked.

The next morning, when he opened his front door to leave, he found a cardboard box. It contained some clothes, two pairs of shoes, a toaster, and an unopened bottle of wine from months ago, his miniature Valentine's card still taped to the side. A roughly folded note stuffed under the box flap read:

Ian,

Your stuff from my place.

If I missed anything, I'll reimburse you.

All the best,

Kate

Ian squeezed the note into his fist. He mumbled, "All the best," as he threw the box inside and slammed the door.

- Sample end -

Get *Guile* at: gneil.co/guile

Let's keep in touch.

To get a Bookbub "New Release Alert" for my next book, follow me here:
gneil.co/bookbub

Instagram:
gneil.co/instagram

Facebook:
gneil.co/facebook

Twitter
gneil.co/twitter

Website:
geoffreyneil.com

Acknowledgments

I want to express my sincere thanks to the following people:

My wonderful wife for her patience, mastery of language and frequent use of that loving, slow-blinking facial expression that gently told me which of my subplot ideas were clearly stupid.

Mom and Dad – You know what you did.

Cyndie Chen for sharing your wonderful eye for logic and uncanny sensitivity to word patterns. Your advice is golden.

Julie "Schmuggums" Harreld for your enthusiasm, sound medical suggestions and constant support.

Courtney Holly for sharing your fantastic voice and incredible creativity and skill by producing the *Wanton Regard* audiobook. The way you brought the characters to life thrilled me!

Michelle Martin-Stroup for sharing your unusual and extraordinary literary talent with me. I'm amazed by your skill and thankful for you.

Craig Wilson for your primer on anesthetic dosage and the feasibility of using pneumatic weapons for intra-muscular delivery of "Special K".

Dean Gamburd for the firearms counsel. Any inaccurate references to firearms or their use in this story is solely the fault of the author because I didn't run it by Dean.

Judith Proffer, Jackie Rankin, Becky Dominguez, Mona Romero and **Frederick James**. In my laziest moments, your encouragement brought me back to the keyboard to write a little more.